BLACK CAT SUNRISE

Richard Rose 1

BLACK CAT SUNRISE

Also by the author:
Vaguely Vivid
Jesus Christ!
Before the Aftermath
Tobias & Osaze
Tai/Dice
Saint Anthony's Firestorm
Tribal Vengeance
The Zoa
Rose City Catastrophe
Rose City Revisited
Bloodlust Paradise
Diminutive Narrative
The Rapture of Corruption

BLACK CAT SUNRISE

Richard Rose 3

BLACK CAT SUNRISE

BLACK CAT SUNRISE
by
Richard Rose

BLACK CAT SUNRISE

Richard Rose 5

BLACK CAT SUNRISE

Black Cat Sunrise is dedicated to my beloved daughter Richelle Mizuki. I'm sorry I wasn't there when you needed me. This book is just for you. As my way of apologizing. I miss you so very much. My kunoichi.

Chapter o
Nightmare
A mangled arm dropped from the sky nearby; falling in among the other dismembered body parts and pieces that had accumulated out there. Some of these chunks of meat were charred and burning. The white of protruding bones; glistening in the sunshine. Paul crouched in a shelter that used to be the corner of a concrete building that had been blown apart. The snow beyond the shelter was more red than white. And absolutely littered with gore. That was about the limit of what he could see; as he cowered and tried to think of what to do next. Probably he'd be dead before he could do anything. He had earplugs in his ears, but the noise was deafening all the same. Every sound; indiscernible from every other sound. Explosions from near and far blended into one another. The strange weapons of the enemy made their strange noises. Electric arcs pop and crackle. Lasers discharge in rapid succession. Other otherworldly sounds defy comprehension. The cacophony; glued together with the screaming and wailing of his peers. The rotors of helicopters could be heard. The roar of jet engines thickened the air. His whole body vibrated and jolted

BLACK CAT SUNRISE

uncontrollably; from torrents of combustions and concussions coming from all directions.

Paul was hyperventilating. His crystal blue eyes were practically rolling back into his skull as he tried to regain control over his overloaded nervous system. His pale skin was slick with the red slime of the fluids he'd slithered through to get into this improvised shell. The enemy hadn't yet realized his position, or they'd have since destroyed him. The thick concrete was preventing detection. This was a good place to be. Occasionally, every few minutes or so, a man would make a run for the rear. Which would soon be the front. These were those who were dying all around him. They were not fighting. There was nobody to fight. They were running, and dying. But if they didn't run, they would die out there. They all knew that. If he didn't run, he would die. That'd be fine. That was what he was born to do. Born to die. That was the creed of his people. It was on the red flag stitched on his sleeve. 'Live to war. War to live.' Along with the image of the hissing and bristling black cat. It didn't bother him to die. It bothered him to die a bad death. That's life, though. Some men die bad deaths. He knew all these corpses around him had died bad deaths. Bad deaths were so easy. Good deaths were so rare.

At his side there was an M-79 grenade launcher. Over his shoulder was slung a bandoleer of 40mm grenades. Slung over his other shoulder was a magazine fed .308 carbine with iron sights. On his hip was a .9mm pistol in a leather holster. There were extra magazines stuffing the pockets of his black uniform. An inconspicuous radio was strapped onto his ear; turned off at the moment. He needed to see what was happening. Since it was difficult to glean much information from what he was hearing. From what he was hearing, the enemy was advancing. Like they had been. Like they would continue to. Inevitably, they'd be on top of him soon. Soon he'd be behind their lines. And his line would be another one, two, or three hundred yards further away. In one minute. In five minutes. In ten minutes. They'd be on top of him. He couldn't guess when. But it was a certainty. Unfortunately, the enemy liked to utilize drone warfare. And the drones were impossible to kill through their shields. The grenade launcher was certainly not helpful in practice. Although it made a good anti-personnel weapon. That was the dream. That was a good death. To kill even one bushi meant a soldier could die a good death. Most soldiers like him never even got to see a bushi. All they ever saw was the drones. If they saw anything at all. It's despicable how the enemy fights, but it's a fact of life, too. Or, a fact of death. More accurately. The bad guys had everything and the good guys had nothing. Or, not nothing. Almost nothing. The confed had the numbers. Their greatest strength was their numbers.

It was dark, where he was. Under that concrete shell. The snow was about six inches deep. The openings- through which he could see the remains of his fallen comrades- were all facing away from the front. Paul needed to get a look back toward the front. There were a couple places where the daylight was seeping through the edges; so he put all his weapons aside, removed his helmet, and used it to dig at the snow at one of these spots- and then he used the helmet as a pillow to lay his head on while he watched through the sliver of light.

BLACK CAT SUNRISE

It was a warzone. It looked like a warzone. The earth was erupting violently. Amorphous balls of fire danced angrily. The enemy drones were engulfed within the chaos; their orange shields shining brilliantly through the hateful atmosphere. Bursts of bright red laser beams chased down pitiful targets. Rockets and missiles and big bore tracer bullets were pouring in from the confed's front. It only now occurred to Paul that he was at just as much risk from his own side's weapons as he was from the enemy's. Where he was at was the front previously. But it had become 'no man's land.' 'No man's land' was continuously expanding. And he was right in the middle of it.

The enemy drones stood about twenty feet tall and they were metallic and spider like; but with six legs instead of eight. At the foot of each of its six legs was one of six phantom-shield generators which enabled the foot to pass through the primary phantom-shield without creating an opening; creating molten craters wherever they stepped. Their arachnoid design enabled them to crawl over the rubble of the battlefield. They bristled with laser cannons that could wipe out a company in under a minute. And each possessed one of several diabolical primary weapon systems.

The war zone was miles and miles in all directions; limited by Long Island Sound to the north and by the Atlantic Ocean to the south. At the rear- at the easternmost tip of the island- the women and children were evacuating. The front- like the island- was about ten miles from north to south. So, there were only two of these drones in his field of vision, but surely there were more elsewhere. And surely there

BLACK CAT SUNRISE

were more up in the sky. And surely there were more out on the sea. The area where he was embattled used to be a quaint urban suburb. Now it was unrecognizable. It was all inferno and pandemonium and the material remains of demolished edifices. What used to be flat ground now undulated with peaks and valleys of destruction and rubble. Only one of the spider drones was an immediate threat to him. The one that had killed all the men around him. The actual machine itself couldn't be seen through the explosions or through the orange light of its phantasma, or through the smoke and the dust. But candy apple laser bolts were still gunning down any men it caught out in the open. He could see the bolts dart out, and he could hear the corresponding slaughter. Some men died louder than others. Some men screamed and screamed unendingly.

The ground outside began to erupt with red light and dirt and snow. Then another soldier came skidding headlong into Paul's concrete shell; a hot wave of air trailing in after. His helmet had collided with the concrete interior. Clutching his rifle in hands filthy with dried blood and black ash; the expression on his grimy face was of mortification and disbelief. His eyes were crazed and his lips looked weird as he gasped for air. Paul expected death to have come along with the newcomer, but nothing happened. The newcomer was probably also expecting to die, because it took him a minute to notice he wasn't alone in there. They didn't say anything, at first, they just exchanged looks. Then Paul went back to peering through the sliver of light.

Something strange was happening. The day- which had already been bright and shining- had

BLACK CAT SUNRISE

become even brighter and even shinier. But the extra illumination was shifting about. Casting shifting shadows of great length. It was as unsettling as it was unnatural. Hard to believe, even under the circumstances.

"We got to go," said the newcomer.

"You just got here."

"This place is going to blow."

"I know that," said Paul.

"We got to go. We got to go now!"

"That spider almost killed you. It's still out there. I'm looking right at it."

"We're going to fucking die in here."

"Die in here. Die out there. What's the difference?"

"We got to make a run for it!"

"Wait. Wait a second. Something's happening. What the fuck?"

The second man could see a blinding white luminescence coming through the viewing sliver and illuminating Paul's face. In fact, that bright white light was seeping in from all the small openings all around them. Paul squinted and braced himself against what he was seeing. Coupled with the gleaming reflection off of what snow there was, it was hard not to look away from the intensity.

"What is it?" the second man asked.

"It's a Hex."

"A white Hex, or a black Hex?"

"I don't know."

"Let me see."

Paul moved over and let the second man take a look. The second man said, "It's a black one."

"How can you tell?"

BLACK CAT SUNRISE

"For one thing, it's going toward them, and away from us."

"That doesn't mean anything," Paul said.

"And it's lit up like the sun. Whites don't do like that. Blacks do."

"How do you know?"

"I don't know. Rumors. It's just what people say."

"Well, whatever. Give me back my window. Make your own window."

The second man moved over and sat up against the wall. Not interested in making his own window; saying, "Just tell me what's happening."

"Something. I can't tell. It's too goddamn bright. And too far away. I can't see nothing."

But then, it became obvious what was happening. Because the spider drones stopped moving, jerked their legs in, squatted down to their standby position, and ceased firing on the confederation forces. "This is it! Come on! We got to go! Now!" Paul said, urgently, and without waiting for the other man to agree or not agree. Paul grabbed his weapons, shimmied out from under the concrete, and ran toward the rear in a mad panic. Meanwhile, other men were simultaneously rushing out from their hiding spaces.

A battlefield that had appeared all but deserted minutes before was now awash with soldiers fleeing from their tormentors. Some sort of ceasefire had accompanied whatever was happening. Not a total ceasefire, but a partial one. The confed had nothing to fire at anyways; not as long as the bakufu shields were up. They wasted a lot of weaponry shooting at targets that couldn't be hit. It was normal. And it was

BLACK CAT SUNRISE

nonsensical. Furthermore; up in the air and out at sea, there were other fights being fought- and these were as loud and as concussive as ever. And as futile, too.

Frantically; Paul scrambled over and around the ruins of the bombarded cityscape; finding himself compelled to scurry up the side of a home that was blown in half and flung far away from its foundations. And while he was atop this ruin, he cast a glance out toward the sea. What he saw stopped him in his tracks. The last time he had seen their navy, it was a triumphant sight to behold. Warships of every variety had been amassed to support the evacuation of civilians from Long Island. Glorious because soldiers didn't usually see the navy. Certainly, they never saw it amassed at maximum strength. That was only a couple of hours ago. Now, their armada had been definitively defeated and reduced to smoldering wreckage. The navy warships were sunk, or sinking. They were burnt, or burning. They were exploding, or exploded. Even as he watched, they remained under attack and all but helpless; being decimated before his very eyes. By a power he couldn't fathom or comprehend.

Another soldier stopped next to him- up there on the side of the house- and asked him, "What the fuck you standing around for?" Paul gestured broadly to the pitiful scenery of flame and smoke; the twisted metal of mangled boat hulls and the violent carnage of bizarre weapons- performing elaborate spectacles of death and destruction before them.

This other soldier- a negro with a scruffy beard and bloodshot eyes- had apparently not realized their navy was destroyed either. For just a second, he stopped and observed what was happening out there, but he snapped out of his surprise quickly. Other men

BLACK CAT SUNRISE

were hurrying past them like so many insects. Not even noticing the navy. Or lack thereof. The considerate soldier grabbed Paul by the arm, and said, "Them boats been on borrowed time for four decades. Come on. We got to go."

Paul didn't hesitate further, or resist at all. He went right along and they joined in with the flow of the others. These military men coalesced fluidly as they fled. They were trickles becoming creeks becoming rills becoming streams becoming rivers becoming lakes. And they ran and they ran. Some of them dropped from exhaustion and were either carried away or abandoned or trampled and crushed. The only goal was to get away from the front; to get toward the rear.

Gradually, they cleared out of the areas where the structures had all been obliterated and they were getting out toward the countryside where there were roads and intact buildings and homes- as well as forests- to take shelter within. Then the siren began. It was an old civil defense siren. An ominous ambient wailing. This was their warning. Some of the soldiers called out, "Double time!" or "Move it! Move it!" The exhausted throng quickened its pace. The gasping men; literally throwing their bodies forward because they were all limping too much to run well enough to move any faster.

Up ahead, Paul could see the green flags of the green zone. That's where they were trying to get to. The green zone was the safe zone. It wasn't particularly safe from the enemy, but it was safe from what the confederation engineers were about to do. The fleeing horde of retreating soldiers trudged across a marsh and made its way to a forested area. They got into the trees and muscled through the stabbing branches and the

Richard Rose 15

BLACK CAT SUNRISE

thick brush as they began to spread out and filter through the woods. Men were collapsing all around him. And soon he collapsed, too. His lungs; gasping for air. His eyes; staring up through the sticks and observing the light show of the aerial combat without any clue as to what exactly he was looking at up there. With the oxygen returning to his bloodstream; his breathing calmed, and he could hear sounds other than his wheezing lungs. Mostly what he heard was the unending thunder of explosions and the deafening sizzling and popping of energetic discharges. Superimposed upon that sinister orchestra was a grizzly chorus of men screaming verses of unspeakable agony. Paul sat up, clutching his rifle and grenade launcher more like a child than like a soldier. Looking around, he could see the red crosses painted on white banners. There was a field hospital set up out in a clearing over there. The wounded men of this sector were being carried- or dragged- over there, or they were carrying- or dragging- themselves over there. Really, these mutilated ones were all around him; he realized. They came on stretchers. They came on triangles of poles. They came hanging by the armpits in the clutches of their rescuers. They came draped over the shoulders of men who struggled to shoulder the burden of the weight. Soldiers with missing limbs. Or limbs hanging by threads of meat. Soldiers with holes shot through their bodies. Men with mangled bones. Men with grotesquely disfigured and deformed faces. Naked men. Burned men.

These sorts of casualties had probably been being moved to this place for hours- ever since the bakufu offensive commenced- but now there was a sudden influx in their numbers, because- as Paul was realizing- these high numbers of casualties constituted the tail end of their retreat. These- for obvious reasons- were the stragglers. That meant there were more of them left behind. Probably a lot more of them. He had to go back. He had to help these people, if he could. Except he couldn't help them. Because they were in the blast zone.

It was that thought in his mind when suddenly he was blown off of his feet. His helmet smashed against a tree. The shockwave had been so intense that he didn't even hear it. His body fell atop the bodies of the other men who were crowded in around him. And they had all fallen atop their weapons as well as atop the rotting logs and the bent saplings and the tangled scrub of the underbrush. A second later, as he came to his senses, he felt burning hot air washing over him. Looking out toward the front; nothing could be seen through a singular grey cloud of dust and smoke and ash. This cloud reached way up into the sky. And it stretched way out to the north, way out to the south, and over their position to the east. The engineers had used unprecedented quantities of explosives to separate the eastern tip of Long Island from the rest of Long Island. And now a new sound emerged through the catastrophic din of the battle. A sound that was as much an earthbound rumbling as it was the rushing and roaring of tons and tons of water filling in the chasm that had been carved through the island.

Underneath him, he heard a man say, "Fucking island ain't so long anymore."

This got a laugh from those who had heard it. And another man said, "Will you people get the fuck off of me?" Naturally, they were all shouting at the top of their voices in order to be heard.

BLACK CAT SUNRISE

Paul tried to get off of the guys beneath him, but there were people on top of him, too. He observed a comical visual: The soldiers were all strewn about in a singular pile of countless heaps; only separated by the trees they'd fallen against. The pile was writhing and struggling to sort itself out; to form into a mass of individuals instead of an individual mass. Burning dust came rushing through the trees. It sizzled against their exposed skin. The engineers had angled the detonation out toward the front and away from the rear, but there was a lot of blowback, nonetheless. Paul struggled to get up to his feet; the pyroclastic ash cloud upon them. Some men cried about the heat, and others remarked that it was not so bad. Relative to a sucking chest wound, the heat was not so bad, but relative to a spring rain shower, it was certainly quite bad. Visibility in Paul's area became very low. There was a new body of water not far off. It was a comfort, because Paul knew the engineers had placed the ocean between him and the enemy. With any luck, those ungodly spider drones were fifty feet under water. Undoubtedly, they'd lost a lot of friendly forces in that monstrous blast.

Thankfully- with help from the biting wind- the smoke soon began to clear. After a minute, he had found his weapons; covered in blood. In fact- he realized- he was covered in blood, also. There were dead and dying men scattered about. Many who'd fallen and simply couldn't get back up. Others had been there all the while. These were the grotesque casualties of the onslaught of the laser barrages. The ones who had made it this far, that is. The more he looked, the more he saw. The overwhelmed medical tents nearby contained but a small fraction of these

BLACK CAT SUNRISE

numbers. All around, these wounded men writhed and wailed in agony; inaudibly calling for their mothers. The soldiers who still possessed a semblance of awareness were looking around in confusion. Nobody knew what to do next.

"What the fuck is that?" a blood-soaked soldier asked. They were all blood-soaked soldiers... Over the sound of the heavy artillery; he had to scream to be heard at the volume of a whisper.

"What the fuck is what?" another blood-soaked soldier called back.

These men were near enough to Paul that he could see what they were referring to. There was a naked body drenched in blood. There were a lot of naked bodies drenched in blood, but this one was special. It was a woman's body. No boots. No tattered clothes. Her figure; a sheen of slick red blood accented by crusts of dried-out black blood. As she rose, it seemed like her forearms, hands, knees, shins, and feet were down in the blood puddles; like the blood puddles were much deeper than they were, and that she was rising up out of them.

"It's a fuckin' hex!" one soldier cried.

"What do we do?" asked another.

Some took off running without a second thought; quickly discovering themselves to be trapped within their own horde. Others raised their rifles and took aim at the woman. Paul just stared. Transfixed. The hex was made of blood. She was naked. And sexy. She had a great pair of glorious tits on her; massive and perfectly round, with painfully exquisite nipples protruding. And her face was lovely; cherubic, with chubby chipmunk cheeks. Its slant eyes indicated oriental origins. Their enemy being- essentially-

Richard Rose 19

BLACK CAT SUNRISE

oriental in origin. Her eyes were shimmering shades of shining blood. There was no white in her incongruous smile; her glossy teeth were made of blood, also. Her silken hair; made of fine strands of crusty black blood. This girl was made of blood, and nothing else. Her features were well defined by viscosities; and this made her seem oddly human. With a hint of sexuality in her expression; she watched them watching her.

Many of these men intended to shoot her, but nobody dared to take a shot, because there was no safe line of fire in any direction. Then, one of them had the idea to throw himself down upon his fallen brethren and to shoot upward at her with his sidearm. The bullets went through her without harming her; coming out of the back of her as if she were made of liquid- because she was made of liquid. One soldier called out; "Get a fucking flamethrower over here! We need a fucking flamethrower!" They all looked around for a flamethrower, but there wasn't one in sight.

With strange skipping steps; the hex approached the soldier who'd shot up at her. He was pulling the trigger on an empty pistol as she reached her arm out toward his face. He pulled away and tried to scurry off, but she leapt on top of him, straddling his chest, placing her hand on his face. Two fingers went up into his nose, and two flowed around his eyeballs and into his eye sockets, and her thumb went into his mouth. The man's gushing blood came flooding out of his facial orifices; the very iron of his essences impelled by a mystical magnetism. It only took ten or fifteen seconds for the hex to suck the life from him.

Others were trying what the first man had tried: Getting low and shooting up at her. She winced as the bullets struck, and it seemed to annoy her, but also not

Richard Rose 20

BLACK CAT SUNRISE

really. She was infuriatingly cutesy; smiling as she got up and flung herself down onto her next victim. Moving like a crimson wave. Draining the life of another man. "Get away from her! Get away from her!" called out one soldier with a grenade in his hand. Of course, there were a lot of helpless soldiers littering the ground who couldn't possibly get away. Others- like a school of fish- were fleeing from her as the grenade was thrown at her. It exploded; sending body parts, bone, blood, dirt, and gear flying in all directions. And in the dust and smoke it seemed she was gone. And she was- in fact- gone. The explosion had blasted her apart entirely. Apparently. The soldier called out, "Fuck! I fucking got her!" And as he said this, another soldier called out, "She's right behind you!" And, indeed, she was; having risen up out of the corpses that this man literally stood upon. He turned to see and she promptly grabbed him by the face; dropping him to his knees as she drew the life out of him.

Bullets began flying in all directions, as- in their panicking- the soldiers abandoned their discretion and took crazed shots at her. The hex flung herself about like water splashing off of rocks in a raging river. She was either staying still and joyfully murdering these men- one by one by one. Or she was fluidly flying around. Rushing forth like how blood surges through veins. Coming apart and coalescing again. This caused a generalized pandemonium. Soldiers were being trampled; they were dropping from friendly fire; and as the moments went on she only killed more and more and more of them.

Paul had taken cover behind a tree, but he called out; "Stop shooting! Stop shooting!" Nobody heard him. It was almost impossible to hear anything

BLACK CAT SUNRISE

over the sounds of the thundering fighter jets being blown out of the sky by the enemy's attack drones. The bloody hex was pursuing the others in a direction that was going away from his position. The grenade launcher was in his hands and loaded as he peered around the tree and wondered what to do. It was chaos out there. Men were jumping into the ocean that had only just moments before appeared out of nowhere; the waters still roiling with rocks and grating silt. The bloody hex had a tendency to herd the soldiers into other soldiers and to keep them running into one another. Wherever she was, the others were all shoved against each other. If he shot a grenade at her, it would kill many men.

Suddenly, a torrent of fire emerged from somewhere within their numbers. Someone had produced a flamethrower. They loosed the flamethrower upon the hex and bone-chilling screams of fiery hell emanated from some men who got caught up in the inferno. Paul observed as the bloody hex melted back into the ground. Several soldiers struggled to extinguish their burning uniforms. Others just roasted without protest. Meanwhile, the bloody hex reappeared behind the wielder of the flamethrower. As she pulled his lifeblood out through his face, his finger squeezed the trigger and his arms flailed about as his body twisted and struggled- and so a wild deluge of flaming napalm washed over the hapless soldiery.

Paul tried to get away, but these woods were filled to capacity with men, and there was nowhere to go except into the backs of other soldiers who were trying to force their way through the jam just the same as him. As Paul realized just how many men were between him and his escape, it also occurred to him

BLACK CAT SUNRISE

just how few men were between him and the hex.
Upon this realization, he turned with reluctance to see
he couldn't see her anywhere. Just burning men. And
gun-shot men. And burning bodies. And a burning
forest. And a carpet of corpses amidst the trees. Then,
like a water spout bubbling up from the ground she
appeared before him. Reaching out for him. When
suddenly a flash of purple light blinded him, and the
clap of a powerful electric discharge hit his ears with a
sharp and stunning slap that briefly knocked him
unconscious. The power of it threw him backward into
the others. A couple seconds later, his eyes opened,
and he again felt the fear of certain death like a vise
crushing his mind. But, what he perceived through his
distorted vision was shocking and he forgot himself as
he looked up in astonishment at a woman made of
purplish-whitish electricity that sizzled like static. It
was a hex. Made out of lightning, apparently. And she
floated through the canopies of the trees, incinerating
branches and leaves- which charred and crumbled
instantaneously- as she descended upon the scene. Her
electric hair stood on end. The bloody hex had
disappeared. The horde of soldiers was slowly
dispersing rearward. Paul couldn't help but admire the
electric hex's nude figure. This hex appeared to be
Nordic in origin; voluptuous and lean, petite, busty
and muscular. And very pretty. She watched him
watching her. There were dead bodies everywhere.
And here was this ghost witch- looking like an angel.
She had saved his life. But the skin on his face hurt
badly, as apparently, he had been burned fiercely.

Chapter 1
Obliteration

BLACK CAT SUNRISE

The Long Island headquarters of the Nyu NyuYoku Bakufu had been established within what used to be a prison on an island called Rikers; specifically, far beneath what used to be the Rose M. Singer women's facility- with the rest of the island functioning as a fire base and troop barracks for Bushi. An airport formerly known as La Guardia is adjacent to the island and this serves as the bakufu air base. And the bakufu naval base is further away at what used to be the South Brooklyn Marine Terminal. Up until recently the enemy front was located along the Meadowbrook State Parkway between Hempstead and East Meadow. Not long ago, the Bakufu broke through the enemy front. This caused the enemy population beyond the front to evacuate, but they could not get very far. And the enemy forces fought futile rear-guard actions as they retreated toward the east. The bakufu pursued the enemy relentlessly; pushing them to the literal ends of the earth. That is; toward eastern Long Island. A mass exodus of over a million civilians: Defended by ground forces numbering upward of 50,000; a militia of twice that many; along with all available air and naval support; along with multiple enemy majo both known and unknown.

Bakufu Forward Battle Command is located far below the hollowed-out remnants of the Singer complex. In a bomb shelter 75 feet underground. A spherical room; like an orb. Elevated on pedestals in the center of the orb there are two virtual reality thrones; one for the Shikken and one for the Shugo. With four additional thrones situated four meters below; each facing one of the four cardinal directions. These thrones can recline 90 degrees back, 45 degrees forward, rotate 360 degrees, and can remotely operate

BLACK CAT SUNRISE

a variety of antigravity attack drones. Each throne has a telescopic lid that engages when pilot mode is initiated and retracts when it is not. The walls of the command center are covered in viewing screens from the zenith to the horizon to the nadir. These viewing screens can present a unified image or be divided into any number of separate views and they are obstructed only by the positions of the four Jonin occupying the lower thrones. The spherical shells of each of the thrones- as well as the requisite walkways- are also made of viewing screens which integrate into the surrounding images.

Seated in the central drone throne is Kazuki Sama; shikken of the Nyu NyuYoku bakufu. Her gaze is piercing and fierce as she peers into the high-definition monitors with feline eyes. The images reflect upon the pitch-black ink of her irises. She possesses the striking Asiatic beauty of her mother, the daimyo; tempered by the softer Caucasian features of her father, the shogu. Leaning forward in her chair, she tenses with the hatred of one billion ghosts. Her knuckles are white as she grips down on the polymer of her joysticks. Her pearl white teeth are gritted and there is a snarl on her blood red lips. Her slender body is adorned in the white denim jumpsuit all drone operators wear; a red Hinomaru circle over the heart. In her ears there are ruby studs, and it is these earrings which serve as the only observable designation of her rank in the bakufu.

Similarly; Xander Sama, the shogu, her father- in the throne beside her- wears a blackened gold thumb ring. Xander was born a confederate, captured early on in his soldiering career, thrown into the slave populations- the Dorei- and elevated to his high position by virtue of skill, chance, and achievement.

BLACK CAT SUNRISE

And seduction. Very few men ever transcend the status of dorei. Theirs is a woman's world. As a rule, a man is typically but little more than a necessary evil. To hear the ladies tell it... Xander is an exemplary exception to the rule. He is a white american man; shaved bald, with a handsome shaven face, gaunt features, intense brown eyes, buck teeth, and a lanky form. The throne's telescopic lid extends out and down and covers up his whole upper body; ditto for the jonin. Only Kazukisama utilizes the magnificent display of the sphere; as she is commanding the drone squadron.

      The jonin are all men who were chosen from the higher ranks of the Bushi. The bushi being chosen from the upper echelons of dorei class structures; or from the lower echelons of bakufu class structures. Jonin function as captains; they are bushi commanders. All drone pilots are jonin. All jonin are nihonjin in origin; which is to say, like the daimyo; they come from Nippon, or- Japan. They've got murky golden skin tones, black eyes with slant eyelids, and are short in height. These are the six pilots of the drone sphere built far below the earth. These six pilots correspond to six antigravity attack drones flying way up high in the sky. Each drone is saucer shaped. Each drone has one of a variety of weapons systems. Each drone is shielded by phantasm. The six drones hover in a pyramidal formation; with the two executive officers' drones at the center, the lead jonin at point and the other three in the rear; each drone occupying a different range of altitude. These six constitute one section of the squadron of 18 drones. The other twelve pilots are operating out of two other spheres located above ground in innocuous hangers out at the airport. Each flying saucer has a band of colored lights encircling the

BLACK CAT SUNRISE

circumference. 16 of the 18 drones glow with blue light and the shikken and the shogu drones glow red. The drones hover high in the sky; holding their position. They're watching the activities down below. It is certainly a vision to behold. A momentous occasion. The exodus of Long Island.

There are millions of people down there. Nobody knows how many, really. But they are all the enemy; all Teki. It is up to the bakufu daimyo whether they live or die. But it is not that simple. Certainly, Kazukisama would like to annihilate them all in one sweeping motion; obliterating the whole swath of them. Like so many insects. But Kazuki must obey the daimyo. And still, the daimyo is not the final authority here. The final authority rests with Tengoku Majo. To anger Tengoku majo is to invite the wrath of the kamikaze. The earth is positively crawling with teki; with the enemy. It would be so easy to incinerate them en masse. Except for that there would be dire consequences.

The speakers of the sphere chime and a voice rings thru; it is the admiral- the Teitoku- of the naval forces, saying "Kazukisama, this is Teitoku Yoko. It looks as though their first transport ships are jettisoning. Are we going to engage, or what? Over."

Kazukisama presses the com button and asks, "Do you know what their majo are doing? Are there any reports? Over."

"Negative. I was going to ask you the same thing. Over."

"Negative. No reports. Over."

Teitoku Yoko asks again, "Do we engage? Over."

From the drone's bird's eye view, this is the scene: At the eastern end of Long Island there is a

BLACK CAT SUNRISE

narrow peninsula. Just over two miles wide at its thickest area; a place called Montauk. And it is over fourteen miles in length from where it joins to the rest of the island. This peninsula is swarming with people. With teki. All teki are the enemy but only some teki are Heishi. Heishi means soldier. The heishi presence is substantial but mostly indiscernible. Except for at the front. The front is where the peninsula begins. There, the bushi- bakufu soldiery- are utilizing automated war machines to stay away from danger. As is their prerogative.

To the north of the peninsula- in Block Island Sound- there is the teki armada; or, this theatre's contingent of it. To the south of the peninsula- in the open ocean- is the bakufu naval strike force. The bakufu naval strike force is indistinguishable from the blue of the water but each craft appears on command monitors with arrow shaped and color-coded demarcations. Red are the heavy destroyers, white are the light, and green are the medium. Each vessel's design being contingent upon its weapons system. Three systems. Three designs. Three of each. Nine in total. And they were not boats in the old sense of the word. They were unmanned drones propelled with anti-gravity technology; floating just over the chop of the waves, looking like sperm whales with no fins or fluke or facial features. Also, these were capable of operating underwater.

The teki armada- alternatively- is not stealth whatsoever. It is an old-world conglomeration of hulking warships; one aircraft carrier, a couple cruisers, several frigates, four destroyers, and three corvettes. Presumably one or two submarines as well. But the submarines had surely sounded at the bottom of the sound where only Umi Majo could possibly reach them. Of course, nobody could guess where umi majo was or what she was doing. Equally as vulnerable as the hopelessly outdated teki warships were the unarmed teki transport vessels. They were innumerable and of all shapes and sizes. These boats were coalescing around the inlet of Montauk lake. The lake, too, being filled with them.

Kazuki pushed the com button and said, "Teitoku Yoko, chotto matte. I have to consult the daimyo."

"Hai hai," Yoko assented.

Kazuki equipped a headset specifically for this purpose. It connected her to her mother- the daimyo- who spoke with a thick Japanese accent. The shogu and jonin could plainly hear Kazuki speaking but they could not hear the daimyo.

"Are you seeing this?" Kazuki asked.

"Of course I am."

"The teitoku wants to know what to do. And so do I."

"Stay away from the evacuations. Let the civilians escape. It is not worth the risk to destroy them. Our bushi have already inflicted severe casualties on the heishi teki, obliterated their defensive lines, forced a retreat, and are in pursuit. That's good enough. As for your squadrons; I want you to give orders to destroy the warships, and to destroy the airships."

"What airships?"

"They haven't deployed yet, but they will. You, my child, are not to engage unless your forces are sustaining losses, and even then, only minimal involvement. Is that understood?"

BLACK CAT SUNRISE

"Hai, wakata."
"Iine."

Kazuki removed the headset and pressed the communications button to address her forces; "This is your shikken. Umi units you are clear to engage. Kuki sections two and three, you are clear to engage. Kuki section three, we're holding position. All units; initiate battle protocols." She did not address the bushi. The bushi were on a different channel; a separate force, under the command of Motosama; Kazuki's aunt.

"Copy that. This is Umi one. Umi units are moving into attack position. Estimated time of arrival, five minutes." 'Umi' meaning 'seagoing.'

"This is Kuki seven. Senso units report in and commence bombardment."

'Senso eight, commencing.' 'Senso nine, commencing.' 'Senso fourteen, commencing.' 'Senso fifteen, commencing.'

All the attack drones now bristled with a defensive array of eight laser cannons each; four topside and four bottom side. Each laser on an aerodynamic rotating turret. The senso units held their positions as the other eight attack drones slowly descended from the heavens; moving toward their respective ranges. From the bottom of each of the senso drones emerged- at a 60-degree angle- a rectangular barrel with a thick disk at the tip. A pulsar cannon. At the tips of these barrels, blue sparks sparked to life and sizzled and frizzled and began to gather and coalesce and grow in size and intensity. They needed twenty seconds to charge. Then they discharged bright blue comets of energy at approximately one third the speed of light.

BLACK CAT SUNRISE

The pulsations tore through their targets like they were nothing; traveling down into the briny depths thereafter. One corvette exploded into dust. A gash like a great ravine was torn through the deck of the aircraft carrier; but all the fighter jets had already launched and were at present inbound to attack their stealthy opponents. A white frigate leaned over with a gaping hole in its hull and its weapons pointed toward the sky; all of which being rendered basically useless. If they weren't to begin with. The conning tower had been shot off of a battleship; like an apple shot off a man's head. Down there amidst the destruction the impact concussions were deafening- to say nothing of the metals and materials being blown apart. Oddly, the weapons themselves emitted only loud zapping noises when they fired; and similarly, the senso created no sonic booms, because they caused a vacuum in the space time continuum by obliterating the fabric of reality itself. If just for an instant.

A team of six F22 Raptors- out of the squadron of 24 which had launched from the aircraft carrier- were flying in a 'V' formation and had been able to sight in on the senso drones using the heat signatures of the pulse cannons. A barrage of 20mm bullets crashed into the shields of the attack drones; creating splashes of vibrantly sparkling orange phantasm as the hot lead liquified and fell to the ocean like rain. This was to be expected. The lasers of the attack drones shot back; bolts of deep red light that emitted a pitch like the note of a guitar string wound right up to the breaking point.

The fighter jets- having already launched a barrage of AMRAAM rockets- were arching back and away evasively. Still, one F-22 was hit and exploded

Richard Rose 31

BLACK CAT SUNRISE

and another was hit and- with its wing torn away- had begun to tailspin; trailing fire and smoke as the pilot ejected and parachuted below. Dozens of rockets were flying into the senso drones now; and the warheads exploded against the forcefields impotently. Throwing the drones harmlessly yet wildly across the sky. Only one senso had managed to discharge its second pulsation into its target; the conning tower of the aircraft carrier; which became a volcanic stump of what it had been only an instant prior. The other pulsations had all discharged out into outer space. Meanwhile, the drones' defensive lasers continued to crazily chase after the maneuvering fighter jets as the drones whirled and spun out; stunned and subdued for a moment.

Kazuki said, "Raijin units, your position is good. I want you to fire into damaged warships; first priority. Second priority; engage fighter jets with your laser system. Report in and commence."

'Raijin Eleven, commencing.' 'Raijin Twelve, commencing.' 'Raijin Sixteen, commencing.' 'Raijin Seventeen, commencing.' Copper rods with tripods at the tips emerged from the bottoms of each of the raijin drones. Each drone harnessed one billion volts of electricity from the zero-point energy of the ether and what happened next was like a lightning storm oddly out of place on a bright shining winter's day. The jagged arcs of electricity danced and dazzled across the warzone to connect with the wounded warships. These were sinking and burning vessels that were littered with scorched and dismembered corpses as well as with desperate men running for their lives, struggling to perform despite injury, or jumping overboard into the freezing waters. Due to damages sustained, the

BLACK CAT SUNRISE

warships had become somewhat vulnerable to lightning strike; insofar as the personnel could be electrified and the circuitry could be broken. The problem with the raijin weapon was that undamaged warships and airships- by design- possessed counter measures against them; lightning rods and electrical grounds.

The raijin attack carried on with ten second charges between discharges. Also, the senso drones had reoriented and were firing their devastating blasts again. The 64 laser cannons of these eight attack drones were all the while automatically targeting and firing on the fighter jets. The fighter jets had circled around to launch another barrage of AMRAAM rockets at the senso. F-22s were coming in from everywhere now; 20mm tracer rounds- as well as laser bolts- could be seen shooting toward all directions. The senso blasts reeked devastation upon several more warships before the rockets exploded against their dazzling orange phantom-shields and sent them spiraling out of control again. Down below were colossal boats with their bows pointing straight in the air, or their propellers pointing straight in the air; and the aircraft carrier had begun to lean over; while other warships had become towering infernos, and still others were just red-hot skeletons of their former glory. Several of the teki warships remained unscathed and these were doing their best to fire the gas-operated 35mm anti-aircraft guns back at the drones- their lasers and radars, given the circumstances, were able to lock on to some of the drones some of the time- but there was no way to penetrate the shields.

Meanwhile, the teki ground forces were using their anti-aircraft weapons to fire into suspected bushi

Richard Rose 33

BLACK CAT SUNRISE

positions and couldn't be troubled by the fight happening above. The warships' 57mm cannons were, however- in some instances- capable of knocking the senso blasts off target. And the warships' surface to air missiles- when not blown up en route by the laser cannons- were capable of hitting hard enough to send the drones spiraling out of control. Temporarily. But also repeatedly, occasionally. The rockets and missiles were coming in torrents, but the laser cannons were fast and accurate. This had been an eventful couple of minutes. The airspace was crowded with tracer bullets, rockets, missiles, explosions, lightning, lasers, phantasmagoric reactions, burning fighter jets breaking apart, and darting senso blasts. Plumes of smoke- rising up from the fiery wreckages accumulating upon the surface of the sound- were drifting on the gentle seabreeze. The air became hazy.

Kazuki said, "Attention dondon kuki. I want you to target whatever has not taken any damage and damage it. Report in, and commence your bombardment." "Dondon seven, commencing. Dondon ten, commencing. Dondon thirteen, commencing. Dondon eighteen, commencing."

Kazuki said, "Attention umi one, what is your status? Where are you?"

"Just another minute, Shikken!" returned umi one.

Besides the standard laser array, the dondon attack drones each possessed a complicated plasma cannon. Its inner workings were encased in a carbon fiber shell, but it was wrapped up in black cables and glowing purple hoses; and at the front of the weapon was an ionized metallic ring which shone with a dusty purple static. The dondon cannons fired radiant purple

BLACK CAT SUNRISE

plasmoids that grew in size as they went along; from about 10 centimeters to about one meter at a kilometer and two meters at two kilometers and so on. Each plasmoid burst forth from the weapon with a concussive blast- or, 'don', before colliding with its target and exploding with tremendous force; generating a secondary 'don.' Hence, dondon. These extremely loud weapons were louder than all the battleground's other extremely loud weapons combined. Every human being down below would feel each of these concussions quite profoundly; some more than others. When the plasmoids slammed into the assorted warships; they impacted with meteoric force. A boat struck by one would be thrown over on its side or cut into two. The weapons transformed otherwise pristine vessels into twisted wreckages and reduced human organisms to boiling vapors. They turned windswept ocean chop into waves rolling like moving mountains; capsizing many civilian vessels in the distance.

Raijin eleven released another arc of lightning from its primary weapon, but the emission never reached the destination. What happened instead was that- in midair- the charge illuminated the manifest spirit of a beautiful woman. Her features; vaguely nordic and somewhat elven- with an upturned button nose. Her bodice; exquisite and naked and made of bright aqua-white electricity. Her short hair; like aqua-tinged fiber optic strands standing straight on end. The energy surged through her and lit up her figure- her legs; together- her arms; stretched out over her head in a V- her breasts; perky, pert, and perfectly full- and even her pubic hair, too, was electrified and standing straight out on end. And there was a smile upon her

BLACK CAT SUNRISE

face; a smile of wonder and awe as she glanced up at the drone that was connected to her left little toe by the jagged, jumping, and jolting lightning. She lit up brilliantly bright and the electricity surged forth from her, out along that arc that enlivened her, and back into the drone from whence it had come; completely bypassing the shields. But now the charge was immeasurably more powerful than could be absorbed by the weapons system and the drone exploded from the center; out into a shower of aqua-white sparks and shrapnel.

This was Denki Majo. As the chaos raged about her, she shifted her gaze toward another raijin drone. Raijin sixteen. Her expression was innocent and joyful. Raijin sixteen discharged its weapon and it diverted wildly from its intended mark and veered directly into her. She lit up with pure aqua-white light and returned the charge back to its source. Blasting a second drone into falling fragments.

Kazuki by now had realized what was happening, and she ordered, "Raijin kuki, cease fire! Raijin kuki, cease fire! Both of you, get out of there. Return to base! Return to base!" "Copy that. Returning to base." "Copy that. Returning to base."

Denki majo dropped her arms to her side and a quizzical expression came over her face. She watched the raijin kuki zipping away and looked a little disappointed. All manner of projectiles darted and soared and shot and screamed all around her. And she looked at the fighter jets and the wreckages of ships and the flashing of the drone shields. But what really caught her eye was the sprawling hellscape that was the combat on the ground on the island. And her expression became one of bashful curiosity and

Richard Rose 36

BLACK CAT SUNRISE

intrigue, with a hint of mischievous glee. She floated away- as majo tend to do- not hurrying at all; down toward the nightmarish slaughter of the front-line confrontation: A beautiful woman made of electricity and nothing else; shimmering and flashing as she went; purple, blue, aqua, and white in turn or all at once or in an undulating amorphous pattern like cuttlefish skin. Her fibrous hair; still standing crazily on end: A silly spectacle to compliment her whimsical demeanor.

Umi one contacted Kazuki, saying, "Umi units in position."

Kazuki ordered, "Umi units, commence bombardment. On the double."

Umi one said, "Copy that. You heard Shikkensama. Commence bombardment."

Umi drones utilized three types of weapon systems. Taiyo umi. Hoshi umi. And Tsuki umi. Sun, star, and moon. All umi possessed four laser cannons; like how kuki possessed eight. Also, umi possessed the same shielding as kuki; the interaction of phantasm and ocean water cast a dull orange glow beneath the vessels. The primary weapon of the umi tsuki was a long rod with ten concentric circles of gold- not attached by anything visible- running up the narrowing length of it, and at the tip there was a golden sphere. The tsuki cannon did not appear to do anything, and it was completely silent. It could fire two or three times each minute. Whatever the cannon locked onto would be struck by an orb of antimatter; about fifteen meters in diameter. These insidious orbs were akin to weaponized black holes. They produced no sound and were completely invisible. What they did was effectively disappear anything and everything

BLACK CAT SUNRISE

within their dimensions. The tsuki orbs struck like blips; instantaneously. A bizarre spectacle to behold up close and in person, but not so shocking in the context of the witch wars. The cannon of the hoshi umi were more like a rectangular arrangement of thousands of micro cannons; and each micro cannon fired a crystalline projectile filled with charged particle flechettes. Each projectile created a cloud of high voltage particulates. The victims of a hoshi cannon would hear an ominous tinkling noise all about them. They would feel dozens of tiny zaps. Then hundreds of tiny zaps. And then thousands of tiny zaps. And then nothing at all. A more painful way to die than simply disappearing, but much more beautiful because of the sparkles. The taiyo cannon was a fission weapon. More akin to a beam than a bomb. It was the quintessential 'death ray' of lore. It roared with a hum like a monotonous siren. The beam was massive; growing from an apple sized point at the tip of the matrix within the weapons cylindrical shell and spreading out from there in a conical shape that doubled in size every one thousand meters. It fired in five second intervals with five second resets. And while it was not especially proficient in causing structural damage- as an anti-personnel weapon, it was extremely potent. Its beam was that of harnessed sunlight. It couldn't be looked at. The brightness of it illuminated the sky in all directions; so as that the day became bright in an otherworldly way. Viewed through special filters, the beam could be seen to shimmer and pulsate with melding frequencies of prismic radiation.

And so it was that the senso and the dondon and the tsuki decimated the teki warships as the hoshi and the taiyo obliterated the 'surviving' crew members

BLACK CAT SUNRISE

and ill-fated passengers. The umi drones immediately took fire just as the kuki drones had. The umi shields blazed so intensely orange that the vessels themselves could not be seen within; they were like domes of sizzling energy afloat on the water; attracting ineffectual machine gun fire and jostling around as missiles and rockets exploded against them. Their red laser bolts; spraying every which way but down. The umi drones were repeatedly engulfed in immense fireballs- some of which came up from below where the water had been blown away; and occasionally they'd be thrown through the air for substantial distances. To no avail, as they'd been designed to be impervious to such conditions.

As the taiyo cannons blazed mercilessly; one of the beams began to malfunction and become distorted as if it was being blocked by something that wasn't there. Only about 50 percent of its force was registering on its targets. Then 25 percent. Then 10 percent. And then it could be gleaned as to what was causing the disturbance. A woman was manifesting within the taiyo ray. At first glance she looked like what the sun looks like; a blindingly bright splotch.

"Shikken. This is umi taiyo two. I have majo activity manifesting in my weapon system. I'm shutting it down. Wait. No. I'm losing control. I think she has it." While he was talking; the radiation majo surged through the death ray, bypassed the shield, and disappeared into the inner workings of the cannon; and from within the cannon, she burned her way through the synthetic materials of the weapon and then through the umi's hull and then through the vital components of the umi's inner workings. The phantom-shield deactivated and before she could get

Richard Rose 39

to the antigravity drive, a sidewinder missile hit the umi drone and blew it into pieces that flung out in all directions. Leaving the radiant majo remaining; glowing brightly within the ball of fire until it dissipated and the wind blew the smoke away.

She illuminated Long Island Sound with an unnatural brilliance. Through the haze of smoke, she could somewhat be seen. Still, it was nearly impossible to determine the shape of her. She had no shadow or contour; only intensity. Her body, hair, face; all shaped and defined by the relative intensity of the light she emitted. Her eyes shone brightest. The radiant majo was a naked young woman; nicely shaped, with short waving hair- or the impression of it, and she was Nordic in her beauty; similar to the electric majo- like they could be sisters.

The battle; it raged on. Pitifully for the teki. Triumphantly for the bakufu. At least in the air and at sea, that was so. The ground forces were fighting a different fight. The Taiyo Majo Teki observed her surroundings, looking all around and all around in the sky. From anywhere in the nearby vicinity, it would appear as though there were two suns now. One up in the heavens, and one down there on earth; out over the water. This taiyo majo held her hands up before her with her palms turned outward and she hovered toward the nearest umi drone. An umi tsuki drone. She descended upon it, but she found herself- firstly- immersed in an ongoing barrage of the explosions of artillery and rocketry; which had no effect on her. And, secondly, she realized she wouldn't be getting through the phantasm of the shield. It just wasn't possible via the conduit of the weapon system; which was typically the only way to break through. Knowing what this

BLACK CAT SUNRISE

magic was, she lingered upon the sizzling orange light for an instant until more explosions exploded and the vessel was blown out from under her foot. After that, she drifted off toward the shore.

Kazuki continued to monitor the situation with the teki fleet. The situation was that there was no situation. There was no teki fleet. All those proud warships had been reduced to proud shipwrecks that were alive with flame and smoke if they were not already down on the bottom of the sound and dead. The innumerable evacuation vessels continued the exodus of Long Island. Many such innocent boats had been damaged or destroyed in the upheaval. But the sheer quantity of these escape-oriented transports made such misfortunes imperceptible at a glance.

Alternatively; the frontline of combative ground forces was visibly catastrophic. It was- of course- a warzone; positively ebullient with the traditional explosions of the teki and the more advanced emissions of the exotic weapon systems of the bakufu. Occasionally a teki fighter jet or two or three would mount an assault upon Kazuki's kuki drone section; up and out where it floated high above the action- but the laser defenses were automatic and deadly and the teki missiles were useless. In just a little over ten minutes, the teki fleet had been reduced to almost nothing. Satisfied with this result; Kazuki ordered, "All umi and all kuki. Cease fire. Cease fire. These are your new orders; kuki dondon seven, kuki senso eight, umi hoshi four, umi tsuki seven- you are to provide support to the bushi kumo. All other kuki and umi, return to base."

Kazuki felt a hollow sense of accomplishment. She wasn't so enraged anymore. But she was still

BLACK CAT SUNRISE

raging. There was still a sneer on her blood red lips. But her hateful gaze had become glossy. The teki were pathetic. She pitied them with disgust.

As she watched the drones moving away from the battlegrounds, and as she watched the candles burning in the water, and as she watched the fireworks performing in the skies; she thought to herself, "How terrible. To be teki. They don't have a prayer."

Of course, in the excitement of the moment she had forgotten to remember about the two teki majo which had emerged from the fighting. Then the island erupted like a volcano; so suddenly and so unexpectedly that it startled her and she started in her seat. On the screens the vision was unbelievable; but the concussive report was muted. A cloud of dust and smoke obscured the area where the explosion had occurred, but outside of the clouds of debris she could see the bushi kumo drones. They weren't doing anything, she realized. Kazuki radioed her mother, the daimyo; "What is happening on the ground?" she asked her. "It's not ideal," the daimyo responded.

Chapter 2
Chaos

Commanding the Nyu NyuYoku bakufu bushi was an eighth dan bushi called Motosama. Moto sat within a stealth command vehicle that utilized advanced camouflage technology to blend in with its surroundings. It had eight wheels made of solid rubber. There were nine other similar vehicles that contained the nine operators for the nine kumo drones. And sharing the space with each kumo drone operator was an assistant who served as a driver as well as a spotter utilizing an airborne surveillance drone.

BLACK CAT SUNRISE

The surveillance drones were simply old-style quadcopters fitted with cameras.

Moto was a severe woman who- like all bushi- wore the white bandana with the red hinomaru dot over the forehead. Her hair was a velvety carpet of black fuzz. She held a cigarette close to her lips. Moto was sister to Maya, the daimyo. Both sisters were in their forties. But Moto was shorter and rounder and Maya was taller and thinner. Both were native Japanese. The bushi uniform was plain white linen pants and shirt and black leather boots. With a black vest and black utility belt to hold gear. Moto surveyed the battlefield primarily through the transmissions of the cameras of the quadcopters and secondarily through the transmissions of the 'heads up' displays of the kumo drones themselves. Heretofore she'd been quite pleased with the progress made on this day. Although they'd destroyed practically all of the infrastructure and although every building that wasn't burning was lying in ruins and although the landscape had been made barren of flora and fauna; they'd succeeded in inflicting heavy teki heishi fatalities, and that was all that really mattered. What was happening now was that the drones were scouring the combat zone for whatever teki heishi they could find, and subsequently eliminating them. Moto had overridden the quadcopter nearest to the north shore in order to watch the dazzling aerial and naval battle which had recently commenced and was already almost over.

So, she was aware of what was happening when the taiyo cannon generated a taiyo majo. This is what caused her to smoke her cigarette so nervously. As opposed to smoking her cigarette nonchalantly. Several of her camera feeds were observing the taiyo

Richard Rose 43

majo; utilizing the darkest filters to see the lovely nude woman made of light. Moto and her forces were aware that this majo had already been responsible for the destruction of one attack drone, and now they watched as it descended toward their positions.

Moto wondered if the majo could see them. They were spread out and relatively invisible. But the majo were unpredictable. Nobody ever really knew what a majo knew or didn't know; what they could do or what they couldn't do; what they could see or what they couldn't see. And it was becoming self-evident that the mojo was perfectly aware of their whereabouts as she was moving directly toward them. Moto's command vehicle was parked inside of the phantom shield generated from a unit mounted on a trailer attached to her ATV. But, sadly and unfortunately, none of the other drone operators enjoyed the same luxury as no additional units could be procured. Without hesitation; the taiyo majo moved straight for one of the kumo drone operator's vehicles. Frantically, Moto struggled to match up the position of the majo with the information on her display in order to ascertain which of her subordinates was being targeted, but it was too late. She soon saw that it was kumo team 7 who was attacked first. The feed from their cameras blacked out.

Through multiple cameras and from several angles, Moto had watched as the taiyo majo simply alighted delicately upon the camouflage 8x8 all-terrain vehicle. Setting it aflame instantaneously. And as the taiyo majo floated up out of the inferno and wafted over to her next target, Moto gave the order; "All kumo units, all kumo units! Abandon your stations! I repeat, abandon your stations, now!"

Kumo team 4 was throwing open their hatch when their vehicle ignited as fast as a puddle of gasoline touched by a match. One bushi fell out onto the asphalt; already a roasting corpse- and the other never made it that far. The taiyo majo didn't seem concerned with the insignificant humans who were running away. But she was very interested in- one by one- torching the 8x8 ATVs. Moto radioed to Maya- asking, "Are you seeing this?" And Maya responded, "Yes." And Moto asked her, "What am I supposed to do?" And Maya replied, "Stay under your shield. What else can you do?"

"I should try to gather up my bushi, if I can."

Maya said, "Don't do that. If you drop your shields, she will kill you. Or a teki rocket will get you."

"It is wrong not to try to save them."

"She will kill you. You will die. And besides, she doesn't want your bushi. She wants the kumo. That's the best she can do. She's going to burn herself out soon."

Moto watched the monitors going black- one after another- as each unit's indicator light disappeared from her map display. Her command vehicle still had cameras to see out of and she still possessed a drone of her own to use to see what was happening. The real fighting was somewhat far away. But this wicked woman was within her very midst. Destroying bakufu assets; disabling their invaluable weapon systems. For the time being, anyway. It wasn't long- perhaps only a few minutes- before the taiyo majo had incinerated every kumo drone command vehicle. Leaving the kumo drones themselves lingering about the battlefield like ominous sentinels; sleeping giants on standby.

BLACK CAT SUNRISE

The taiyo majo then wafted over to where Moto was. Moto didn't like to be near her. The phantasma-shield flared with orange spectra as the majo came close. And it was positively roaring when the majo put her hand out to touch it. The ATV vibrated. Moto's molars ached and her eyes strained. She took a long pull off her cigarette and asked her sister, "Are you seeing this?"

"She can't hurt you. Or you'd be dead already," said the daimyo.

"She's so pretty."

"Yes. Very pretty. Very ugly."

After another ten seconds of pressing against the shield, an irritated expression came over the face of the taiyo majo; who shrugged her shoulders, floated up into the sky, became one with the bright midday sun, and then disappeared entirely. It was at this point that the island exploded. The ground had been shaking beneath her for quite some time- especially in the preceding minutes- but, the force of this sudden blast bounced her out of her seat and onto the floor of the cabin.

"What was that?" she asked her sister.

"They blew a channel through the island, to cut off the kumo. Smart move, but unnecessary, considering the kumo are disabled," said the daimyo.

Moto said, "I could still operate one, if I wanted to. I will have the technicians repair the control modules in the facility at headquarters. It should have been done months ago. Anyways, I think our work is done for today."

"Indeed, I think so, too. You did good, Moto."

"Good enough, I suppose. I got to go. I'm getting out of here."

BLACK CAT SUNRISE

"Hai. Keep me posted."

"Hai."

Moto- chain smoking, and thinking about her dead bushi- drove through snowy blood-stained streets lined with blackened ruins and burning tree trunks and littered with body parts and smoldering rubble and windblown debris; heading back to the forward command post; which was an old high school gymnasium filled with electronics and weapons. On her way, she passed by several of her bushi marching toward the rear. But, she wouldn't let these men into her vehicle because she couldn't drop her shield for fear of teki ordnance, and so- much to their lament- she didn't stop for them. Instead, she radioed for a subordinate to come and retrieve them in a troop transport with a kuki as an escort.

Before he could collect his wits, Paul saw the blood witch appear again on the other side of the carpet of corpses. And the lightning witch- who illuminated the shadowy forest with flashing purple light- struck the blood witch with a seething jolt of jagged plasma that looked almost liquid and crackled with a loud throbbing sizzle. As the blood witch was burning and disappearing; Paul turned and joined in with the horde of soldiers who were desperately trying to escape the situation. They were pushing and shoving one another; scraping against trees and struggling to stay on their feet lest they fall and get crushed underfoot. Paul wanted to get to the boats. The boats were the only way off of this terrible island. Except he had no idea where he was going. Nor did he know which direction he was hurrying toward. Not until the wave that was the lot of them collided and

BLACK CAT SUNRISE

clashed with a different wave of further droves of men going in the opposite direction. These other men were calling out, 'North! Go north!' So, that told him he was going south. The wrong way. He needed to go northeast.

It was all chaos now. Pressing and squeezing, and falling and getting trampled, and pulling others down to lift himself back up. They were all doing the same. It had become a blind panic. A tsunami of humanity. And just when it seemed as though he would suffocate, the northward bound opposition succeeded in traversing the distance up and over his conglomeration, which had essentially been trampled before it could reorient itself. Paul had heard something about what they were shouting about; 'They killed everybody!', 'It's a bloodbath!', 'Save yourselves!', 'They're bombarding the shoreline!'

Paul finally got back up on his feet and was turning to run after everybody else, and then he caught a glimpse of what they were running from, and it stopped him in his tracks. Not far off; at the crest of a ridge- the forest stopped abruptly. From his position- if he peered through the smoke- he could see up over the edge. What lay beyond was scorched earth, and beyond that was the sea. And upon the sea were the enemy drones. He saw clusters of craters within craters. Splintered pine trees thrown around like twigs and burning. And the remains of soldiers stretching from the west all the way to the east. Pieces and parts, and halves and wholes. Bodies split straight up the middle, or bodies torn apart at the waist. Arms and legs in mangled contortions. Bodies missing chunks. Or, chunks missing bodies. And these remains gathered about in heaps where they'd collected like snow drifts. Or they were strewn over the terrain with gruesome abandon. All bloodied and broken; ragged flesh and sharp shards of bones. Some of them were on fire. The more he looked, the more he noticed the staggering quantity of disembodied heads that used to have faces, and that now instead wore horrid masks only vaguely reminiscent of their former selves.

Maybe the bombardment was over. Or maybe it was not. Maybe the enemy artillery would shell them through the ridge, or maybe it would not. Paul didn't want to find out. He turned and ran away and hurried to be absorbed into the numbers of the horde. For reasons known and unknown, these embattled souls would spontaneously release crescendos of outcries of abject terror. Earth quaking and ear shattering artillery strikes were coming from all directions and seemingly hedging in toward Paul's position. At any given moment, he could look upward and see the bodies of men soaring through the sky, limp and blown to pieces; some aflame. The blue flames of the discharges of the impacts of the enemy shelling burst up out of the ground and towered overhead; shrouded in dirt and dust and smoke. These weapons sent shockwaves through the terrain that dropped the horde to its knees in its tracks; this happened over and over. Paul wasn't thinking about any of it. It wasn't registering. All he could think was to keep moving forward. Even when about a dozen or two dozen soldiers instantaneously disappeared into thin air right in front of him- with others close by having their limbs and portions of their bodies similarly suddenly vanish; Paul just kept moving forward; passively ignoring their grotesque injuries. Their horrid cries of agony; sharp in his ringing ears. The shelling continued to explode all

BLACK CAT SUNRISE

around them. To Paul, these were unprecedented detonations; he could hear them coming like sonic hatred. They hit the earth like meteors.

Along with the bodies of the other soldiers; entire trees, too, were falling out of the sky. Along with boulders and stones. Paul hadn't considered the possibility of one of these rocks falling on him until it happened. He'd been hunched over- crawling over dead bodies- and a rock struck him in the back; taking the strength from him- dropping him down upon the dead. Through all the confusion, he knew he had to keep moving. His shoulder blade knotted up with an awful pain, but he had to keep going.

Shadows stirred wildly and he wondered what could cause that. Looking skyward, he got his answer. The witch that burned bright like sunlight was soaring over the killing field. Further illuminating the bright snowy landscape. 'Thank goodness for the witches,' he thought, 'they're all we got.' As if to mock his uplifting sentiment- his eye caught sight of the voluptuous oriental blood witch; who smiled seductively as she moved through his army's chaotic retreat, almost unnoticed. Men were dying all around; burning in fires, vaporizing in blasts, disappearing into or being dismembered by the sickeningly strange deatomizing void generators. While many other men were simply struck by falling rocks. Or regrettably trampled by one another. Paul surely had no idea if those he was stepping on were alive or dead.

But the blood witch saw him see her. And she seemed to remember him. Her hand was pulling the life out of a soldier through his nose and mouth, but she dropped that one, sank down into the bloody ground, and reemerged beside Paul; reaching out for

BLACK CAT SUNRISE

him. However, thanks to the deatomizer- there was a vacant area directly to his left. He jumped over into it. And the blood witch leaped after him. But she was caught midair, by the arms of the sunshine witch. In her grasp, the blood witch vaporized instantaneously. Paul was in a smooth crater that had pooled with the blood of the lain out and bleeding out men who were dead and dying along the edges of it. He could feel the heat of the sunshine witch. It was blistering. He rolled around in the blood to stop his skin from burning. He wasn't the only one searing in her heat and she seemed to realize this and so ascended to relieve them. In the confusion, he had dropped his .308 rifle and wasn't inclined to attempt to locate it. He still had the grenade launcher, the grenades, and his side arm.

There was nothing left to do except to keep running. His pain was extreme. His burns were severe. In a way, this was a good thing. It removed him from his situation. The rest of the ordeal happened in slow excruciating motion- but, at the same time, it was over in an instant. As he ran, his army was assailed relentlessly. Over and over, swaths of helpless men were being eradicated all around him. The ground all around burst and danced with the sky above; a cataclysmic Charleston. He just kept moving. Not praying, not wishing, not hoping. Devoid of all emotion and thought. Except for maybe the expectation that each instant would be his last. The lightning witch and the sunshine witch continued to thwart the blood witch's attacks, but- because she could slither across the bloodied ground quickly and invisibly- often times they couldn't spot her until it was too late. And so she killed many men.

Richard Rose 51

Ultimately, a great many soldiers survived the bombardment. But it was only a small fraction of the force that had been stationed on the island earlier that morning. Paul broke out of the forest and stumbled through a chaotic scene where all manner of civilians rushed around in every direction; trying to get to where there was a boat that could evacuate them. Paul was limping, and every step required a concerted effort, and he felt as though he might collapse from pain and exhaustion; but through the fog of his suffering, he remembered what was happening in this place. It was an evacuation. Maybe a million people. Maybe more than that. He wondered if the enemy would murder these innocent people, now that the military was defeated.

Some of the other soldiers melded into the crowds. Others meandered about aimlessly. Others tried to identify some semblance of the former command structure. What Paul did was to wander into the yard of a house on a side street; to an area where the snow was undisturbed; albeit it was somewhat icy. He fell down and laid there on his side. He saw the blood on his hands and it bothered him, so he used snow to clean it off. It hurt, but everything hurt. There was nothing he could do about his blood drenched clothes. His eyes closed. And against his will, he slept.

When he awoke, he thought, 'I can't believe how much this hurts.' His face was the worst part. But his hands hurt, too. The rest of him had been protected by his uniform. He thought, 'I got burned by that damned hex.' There were so many grotesque images flashing through his mind that he couldn't focus on any one of them for more than a second. It made him feel sad; despairing to consider the senseless loss.

BLACK CAT SUNRISE

They'd accomplished nothing. It wasn't a fight. It was a massacre. So it came as a surprise to him when he found himself smiling. He smiled at the thought that he'd been saved from that blood witch bitch not once, but twice. Then he wondered if it was even over; realizing he had no idea what was going on and even less idea what to do next. Despite his smoldering burns, his body temperature had dropped. He knew enough to know he needed to move if he didn't want to freeze. Standing; he wandered off.

It occurred to him that the constant din of energy weapons and explosives had abated. And the wailing of the lamentations of the pains of the soldiery, too, had abated. Those men were elsewhere now. Noticeably fewer people could be seen moving around compared to before he fell asleep. This island belonged to the enemy now. The only thing to do was to get away from it. So he searched out some other soldiers to fall in with. The soldiers were distinct from the civilians because the civilians kept their distance from the soldiers like the soldiers would get them killed just by virtue of their close proximity. Which was an entirely reasonable assumption. What civilians remained- a teaming multitude- had made their way further and further east; accumulating around the docks. While the soldiery lingered about the western areas of the north shore Montauk beaches.

Paul got his first glimpse of the ocean since his last glimpse of the ocean. Near, far, out toward New York, out toward Rhode Island; absolute devastation. The skeletons and carcasses of the pride of an old world burned and smoked. Enormous warships; reduced to monuments of defeat. Smaller vessels- more numerous and equally destroyed- gave some idea

Richard Rose 53

of the gigantism of the once impotent and now dead giants. Many were lost beneath the surface, but had left bits and pieces afloat to evidence their demise. A cabaret of wreckage and ruin. The scene served as a reminder of what was generally a well-known fact; the enemy was invincible. Everywhere; acrid smoke hung thick in the air. The enemy; ominously absent. Apparently, all fighting had ceased. Up and down the beach were strange mementos; half of a fighter jet, countless dead bodies, random flaming debris, and soldiers staggering about like drunks.

It was a strange moment. He should be dead. So many were dead. Those behemoths had been ineffectual at best. The whole day was a loss. Even for a people accustomed to losing. Set against the backdrop of a disastrous naval battle, was the evacuation of the entire civilian population of confederate Long Island. These harmless boats came and went unmolested in several uniform lines. Helicopters and airplanes, too, were coming and going. If he looked closely, Paul could see tiny little men struggling to survive in the icy waters; adrift on anything that floated- waiting to be rescued. And then he noticed there were boats out there collecting those men to the best of their ability.

Paul found a group of soldiers huddled inside a house with no windows that overlooked the sound. They were waiting for a boat, presumably. 'Fuck. I want to get out of here. If I never see this island again, it'll be too soon,' Paul thought. None of these men looked any better than him and several looked much worse. One was missing a hand. Another cradled a fractured arm. These things weren't so bad; considering. It stood to reason that many of the wounded had been left for dead. Nobody was saying anything.

BLACK CAT SUNRISE

Paul asked, "Those men. In the woods. We're leaving them out there? Or what?"

The soldiers ignored him. All but one soot-caked younger guy- almost a kid- who said, "You want to go pull them out, then more power to you."

Paul looked beyond the township, back toward the forests, which were hidden by buildings, but which he could see were burning in places.

"There's no search and rescue coming?" Paul asked.

The kid- who sat huddled against a wall; blackened face devoid of emotion and with a shiver in his voice- said, "We can't go back into that hell hole. The samurai are probably out there right now."

"There's no samurai out there. Samurai don't expose themselves. I wish they would."

"Yeah. The fuckers. I meant the drones. I guess. The drones are out there. Hey. You know your face is all fucked up, right?"

"Yeah. Got burnt to shit. By a damn hex."

"Oh. That's good luck."

"Really?"

"No. But don't feel bad. My fuckin' ankles broke. I can't walk on it. Hey. You mind helping me up onto the boat? When it gets here, I mean?"

"Yeah. Sure."

"Thanks, bro. What's your name?"

"Paul."

"My name's Jacob."

Nyu NyuYoku is a city that is only the hollow shell- an empty husk- of its former self; operated and maintained by a complicated caste system of dorei; slaves and slaves' slaves and slaves' slaves' slaves. A

Richard Rose 55

BLACK CAT SUNRISE

tremendous workforce, but a skeleton crew relative to what the city once necessitated. This city- like most major cities, now- is lorded over by the bakufu.

1,700 feet above Nyu NyuYoku; there is a garden of colossal stones, neatly raked gravel, bamboo, azaleas like orbs, and evergreens windswept eastward by perpetual high-altitude gusting. Amidst this garden are the local bakufu rulers. The Naito. Deep in meditation. Kneeling upon tatami mats. Statuesque; enshrouded in white cloaks. Exposed to extreme cold and wet. Kazuki, Moto, and Maya. And also, Xander and Michio. Michio is the shokicho- a secretary general, in essence; who oversees a cadre of underlings who facilitate all manner of mundane and practical details; often by cruel and unusual means. Michio is also the younger brother of Moto and Maya and has two young children- a boy and a girl- who are elsewhere. The night air is blustering, but these people are as still as the dead; their garments rippling upon them. For several hours they have sat. At one with the oneness that is all there is.

Without warning, an old woman appears before them; in a split second she manifests from out of the nothingness. She appears silently, and observes them; as they do not realize she is there. This is Yoshiko Naito Majo. She is small, frail, with wrinkles, and the subtle jowls of the aged. She, too, is adorned in a white cloak. Her hair is short and black, with some white in it. She smiles. Even from the perspective of her otherworldly disposition, it is a joy to see her children. Even with the vibrations of mass death still buzzing through the ether. Her children call to mind her own childhood. She remembers the innocence of her first

Richard Rose 56

years. The only time she'd ever been oblivious about what is and what must be. A fond memory.

Yoshiko Naito majo speaks loudly, to be heard over the rain, "My children. I have returned."

Their eyes open and they smile to see her smiling face. In their minds, they remain in a dreamlike state of pseudo-hypnagogic trance. The mystical radiance of the majo furthers the effect. The majo says, "Please, hear me well. For I am tired and cannot stay long. You've attained a respectable victory. Our kovun of the white is pleased with your success. But I have summoned you all here to deliver a grave warning. The heavens are resentful of these recent events. The coven of the grey is of the mind that to force the confederates off the island was to upset the sacred balance."

Maya objected, "They were a threat! They had to be removed!"

"This, I understand. And in this our white kovun is in agreement. Unfortunately- as an indirect result- the situation is this city will remain as untenable as it had been previously. For we have fallen out of favor with the coven of the grey. And as you can well imagine, this is a serious problem for the Nyu NyuYoku bakufu."

"What are we supposed to do?" Maya asked.

The majo replied- her voice; a rasping timbre, "Do not forget, you are the custodians of warfare. Our coven has given you all the tools and all the means. You must multiply the bushi by one hundred-fold. You must fortify the city to its outermost limits; every crack and every crevice must be as the web of a spider. You must reinforce and entrench and concentrate your forces. You must refer to the wisdom of bygone bushi

BLACK CAT SUNRISE

masters. I am just an old wicca. I cannot fight your fight for you."

Maya said, "Mother! We cannot fight the coven of the grey! We will be annihilated!"

"You will not have to. The kovun of the white will yield to the coven of the grey. If we must. Such a travesty will not ever come to pass. Do not forget the sacred balance. Without the balance, there can be no white, no grey. No black. But the coven of the grey is not the bakufu teki. Bakufu teki wa bakufu teki desu yo! Do not underestimate your enemy. Anticipate the hordes. Do not place such reliance on our technologies of death. One day you will face the horde on the terms of the horde. And on that day will come your judgment."

The bakufu overlords considered these words. Yoshiko majo looked around at the garden with approval, she studied each of their faces, and then she said to them, "I must go. I am old. I am tired. I love you all. My children."

They watched her turn and walk to the edge of the building and crawl up upon the ledge and sort of just fall over the other side. Into the abyss. A curious old woman. Their blood was rushing now. Their faces flushed by the cold. Their inhalations and exhalations becoming more rapid. Their minds; returning to their skulls, like vapors moving in reverse.

Kazuki said what they were all thinking, "It's freezing out here and I am soaked. Let's go inside."

Moto said, "Yes, come on. We will drink sake. There is a lot to discuss."

Chapter 3
Phantom

BLACK CAT SUNRISE

A swarm of surveillance drones monitored the ongoing Long Island exodus from high up in the sky. For two reasons, the drones were spread out over significant distances; so as to not all be shot out of the sky at once, and so as to take account of which throngs were traveling along which roadways and in what densities. This was of interest not only to the Nyu NyuYoku bakufu but also to the Bosuton bakufu, who had their own drones to watch with. The refugees moved like a river, but in reverse; stemming from the ocean at Old New London and dispersing into tributaries that spread out over the land as they went along. A thick vein went north- walking on Interstate 395, weaving between the omnipresent rusted out shells of abandoned cars and gradually veering off toward the forests in the northwest. Presumably to avoid Old Worcester while still making their way toward Old Springfield. Most refugees went along Route 2 toward Old Hartford and then on up toward Old Springfield. Other throngs took a myriad of alternate routes through the decimated townships of yore. It seemed they were converging on the area surrounding Old Springfield, but a sizable contingent was departing from Old Hartford on a separate course toward an area between Old Springfield and Old Albany, called Old Pittsfield.

These smaller type cities were targeted for destruction long ago, during the preliminary escalations of the perpetual conflict. With the megacities invaded and overrun and with the smaller cities predominantly decimated; a humanitarian crisis inevitably ensued as confederates were driven into the wilds to perish. The dying off en masse of the teki civilians was by design, of course. But the staggering

BLACK CAT SUNRISE

losses suffered unto the confederacy began to threaten the balance of the two warring covens. And the third coven- which is the fulcrum for the contesting two- eventually began to take more and more offense to the ethnic cleansing of the confederates. It was considered unacceptable for the whites to eliminate the blacks to such a degree that it would tilt the balance of power. And so- under the protection of the greys- the black populations swelled into the hordes of the present day.

"We're thinking the army will be using the Old Springfield area to regroup. And that Old Pittsfield will become the refugee encampment," Kazuki- biting her nails- tells her mother.

They're wearing plain white bushi uniforms with hinomaru headbands. They're standing with Xander before an array of monitors in an otherwise nondescript white room in the upper floors of their Manhattan headquarters. The drone operators themselves being located elsewhere. Maya sips a cup of tea. Xander smokes. Him and Kazuki have been examining the screens for a couple of hours. This is five days since the battle of Long Island.

"Many of them will freeze to death before they get where they are going," said Maya.

"They're more resilient than that, mother," said Kazuki.

"Yes, well. Wishful thinking, I suppose," said Maya.

Xander said, "We've not been able to identify any targets of strategic significance. That is, of course, because it's all underground. We map the entrances and exits of their subterranean facilities insofar as we're able to discover them, but this is of limited practical benefit because for every thing we find there are countless things we don't find."

Kazuki said, "We do know they're very active in these hundred square miles surrounding Old Pittsfield. In these hills to the west, in these forests by this lake, and all along this mountain ridge to the north. They've got earth moving machines all over. We could take those out. Make it harder for them to dig in."

"I'll consider it. It's a smart move. But it exposes our resources to grey retaliation and peril."

Xander offered, "It's simple to locate where they're actively blasting through the rock to make their fortifications. They do that all over. But, there's no way to distinguish between civil and military operations."

One of the screens went haywire with whirling images of spiraling motions as the corresponding drone plummeted to the earth; having been shot out of the sky. Maya rolled her eyes, frustrated, asking, "How many of these have we lost today?"

"That would be the fourth," Xander said.

"Alright. We're not made of drones. Shut it down for the day. Send them out again tonight. I want to know where their tanks are. I want to know where their ammunition dumps are. Where their armories are. I want to know where their planes are. I want to know where their weapons systems are hiding."

Xander said, "It's all underground. Disassembled. In pieces. All over the place. Getting shifted around bit by bit."

A communication device in Maya's ear goes 'ding, ding, ding.' She presses the button to answer. Her sister informs her that their transport is inbound and the akachan bushi are prepared for exhibition. "Hai, hai. See you soon," she says to the earpiece. And

BLACK CAT SUNRISE

then she tells her daughter and her daughter's father, "I've got to go. Have the drones in position at midnight, and I will meet you back here then."

'Hai,' the two repeated in unison.

Maya turned and left abruptly. She went to the stairs and hiked up a multitude of flights until she came to a door where her thick white winter jacket was hanging. She put it on and went out into the garden; traversing through to where a platform was located. She ascended the stairs to get up on it just as a transport drone was descending to carry her away. This drone looked like a helicopter, but with no rotor or blade or anything like that; all silver and with a pointed tail. No windows on it, but from within the interior all the outside world was visible via a system of cameras and high-definition screens. Moto was seated inside and operating the controls.

"Sister. We've done quite well. You will be impressed," Moto said.

"However many we've got. It won't be enough."

Kuki attack drones patrolled the skies above the city. And umi drones patrolled the waters, as well. Keisatsu security drones- reminiscent of flying saucers, but just a meter across- patrolled the streets, as per usual; hovering ten feet above ground and indiscriminately aiming their laser cannons at whoever they happened upon. Because their surveillance camera, targeting system, and cannon shared a singular tubular protrusion of an apparatus. Slaves- wearing all red uniforms, coats, and hats- traversed the sidewalks on their way to and from their dismal purposes; not daring to think any rebellious thoughts. The weather was blustering and blowing yesterday's icy snow through the skyscrapers and everywhere was a

BLACK CAT SUNRISE

wind tunnel. The transport drone compensated for this but it made for a subtly sickening jostling sensation within the interior.

What the sisters were observing was an assortment of collections of bushi which were gathered all over the city; congregating in parks, gardens, courtyards, and quadrangles. These men were kneeling in meditation and facing eastward. However, because these men were only recently lifted from the dregs of the dorei- the slave cast- it was not comfortable for them to be seated on their knees in this traditional fashion and so many of them were suffering greatly; as the recourse for their squirming and shifting was a stinging slap in the face from the riding crop of the lieutenant of their contingent.

These lieutenants were to be the glue that would hold the bushi together. Up until a few days ago, they were the entirety of the bushi. These lieutenants were men of distinction and elevated regard- most of whom were of Japanese descent- who collected their contingents from what manpower was available and then made it their responsibility to raise the individuals into fighting men worthy of the title. Doing so by utilizing a variety of fundamental martial arts practices coupled with education, conditioning, and drilling. It was a daunting proposal but the only thing particularly unrealistic about it was that in this case the processes were to be rapidly expedited. Whether the rushing of the growth spurt was necessary or unnecessary would remain to be seen.

Maya and Moto drifted through Nyu Nyu Yoku and observed the collections of bushi as they knelt close together and suffered the elements and the discomforts; the lieutenants standing apart and

Richard Rose 63

enforcing discipline as necessary. All bakufu wore white uniforms with hinomaru headbands; same as the exalted sisters. Their warm outerwear; also in white. Warm white hats covered their headbands. The city itself remained more or less like it always had. Mostly less. Although, it had become surprisingly clean, tidy, and orderly. What was once a dystopian wasteland of wreckage and ruin had slowly been cleared out, cleaned up, and well organized; thereafter thrust into an ongoing stasis complemented by a low impact largely nonexistent citizenry. The place- like all bakufu cities- was a monument to its former self. A hollow shell of what it once was.

"They've done better than I thought they would," Maya remarked.

"These men were dorei. Now they are bushi. They were eager to sign on."

"Maybe foolishly so."

"I suppose, but they will eat better. And their loved ones will prosper."

"Hai. This is a splendid display."

"Hai. Yoshikosama said to multiply by one hundred. So we multiplied by one hundred. Or, near to it. Of course now we will have a shortage in menial labor."

"What about skilled labor?" Maya asked.

"Skilled labor has not been affected."

"Good. Good. It's not hard to get more dorei. There's always more dorei. And the prisoner of war transfers, too. For whatever they're worth. Michio will have his people bring them in. And we can use the akachan bushi as needed."

"It's not good to interrupt their training."

BLACK CAT SUNRISE

"If it is important, we will have no choice. At least, for this next week or two."

"Hai."

"How many bushi do we have now?"

"Some of these will wash out. Some people are just garbage. But, tentatively, we've got 50,000."

"Big difference."

"Hai. Things are changing. It's going to be bad," said Moto.

"Hai," Maya agreed.

"The kovun will send the ninja."

"Hai," Maya agreed with a sigh. The ninja would usher in a new era. The ninja were a precursor to cataclysm. But so long as the hinomaru flew over the city- or even over its remains- that was what mattered most. Her feelings were irrelevant.

Maya's mind reeled; trying to figure out if all the pieces were fitting together or not. It was not unusual for her- or for her family- to feel a little clueless about bakufu operations in general. It was an empire operated by underlings and an irritating disconnect persisted between those below and those above. But they were used to it. From her commanding perspective, this obfuscation was the proverbial fog of war. Bakufu systems of organization were more akin to invaders occupying foreign territory than to the refined war machines of the late old world. It was easy to wield authority, but it was difficult to manifest desired results.

Moto maneuvered the transport up and out over central park. This is where the largest collections of bushi recruits were gathered. The trees had no leaves. The grand lawns were white with snow. The akachan bushi were inadvertently camouflaged by

Richard Rose 65

BLACK CAT SUNRISE

their white clothes. The baby samurai created a hopeful display as they knelt in miserable forced meditation. Suddenly, a squawking radio communique burst through the speakers of the transport and through the speakers in Maya and Moto's earpieces; "All units, all units, battle stations, battle stations, under attack, under attack."

Hearing this; Maya told Moto, "Return us to the garden. Hayaku. Hayaku."

"Hai," Moto said, grabbing at the transport's stick and wrenching it back and over and veering up and away on a reverse arcing trajectory; the buildings of Nyu NyuYoku becoming a blur through the window monitors. Soon they gained some altitude and Maya could see for herself what had sounded the alarm. Far away; an incoming enemy missile trailed black smoke through the bright blue sky.

"Wait. Stop. Look," Maya told Moto. The transport spun to a gentle halt in midair. Maya pointed to the missile, which was coming at them from the north. "What is it? I don't see it," Moto said, but before Maya could point it out to her any better, the missile had already collided with the phantasma-shield of one of the kuki drones. They were above lower Manhattan by now and the explosion had occurred out toward Old Harlem; just north of Central Park. Even at this distance they felt the shock and heard the boom. It wasn't an unusual thing to see a missile hit a kuki drone, but what happened next turned Maya's blood to ice water.

The shield's field of phantasm splashed away with the blast; looking something like an orange firework bursting sideways. Which was unprecedented in and of itself but what was worse was that

BLACK CAT SUNRISE

phantasmosis began to gravitate toward a single coalescing point that sucked the dazzling light toward it like a vacuum. The shield had served its purpose, and the kuki drone remained in flight and in position; but all that changed in an instant, when- like a glowing fairy trailing pixie dust- the concentrated phantasm darted into, through, and out of the hull of the drone; trailing flaming wreckage and orange energy behind it. In an instant; the kuki drone was dropping like a blazing brimstone.

Maya's gaze went to the footwell. She couldn't watch. Because she understood. This changed everything. Moto asked her, "Is that what I think it is?"

"That, my sister, is exactly what it looks like. Our worst nightmare."

"Phantom Majo desu yo... They finally did it. We shouldn't be out here."

"Get back beneath the skyline. Take us to Riker's. Hayaku. Hayaku."

Moto cut the antigravity drive. The craft fell at freefall speed for a second. Then she reengaged the power; flying away through the city streets. Making their way to the underground command and control bunker. They had no way to know it, but the newborn phantom witch wasn't currently interested in them. It didn't pursue them and, in fact, it hadn't noticed them at all.

This phantom witch had the likeness of a nordic woman. Such as all teki majo possessed. She was a short woman with round features and her sizzling eyes were soft in their watchfulness. Her restrained smile was one of feigned naivety, ironic innocence, and good humor. Her short ionic hair wafted about her head like she was underwater. Nude; her breasts were supple,

BLACK CAT SUNRISE

pert, and round. Her figure was an hourglass; shapely and full. She held her hands up before her as she glanced about curiously. Looking down, she saw thousands of men looking back up at her. These drew her attention. Her smile shifted to that of wickedly pleasing malevolence. The phantom witch descended on central park; her radiant form emitting a shower of sparkles as she went. These thousands of men in the park made great haste to scatter, but there were too many of them, and they were tripping over one another and slipping on the ice and running in the wrong directions.

Her feet came down through the bodies of struggling individuals and left holes and channels and ravines in their flesh as she literally stepped through them. Those who did not die screamed in agony while others screamed with fear and panic. She drifted through them with her arms out. A ghostly apparition; she moved without much motion. Only reaching for them a little. At first. As her excitement grew, her behavior changed. She began to enjoy herself. Pieces, parts, and portions of human men vanished in bursts of ghastly orange sparkles. Her gentle movements removed heads from torsos and torsos from legs. Her gliding ankles would slice through a man as if he wasn't there. She took chunks out of them as a laser might. Ropes and sprays and mists of crimson blood splashed about her. Men fell before her. And behind her. She was having fun; doing graceful ballet types of leaps and bounds through her dying and suffering victims.

The slave-soldier recruits fled to all directions as fast as they could. The hardened bushi, too, fled just the same. Still, there had been so many of them within

Richard Rose 68

BLACK CAT SUNRISE

the area that the phantom witch found herself in no short supply of persons to eliminate. And eliminating these was, of course, her reason for being there.

The phantom witch began to toy with them. She could move with otherworldly speed and she would block their exits and force them back and in this way corral them into clusters of clusters. And she'd move through these clusters as a bringer of doom. Effortlessly disappearing tremendous quantities of human flesh. Innumerable salvos of glistening orange sparkles flared up and disappeared amidst torrential fountains of blood.

The whites of the clothes of the men who had thus far somehow survived were now stained red with blood. Many of them were missing hands and feet or arms or legs; or missing areas of their bodies. There were dozens of these such men; scrambling over the strewn about corpses of hundreds of those who weren't so lucky. Some; the phantom witch would reach for them individually; running her fingers through their skulls leaving only chard and cauterized fragments thereafter. Her toes drifted through the remains of these men; sizzling and scorching with an unnatural burning that had less to do with thermodynamics and more to do with trans dimensional forces of mystical origin.

The phantom witch began to fizzle out. Her intensity diminishing suddenly. She realized this and stopped and shrugged and observed her surroundings. Many dead men strewn in pieces and gathered in heaps all across a field of blood drenched snows. Many suffering and struggling to flee. 'How beautiful,' she thought, as she disappeared.

Richard Rose 69

BLACK CAT SUNRISE

It would be some time before Jacob could walk without assistance. His broken ankle had been set and bound by a field surgeon after crossing the Long Island Sound and it would- more or less- heal eventually, but not any time soon. The same surgeon applied a creamy white substance to Paul's burns and gave him a jar of the stuff to take with him. Some of the burns were dressed with gauze and linen, and others remained exposed to the air. It took a full day and night for the throngs of women and children to coordinate with the surviving militia men and disembark on their various nightmarish flights. The military followed behind them. Thusly, these civilians were omnipresent fixtures. And always there were lingering scavengers or dead and dying stragglers strewn about the landscape. Jacob and Paul had been assimilated into a company with other surviving soldiers who had successfully escaped from the island. Jacob hung on Paul's shoulder and limped along as they painstakingly traversed winding forest roads that were slick with ice- moving from one major thoroughfare toward another; slowly making their way northwest. On the second night after the battle, they sheltered in an overgrown development of abandoned homes that were destroyed by time and by the elements and overtaken by thorny vines and tangled bushes. Entire houses were burned for warmth. They built windbreaks from scrap metal and huddled close to these sizable fires.

Their company was called Delta and it consisted of 75 men divided into four platoons. Seven such companies were the entirety of the remains of the confederate forces of Long Island; forces which had previously numbered in the tens of thousands had been divided into multiple divisions. The companies traveled separately and along different routes. Their mission, now, was to rejoin the rest of the army. Which meant an arduous march cross-country in blinding cold and driving snow; while suffering from incredible injuries. Often, wounded men fell behind and were left to their own devices- or lack thereof. It was a dismal situation, but these were soldiers accustomed to all the worst horrors of this world. Thankfully, they were able to sustain themselves on an abundance of venison. There were deer everywhere and these were easily shot and roasted and made into soups. And being as that there were so few mouths to feed, there was always enough to go around. That, and also, of all their myriad problems- running out of hardtack was never among them.

On the third night they made it to an underground outpost in the middle of nowhere. The confederacy possessed untold numbers of such facilities; cavernous concrete caves with endless corridors and all manner of chambers. Their civilization tended to live underground more so than it did above, and this had been so for decades. They'd learned to thrive down there. Within the security of the outpost they were able to eat real food, sleep in real warmth and relative comfort, and generally feel a modicum of safety. Free- at least- from the threat of succumbing to exposure to a vicious Old New England winter. Here they remained for a further second evening so that it was the fifth day after the battle when they disembarked. The fifth night was a repeat of the second night- with more campfire houses- but the experience wasn't nearly so spiritually crushing as that of just a few days prior. Much had been lost, but these

BLACK CAT SUNRISE

men were still alive. And that meant something. It meant a lot. It meant more than words can express.

Through all of this, Jacob remained close to Paul. They'd bonded; whether they knew it or not. Something about their having met when they had and how they had; it had connected them. Jacob was smaller and younger and his skin was brown due to southwestern ethnic heritage. Nobody looked to him for help or assistance, but his disposition was incongruously cheerful and Paul appreciated him for that as well as for his cunning insight and keen powers of observation. Jacob was also strangely handsome, and so he attracted unwanted attention- if only as a target of derision. His many positive character traits were, of course, obscured and subdued by the awful circumstances, but even men who suffered like this still filled their time with gallows' humor and nihilistic chiding. These marching days were grueling days overflowing with sadness, pain, and misery.

Jacob liked Paul because Paul was a sympathetic character. Half of Paul's face was pink and raw and shining with ooze as well as black with dry bloody scabs. Perpetually; Paul seemed as though he might pass out from the pain, but- paradoxically- he didn't seem to notice. Despite his torment, Paul was friendly. And he appreciated Jacob being there. Simultaneously smart and oblivious; Paul knew all kinds of abstract information, but seemed blissfully ignorant about the war and the state of world affairs. Also, not for nothing, Paul was as tall and strong as Jacob was short and delicate. More so than that, it was generally understood that if it weren't for one another, a soldier would have nobody at all. And these two evidenced that.

BLACK CAT SUNRISE

On the seventh day, Paul and Jacob's company- in accordance with the mission plan devised at the outset- regrouped and joined up with the other companies of the Long Island Battalion. They finished their marches in concert and were funneled down underground into an immense dome chamber to where they were given soup to eat. Their clothes were soaking wet, like usual. But it was warm in there and it was good to take their boots and soaking layers off. A lot of these men were in terrible condition. Besides their wounds and injuries, many suffered from hypothermia and frostbite. Many were passing out from exhaustion and their peers were kicking them and shoving them to get them to wake up because a pedestal had been carried out and a PA system had been set up and their new commanding officer was evidently preparing to address the lot of them.

Having suffered through the same ordeal as them, the lieutenant colonel looked about the same as them. The main difference being that his health was holding up whereas theirs was failing them. And the man had shaved his face, which would have been odd were he not an officer. He had a strong jaw that gave him big cheeks. His ear-length black hair was nicely cut. His black uniform was clean and fresh. He'd obviously obtained and changed into a fresh one. A little red leaf-looking symbol on his breast pocket marked him for what he was, but besides that he was just like them. His blue eyes scanned the room, trying to take in what he was seeing. Paul watched him looking at them.

The officer called out, "Attention!" and their heads turned to him and that was about the best he could hope for, so he carried on, "Good enough. Good

Richard Rose 73

BLACK CAT SUNRISE

to be out of the weather, yes? Okay. I am Lieutenant Colonel Anderson. I was Captain Anderson, but they needed a guy to head the battalion, and I was the guy. Listen, I have got some good news for you all. Let me say a couple things, first, and then I'll get to that last. But let me tell you this; this is some good good news. Many of us live our entire lives and don't hear any news this good. But I got to sort out orders and speak my piece, first.

"The rest of this god-awful march will commence tomorrow morning at 0500 hours. Until then, eat your fill, and get some rest. I am sure you'll find the facility hospitable. We'll be heading northwest to meet up with and be absorbed by Colonel Alan Blake's regiment. For whatever it is worth, the Long Island battalion will remain intact. You will receive as much R&R as possible. You will be fed well. You will be outfitted with fresh gear and new equipment. And then probably you will be thrown right back into the meat grinder.

"I know it might seem impossible to put yourself out there again but you have to remember what is written on our shirts. We live to war. We war to live. Obviously, what happened back on Long Island was a sad thing. A bad thing. Even measured against the unending hell we are accustomed to. But you know, they always tell you that. They say, 'it can always get worse.' I'd say they're right about that. There ain't no words that can bring back what those snake skinned neeps took away from us. All I ask is you keep your hatred- your anger, your rage, your wrath- you keep it burning inside you, like a little candle. And no matter what, you don't never let that candle burn out.

Richard Rose 74

BLACK CAT SUNRISE

Because if that candle won't win this fight, then there is nothing that will.

"Alright, I said I got some good good news, so here it is..."

Paul wasn't thinking about the good good news. Paul was thinking about how his angry little candle isn't going to win the fight because the fight can't actually be won. It's a well-known fact that while the upper management never shut up about winning the war- it wasn't ever going to happen. And it's no small consolation that while they cannot ever win, they won't ever lose, either. And then, suddenly, the lighting began to flicker, and everybody's heads looked upward as all across the ceiling of the dome the lightbulbs began to pop and burst. Glass shards rained down upon them.

Only a fraction of the men of the battalion saw what happened next- and none of them were fast enough to react to it- when; the shadowy figure of an old oriental woman in a black cloak suddenly appeared- hovering in thin air, as it were- behind the lieutenant colonel's back. Her hostile eyes were glowing radioactive green and there was a hateful sneer on her lips. In a singular motion she effortlessly sunk her razorlike claws into Anderson's throat and tore them clean through his jugular vein. His blood; splashing over all those who were near to him. And then the woman vanished as suddenly as she had appeared. Some of the men pulled guns but there was nothing remaining to be fired at. The officer lay on the floor bleeding out with eyes wide like a suffocating fish's and his mouth gaping like a suffocating fish's.

It was still possible to see what was going on because a small number of lights hadn't blown out.

Richard Rose 75

That, and because flashlight beams were beaming all over the place. One soldier called out; 'We need a medic!' and another replied, 'Don't bother. This guy's dead,' and another called out, 'I got glass in my soup!' and another replied, 'Can I have it?' Paul turned on his flashlight and checked his bowl and Jacob's bowl. They had both finished their soup, already. But, indeed, glass had gotten all over everything. Nobody was especially upset about or surprised by what had happened to the officer. Wasn't the first time, and it wouldn't be the last. Officers had a way of randomly getting picked off. It was a well-known fact that they were high priority targets. As a result, nobody ever wanted to hold those positions. A soldier called out, 'What's the goddamn good news?'

Jacob said to Paul, "Hey, check me for glass and I will check you." "Yeah," Paul agreed and they shined their flashlights on each other; scouring their clothes and bodies, searching for bits and pieces and shards of glass. Of which there were plenty. One soldier nearby remarked, 'Those fuckin' witches are weird as shit. What the fuck?' Paul remembered his close encounters. Weird wasn't all they were. They were as frightening as any war machine.

Another officer climbed up on the pedestal. In his black battle dress uniform he looked just like an ordinary enlisted man. Except for his breast pocket's red oak leaf insignia. This was a tall and broad man; bulky, with shaggy blonde hair coming out from a warm black wool cap; blue eyed and with a face like carved stone. He took the microphone and said, "Gentleman. I am Major Arnold. I presume I will be your new lieutenant colonel in a few minutes here. Lieutenant colonel Anderson would have wanted me to

BLACK CAT SUNRISE

share the good news. I don't know why that bitch was so inclined to kill the man, but fuck it. Who knows why a hex does anything it does? Not like what I'm going to tell you is some big secret. I think they're just pissed off about it, is all. Fucking bitch. Anyways. The good news is that those geniuses in the Netherlands have finally synthesized a phantom witch. This means that, for the first time in all these decades of global warfare, our side finally has a weapon with which to break through the enemy phantasma-shields."

A silence fell over the men. A silence as brief as it was heavy. Because just a second later they were up on their feet and cheering and clapping and hooting and hollering with joy. For many of them this was the happiest moment of their lives. For many of them this was the first time they'd ever felt what hope feels like. Some of them couldn't help but to burst into tears. After all they'd been through, and given the context, it was easy to understand how so many hardened men could break down at these words. Those shields were the worst thing in the world. Even worse than the witches, in a practical sense. Paul, too, was on his feet and clapping his hands up over his head, with tears running down his scabbed-over face. He couldn't believe it. It sounded too good to be true.

Chapter 4
Initiative
Some busy weeks passed by, during which all manner of preparations transpired. It had been decided to mount an offensive against the Nyu NyuYoku Bakufu and take the city, if at all possible. The Long Island battalion- it was decided- was to remain intact. And it was subsequently absorbed into

BLACK CAT SUNRISE

Colonel Dorph's regiment of Major General Atkin's 46th infantry division; the Quinetucket Killers. There were fifteen thousand soldiers in the 46th infantry. And that was less than 10 percent of the official strike force of 160,000 men; divided into infantry, artillery, and cavalry. All of which was to be supported by what air cavalry remained available to this theatre after the disastrous battle of Long Island. There would be practically no naval support aside from what civilian boats could be commandeered for military purposes.

On standby to reinforce the 160,000 enlisted men was a contingent of 80,000 militia men- many of which were retired soldiery- who'd come down from the northern territories where confederation women make babies and manufacture war materials in relative safety. Some of these militia men possessed no better weapon than a bludgeoning object or a kitchen knife, but they all knew they would find something somewhere eventually. The confederate militia of the world could be counted in the hundreds of millions, but it was the army's standard operating procedure to request %50 of committed troop numbers in committed militia so as that the supply would never run dry. For all operations were prone to heavy losses and if the militia were lost then their sad facsimile of a civilization would be entirely lost, as well.

It was night time. The offensive was slated to begin in the morning, with no word yet as to how the commanders intended to penetrate the enemy defenses. It was supposed the new phantasma witch would make this impossibility possible, but nobody had much faith in the theory. Paul and Jacob sat around a small cook fire with their fireteam. The other two men were Elijah and Yoshic. Elijah- a noticeably

Richard Rose 78

muscular pasty-skinned guy with a round and high foreheaded head, a stubbly face, fuzzy hair, a perpetually crazed smile, and deranged eyes- would serve as the automatic rifleman; utilizing a belt-fed M240; the belts themselves to be carried in a heavy box slung over his shoulder. Yoshic- a tall and slender tan-skinned man of 27- with chiseled cheekbones, a stylish goatee, short sandy hair, piercing eyes, a wry grin, and a positive demeanor- would serve as team leader. His primary weapon would be the familiar M4 automatic chambered in 5.56 with a drum magazine, red dot sight, and a modular M26 bolt action magazine-fed shotgun mounted under the barrel. As a result of this impractical configuration, Yoshic had to fire the weapon sideways when in the prone position. But he was used to it.

Paul would serve as grenadier, because he still had his thumper and bandelier of shells; although he'd traded out some of his red tip explosive rounds for blue tip flechette rounds. Jacob had been re-outfitted with an M110; a high caliber magazine-fed semi-automatic sniper rifle with a long-range scope. At any given time, Jacob could be observed cradling the weapon like a baby, because the scope was such a delicate instrument. Jacob thought about that scope before anything else. He wouldn't let people near him, and he wouldn't do anything unless he first placed the rifle in a soft and safe place. It made him difficult company, and a weird soldier, but they all understood.

All around them there were other teams positioned around cookfires. This was their way. Each team was like a family. Three teams to a squad. Three squads to a platoon. Their platoon- second platoon-was commanded by Lieutenant Darby; who always

BLACK CAT SUNRISE

seemed to be elsewhere. The squad was- in theory- the extended family, but beyond the fireteam, even familiar faces tended to blur into the swarm. The platoons bled into one another to form the company and the companies bled into one another to form the battalion and so on.

As per usual, there wasn't any electricity out where they were in the ruins of what was once an expanse of suburban developments and which had long since been burned-out and reduced to tracts of rotting ruins overgrown with forests. Quietude lingered in the air. The silence of exhausted men granted a reprieve. This was the culmination of several days marching. And while the harsh winter was finally calming its fury, it had been quite cold all the same. Their little cook fires were their greatest joy in the world. Producing hot food for their stomachs, and hot heat for their hands to absorb. Throughout the sprawling encampment, these little fires burned in their little rocket stoves and produced countless little candles of light; creating a tapestry woven throughout the trees and betraying their positions to nobody in particular.

Paul was savoring each spoonful of his stew- the warmth, the flavor, the energy- when he heard a strange sound. "You fuckin' hear that?" Yoshic asked. They were all hearing it. "What is that, like, coyotes?" Jacob asked. "Or, bats, maybe?" Elijah suggested. Paul said, "It sounds like... laughter..." The sound was faint at the moment, but it did not remain faint for long. Rapidly, it got louder and louder. It was laughter, but, the laughter of chipmunks or squirrels or something. It seemed to be coming from everywhere. From all around them, and even from amidst them.

BLACK CAT SUNRISE

"It's a hex," Yoshic shouted. "It's more than one," Paul added, as he took out his flashlight. "Always got to be something," Elijah noted. Jacob clutched his rifle against his body and looked around him. All the men who were in this area were having more or less the same conversation. All swinging flashlight beams about and searching for some explanation or indication of what was happening. The laughter was sharp and small. It was the laughter of children. Many, many children. And these children were simultaneously on top of their position and nowhere to be found. The laughing voices possessed an ethereal quality as well as a very distinct piercing lilt that betrayed their origins. This was the striking laughter of multitudes of Japanese children; rising to a fever pitch.

Then the little flame from their little rocket stove flared up into the air, shot up into the night, and took the form of a small boy made of blue fire who at once fell to the icy ground and then quickly stood up to his full three-foot height. The fiery child looked around, and- squealing wildly- jumped at Yoshic. Yoshic struggled but the boy was made of flame and there was nothing to fight against. "Get a blanket! Use a blanket!" Paul called to his teammates as he himself struggled to unstrap his own wool blanket from his pack.

Elijah- who'd been warming his legs a minute ago- happened to have his blanket at the ready. Yoshic was rolling around on the icy ground now; his clothes burning bright and hot. The flames; growing and dancing. And the little Japanese boy made of blue fire was laughing like a crazy person and leaping hurrying toward Paul when Elijah jumped on him and wrapped the blanket around him and pushed him to the

Richard Rose 81

BLACK CAT SUNRISE

ground. Still, the boy laughed and laughed; but now more like a deranged child than like a happy child. And, still, the shrill and bizarre sensory-overloading laughter was coming from all around them; intermingled with the shouts of panic-stricken men and the screams of the searing torment of men whose clothes were also on fire now.

Elijah wrestled with the crazed figure of blue fire. It possessed no mass but its amorphousness allowed it to burst forth from beneath the blanket with which it was being smothered. Elijah did a commendable job of wrangling the slick thing, but even still- when he thought he'd finally vanquished the demon- it again seethed into being and stood to its full short height and maniacally leapt upon its combatant; catching Elijah's clothes afire and sending him falling to the ice to roll around in desperation. Jacob- meanwhile- had delicately secured his fragile weapon and was now equipping Elijah's blanket to extinguish the fires burning on Elijah's clothes. Paul by now had his own blanket at the ready and he was able to finish the task of snuffing out the fiery boy who was apparently sufficiently weakened so as to not have much fight remaining in him. Soon, the flaming child had vanished entirely, but- having not realized this- Paul continued fighting against it for a spell. When he eventually noticed that the thing was gone, he looked up and first saw Yoshic- his clothes smoking from the legs- and then saw Elijah with Jacob on top of him and still tamping out the fires with the blanket. And then he looked around and saw that the area was lit up bright with a myriad of minor blazes, and all throughout the crowd there were men wrestling these laughing child devils back into the oblivion from

Richard Rose 82

BLACK CAT SUNRISE

whence they'd come whilst other child devils were still running free and squealing with delight as they ignited the clothing of whoever so crossed their paths, as well as the tents that sheltered precious supplies, as well as the gear that was piled everywhere. This scene could be multiplied and extrapolated all through the forests and all through the rubble of Old Dover. Thousands of fires. Thousands of fiery children.

The vicinity was seemingly teeming with these pyromaniacal apparitions who were all laughing like only children do; their high-pitched mirth as grating as it was ghastly. And many of these demons succeeded in inflicting severe casualties. It took some twenty minutes before the most wiley of them could finally be subdued; during which time the soldiers were running around with blankets and interchangeably smothering the flaming children and keeping their fellows from burning to death in their clothes. Paul and Jacob both further participated in the effort; eliminating one more demon between the two of them, and helping several men to extinguish their afire clothing. Yoshic and Elijah were still coming to their senses; both in a lot of pain as a result of these events. Somewhere; an ammunition truck exploded; killing and injuring many men who were nearby. Some men had burned alive because there was nobody available to help them. Many men were suffering from serious scorching. Yoshic not among the least of which.

The smoke lingered and the chaos settled down. Yoshic's fire team reconvened. They examined each other's clothes and wounds. Yoshic said, "It fucking hurts like all hell, but look at my goddamn pants. How I'm supposed to fight a war with half my ass hanging out?" "You can probably fight the war naked. Unless

Richard Rose 83

BLACK CAT SUNRISE

your balls freeze off," Elijah said. Paul- with a prophetic observation- stated, "They just attacked us. They're going to keep attacking us. Wait ten minutes and you can pull the pants off a dead body."

Lieutenant Darby was a weirdly feminine man, wearing the same black battle dress uniform as everybody else, with silky tan skin, a gaunt shaved face, and a silly poof of sandy blonde hair that sat like a parted sea upon his skull. He came sauntering through the platoon shouting, "In light of recent events, R&R has been canceled! Pack up your gear! We're moving out in fifteen minutes!"

In response to this announcement the men groaned and moaned and swore oaths and complained to each other. They'd been marching forever. They'd been so happy to stop. But they should have known better than to feel any sense of relief as so often such a sense is as fleeting as it is illusory. They did what he said, and soon the platoon had gathered together. Darby gave the order to move out, and- with their packs on and weapons in hand- that is what they did.

Then the ground shook and the sky lit up to the south and the 'whoosh' of a shock wave washed over them. Many who hadn't the footing to brace against this rushing wind were- as a result- knocked over. The trees flailed above them. The soundwave came after like a tremendous thundering 'ka-kow!' All four men recognized the dondon immediately. The lieutenant called out, "Platoon, halt! Take cover!" A call that echoed throughout the divisions.

From one of several multi-purpose battle stations within the Nyu NyuYoku Bakufu headquarters- a small darkened room full of glowing

BLACK CAT SUNRISE

touchpad screens serving a myriad of purposes, and all positioned on a long half circle desk- Xander and Kazuki sat drinking coffee and monitoring the feedback from a single dondon kuki drone that had been dispatched to intercept the teki; now that it had emerged from its tunnels and made its intentions clear. The purplish thermal imaging of a high-altitude surveillance drone showed clearly that the colorful figures of the teki were on the move again; now that the fiery Hi Majo had done their business.

The bakufu commanders sat in lush leather chairs. Wearing the bakufu uniform. Hinomaru headbands on. Kazuki wasn't optimistic. Her expression was wearisome. A sneer of disgust on her lips. Hatred in her eyes. The teki were a nightmare. If only they'd just stop fighting. It had been a tense and uncertain period of time since the bakufu learned about the phantom teki majo. Her whole world had been turned upside down. But, still, she was her mother's daughter and the war was hers to fight and that was that. She said to Xander, "We should have sent out a raijin. This is going to be a waste of a dondon." "It's not a waste if we eliminate those tanks," he replied. Sweat trickled down his face. Xander loved his daughter. It was a bitter time and it made him sick. He only wished she could be a normal girl doing anything else. But he had no say in it. This was a woman's world.

The slant-eyed and shaved-headed drone pilot on Rikers Island could be seen on one of the screens. A hinomaru over his forehead. Working his controls. Kazuki pressed the com button and gave him the order, "Dondon one, fire at will." The pilot's primary objective was to decimate the enemy's armored

BLACK CAT SUNRISE

vehicles and his secondary objective was to reap as many fatalities as possible; so he moved forward until the lasers were in range and as- in rapid succession- the array of laser cannons automatically locked onto and fired red bolts into their human targets, the pilot manually aimed and fired the dondon at the formations of tanks and armored vehicles.

Many enemy soldiers disappeared from the screen and, of course, they were just hiding; but, there was too many of them and not all of them could hide sufficiently and so the lasers wreaked havoc and the death toll continued to rise as the dondon cannon delivered punishing blows to the enemy's mechanized forces; disappearing 70 ton metal monsters in an instant and throwing others through the air to land down upon the hordes they'd been there to protect.

"Ah, hell, here it comes," Xander said, pointing to the radar screen that displayed a triangular configuration of multiple white arrows that indicated a barrage of incoming projectiles. These projectiles were a hundred miles out, moving fast, and inbound from the north. Kazuki alerted the pilot; "Dondon one, activate your anti-missile protocol and continue your barrage." "Copy that, Shikken," said the pilot. The lasers continued to tear into the infantry and the dondon continued to pulverize its targets. The enemy was firing into the phantasma-shields with an array of four-barrelled .50 caliber anti-aircraft guns, but they weren't having any effect. Some of the tanks were taking pot-shots at the drone, but often they'd be blown out of existence after only a couple volleys. The teki began booting up their truck mounted surface to air missile launchers, but they did not release the payloads because there were cruise missiles incoming

Richard Rose 86

BLACK CAT SUNRISE

and the plan was to overwhelm the drone's defenses in order to secure a sufficient strike.

Two saucer shaped surveillance drones were broadcasting video from points southwest and northwest. These images portrayed a dazzling spectacle. The dondon drone's shields glowed orange from bullets and tank rounds impacting. The four laser cannons discharged bright red laser bolts in rapid succession. The dondon bursts glowed purple as they thrust through the sky; leaving trails of burning air behind them. The earth erupted in fire and fury when the tremendous blasts impacted. Fires burned where the ruins of the dondon's targets smoldered. Smoke plumes wafted about.

The drone's lasers were limited in range only by the limitations of their targeting technology. The problem with them was that beyond four or five miles, there was too much mitigation to maintain the precision accuracy the weapon required. When the teki cruise missiles- traveling 500 miles per hour- were calculated to be in the appropriate position, the teki artillery commander gave the order to launch the truck mounted sidewinder missiles as well as some shoulder fired stinger missiles. The teki had rehearsed a strategy for exactly this situation. Intending to overwhelm the laser's targeting system.

The drone's lasers had only a few seconds to shoot down 30 missiles, and it wasn't enough time. What happened was that the sky over an unpopulated area began to fill with a cascading procession of massive explosions with flaring debris propelled outward in fractal dispositions; their shockwaves pushing and shoving amongst one another. While above the heads of the infantry the same thing occurred, but on a smaller scale; claiming many lives. The counter-strike was a success. Several missiles collided with their target. And this achieved the desired result. The glowing orange phantasma-shield flew away from the drone like a blanket in the wind and coalesced into the seething luminescent figure of a lean, muscular, and voluptuous goddess. The drone itself was immediately decimated by the force of further detonating missiles.

The phantom majo swirled in a dazzling spectacle of orange light; evidently trying to orient herself. What sort of senses she possessed, Kazuki could only guess at- but the majo didn't take long to get her bearings, realize the immediate vicinity possessed no important targets, divine her new objective, and gear herself toward achieving that end. The flying nude woman made of particles of luminous phantasmagoria focused her gaze in the direction of Nyu NyuYoku and then shot off toward that direction in a blur of glistening neon orange.

Xander said, "We have to get underground! Now! Come on!"

Kazuki's father pressed a button to alert the others, took Kazuki's hand, and they ran to the polyvinyl emergency escape tubes. He touched his thumb to a hidden doorway, checked for a green light, and pushed Kazuki in through the opening. She descended rapidly as a rush of sterile smelling air whipped against her clothes and a sickening sinking sensation rose up through her guts and into her throat. She emerged from the tube on a slide and found herself in a familiar underground concourse of mirror-finished stainless steel. This sort of evacuation was occasionally drilled, but this was the first time she'd

BLACK CAT SUNRISE

ever had to do it for real. Her father arrived in a second slide beside her shortly thereafter.

"Father! What about mother? And auntie and uncle!"

Before he could respond, these people were emerging from the tubes. Nobody else had access to them. Maya asked Xander, "What happened?"

"The phantom majo is inbound. We have to get out of here," Xander said.

"Hai," Maya agreed.

The family climbed into a white and cylindrical maglev rail tram and- after the circular door sealed shut- Maya selected one of several red buttons, pushed it, and the pod zoomed away toward the Bronx; otherwise known as 'Location B.' The tower being Location A. The pod was lit dimly red. The tunnels were dark. There was an interface module in the escape pod and Maya utilized it to scan the video streaming from surveillance drones. The others watched over Maya's shoulder. The phantom majo was plainly visible streaking across the sky.

What happened next didn't look especially magnificent when viewed through a screen. But the result was clear. High up in the sky a blazing green slash could be seen cutting down from outer space. It moved with the speed of a shooting star and was traced by a miles long trail of brilliant color. The neon green beam was much the same as the neon orange beam, but bigger and faster. It collided with the phantom majo and the greater force of this green entity drove the orange entity down into the Hudson River.

"Oh, kami arigato," Moto said, as they all let out a sigh of relief.

Richard Rose 89

BLACK CAT SUNRISE

They continued to observe the monitor and eventually the green entity shot up out of the water and flew off into the sky. The orange entity did not reemerge. They spent the remainder of their duration within the escape pod examining and assessing teki troop positions and strength. As for bakufu positions and strength; it was under control and as it should be. With the exception of the high command having been driven underground for the time being. The pod arrived in a mirror polished concourse similar to that which they'd departed from, and Michio- Kazuki's uncle- said, "Well, it seems we've got some time before all hell breaks loose; might we enjoy a nice meal, while we're all together?"

Maya said, "Yes. Just... wait here. Moto and I will go give the men their orders, and then we can eat."

Before Maya and Moto walked away, Kazuki asked, "Was that thing coming for us, do you think?"

"In all likelihood, yes," Maya said, and then her and her sister turned and walked away. A chill ran up and down Kazuki's spine, her pleading eyes widened with dread, her skin crawled with goosebumps, the fuzzy hair on her neck stood on end, and she felt her heart pounding in her chest.

From overhead and through the trees and between the houses, Paul could see glowing red laser bolts flashing all around him; the laser light was the only light in the dark of night and it created a fearful strobing effect on all sides. Off yonder, a luminescent blue emanation shone through. The other men of his fire team kept close to him, and he kept close to them. From behind, a dense crowd of soldiers were rushing into them and they, too, were a portion of a dense

BLACK CAT SUNRISE

crowd which was rushing forward and pushing the men before it into the crowd of men before it. The density of their numbers meant that a single laser bolt could shoot through multiple individuals, but there was no helping that. These crowds filtered through the skeletons of decaying old homes and over tangled brush and through the trunks of trees and between multitudinous rusted out husks of automobiles; through graveyards, through parking lots, through school yards, down long avenues; they ran without thinking. Not even realizing their own fear. Numb to the world; their beating hearts already dead in spirit. And the laser bolts rained down from on high. The catastrophic explosions of the dondon were such that nothing could be heard except for wave after wave of deafening shockwaves washing over the landscape. But as to where the plasmoids were striking exactly, that couldn't be ascertained and was of minimal importance to these men who were preoccupied trying to avoid stepping on the bodies of dead, dying, and wounded soldiers. If they could hear anything at all, all they would hear would be the screams of these agonized soldiers who were getting chewed apart by the lasers. The enemy drone was positioned toward the east, evidently. They were moving toward it and the lasers were coming at them from straight ahead. Paul could have been looking right at it, but all that could be seen were the lasers. The dondon plasmoids were like shooting stars, except up close and personal; at one instant overwhelming in their radiance and intensity, and then in the next instant only the faint trail of its tail's purplish emanation remained. When a dondon plasmoid passed overhead, the air rushed toward the vacuum it created. And then the air rushed

BLACK CAT SUNRISE

back the other way when the shockwave came. Always these winds were hot, which was actually nice, because it was so cold otherwise.

Suddenly- out ahead through the trees- the sky lit up bright with a fiery explosion that seemed to morph into a shimmering orange substance. The laser bolts stopped coming at them. The roar of the final dondon blast quieted. A chorus of tortured screams and cries rose up from all around; as if the ground itself was human and alive and suffering extreme pain. Still running; Paul tried to get a glimpse of what was going on up there, but it was too far out and too obscured to see clearly. He was able to glean that the flaming wreckage of the drone was falling toward the earth. And it was a beautiful thing that caused him to notice the presence of an unfamiliar feeling; hope. Hope; like a spark in a black void. The hex was up there; Paul could see her orange luminescence, but could not distinguish any of her 'physical' features. Then she darted off and pretty soon she was completely out of sight.

The unit continued to move forward, but it slowed its pace. Paul, Jacob, Elijah, and Yoshic took a second to confirm that they had remained together. And it was a relief to know that they had. After a brief march, all the injured were behind them and the night was eerily quiet except for the symphony of the troops' movement; the dull rumble of thousands of boots crunching icy snow, the percussion of gear clattering against gear, the deep rhythms of men breathing heavily, and occasionally the percussion of a few words being exchanged.

"So, this is it, then? We don't get to sleep, or nothing?" Jacob asked Yoshic.

BLACK CAT SUNRISE

"Depends. Right now the orders are to march. So, we march," said Yoshic.

Paul, to reassure Jacob- and himself- said, "If they're smart, they'll let us sleep. Can't shoot the neeps if we can't see straight down the barrel."

Jacob asked, "You'll think we'll get a shot at 'em, for once in our lives?"

Paul said, "If we survive long enough, then yeah."

Elijah reiterated what they all knew, "Sons of witches can't hide behind their shields anymore. We're going to exterminate the motherfuckers."

Yoshic corrected his team, saying, "Don't get too excited. A lot of them motherfuckers are just slaves and prisoners. Guys like us, but from the other theatres."

But then Paul added, and correctly, "Not the slant eyes. The slant eyes are the real samurai. You get a shot at one of them, it's a shot worth dying for." And in that moment, more than sleep or food or warmth; all he wanted was to kill a slant eyed neep.

And then Yoshic said, "All we ever think about is when and how we're going to die. Is that any way to live? Is any of this shit worth dying for? Fucking war can't even be won. If you get a chance to survive, then you take it. Even if that means conscription."

Paul thought about this for a while before deciding that he had to agree.

Meanwhile; troops and mechanized weaponry continued to pour out of the mouth of the tunnel. Yoshic and his team were positioned near the front of the assault force, but the operation stretched back across the town of Old Dover and out into the forests and then down into the primary tunnel and far out into the tributary tunnels. There were tanks rolling on clanking tracks. There were half-track trucks mounted with heavy machine guns, anti-aircraft systems, large caliber kinetic energy guns, and guided missile systems. There were fleets of HMMWV; high mobility multi-purpose wheeled vehicles- as well as fleets of the newer and better LCATV; light combat all-terrain vehicles. Plus, jeeps and different sorts of motorcycles and quads. These assorted sorts of vehicles possessed all manner and variety of machine guns, gatling guns, cannons, rocket launchers, grenade launchers, mortars, and whatever else could be strapped onto them; including, of course, plates of armor and bullet proof glass. They towed trailers with mounted weapon systems, as well. There were also fleets of big ten-wheel trucks tasked with transporting ammunition, food, and supplies out to the front and bringing wounded men back to the rear.

The soldiers themselves appeared to be moving like swarms of army ants; indistinguishable from one another; an undulating mass of humans seething along the path of least resistance. The onslaught of the dondon had succeeded in eliminating a significant quantity of the confederate's equipment, but it was just a small fraction. And while it succeeded in killing hundreds of men; there were many tens of thousands more left unscathed. But, also, that was just one drone. Its purpose was to test the phantom witch, and that it did. The confederates had gained the initiative, and now the enemy would try to retake it. The enemy's objective would be to destroy the confederate's mechanized equipment as well as to destroy as many soldiers as possible. To destroy every last little asset, if at all possible. But it wasn't going to be as easy as it

BLACK CAT SUNRISE

used to be, now that the phantom witch had been inserted into the equation.

After no further enemy attack had presented itself, orders were given to make camp around the Boonton reservoir; for there wasn't a foot soldier within the ranks who wasn't about to drop from the exhaustion of the long march. This delay granted the enemy a beneficial reprieve, but it was a necessary thing. With an added benefit to the confederates; the respite would provide an opportunity to concentrate and organize their forces before moving on toward their mission; the retaking of Old New York City.

Chapter 5

Aglow

The Boonton reservoir was radiant with a neon green glow. There was no ice on the hot radioactive water. And the water itself was not actually glowing. It was the air directly above the water that was glowing green; a hazy film that vaguely vibrated with a subtle hum and stretched out far and wide and dimly illuminated the black of the night. Worse than that, the whole area was abnormally hot. Paul and his fireteam were close enough to the vanguard that they were able to turn and head back into the throngs instead of getting any closer to the intimidating body of water. So, the ranks were pushing forward toward their rendezvous point while simultaneously retreating back into themselves to get away from the hostile reservoir. No order had been given, but every man intuited the problem there. The end result was a huge mess of confusion. But this confusion was a relatively normal occurrence and eventually Yoshic's fireteam met up with its company and staked out some space to

Richard Rose 95

BLACK CAT SUNRISE

bed down. Nobody would venture nearer than about a kilometer to the reservoir. That was the point just beyond where the heat and the glow weren't noticeable. It was obvious to everybody that concentrating their forces in this area was a colossal blunder, but there was nothing anybody could do about it. 'At least we're up wind,' was the utterance upon many a man's lips; just before passing out from exhaustion.

The rear continued to compound upon the front; bringing forward their weapons, their vehicles, their supplies, and their numbers. The army formed something of a crescent moon around the reservoir and it waxed larger as the night went on. The southern tip of the crescent reached all the way down to Lake Parsippany, which- to the relief of the soldiers down there- did not suffer from the same malady as the reservoir; but was, of course, frozen over. Other than the droning of machines, and the occasional shouting of men going about their duties; it had become an oddly peaceful evening. Thousands of stars shone in the sky. Tens of thousands of men were sleeping in pig piles. Tens of thousands more were just trying to find their bit of frozen ground to fall over and pass out on. The frozen ground subsequently turned to wet ground from the warmth of their bodies; but they were used to the wet and outfitted against it as their snow pants and parkas were coated with expanded polytetrafluoroethylene.

A swath of beech-maple forest banked the eastern shore of the reservoir. The trees closest to the water had died, but this was winter and the living trees appeared almost as dead as the dead trees. Smooth and pale bark absorbed the green light emanating from the waters and their trunks cast soft shadows. From within the forest, a figure emerged; shroud in a white cloak that shone neon green. Naito majo approached the rocky shoreline. Her black eyes reflected the eerie spectacle. A reserved smile adorned the thin lips of a timeworn face crinkled by fine lines. Once an immaculate beauty, she was now so very old. Still tremendously beautiful, but in a different way. It was a beauty akin to an ancient bonsai tree; majestic in the strength of its spirit. And her spirit was nothing if not strong. A profound and delicate strength; like the silk of a spider. It was the enchanted strength of the power of magic. The gaze of her slant eyes lifted from the glowing surface of the water and peered across.

In the distance, she could see the orange of the lights of the teki equipment. She looked to the north, and then to the south. The gentle breeze began to shift and whirl. The branches of the trees knocked about one another. Some snapped and fell. There were no words in her thoughts. Her mind was that of the atmosphere. Although, like the atmosphere, she could be described as turbulent. The turbulence rose up into a driving wrath. The winds gusted to the north. Back to the south. East. West. Around and around. Beneath the discordant stillness of the neon glow, the waters roiled into a frenzied chop. The haze of green light only hovered there unmoving; gently throbbing with the high frequency pulsations of radioactive decay.

Overhead; clouds from the surrounding area began to coalesce and converge upon the vicinity. Moments ago there wasn't a cloud in the sky, and within a few minutes all the heavens had become blotted out by a singular disk shaped cloud that was gargantuan in depth and breadth and divided into

BLACK CAT SUNRISE

several bands that were wrapped about one another in a spiral configuration. The entirety of the cloud mass was rotating slowly at the peripheries and whirling somewhat faster toward the interior.

Within the encampment of the confederates, those who were not asleep observed this bizarre weather transformation with growing alarm. The younger men didn't know what was happening but the older men more or less understood. Because it was dark and because the enormous cloud had blotted out the moonlight, it could be presumed that they wouldn't be able to see what was coming at them, but this was not the case. The radiant green glow of the reservoir produced a bright enough light to reflect off of the water vapors of the low hanging clouds, and, too, the artificial lights of the military strike force gave off a comparable luminescence and the combination of green and amber lit up the sky enough to observe what was occurring. And several units were beaming spotlights up at it to watch it. What they saw was a modest funnel emerging and descending from the center. The center being up over the northernmost of the troops, at the time. The funnel looked like it would be coming down directly upon them. It was at this point that multiple air raid sirens were sounded; awakening the exhausted soldiery.

The funnel did not- however- come down upon the soldiers beneath it. What happened was that half way down the funnel swung out toward the east. The sidewinding vortex then stretched toward the earth and touched down in the reservoir. The suction of the tornadic waterspout pulled the radioactive water up into its structure. Paul and his team were observing

BLACK CAT SUNRISE

this from their position within their company. Nobody knew what to do or where to go. They knew enough to know not to panic. But they felt panicky just the same. The army was concentrated. This was a vulnerable situation. There was really nowhere to go and nothing to be done. Except to watch. So they watched as this long, narrow, and tubular waterspout filled itself with radioactive water and lit up like a green pit viper from hell. An image seared into the memories of all who saw it. Paul was fortunate enough to be further to the south, but all the forces in the north were being pelted by the toxic water droplets being whipped around by the raging winds. Certainly, that had been the witch's intention. The waters being ejected from the funnel cloud were drenching thousands of men with ionizing radiation.

Lieutenant Darby was stomping through the ranks and shouting out, "Hold your positions! Nobody move! Lay on the ground! Keep your heads down! Hold your positions! Nobody move! Lay on the ground! Keep your heads down!"

"What the hell are we supposed to do?" Jacob asked Paul; shouting over the wind. Crystalline ice particulates; thrashing their faces.

"There's nothing we can do. Not unless they coordinate a retreat, but by the time they do that, this will be over!" Paul shouted back.

All around them, in every direction, other men were having this same conversation.

"Fucking Jap bitches are dousing us with that fucked up water," Elijah said.

"We're supposed to sit here and wait to get sucked up into a tornado?" Jacob asked.

BLACK CAT SUNRISE

"It's the water. They're throwing the water at us," Paul said.

"For now, but look. It's moving. It's coming this way," Yoshic said. The crown of the funnel was slowly drifting northeastward, but the root of the funnel was curving back toward the west. Toward them. When the waterspout made landfall, it hit the snow and so it wasn't sucking up the radioactive water any longer and so it stopped glowing and partially disappeared into the night; except for what aspects of its twisting snaking motion were being shined on with spotlights. It was a tornado, so it moved fast. It blew across the land like a wind. Because it was a wind.

From the distance, beneath the din, came the first screams of terrified men. Paul had heard many men scream for many reasons, but this was different. Some were the same as always; ending abruptly. But others possessed a unique quality as their screams would end not abruptly, but instead would fade away as the man was thrown off into the distance. Or, as was also the case, the scream would become louder as the man was thrown toward where Paul's team was hunkered down at. In all directions, these men were thrown. The spotlights lit up some of these men so as that they could well be seen orbiting eerily around the funnel; upside down, arms flailing, legs kicking- their rifles tethered to them.

From out of the darkness these flung men came like projectiles launched out of catapults; some fell gently, softly, and without injury, while most came down like cannonballs. The far-flung individuals were a hazard unto themselves, but what was worse was the equipment that was being thrown about; anything and everything that had been stationary was now falling

Richard Rose 100

BLACK CAT SUNRISE

out of the heavens; trucks, gear, crates, weapons, etcetera. Many soldiers were doomed to be crushed where they lay. The air raid sirens continued to wail.

"Why the fuck aren't we fucking running?" Elijah shouted.

"The army can absorb these losses. If we all run, we'll stampede, we'll all crush each other. All our shit will get fucked up. It'd make everything worse," Paul responded.

"Worse than this?" Jacob asked, pointing toward the monster that was now looming into proximity. It breathed on them; raspy breaths laced with grit and shrapnel.

It was close enough that in the camp lighting they could plainly see as men were being pulled up off of the ground and sucked up into the vortex. Paul watched it somewhat dispassionately. He'd never seen anything like this. But he'd seen it all before, just the same. Men dying. So many men dying. And he wondered if this was when he would die. Certainly an unpredictable way to go out. He never thought he'd die in a tornado. He always figured it'd be a laser. The lasers were what took out most guys.

Thankfully, the tornado drifted away from their position. And after another minute or so, the funnel lifted off of the ground and disappeared up into the sky from whence it had come. Paul and Yoshic and Elijah and Jacob all checked each other with flashlights. They'd made it through unscathed, but their clothes were coated with grime. Seeing that they were all alright, they were anxious to get back to sleep. Paul dropped his head to the ground and breathed a sigh of relief. The camp was in chaos and turmoil. But he didn't care. He was glad to be alive and still so very

BLACK CAT SUNRISE

tired. All around, men were suffering grotesque and unfathomable injuries. Nearby and further off. There were many casualties. Many fatalities. But he wasn't a medic. The confederates had entire companies of medics for exactly this reason. The unfortunate ones weren't his problem. He needed to sleep. And that was that. But then he remembered all the green water droplets that came down on all those thousands of soldiers and his eyes shot open. That was going to come up again. That was going to change things.

Location B was a bunker within a bunker within a bunker and far beneath a prisoner of war camp in the Bronx. Similarly, location Y was a bunker far beneath a civilian internment camp in White Plains. The prisoners of war were conscripted and sent away to far off theatres to fight or slave for the bakufu and those who would not comply were executed. The interned civilians were assimilated into the bakufu labor force. And those who would not comply were executed. Along with those who displayed any other sort of undesirable characteristics. The bakufu labor force was a complicated caste system, but it shared a commonality with the confederate way of life in that the highest reward for a lifetime of service was the privilege to procreate. The difference being that the confederates had many persons breeding and the bakufu had a relatively small breeding population.

The bunker they were in was 300 feet below the surface of the Earth. A lavish affair in the sense that it was styled to resemble a traditional Japanese dwelling. The floors were tatami. There were wooden beams to replicate a real home and create the impression the occupant was not in a reinforced concrete box

BLACK CAT SUNRISE

underground. One wall was wallpapered with a realistic image of a glorious landscape of knolls of manicured grass, a pleasingly oblong pond, silvery rock formations, cloud pines, and spherical boxwoods; puffy clouds drifting across a blue sky. One wall displayed a fresh ikebana. Another wall was shoji doors that opened into a more practical area designed for people who were to be trapped in there for a very long time.

Five heads shaved bald. Five plain white uniforms. Five hinomaru headbands. Four sets of slanted eyes, and one set of round ones. They were seated seiza style on the floor, at a table that was low to the ground, and eating a meal of tori no karaage, onigiri, miso soup, daikon, gyoza, and sake. They ate quietly and with little discussion of transpiring events. There was a lot to be said, but nobody really knew what to say. Maya, especially, was feeling the burden heavily. She couldn't really taste her food. Her mind was someplace else. Kazuki watched her mother chewing with a blank stare on her face. And her aunt Moto, too, seemed lost in her own thoughts. Kazuki looked to Xander who was watching her watch them. He smiled at her. And she smiled at him. Her father only ever wanted her to be happy. He never cared anything for the forever wars. He only ever thought about her. Her uncle Michio was devouring his food hastily and drinking sake heavily. Michio had evacuated his wife and children to Bosuton and was anxious to get to them. In Michio's mind, Nyu NyuYoku was already lost. All was lost.

Kazuki took a bite of her chicken- crunchy, moist, flavorful- and remarked to herself, "Oishi desu yo..."

Richard Rose 103

Kazuki was swallowing that bite when something shocking occurred, and it caused her to choke and cough and struggle to swallow. She was desperately trying to drink some water and wash down her food as the others were realizing that an old woman had appeared in the room. The adults were less surprised to see this person. They simply lifted their gaze to her expectantly. Maya had a somewhat bemused and somewhat resentful expression on her face.

The old woman stood before them and smiled warmly. She wore a black cloak of a special material unique to witches. But the hood was down and her pale and wrinkled face wasn't malicious in the least. Short white hair fluffed about her head. Her eyes were sunken and the flesh about them was pinkish. The witch smiled when she spoke; she seemed pleased to make their acquaintance.

"Do you know where your mother is right now?" she asked; her words thick with a German accent, and so the word 'where' sounded like 'vere.'

Maya answered, "No. When she's not here with us, I have no idea where she goes."

"Your mother is attacking the confederate army with a tornado. Showering them with radioactive water."

"They're invading. That's her prerogative."

"Yes, that is so. I just wanted to know if you knew."

"Well, we know now. Have you come here to gossip, or are you going to kill us?"

"Oh, no no no. Nothing like that. I wouldn't dare."

"Your phantom wicca. She would dare. It looked as though she had every intention of killing us, earlier today."

"These are willful beings. Surely she intended your destruction. But of course, her attempt was thwarted. And if she tries again, she will be thwarted again. Do not fear your enemy. Fear your war against your enemy. These are dangerous days. There may come an occasion, when all the magic of the heavens cannot save you from obliteration."

"Well, that's reassuring, I suppose," said Maya.

"I only wish for a few moments of your time. And then I will take my leave."

"By all means. We are a captive audience," Maya said.

"I was a woman, like you, once. In a time before the bakufu created the phantasm manifestors. Those were simpler times. Worse, but simpler. Our coven has always lamented the imbalance of the phantasm. But, what is this war if not an exercise in balance? It seems we're returning to the past."

The witch paused and Maya asked, "This turn of events pleases you?"

"More than words can say, yes. But the ironic fact is it changes very little. It changes everything, to be sure. But, fundamentally, it will not change the war because it cannot change the war. You will push, we will push. We will pull, you will pull. The women's war will never end. Because a woman's war is never done."

"Okay. But, why? Why do we do it?" Maya asked.

"Nobody truly knows why. All we know is that there are powerful beings- in this world and beyond-

BLACK CAT SUNRISE

and that this is what they want. This is what they want, so this is what we do."

"This invasion is going to destroy this city," Maya said.

"Yes, and you will destroy the invaders."

"Why not let us keep the city? Why waste an army, for this?"

"It's not a waste. It's part of the process. We want the vicinity. Not the city."

"Is there no way we can come to terms? Come to an agreement? You take the land? We keep the city?" Maya asked.

"Will you disarm yourselves, and submit to our authority?"

"Of course not."

"Then that is your answer," said the old witch, shifting her gaze to Kazuki, and, after a pause, adding, "Your daughter. How beautiful she is. Like a feline. As fierce as a tiger." Kazuki glared at the supernatural woman with an icy gaze that smoldered. "Her youth, it will not allow her the understanding of an old woman's wisdom. My dear. I can feel your anger. Your hatred. Your rage; burning like an inferno within you. But come now, hear my words. This is not the mindset of a proper lady. Your mother. She does not hate me, like you hate me. She does not hate your enemy like you hate your enemy. One day, you will realize, you have no enemy. I know you feel guilty. I know you feel that you are the wicked one. You feel that the entire world is against you. That you must tear asunder the armies of men until the rising sun flies over all the land of all the world. That you have been cursed to bear this hideous burden."

BLACK CAT SUNRISE

That was all true. Kazuki realized that this woman could peer down into the depths of her soul. There was no reason to disagree or argue. What the woman was saying was correct. The bakufu terrorized the many for the benefit of the few. It was wrong. Kazuki always thought so, but she pretended to take pride in it to avoid facing the reality of it. Kazuki's gaze fell from the woman to her plate of food. Her vision blurred, and she drifted to a far-off place where it was only her and these few wise words.

"Let this wicca put your young mind at ease. We are not your enemy. We need you. Without you, our world would have no purpose. Our hordes of free men would turn against one another and fight and die until only the bones of what we are will remain. You give us direction, drive, motivation, cohesion. You do not appreciate the simple truth. A truth so obvious, it goes without notice. The truth is, this is a woman's world. Even in your concentration camps and ghettos, do the women suffer? Do they starve? Do they slave? No. They make babies. They raise babies. Well. That is the same for us. Our women do not fight. They do not die like ants under foot. Like these men do."

"My aunt Moto fights," Kazuki said.

"Well, there are exceptions to every rule. Without women like your aunt, these men would be hopelessly lost. It is the same on our side. My daughter is like your aunt, and like your mother. And my granddaughter, she is like you. And yes, of course, women suffer. But minimally. We minimize their torment. Their sons may die, but their daughters will live. We shelter them from the storm. We protect them from the holocausts of men. To the best of our ability. Well. Ideally. I mean."

BLACK CAT SUNRISE

"Yeah, ideally. In reality, we got women dying by the truckloads," Kazuki said.

"The war is upon you, child, that is unavoidable. But remember back to two or three years ago. Things were good, were they not? Your city is lost, but you will find new life in a new city. And things will be good again. One day. Please, just think about what I said. I want you to have peace of mind. I don't want you to feel bad. The bakufu is as important to the confederacy as night is to day or as up is to down. The world may be a great big war machine. But the great big war machine is a way of life for billions of people. You are not bad. You are not evil. You are the champion of every little girl and every little girl's mother. You must never forget this. Wakata?"

Kazuki nodded affirmatively and said, "Hai, wakari masu."

In this instant, like the blinking of an eye, another presence appeared in the room. Yoshikosama, the Naito majo. She wore a white cloak with the hood up. The smell of the fresh air and rain emanated from her. The wrinkles of her face hid in the shadow of her hood, but her expression wasn't angry or malicious. Her eyes were soft and her lips wore a smirk. In a soft elderly voice, the Naito majo said, "Helga. Nice to see you. To what do we owe the pleasure of your visit?"

Helga bowed to Yoshiko- who bowed back- and said, "I was offering your daughter terms of surrender. She, of course, declined."

"Of course she did. You knew she would."

"Indeed. Well, I know you must be fatigued after such a grand performance. And I am sure your family is happy for your visit, so please enjoy and I will be on my way," Helga said, and then she bowed to

BLACK CAT SUNRISE

Yoshiko again and then to each of the ladies- but not to the men- saying, "Maya, Moto, Kazuki." And then she vanished before their eyes.

A stunned silence followed Helga's departure. Yoshiko knelt at the table. Moto poured her mother a cup of sake. Kazuki asked, "Obachan? Are you going to stay for a little while?" And Yoshiko told her, "Hai, Kazuchan, for a little while, I can stay."

Helga reappeared in a spherical cave with surfaces of glass that shone grey from the solid rock that lay behind. This was the rear control room. Within the cavernous void of the cave there was a small woman seated by herself in a simple wooden chair and at a little wooden table. The woman observed the glowing images of several tablets laid out before her; comparing and contrasting different sorts of maps and charts and tables of data. This was Helga's granddaughter, Olga. Her skin; a dark shade of white. Her eyes; ice blue. The cave was dimly lit by the bright white light of a single lantern and the tablets' shining screens gave her a blue aura. She wore a black uniform with three red stars embroidered into the collar. This was the lieutenant general of the formation. Long black hair; tied up in a ponytail. Her ovular face was symmetrical and angular, with high cheekbones, luscious lips, and an upturned nose. Her expression was stern. She'd not noticed her grandmother's arrival. But she wasn't startled when the old witch spoke to her.

"I am sure you know we've been attacked," the witch said.

"Yes. By a radioactive waterspout? Arnold should have a preliminary damage assessment,

BLACK CAT SUNRISE

momentarily." Arnold was her twin brother. The major general of the formation.

"It was the Naito witch."

Olga looked up and off into space; considering this. "Interesting. I don't know why that hadn't occurred to me. We knew they'd do something while our forces were concentrated and vulnerable," she said.

"Yes, well... It had to be done. The concentration, I mean. How are your tunnels coming?" Helga asked her.

"We've got 27 out of 30 moleholes in position to breach by h-hour. That'll give us 270 wormholes, ideally. Better than we thought we would do. Here, you can see their positions on this one," Olga said, pointing to one of the tablets. The nuclear boring machines were indicated by crosshair icons. Most were situated beneath the island of Manhattan itself, but a few were on the New Jersey side of the Hudson River; positioned at the Lincoln and Holland tunnels and the George Washington and Tappan Zee bridges.

"They're going to attack again, before the men can disperse," Helga said.

"I know, but what can we do?"

"Unfortunately, the army hasn't slept, and it needs to sleep, and that's just the way it is. Now. Whatever the enemy will do, it will be doing it soon. Nonetheless, we must get our people underground. Has the breach been opened?"

"It has. Just a few minutes ago. I intended to get the heavy assets down in there before the men. But I don't suppose this maneuver is going to be as orderly as I was hoping it would," Olga said.

Helga said, "No. It doesn't matter who or what gets down in there first. Expediency is more important.

BLACK CAT SUNRISE

We need everything underground as soon as possible. Humans and machines alike. So long as they are not trampling one another, that will be sufficient. You will have to wake them at 0330 instead of 0400."

Olga said, "Yeah. I will. But, you know... I actually want the bakufu to attack. The sooner they throw their pods and saucers and spiders at us, then the sooner the phantom wicca can destroy the damn things."

"That's true, but we need to disperse our forces. This is a bad situation; to have them as they are. And the attack hasn't even begun."

"Yes. Bad. But necessary."

"Yes. Unfortunately."

Arnold appeared. He had frizzy curly hair, cut high and tight. His face was like Olga's face. Handsome, ovular, and sly. With a soul patch under his bottom lip and a thin mustache above his top lip. His countenance was suave and debonair; which made him look out of place when he moved throughout the disheveled forces. On his black collar were two red stars. "It's worse than I thought, but not as bad as it could have been," said Arnold.

"Not as bad, yet... You will have many dying men. Dying men cannot endure. Dying men can only die," Helga told her grandson.

"They're going to have to try to hang in there, at least," Arnold said.

"How many dead?" Olga asked.

"Over a thousand, is the estimate. And we lost some trucks and heavy guns, too."

"How many were exposed to the toxic waters?" Helga asked him.

Richard Rose 111

BLACK CAT SUNRISE

"Probably about five thousand. Give or take one thousand."

"Many of them will die. Perhaps most. And in not too long a time," Helga said.

"Divert those men to the bridges," Olga said.

Chapter 6

Dread

What would come to be recollected as the first horrific disaster of the ensuing horrific series of increasingly horrific disasters that would define the campaign; was ultimately the result of a miscalculation. When the troops were gathered up north, the tunnel diggers had said that the tunnels would be complete by the time the troops had gotten down south. There was an important connection that had to be made between the tunnels being dug to attack the city and the old tunnels that were already in place. Due to technical difficulties, this connection had not been made. The result of this failure was that the entirety of the attack force had been forced to trek overland from the exit of the old tunnel to the location where the new tunnel was now being made to open up at as a result of the constraints imposed by the miscalculation. Midway between the exit of the old tunnels and the entrance of the new tunnels; they concentrated their forces and bivouacked for a brief interim. It was in this unfortunate position that the enemy had assaulted them first with a drone and then again with a radioactive waterspout. An ongoing ordeal, that, as it would turn out.

As for those men who had sustained the severest exposure to the deadly radioactive waters; these were being separated and reorganized into their

Richard Rose 112

own contingent which would be directed toward the bridges. It was an obvious suicide mission, but somebody had to do it and these soldiers understood from their own reduced condition that it may as well be them; as they were all more or less struck by a grievous radiation sickness basically immediately after having had been exposed. Also, not for nothing, most in the theatre regarded the entirety of the operation to be a suicide mission.

Regarding the rest of the tens of thousands of troops; they weren't even so lucky as to receive their full partial ration of sleep. Because at about 0345 hours they again came under attack and the order was given to make haste for the breach, toward which the heavy assets had already been rolling. The attack was a restrained one having been ordered by Motosama from down in the bunker. The bakufu didn't want to waste their drones but they also didn't want to waste a golden opportunity to inflict casualties and damage. It was obvious they'd be losing their drones sooner or later anyhow, as there was no defense against the phantom majo save for the Tsuki Majo and the tsuki majo- evidently and for whatever reason- wasn't interested in preserving the bakufu drones. The tsuki majo dwelt outside the atmosphere. She wasn't confederate or bakufu. She wasn't white or black. The tsuki majo was grey. A creature of unfathomable power; she belonged to the third coven. The third coven was known as the equilibrium to the confederates and as the Hitoshi to the bakufu. The equilibrium served as the de facto deciding factor in the war of the women and they also shepherded the ever-diminishing populations of human tribes which possessed neither allegiance nor obligation to either

BLACK CAT SUNRISE

side and whom existed in the crossfire as a way of life. The equilibrium had their own prerogatives, and so too, subsequently, did the tsuki majo.

The drone strikes transpired as was to be expected. First, a kuki raijin was sent in. Its antigravity systems shimmered neon blue in the black of night. The snow below, too, reflected the blue and glowed faintly. The weapon systems of the kuki raijin targeted the infantry specifically; raining down purple lightning bolts and red laser beams. This produced a devastating effect as a single lightning bolt was enough to kill every man within a fifteen-foot radius. The killing quality was as much due to the transmission of electricity as it was due to the concussive jolt of the electric arc. The confederates launched a surface to air missile at the drone. The missile exploded against the forcefield. The forcefield lit up with bright liquid orange light. The bright liquid orange light was displaced from its moorings and flung away by the shockwave of the blast. The drone wasn't much influenced by the loss of its shield and for another short spell it continued to inflict death from above. But, soon, the liquid light of the shield had morphed into the orange phantom witch which darted through the drone like it was nothing. A gaping smoldering hole; bored through its width. The final tragedy of that particular kuki raijin was that its hulking mass fell upon a cluster of about a dozen soldiers who were instantly crushed. The phantom majo- or phantom hex, depending on one's perspective- again bolted toward Manhattan. Again heading directly for the Freedom tower. Again the tsuki majo- or, moon witch- descended like a blazing neon green comet and intercepted the phantom majo; driving her down into the Hudson river before again

Richard Rose 114

BLACK CAT SUNRISE

rising back up into outer space like a green meteor in reverse. The phantom witch had again been extinguished and vanished beneath the surface. The losses of that drone strike were estimated to be about one hundred and twenty. The army couldn't stop advancing and so the dead were stacked in a macabre pile and abandoned.

The second drone Motosama sent at them was a kuki tsuki. Its primary weapon was an antimatter cannon. All of the weapon systems of the bakufu were monstrous in nature, but some were worse than others and the tsuki cannon was especially feared for the way in which it would cut portions out of men and leave them in bloody pieces like chunks of meat; either dead or screaming or something in between. The lucky ones- it was said- were those who simply disappeared. And- as always with the bakufu drones- the laser bolts of eight laser guns shot down in rapid succession and with deadly accuracy. Then, again, came the surface to air missile, and the phantom witch, and the falling hull of the destroyed drone, and the crushed men, and finally the tsuki majo to drive the phantom witch into the river before she could destroy the Freedom tower. The death toll of the second drone was estimated to be over two hundred. Again, the bodies were heaped-up and abandoned. It would have been a simple thing to repeat this process, but Moto didn't want to lose any more drones that night. In her mind she hoped for better circumstances in the future. But as far as anybody could tell, it was just a matter of time until the phantom witch destroyed every last drone they had.

Typically, it was the witches who directed and determined the course of history. The three great

BLACK CAT SUNRISE

covens were the end-all and be-all of mankind and aside from a few stipulations they were mostly concerned with keeping the wheels turning and the meat grinding. However, once in a while certain occurrences occurred which were outside the sphere of influence of even these masters of the universe. Nothing so significant as to change the way of things. But, nonetheless, events which weren't anticipated and which were generally against the will of one, two, or all of the covens. It was the will of the covens for their bloodlines and lineages to remain unharmed, and this was an aspect of the women's war which dictated certain terms of engagement. The third coven- as has already been demonstrated- wasn't willing to let any witch attack any human of any clan on either side. However, the third coven also wasn't inclined to deign to confront the lowly likes of plain and simple humans whom they considered subhuman- which is to say; subwitch. The nature of the third coven was radically different from the other two covens which were relatively similar to one another by comparison. All three covens took it as a given that the Naito clan were untouchable and would remain out of harm's way. Same went for any and all of the myriad dynasties existing in the fray. As such; there was infrastructure in place to ensure the Naito wouldn't be exposed to danger. These infrastructures would serve to deliver the Naito from the warzone when the cause was lost and the situation was too far gone.

Specifically; the Naito were relying on a tunnel to another bunker- Location Y- beneath the slave city in White Plains. And from there they'd fly to Bosuton. And while Maya and Moto and Kazuki were consulting one another about which drones to send or not send

BLACK CAT SUNRISE

against the enemy; something had occurred at the periphery of their awareness which would alter the course of their lives forever. What had happened- what had gone wrong- was that one of the teki's primary nuclear boring machines had inadvertently and accidentally cut a tunnel through their escape tunnel. The system registered this, automatically sealed off the passages with blast doors, and simultaneously notified the family via an alert that went unnoticed for some time. The Naito weren't trapped, but their alternative escape routes would compel them to expose themselves to danger. They could return to the Freedom tower and attempt an escape by air, or they could take an elevator straight up to the surface and attempt an escape by land, or they could travel to Rikers Island and attempt an escape via air or sea. None of these limited options was remotely safe and each would compel the Naito to expose themselves to extreme danger. And so, once they noticed the notification- which should have been an alarm but was just a negligible flashing icon on a monitor's desktop; the Naito decided to remain down in the bunker and fight the war from the relative safety which it afforded. The main reason for this being that their current position was equipped with all manner of equipment necessary to conduct operations; they could address their officers, they could operate their battle drones, they could program their security drones, they could observe all cameras and microphones, and they could direct troops and assess troop positions and weapon capabilities. All of which could be done from the island or the tower, but this position had the added benefit of aforementioned subterranean safety as well as access to all remaining escape routes.

Richard Rose 117

BLACK CAT SUNRISE

Kazuki and her mother monitored an array of surveillance cameras as the invasion began in earnest. Teki forces marched on the George Washington bridge toward the Bronx and on the Tappan Zee toward White Plains. These forces consisted of ragged and haggard men who walked tall and proud and with honor and dignity despite the fact that some of them were falling dead in their tracks and others were vomiting and soiling themselves. Many of them had no more weapons than a side arm. Some not even that. They were all thirsty. Always drinking water in a futile attempt to quench their burning radiation sickness. And they were curiously devoid of battlefield accoutrement such as tanks, trucks, and armored vehicles. Their eyes were bloodshot, their cheeks were sunken, and their skins were speckled with blood red pin pricks and blotchy red rashes. Their hair was falling out of their heads.

Moto had traveled back to the Freedom tower to meet with bushi high command. Xander and Kazuki's uncle- Michio- sat at a desk and made ink marks on paper maps; drawing up a variety of contingency plans based on present troop and asset positions. They were all sipping cold barley tea and enjoying a peaceful- albeit tense- afternoon in the bunker. The teki soldiers had been marching nonstop since before dawn. Earlier- when the southerly teki forces were on the interstate bridge over the Hackensack river- the bakufu had initiated a senso kuki drone attack upon the procession. The senso weapon system produced a devastating effect upon men clustered together such as they were. The drone came in low and touched down directly in front of

Richard Rose 118

BLACK CAT SUNRISE

them. It fired its puslar cannon directly into their numbers. The blazing blue beam passed through them and through the buildings and forests and hills behind them, until eventually being fully absorbed by the landscape. Most of the teki heishi survived the blast, but many were dead and all that remained of them was a stain like a brushstroke of blood bespeckled with a more or less indistinguishable assortment of human remains. Over two thousand men died in just that instant. The others scattered in all directions but there was nowhere to go except over the sides and into the frigid water; many drowned and others succumbed to hypothermia shortly thereafter. The senso drone also rapid-fired laser bolts into the crowd and succeeded in releasing one more pulsar blast; killing perhaps a thousand more. A rocketeer- prior to a laser bolt blasting a hole through his chest- was able to fire off an 84mm high explosive rocket at the drone, and the explosion was sufficient to produce enough reactive phantasm so as to manifest the phantom witch, who immediately and effortlessly drove her seething form through the hull- disabling the drone- before darting off toward the Freedom tower, only to again be driven down into the Hudson River by the tsuki majo. The surviving heishi picked themselves up, pulled themselves together, and continued on their dismal march. Shortly thereafter, the bakufu sent a raijin kuki drone at the northerly contingent. That scenario produced a similar result, but the death toll was far lower. That, and also the tsuki majo had less distance to traverse the second time, as she was already lingering nearby; ominously hovering in low earth orbit- a radiant feminine figure of undefined features; eyeless and mouthless, with no orifices of any sort, or

Richard Rose 119

BLACK CAT SUNRISE

nipples or hair or fingernails, either... The northern contingent wasn't even part of the assault proper. They were evidently attempting to reach the slave city at White Plains. Presumably to sequester manpower.

Early in the morning, assemblages of slaves had been dispatched to barricade the bridges on their eastern sides. So the way into Nyu NyuYoku was barred by jackknifed tractor-trailers with box trucks wedged in between. And now the time had come. The enemy was at the gates. But it was a piteous display. Kazuki asked her mother, "What do they think they're going to accomplish?"

Maya answered, "They want us to send drones at them. They want us to blow the bridges. It's a diversion. They'll be coming up out of their holes soon."

"Do we have to blow the bridges?"

"They're going to take the city. One way or another. And they're going to destroy the place in the process. We don't really need the bridges. And if we don't blow them then they'll be crawling with heishi."

"Sick and dying radioactive heishi," Kazuki said.

"A threat is a threat. Big or small. At least we can hit these with umi. We don't have to waste kuki on them," Maya said.

"We'll have to sacrifice a senso."

"It's got to be done."

Kazuki transmitted the order and an umi drone floated up out of the water. It fired a senso pulsar cannon at the side of the bridge where the teki heishi had clustered into a teaming swarm at the barricades. The blazing blue plasmoid darted from the seagoing vessel and tore through the George Washington bridge with a concussive fury that blasted its fragmented iron

BLACK CAT SUNRISE

and steel and concrete and asphalt far out into the sky over the Hudson River, and, too, went flying the remains of so many teki heishi; the blood of their myriad bits and pieces showering down upon the survivors in a windswept mist. The plasmoid itself; continuing off into the stratosphere. The survivors were faced with a gaping hole in the structure and as they were trying to figure out how to maneuver around this formidable obstacle a second senso plasmoid tore through the bridge like it was nothing; taking another measure of soldiery along with it; most of whom were outright obliterated and others of which were blown apart into fragmented portions. Now there were two ragged and gaping holes that were somewhat kiddy-cornered to one another. The bridge was all but impassable except to be scaled at great risk by only the most daring and nimble of individuals. Or, more realistically, by climbers with rigging.

The umi drone lowered its cannon and fired a third plasmoid far down river at the Tappan Zee bridge. A somewhat long shot, but not a problem for its advanced targeting system. And so, too, was a gaping hole blown through that bridge. Killing dozens and wounding more. What happened next was that a teki F-14 Tomcat fighter jet came screaming out of the west with its wings folded back and it launched a single sparrow missile into the senso umi. The drone pilot had been lining up a fourth shot and by the time bakufu reconnaissance identified the incoming plane and issued a warning, it was too late. The missile collided with the vessel's shield and the teki phantom majo emerged from the explosion; all shimmering orange. Immediately she shot down into and out of the drone and through the water. Then, as the phantom

BLACK CAT SUNRISE

majo came up out of the water, the neon green tsuki majo was immediately upon her, driving her back down in, and further down still; deep into the inky depths of the Hudson to administer her dark medicine unto her. With a smoldering hole through its core; the drone sank in a cloud of steam. Many of the sickened troops remained on the Tappan Zee; still crossing over on their mission to liberate the White Plains' slave city, or die trying.

Paul- his squad, and others- had been re-outfitted with the weapons from the poisoned troops, who, as luck would have it, were significantly better equipped. Paul was given a six shot M32A1 grenade launcher to replace his ancient single shot M79. And he accepted an automatic MP5 9mm to supplement the loadout; turning over his pistol, because it became redundant. Jacob kept his sniper rifle because he was 'tuned into it' but exchanged his Smith and Wesson pistol for a Glock. None of these old brands meant anything to these people except by reputation. Everybody knew a Glock was a desirable pistol to carry. Not many of them could read, but they knew the insignias. Elijah was able to exchange his large and unwieldy M240 for a more compact and faster firing M249, but he still had to hump a box of bullet belts over his shoulder. And he kept his M9 pistol because he liked it fine. Yoshic wasn't interested in exchanging his M4 with modular shotgun attachment, but he was happy to inherit a quantity of 3 inch slugs as well as to exchange his shoddy polymer 9mm for a well-maintained M1911A1 .45 ACP.

They'd also received a full complement of relatively advanced form-fitting body armor as well as

BLACK CAT SUNRISE

better helmets and newer boots and less worn pants and warmer shirts and field jackets in better condition. Plus, combat knives and grenades. So, now their outfits were clean and black instead of filthy greenish-brown. The squad even received a thermal imaging scope to be shared amongst themselves. Plus, they got extra ration packages, too. All of this gear had been exposed to toxic levels of radioactivity and had indeed been radioactive itself, but the engineers had devised an impromptu method for decontaminating all these assets and it was just too bad that they couldn't decontaminate the soldiers as well because the process wasn't something a human being could endure.

Now- as a result of the extreme exhaustion- the seconds lingered like minutes and the minutes lingered like hours and the hours dragged on like eternities. But it wasn't all bad. They had slept for a little bit, and that was something. Even though that was a long time ago by this point. They'd since moved underground. The cavernous tunnels had walls of black glass and seemed to go on forever. The lighting was minimal, but crisp and white and adequate. The air was ventilated, except not adequately, and so hung heavy and thick and felt hard to breathe at times. And the men were jammed in there and jostling just to move forward and their gear was becoming entangled with one another's. The moisture crept under their clothes and chafed their skin. Water droplets dripped on them from the ceiling. But at least it was hot. Soon they'd be freezing and they all knew it. As awful as the marching was, it was nice to be alive. And not bleeding out. Or succumbing to exposure. But this was the end of winter and they'd endured the worst of it, so it was

BLACK CAT SUNRISE

unlikely the cold would threaten them the same as how it had been doing as of late.

Along the floor- which was flat for a twenty foot width- the dripping droplets were gathering into tiny rivulets that flowed downward toward the lowest most point and there formed puddles. This was happening in every tunnel. And the engineers were keen to it and they were sucking the puddles out with vacuums. But in the tunnel that Yoshic's squad was marching through, the motor of the vacuum had blown out. It was an industrial vacuum; with hoses that ran for miles. So it wasn't a simple thing to get a new machine into position. It'd be simpler to splice the hoses with another tunnel's unit and run that one at reduced power. And that's what was being done. In the meanwhile, the puddles were gathering. And the soldiers who trudged through them couldn't help but chuckle under their breath about their fear of a little puddle that didn't even come up over their boot laces. But fear it was. And afraid they were.

Paul had just passed beyond that lowest point. He had stepped through the waters and felt the icy chill running up his spine. He'd heard the murmurs of the others. They knew instinctively. Something was coming. And they were right. Because about ten minutes later men were screaming back there. It was far away, but it was a lot of screaming.

What was coming up out of the puddles resembled adolescent male humans made of water; naked and somewhat featureless, but it was irrelevant what they looked like because they didn't retain their shape for more than a second or two at a time, as they were breaking apart like waves upon the shores of the bodies of the soldiers while simultaneously succeeding

BLACK CAT SUNRISE

in thrusting their arms down the throats of these men who could not escape them. Some began shouting for blankets. It was all they could think to do; to throw blankets on their assailants and hope to absorb them. So as these men were choking and suffocating, other men were attempting to soak up the water with blankets. But it wasn't exactly possible. There weren't enough blankets, there was too much water, and the menace was literally fluid.

With every soldier who fell down dead, the situation grew more dire. And other men- according to their duty- were utilizing their discipline to stand firm against the onslaught of crazed men who were fleeing for their lives. Panic was often just as dangerous as the water devils. So, there was a sopping wet tangle of blankets and dead men and a few handfuls of heroic souls who were descending upon the ordeal to toss in their lot with the imperiled. Still, men cried out for blankets and when no blankets were forthcoming, they stripped from their clothes and tried to soak up the water with these.

The liquidic fiends were relentless. It was a simple thing for a man to force one asunder with a blanket but it wasn't so simple to defend against the onslaught. The attackers didn't need to be a towering figure to kill a man; they only needed to be manifest within the water, and that they certainly were. It seemed as though the tunnel would never cease to echo with the horrid cries of mortal terror. This carried on for a substantial amount of time, and the men who were dying now were the men who had been trying to rescue those who were dying before them, and this cycle went on and on until the bodies were as a vast and lush carpet of soggy moss. And then- without any

BLACK CAT SUNRISE

pomp or circumstance- it was over, and the devils receded back into the nothingness from whence they'd come. Those who were close by fell down in place and laughed or wept with sweet remorse or sorrowful rejoicing. Just a moment later, with a sudden wet wheezing, the vacuum hoses start sucking and slurping again; pulling the water out of the area.

Paul kept marching. It wasn't difficult. He was numb. His body knew to march. His mind knew to project itself out into the void for peace. Yoshic knew where they were going, kind of, but he still had no real idea where they'd be when they got there. He knew they'd be climbing out of a wormhole. The commanders wouldn't breach the molehole until the area was secure. Although, how they intended to secure the area without breaching the molehole had not been adequately explained. But it wasn't hard to guess. The upper echelons had a default solution for challenging problems. Throw human bodies at it. The micro-TBMs, the worms, were powered by the macro-TBMs, the moles. Each nuclear powered macro-TBM supported ten micro-TBMs by means of stainless-steel encased power cables. At a subterranean area close to- but not too close to- where the breach was expected to open up at; an extra nook would be bored out. This area resembled a barb. There, the tunnel boring machine would be parked in case the breach became sealed and needed to be reopened.

When the marching was finally over, and all units were finally in position, Yoshic's squad was waiting in the line that led to where their wormhole opened up into this sector's molehole. The entirety of his battalion- and several other battalions- were positioned in this area. The tunnel stretched far back

Richard Rose 126

BLACK CAT SUNRISE

and so too did their single file ranks. They remained positioned against the wall because tanks and tactical vehicles and improvised fighting vehicles and utility vehicles and different sorts of supply trucks were all being positioned for when the molehole opened up. While waiting for their orders, they examined a 100-meter 4QFJ MGRS map of lower Manhattan. They studied the area where their breach would open up at, but it didn't explain- and nobody seemed to know- whether or not they'd breach into a subway tunnel, into a basement, or into the open air. There were rumors, though. The rumor was a different tunnel had breached into open air, and they were greeted by a certain sort of tactical drone; a silver saucer- smaller than a steering wheel- that flew very fast and shot off rapid fire laser bolts with deathly precision. They were called murder-hornets. A lot of guys had seen these things in other theatres in distant lands. Anybody who had ever gotten close to the bakufu had encountered them.

These rumors were something of an informal briefing, as they hadn't received any real briefing and this was the best they could hope for. Apparently. Basically, the lieutenant pointed them where to go and they went and that was about the extent of it. The task at hand was to secure their sector. That is, X amount of grid squares. And so, because the soldiers were eager to know, there were other things being said about the enemy, too. It was said that the samurai- that's what they called them, the samurai. Or, bushi, at other times. It was said that the samurai would be few in number, but there would be a lot of slaves. The slaves were terrible soldiers but the samurai knew this, and expected this. The slaves would be wearing collars; like

BLACK CAT SUNRISE

dog collars. High-tech and extremely dangerous dog collars. This was how the samurai controlled the slaves; by utilizing a remote-control device to effortlessly kill whoever was wearing the thing. Be they deserter or insubordinate or traitor or whatever. These collars were an exceptionally dangerous aspect of fighting the bakufu. The collars released something like an electro-magnetic pulse, but it targeted the bio-electricity of the human body. The enemy all had surgical implants that protected them against the effect, but if a confederate soldier got within ten feet of an enemy slave, then their heart would stop and they would die instantly. These were called 'god-collars,' because they'll send you to God if you get close enough to one. The weapon of the slave was basically a silver sphere on a stick that they held out in front of them. This used the same technology as the god-collar but it could hit a man at a distance as long as it got a clear shot at them. The weapon was fully automated. The slave didn't have to aim it; it aimed itself just fine. Nor was there a trigger to pull. It killed and that's all it did and if you didn't have the implant then you died. But the confederates couldn't use them because they were linked to the surgical implants and powerless against those so implanted. These handheld devices were called 'circuit-breakers.' Meanwhile- their limited understanding informed them- certain exceptional slaves carried the same laser rifles that the actual samurai were equipped with. These looked more or less like the more technologically advanced rifles the confederate sometimes issued- but with capability surpassing anything the confederates produced in several ways. Firstly, it could target instantly and automatically- secondly, it fired laser bolts- and

Richard Rose 128

thirdly, it could use reflections to triangulate targets and bounce laser bolts off surfaces to hit targets hiding behind cover. They called these laser rifles 'reapers.' Of course, the bakufu had other weaponry, but these systems were the most common and the most feared.

Chapter 7

Go

And then there was the problem of the ninja. Nobody had much to say about the ninja. Nobody knew very much about them. A few things were known. They came out of Japan explicitly. There were no local ninja. They were always imported. And when they killed, the victim never saw it coming. Some people claimed to have seen them kill others, but all they could say about what they looked like was that they were invisible. This made a lot of people wonder if the ninja even exist, because it seemed more plausible that those people were dying from circuit breakers or god-collars than that there were invisible assailants out there. But high command maintained that they were real and so it was taken as gospel that this was so. These stories were the same stories which these men had been hearing since they were small children. Except, suddenly more pertinent than ever before. Few men in the ranks had ever been this close to the enemy. Most had only known the bombardments of the drones, if anything. The witches, however; these had been becoming familiar. Thankfully, Paul's burns were healing better than he had thought that they would.

The guys ate their ration and didn't need to be told to collapse in a heap of guns and gear and go to sleep. They were someplace beneath Wall Street.

BLACK CAT SUNRISE

Where there were all manner of underground bunkers and vaults, but such places were emptied and irrelevant. The civilization that had created these places and gave them meaning and purpose; that civilization was all but disappeared. Only the skeletons of their cities remained. And here and now, even, yet another such skeleton was scheduled to be demolished. Well, really, everything the confederates possessed was a product of or an extension of the artifacts of the old world. So, in a lot of ways, it lived on after all. Nobody liked to think about it. They were only ever trying to forget everything they heard about it. It was all too good to be true. It was demoralizing to contrast the beautiful stories of old against the grim realities of the present.

Paul awoke to Yoshic shoving him. He felt good because his omnipresent sleep deprivation headache seemed to have subsided. Looking back down the ranks, he saw that everybody else was looking forward up the ranks. The others were looking forward, so he turned his attention forward, too. Then he zoned out and kind of went back to sleep with his glazed over eyes open. It was quiet, for a small area filled with many humans. A palpable anticipation weighed heavily upon the hot and humid air. Paul remembered the other times he'd gone into battle. It was so ordinary right up until all hell broke loose. And then it was nightmarish. This tunnel was ordinary. He'd lived his whole life in and out of tunnels identical to this one. These men were ordinary. They were strangers, but they weren't any different than the guys he was brought up around. They were all raised with this end in mind. As soon as they could walk, they were learning bushcraft. How to survive with only a knife.

Richard Rose 130

BLACK CAT SUNRISE

What roots, stems, leaves, flowers, and fruit could sustain them. All the different ways to catch a fish. How to make a bow and arrow out of whatever one could find. They were little children marching across the arctic countryside from sun up until sun down. They built different kinds of shelters with sticks and ice and rocks and sod and logs. They killed caribou and made the skin into shoes or rudimentary clothing. They made bo staffs out of saplings and fought their friends in contests that carried on for years. They practiced a new martial art unique to their time and place, called 'Synthesis' because it was the official confederate distillation of an assortment of practical hand to hand combat techniques that were salvaged from the old world. And so martial skill, too, was an unending contest. They starved. They froze. They suffered unendingly to develop maximum strength and resilience. They thought mostly of the enemy. The neep. The neep was a constant obsession for each and every one of them. Their greatest ambition was to kill a neep. And, similarly, the witches were a bewildering source of endless fascination. And fear. And resentment. As well as gratitude and reverence and even worship. It was the witch's world. They were just living in it. They learned guns but almost never fired the ever-precious bullets. They learned weapon systems they'd probably never have to use. They learned equipment they'd never have to operate. They were all expected to know everything that didn't require overly-extensive training and specialization. This was up in Old Canada. Within- and southward of- the boreal forests. Where the bakufu had no interest in going. There were underground facilities for women to raise girls and to birth babies; their sacred and

Richard Rose 131

BLACK CAT SUNRISE

imperative calling; their raison d'etre. And there were underground facilities where boys grew into soldiers; suffering one miserable day after another. Like men. And there was a place called Valhalla. But it wasn't the mythic Valhalla of old-world legend. It was a real place where women went to couple with soldiers who had survived beyond the age of thirty. Valhalla was the dream the grunts would not dare to dream. Some wanted to kill a neep. Some wanted to get to Valhalla. All wanted both, but each wanted one more than the other, or vise-versa.

Paul's mind wandered. Daydreaming about killing neeps. Daydreaming about Valhalla. It seemed unlikely he'd ever get to Valhalla. Killing a neep was within reach. Especially now. Now that their shields were down and everything had changed. Yoshic snapped Paul out of his reverie as he passed the marching orders off to the next team behind them. A cold wind had begun to blow, over the last hour, or so. But that was a welcome change, after the dank suffocating air of before. Three of the ten wormholes had breached into a subway tunnel. Theirs was one of the three. Their only purpose- for now- was to secure their sector. There was no real way to do it, but it had to be done. Ultimately, the witches had to take out the drones. Until that was done, their outlook was limited. What the colonel wanted was that they get into a better position. Once they were in the subway, they'd be in a better position to position themselves better. Yoshic's squad was somewhere in the middle of the line for this tunnel and the line was- by Paul's estimation- about one thousand five hundred men long. That would fit with confederate logic. 1,500

BLACK CAT SUNRISE

bodies to a hole. Ten holes. Fifteen thousand bodies. One division per macro-TBM.

Already, fighters were fighting in other sectors. Paul didn't know anything about it, but skirmishes were breaking out wherever a wormhole was breaching the surface. It had begun and it was raging but for Paul and his division; they still had a moment to breathe.

Soon, the enemy would know these holes had been opened. He didn't know how they'd know, but he knew they'd know. And he was right. The enemy had eyes and ears in every crack and crevice of the city. All it took was one slave with a circuit-breaker to plug the wormhole with dead men. Of course, there were techniques for this situation. The first men to breach the hole were not men at all. They were remote controlled robots that ran on two rubber tracks and which were typically armed with an automatic shotgun and a silenced 9mm automatic carbine mounted on a rotating turret and which utilized multiple cameras to monitor different spectrums of light. The nice part about these was that the average slave couldn't easily destroy them. Not without a reaper. Or a bug-zapper. A bug-zapper was the standard enemy grenade. It was a scary thing. Essentially, it was lightning in a bottle. Its power came from the concussion it produced. They were known to send tanks flying through the air and blast craters big enough to land helicopters in. Again, this was information based on rumors from men who had fought against the bakufu, but the rumors had to be balanced against the fact that such knowledgeable men were few and far-between and for all intent and purpose virtually nonexistent; because the bakufu did the vast majority of its fighting with kuki and kumo drones; not boots on the ground. However,

BLACK CAT SUNRISE

confederate intelligence confirmed the stories by training the soldiers to defend against these enemy technologies. The fact was that battles such as these were fought long ago in the time before the forcefields. And that was a different era and obfuscated by a haze of a generation passed.

The remote-control bots of the confederacy were called vampire-cats and the men who operated them did so with a special head unit like a full-face helmet as well as with an elaborate handheld device. They'd been training with these remote vehicles for many years, and were impressively proficient in maneuvering and fighting with them. Being that these were the de facto vanguard, their operators were positioned toward the front, but behind the vanguard infantry.

The three wormholes had breached at different areas along the same span of subway tunnel. The tunnel had a single track of rails running along the bottom as well as- running down the side- a narrow platform that could be walked along. There were lights on the walls, but they were lifeless and it was pitch black in there. Four of the vampire-cats were able to get situated on the platform but the other two were spat out down on the tracks and so couldn't move as smoothly due to bumping and crawling up and over the track's fixtures. The operators were able to communicate with one another and so they sent three to the east and three to the west. Meanwhile, the troops kept waiting and facing forward and wondering why they couldn't be sleeping right then. Some of them did indeed go back to sleep. The vampire-cat cameras looked around and noted the presence of escape hatches that were about one hundred yards apart. The

Richard Rose 134

BLACK CAT SUNRISE

eastward span of the subway tunnel soon met up with another tunnel and another line of tracks and these opened into a station which was dimly lit; with spacious platforms on either side. It was there that this sector made contact with the enemy. The vampire-cats stopped suddenly when they encountered the sentry. The sentry had not spotted the robots and he seemed to be the only one there.

If the confederates killed the guard, then his god-collar would signal the samurai. If they didn't kill him, he would signal the samurai. They had eyes on him, and he was unaware of that fact, and that was good enough. Conveniently, the exact same thing happened in the westward span of the tunnel. The sentries seemed oblivious to their surroundings. They stood with their shoulders slumped and their heads down and their circuit breakers held by flaccid hands. They wore white from head to toe, with red hinomaru circles on their white winter hats. Their skin was pale as milk.

This was when the line started to move. The first men out were minigunners and each of them had a sharp shooter to watch their back and to pick off any targets the minigunner wasn't seeing. The flame-throwers piled out up front, too, but that was mainly to get their fuel tanks out of the tunnel and into the field. Backing up the minigunners were machine-gunners and grenadiers as well as heavy machine-gunners with their .50 calibers mounted on shielded turrets. All this heavy weaponry was being maneuvered into position rearward of the vampire-cats which were positioned just out of sight and sound of the sentries. However, despite their best efforts, it wasn't exactly a silent endeavor. It was the westward bakufu guard who

BLACK CAT SUNRISE

became alerted first. He heard a clank of metal down in the tunnel and it aroused his interest. Nobody was in position to fire at him, except for the vampire-cat, whose operator sent the remote vehicle charging forward and fired a burst of 9mm bullets into the man as he turned to run away. The man fell dead and the vampire-cat advanced on him in order to shoot up the circuit-breaker and the god-collar around his neck. The things were harmless with a few bullets in them. After that, the units who were advancing toward the westward subway station were ordered to rush in, position their heavy weapons, and secure the entrances and exits.

In the eastward tunnel; the vampire-cat seized the initiative and eliminated the threat of the semi-alarmed slave soldier who was posted over there. Now the enemy was aware of their presence in two places in this sector and so the mission commanders gave orders to breach an extra wormhole a few blocks over in order to further divide the strength of the opposition.

Paul's line began crawling toward the mouth of the wormhole. Approximately three feet in diameter; the tunnel was cramped, but not claustrophobic. For the gear Paul was packing, it was easy. Only Elijah would find it challenging because he'd have to make the ascent with his ammo box dragging between his legs. They squirmed through on their bellies; weapons in hand or strapped on their packs; working their shoulders and elbows and hips and knees and pushing with their feet and pulling with their wrists. Paul had been in wormholes that were overly vertical and those could be daunting and exhausting. This one had a pretty good angle. In his right hand he held a flashlight and the illumination was preventing him from

Richard Rose 136

BLACK CAT SUNRISE

crawling into Yoshic's boot. His bandolier of grenade shells was the heaviest gear he had. His pack was relatively light. Bullets were heavy. Weapons were heavy. It was nothing. Soon he was out in the open and the lieutenant was screaming, "Go, go, go!", and so they went. Their hole was closest to the western objective and so to the west they ran with the others. Paul slung his grenade launcher and equipped his MP5; double checking the chamber and the safety. There was space on the platform but it was crowded and so they ran out onto the tracks where it was more open. They fell in with Second platoon and Second platoon fell in with Delta company and Delta company joined several other companies and soon the entirety of Long Island battalion- and a good measure of Poughkeepsie battalion- were all crammed into that station down there.

　　　　The colonel decided he didn't want all the men in one place and- utilizing a complicated communication system of radios and cables and transponders- passed down the order to get out of the tunnel and take up positions in the buildings surrounding the subway's exit to the street. Paul didn't have a clue exactly what was happening, but he could guess; because he could hear screaming and confused shouting, and occasionally the boom of guns blasting; but mostly, just a chorus of men crying out, "Where are they? Where are they?" and others replying, "Just fucking go! Go! Go! Go!" Yoshic's squad jumped up onto the platform and saw there was one sergeant ordering his men to pull the dead bodies down off of the stairs and heap them against the wall. The sergeant was explaining how to stack them so the stack wouldn't take up too much space or fall over. A grunt

Richard Rose 137

BLACK CAT SUNRISE

was pulling another grunt down the steps and saying, "Not off the street, just off the stairs!" And then Yoshic's squad squeezed out into the crisp and chilly open air to find Lieutenant Darby doing hand signals and yelling, "Second platoon! Stay with me! Second platoon! Stay with me!" They trampled over dead men. It wasn't the first time, and it wouldn't be the last.

There was a lot going on around him, but Paul couldn't absorb hardly any of it. There was wet snow everywhere. It was cold, but not very. The sky was blue and clear. The impossibly tall buildings cast shadows over the streets. The sun reflected off the glass. He knew other soldiers were following other officers into other buildings. And it was impossible to ignore the corpses sprawled out everywhere he looked. And, like everybody else, he was searching around for an enemy, but he wasn't seeing any. Nonetheless, men were dropping dead in their tracks. Not as many as he feared, but definitely enough to make him afraid. He remembered something about the circuit-breakers; they had a slow rate of fire. They needed to recharge after each discharge. This wasn't so bad. It would get a lot worse. It had to.

The door they were gearing toward was a few hundred feet away. He could see the glass had been shot out and the rest of his company was filing in through there. And then he heard a sound he really hated. An unmistakable sound he knew all too well. Lasers. But an unfamiliar and different sort of pitch that signified an unfamiliar and different sort of laser. A smaller caliber, presumably. He turned his head as he ran and saw the needling red bolts flying through the air but he couldn't see where they were coming from; but he could hear. It was the swooshing whistle

BLACK CAT SUNRISE

of a silent object moving at high speed. He heard this again and again, from multiple sources. And the laser bolts were raining down in rapid and methodical succession. As he entered the building he turned back and got a better look. At a glance, he saw there were three or four of them just in this vicinity. Or, likely, even more than that which he could not see. But him and his people were inside and they were flooding up into the building now. Still; wild commotions arose from every direction. Evidently, they were making contact with the enemy. But there were so many people filling up these corridors and rooms that he couldn't figure out exactly where the action was happening at. The gunshots rang out from outside as well as from inside. From near and from afar. And laser bolts came in through the windows. Men were screaming outside the building. Men were screaming inside the building. And then he heard something strange. It was the whooping and wailing of soldiers who were overcome with joy and excitement. And he knew what it was. And it was close by. And he knew he wanted to see. He had to see. Because he could die at any second. There were six or seven dead confederates, but turning the corner- and going into what was once a boardroom- there was a truly beautiful vision to behold. A dead man with dark skin and slanted eyes. And a sword on his hip. A hinomaru on his headband and a bloody red hole through his chest. It was a neep. A real bushi. A real samurai. His wrist was shot to a gory mess because they wear their kill-switch device like a watch and it was deadly to anybody without the surgical implant. The reaper laser rifle was there, too, but they were weary of it. One soldier said he was

Richard Rose 139

BLACK CAT SUNRISE

going to try to use it but he wasn't able to before another soldier shot the gun to hell.

Paul wanted to laugh. He wanted to cry. He knew what he had to do but he didn't know how he was supposed to do it. There were enemies in the vicinity. They were everywhere and nowhere. The only way to find them was to die. To stumble into one and die. But the lieutenant was calling out "Delta company! Delta company! Fourth floor! Fourth floor! Delta company! Fourth floor!" He thought about what he had seen and he reasoned, "Look for the dead men, and you'll find the enemy..." Yoshic grabbed him and pulled him- along with Elijah and Jacob- over toward the stairwell. This was the second floor, he noticed.

They funneled upward like a frenzied column of ants. Into the interior of the third floor and toward the center where they huddled together to keep away from the windows. Many of those who came too close to the windows did not live to regret it. Lasers penetrated; piercing clean holes through glass and men alike. Soldiers were calling out- some screaming crazily- and gunshots were ringing out from multiple positions. The area they were in was a maze of partitions. It was a vast array of cubicles; but none of them knew what a cubicle was.

Sergeant DeVille had stubbly black facial hair, greasy pale skin that always looked sweaty, and he wore a perpetual scowl because he was bitter to be so close to Valhalla and still about to eat shit in the warzone. DeVille came pushing and shoving through the crowd and giving the order to, "Quit dicking around and sweep the fucking area!" As if that wasn't what they were already doing. There was nothing to sweep. They were the fucking area. Paul knew from the

BLACK CAT SUNRISE

gunshots and the screaming that some guys somewhere had already found the enemy in at least two places on this floor. But all he could see was the gear and the skin and the wide searching eyes of the men who were shoved up against him.

Yoshic said, "Hey sarge! Why don't we throw these partitions up against the windows! You know, so the lasers can't target us?"

Sergeant DeVille replied, "Brilliant idea. I'm glad I thought of it. Get started. But stay low and watch your fucking heads. Them windows is taller than that cover."

And so this was done. Every soldier to a man was eager to see this task completed. Not only did it give them something to do and make them feel less helpless; it also opened up the area and- subsequently- exposed this floor's remaining enemy slave soldier who was shot dead within the pile of corpses which had accumulated around him. This story of the building had floor to ceiling windows but thankfully only on one side. The other three sides were just drywall walls. But the partitions couldn't cover those high windows and lasers were still finding their way in through the glass and reaching all the way out to the back of the space. So a second length of partitions was set up about half way across the room and the angling of this arrangement allowed the troops to occupy the back half without being threatened by the murder-hornets' lasers.

As he helped Yoshic to stack up the dead bodies, Paul lamented the absence of a heartbeat detector. They shouldn't have gone in without one. That was a blunder. He hoped the devices would arrive soon.

BLACK CAT SUNRISE

The dead reeked of piss and shit. Paul noticed the expressions on their faces. Many of them looked perplexed. As though they were only just noticing something was wrong, and then an instant later they were dead. Some of them, of course, looked mortified in the figurative sense as well as the literal sense. The dead enemy slave soldiers- of which there were three on this floor- were separated into their own pile. They were bloodied and mangled by bullets, but the men seemed to enjoy looking at them. Each confederate to the last had been born and bred to admire the beauty of a vanquished foe. But it was bitter sweet, for each of these dead enemies had extracted an expensive toll in confederate blood.

Paul thought back on all the men who had died around him. The sheer quantity of them astounded him. It seemed strange that he was still alive. This heap of bodies was just a small fraction, he realized. And now a whole division was coming up out of the tunnels directly below him. Another nine divisions in the surrounding areas. A 100,000 man corps was ascending toward this sun-bleached skeleton of a civilization; the doomed metropolis called Manhattan. It didn't seem likely the bakufu could repel such a force. Not without their shields. Paul tried to guess how many had died just to get up into this building. He had personally seen more than one hundred dead confederates; just along the path he'd traversed en route.

Outside; the din and cacophony of war rang out through the streets and echoed off the buildings. It was a symphony. Of destruction... Indistinct explosions of major and minor magnitude punctuated the sing-song rattle of distant gunfire. And heavy and light lasers alike sang an otherworldly synthesizer song. Men who

BLACK CAT SUNRISE

were conditioned to absorb pain in silent surrender wailed wildly with soul-rending agony. The murder-hornets whistled through the streets. Glass shattered. The earth trembled and rumbled. Bricks and beams and girders fell from thin air. Artificial thunder rolled across the sky. The artillery of bakufu drones made strange sounds that menaced sound minds.

Lieutenant Darby appeared and gathered second platoon around him and commenced briefing them; "Listen up, men. You all know what we're here to do. We're here to kill neeps or die trying. High command doesn't want us concentrated. We don't want to make it easy for them. If they hit this building with a pulse cannon or a kinetic projectile, they could take out a hell of a lot of us. So we have to spread out. This whole operation is a glorified seek and destroy mission. Delta company has been assigned to the New York Stock Exchange. Whatever that's supposed to be... It's a building. It's just next door. The colonel wants it for a forward command post. He seems to have a sentimental attachment to it, but I think it's too exposed. I think it's useless to us. At any rate, our objective is to take it, and hold it, and after that we'll be clearing out buildings just like this one. We will eradicate the enemy in our sector. But it won't be easy. They're like fleas. Hard to get rid of. Now, I got a couple surprises for you. These were expedited up the supply chain."

A grunt had dropped a case by the lieutenant, who then opened it. Inside was a lot of clear baggies and inside the baggies were silver bundles. He held a baggie in his hand and said, "Now, you're going to be wondering where these have been all your life, and I know it's a shame we didn't have them earlier today,

BLACK CAT SUNRISE

but we have them now, and like they say, 'It's better late than never.' What this is is a mylar blanket." Darby opened it up and kept talking, "Each of these is big enough to fit a fire team under it. Each man holds a corner and the idea is to keep the blanket between you and the laser that is targeting you. But keep your fingers rolled up in the corner or you'll get your damn hand shot off. Now, team leaders, come and take one. I got the goddamn heartbeat detectors over here for you, also. We're moving out in ten minutes."

First platoon crowded around the door, and second platoon gathered around first, and then third and then fourth. The plan was to bum rush the stock exchange. A plan elegant in its simplicity. But nothing much about this situation was particularly complicated. Live to war. War to live. Simple.

Chapter 8
Extermination
Each fire team in Delta company oriented themselves beneath the mylar blankets they had been given. Each person held a corner with one hand. In this manner, they filed through the doorway, down the stairwell, past the first-floor garrison and their defenses, and out into the early evening shadows of the open air. Dead bodies strewn the ground everywhere. It wasn't worth sacrificing the living to collect the deceased. Overhead, the murder-hornets whistled. The blankets were tilted toward the drones as they whizzed by but the drones moved too fast and they targeted too fast and they fired too fast and so their lasers were zipping in and out of human fleshes nonetheless. And the murder-hornets were smart, too. They seemed to intuit that when one man fell, the other members of

BLACK CAT SUNRISE

that fire team were then exposed thereafter. And they didn't waste the opportunity. They'd stop on a dime and then zoom straight toward the sky as they pelted their targets with laser bolts; and then they'd zip off again. Flying so fast, there wasn't any way to shoot them down, and so nobody tried to.

At least it wasn't a long walk. They were soon upon the stock exchange steps. The guys on point shot out the glass and the company filed in; taking up positions along the walls. A wall of glass towered overhead- so they couldn't go out into the open space- but they did have cover where they were at. The area was filled with circular structures of some sort and these were adorned with arrays of televisions. As Paul was coming inside, he noticed- because it was hard to miss- that some of the men of first platoon were falling down dead. Paul also saw that toward the back of the room- behind one of the structures- a hand was sticking out. He slapped Jacob and pointed. Jacob saw it immediately, picked up his rifle, steadied himself despite the flow of men all around him, and shot the circuit-breaker out of the enemy's hand. Paul grasped him by the shoulder and shook him, saying, "Nice shot, man." To which Jacob replied, "It was nothing. Easy." Paul didn't see the enemy soldier retreat, so he was probably still back there. Thinking about it for a second, Paul figured; 'This isn't a good place to run a command out of. There's too much stuff in here and that wall of windows is an insurmountable hazard. The enemy might descend on us at any second. This building isn't worth much to us and that neep is a threat I have to eliminate.'

Yoshic and Jacob and Elijah watched as Paul shouldered the grenade launcher, figured out the

BLACK CAT SUNRISE

distance, calculated the trajectory of his projectile, aimed the launcher and fired the round. It thumped out of the barrel, wafted through the air, fell beside the enemy, and blasted that neep fifteen feet across the floor in a bloody smear. Just to be sure, Jacob put a bullet through the collar around the dead enemy's neck. Paul looked at Lieutenant Darby to see if he approved or disapproved but Darby was too busy shrieking into his headset; something about this position is untenable, something about how they needed to get out of here yesterday, and something about how the colonel sent them in there to draw fire and die. And that couldn't be far from the truth because Paul could hear the murder-hornets whistling by outside the window. Meanwhile, more men were dropping dead and some of the other guys were throwing flash bangs around trying to flush a neep out of his stone fixture hiding place. The fourth flash bang went off close enough to the neep that he stumbled backward to where a machine-gunner was able to unload on him.

Shortly thereafter; the platoon lieutenants were rounding up the men and gearing up to evacuate the stock exchange. It seemed the imperative was to get to where the murder-hornets couldn't attack them at. But the colonel- since he couldn't hold his precious stock exchange- decided that he wanted to split the company up, and so assigned each platoon to a building in the area. Second platoon would be making a mad dash around the corner to a close-by 72 story skyscraper called Trump. None of them knew what or who a Trump was. First platoon took off toward their objective. Second platoon fell out shortly thereafter. The murder-hornets made darting passes overhead,

BLACK CAT SUNRISE

but the mylar was protecting them and soon they were at the door. It was a strange rotary contraption as much as it was a door but it wasn't moving and so their demolition man took it upon himself to blow the thing out with C4. Nobody dared look up at the sky, but on the ground, they saw an ominous shadow approaching them and lingering above them. The turnstile door exploded out into the building's interior and as they rushed in through the charred ruin of the entrance, Paul heard the snaps of an electronic tinkling coming from behind him.

He looked back through the smoke and saw blue sparkles. Hundreds and thousands of tiny electrical discharges. Looked to be about five guys who'd been struck down by the weapon. A hoshi cannon..., if Paul was remembering correctly. Sergeant DeVille was among the slain. Yoshic was pulling on his shirt, and Darby was shouting, "Get away from the windows. Get into the stairwell!" Paul observed that he liked this building a lot better than the other two they'd been in. There weren't very many windows and there was a lot of stone- marble- that provided a false sense of security which he found comforting.

In the stairwell; Darby fell against the wall and slid down into a pile. It was pitch black in there, so the soldiers turned on headlamps and flashlights. Darby held one hand up to halt the platoon and he rubbed the corner of his eye with his other hand; he didn't say anything for a minute. Then he stood, gave his men a cursory examination, and, addressing them, said; "Look. We're down a team and Adam's team is down a man. Let's just hope it doesn't get any worse. Now. We don't want to stick together. All it takes is one neep to get too close and we're all toast. So, like it or not, we're

BLACK CAT SUNRISE

splitting up. Seems to be a theme. Anyways. I want you to check in every half hour. I'll cover the second floor up to the 11th and we'll worry about the street, too. Bill, you're responsible for the 12th to 21st floors. And backing me up if need be. Keenan, you're taking the 22nd to 31st, and backing up above or below, depending. Adam, you're taking the 32nd to 41st. Yoshic, you get the 42nd and the thirty floors above it. Adam, you'll have to back Yoshic up, if he needs it. You all see what I'm getting at here? Good. Fire team leaders, you were recently issued heartbeat detectors. Now's the time to break them out. Once we secure the building, we'll reconvene, make camp, and wait for morning. Or new orders. Whatever comes first. Now fall out."

Yoshic led the way, holding the heartbeat detector out in front of him. A simple digital device that told the user how many heartbeats were within one hundred feet and the approximate distance to each one. There were 16 men and it was picking up 16 heartbeats. All were close. With the departure of Bill's squad at the 12th floor, that number dropped to 12. On the 20th floor, another heartbeat appeared- making 13- but it wasn't close by. Or, they'd be dead. Yoshic made sure Keenan was aware of it, which he was. And the rest of them kept moving. Adam and his men stopped at the 30th floor, and Yoshic and his squad carried on to the 40th floor. Outside; an amorphous battle continued to rage unabating. The symphony carried on; intimidating and immediate, but muffled by the edifice of the skyscraper.

At the 40th floor, another heartbeat appeared on the detector. Yoshic made sure they were all seeing it; which they were. And then he told them; "Drink

BLACK CAT SUNRISE

some water. Drop your packs. We gotta get this fucker before we do anything else. Now hang on a second." Yoshic did what he had seen Keenan do twenty floors down. That is, he walked up another flight to see how the heartbeat detector reacted. The heartbeat disappeared. That was a good indication the neep was on the 40th floor. Also, 40 was an unimaginative number that correlated to the number 20; also an unimaginative number, and where the other neep had been located. This raised the question as to whether there'd be another one on the 60th floor.

Yoshic produced a tube labeled 'fogger' and a small laser pointer. The fog was known to disturb the effect of the circuit-breakers but more importantly its purpose was to locate the neep. With the butt of his combat knife, he wedged the door wide open and they all hid behind the walls as he emptied the canister into the cavernous corridor. It was a long and straight hall; dimly illuminated by fading daylight coming in through the windows in the doors. All the doors seemed to be closed. That would have to do, then. He shone the laser light through the fog and searched for disturbances in the air currents. For five minutes, nothing happened. But then, there was a subtle and sudden change. At the foot of one of the midway doors; the fog wafted incongruously. Yoshic twitched his hand to make the laser light dance on the number plate beside the door in question. Elijah held up a grenade as a suggestion. Yoshic pointed at Paul's grenade launcher and then held up one finger. Then he pointed at Elijah's grenade and held up two fingers.

This was the wrong thing to do, so there was no right way to do it. With that in mind, Paul approached the door as close as he dared to; not too close at all.

BLACK CAT SUNRISE

Expecting to drop dead at any second. For lack of any other idea, he aimed at the handle and fired. The grenade blasted the door in and Elijah- who was anxious to make a contribution- didn't hesitate to rip the fragmentation grenade's pin out with his teeth, let the charging handle pop off, and then chuck the thing through the door in such a way as to bounce it off a wall. As it exploded, Yoshic was checking some nearby rooms in order to make a better guess at the approximate size of the room they had just assaulted. These rooms were more like halls than they were like rooms. But the neep had to have been near the door to disturb the air current outside of it, so there was that.

"You think he's dead?" Jacob asked nobody in particular.

Elijah said yes. Paul said maybe. And Yoshic said no. And they all kind of looked at each other for a second. But then the question answered itself, because the neep was choking and gasping and wheezing and squealing in agony, saying, "Help. I surrender. Help." But these words weren't intelligible, only obvious given the context.

"What the hell do we do now?" Elijah asked.

They all exchanged looks. Nobody really knew. Yoshic said, "I have an idea," and then he positioned everybody back behind the stairwell walls and shouted out, "Show us your feet!"

And then the neep called back in his choking and gurgling voice, "My feet?"

"That's what I said! Show us your feet!"

For a second, they each wondered why Yoshic had said feet and not hands, but it didn't take long to remember that the neep could be holding a circuit-breaker. Yoshic utilized a tiny mirror on a retractable pole to look out through the doorway and shortly thereafter a pair of boots poked out into the hallway. Yoshic thumped Elijah on the chest with his fist and pointed at his M249.

Elijah didn't hesitate to step out into the hall, approach as close as he dared to, and then open fire on the enemy; spraying bullets into and through the wall where the neep was at. The machine gun raged; star-shaped fire flashing at its muzzle, hot shell casings bouncing off the walls, the hall filling with a rapid rhythm of deafening booms, holes appearing in the wall, the boots of the target jerking spasmodically and then falling limp. These men would have gone deaf ten times over if they weren't wearing ear protection at all times.

The gun fell silent and Elijah asked the dead man, "You still want to surrender?" Then he turned and walked back to the team; smiling, and saying, "Holy fuck. That felt good. I don't know what pussy is like, but it can't be any better than that."

The guys just smiled at him, and Jacob said, "Okay, but what do we do now? We can't go near him. We don't know if his collar is still going, or what."

Yoshic said, "I got something for that." He dug through his pack and pulled out a silver canister with a red cap. Then he closed the door, spray painted a red 'X' over it, went downstairs and spray painted an X on that door, went up two flights and spray painted an X on that door, and then went back to the team and placed the canister back in his pack. Then he radioed Darby to let him know that they got one and that they're proceeding upward.

"We found one on twenty, we found one on forty. I am guessing there's another one on 60. You

BLACK CAT SUNRISE

guys ready to do that all over again?" Yoshic asked his team.

They groaned and Paul rhetorically asked, "Why can't they just fight us like normal people? With normal weapons?"

"They didn't conquer half the planet by making it easy for us," Yoshic said.

"There's got to be a better way," Jacob said.

"Yeah? Like what?" Yoshic asked.

"Let's just set the building on fire," Jacob replied.

"No way, Jose. This fucker's ours now. Or, it will be. Soon."

"We should've burned down this whole goddamn city," Paul said.

"High command wanted to save some of it, if we can," Yoshic said.

"That's a big 'if.' I don't think we can," said Paul.

"Me neither," said Yoshic, adding, "We can't save this place. We can't even save ourselves. Come on. I don't want to do this either. Let's just play the next one exactly how we played this one, and hope for the best, I guess."

Elijah said, "Wait. I got a lot of bullets here. I can flush him out. I think. And then Paul can hit him with the grenade."

Yoshic asked Paul, "What do you think?"

"Fuck... Worth a try, I guess."

And so, about ten minutes later, they were twenty floors higher, with an extra heartbeat on the detector, and executing their plan according to their plan. The neep was practically on top of them. Essentially, right up against the stairwell. They all backed way off when they realized this. It was a

Richard Rose 152

BLACK CAT SUNRISE

miracle the man's god-collar hadn't eliminated the lot of them. Elijah started close with a couple exploratory shots. That was all it took. He heard the target shrieking and scuffling and from a kneeling position he held the weapon low and opened fire with a slight upward angle; unleashing a barrage of bullets into the vicinity of what he was trying to hit. After about sixty rounds, the firing stopped. The fireteam peered through the bullet holes in the wall. There was a body, lying limp and still, in a pool of its own blood. Yoshic fired another spray directly into the corpse just to be sure it was- in fact- a corpse; saying afterward, "Good enough for me. Come on. If there's another one, we'll do it Elijah's way. Seems pretty good. I guess."

Paul found himself wondering if there was a better way they could be serving the confederate. If there was something more they could be doing with themselves. But he'd seen these god-collars drop a lot of guys. Each one of these neeps could eliminate a fireteam or two or three. Theoretically. So, maybe one of them really was worth four of him. But the intel was that the god-collars killed through the walls. And the first-hand experience was indicating otherwise. If the collars killed through walls, then they should all be dead right now.

Yoshic spray painted red Xs on the door and the doors above and below and then the fireteam continued marching upwards. It wasn't easy climbing all those stairs, but they didn't notice. It was easier than the unending marching they'd been doing all winter long. Easier by a lot. They'd climbed all the way to the top and the heartbeat detector didn't detect any more enemy heartbeats; so they started walking back

BLACK CAT SUNRISE

down. And now they were at the 69th floor. But still in the stairwell.

Elijah couldn't resist the temptation and suggested to the others, "Hey. I want to go look out the windows. You guys want to go look out the windows?"

'Kind of.' 'Yeah.'

Yoshic said, "I don't think the muder-hornets are patrolling this high up, but if you see a drone then you better move your ass. It'll put a bolt in you from the other side of the city. Fuck around and find out."

Chapter 9

Dead

They crept cautiously into the nearest room; a typical boardroom type office with a long table and chairs around it. Every surface; coated in a thick blanket of dust. The air had a bad taste. It was dark out but the moon was full- or close to full- and the city glowed in its pale luminescence. The city itself being devoid of electricity, there was little to no artificial light. But there were dozens of areas of the city which were ablaze and casting bright orange glow over their surroundings. There were more skyscrapers than Paul would've thought possible; several of which were now reduced to the indignity of a towering inferno. He wondered about the people who built these things. They must have been like gods. And now they were like ghosts. The team found themselves staring into the shadowy edifice of the nearby Freedom tower; the largest building in the city. They didn't know what it was called or that it was the biggest, but it certainly looked like the biggest. Down in the streets, they saw the bodies of their fallen compatriots; strewn about like leaves, or litter. There was at least one kuki drone

Richard Rose 154

BLACK CAT SUNRISE

out there, moving amongst the skyscrapers, but the team couldn't see it and so it couldn't see them. What they saw were the reflections of its lasers in the area where it was operating; further to the north. The murder-hornets were harder to spot, but there were more of them; casting flitting fits and starts of red illumination. It was a sad thing to see because they knew that those lasers didn't usually miss what they were aiming at and they didn't waste any energy, either. When those lasers were going off, men were dying. Seeing this, Paul began to appreciate their cushy assignment. Clearing buildings wasn't so bad. If it kept them out of the laser sights. Then the kuki drone came into view and Yoshic was about to start pulling on his men to get them out of sight; when a bright whitish-orange orb dashed across the sky. It was a missile. But they didn't see where it came from. It collided with the kuki and exploded into orange flame as well as orange phantasm. It was far off, but as the flame dissipated and died out, they could see the forcefield's phantasm coalescing into a tiny figure that was presumably the form of a woman. This woman- this witch- then thrust herself through the fuselage of the kuki drone and the saucer burst into flame and dropped out of the sky. Then the witch dashed toward their area; trailing a tail of orange light. Heading for the Freedom tower; unbeknownst to them. But then a neon green shooting star came shooting down from outer space- tailing an arcing neon green streak. It collided with the orange phantasm and drove it down into the waters of the Hudson.

Then the floor trembled beneath their feet and their faces lit up blue, as- uncomfortably close- a radiant plasmoid ripped through the hull of a

BLACK CAT SUNRISE

skyscraper and carried on off out into the stratosphere; leaving a smoldering three or four story tall circular hole punched through whatever building that was. And whatever building materials had been filling that hole; these were vaporized now. And with that, Paul began to notice other buildings with fiery holes and molten gouges shorn through them. It seemed like a waste. These old world treasures. But maybe this was for the better. Nobody wanted to be reminded of how it used to be, for other people. They were more concerned with forgetting the way it always had been, for them.

Yoshic put his finger to his ear and spoke into his earpiece, "Yoshic reporting. Top of the building is clear. What now, lieutenant?"

Darby radioed back, "Nice work, soldiers. We're regrouping on the fifth floor. Floor number five. See you there."

When they got down to floor number five, Darby gave Yoshic a small cigar to share with his fireteam. It was the custom of confederate lieutenants to carry packs of these little cigars to amplify these little reprieves. It wasn't much, but it was something, and the meaning wasn't lost on the troops. Death was just a heartbeat away. Smoke them if you got them wasn't just an archaic quip. It was a way of life.

Yoshic lit it and puffed it and tasted it and savored it and puffed it some more and then passed it off to Paul and then asked Darby, "What's next, lieutenant?"

Darby replied, "Well, it's good news or it's bad news. Depending on how you look at it. Second platoon is assigned to clear out another building next door. We're leaving one fireteam to garrison this

BLACK CAT SUNRISE

building. You guys 86ed two neeps to Keenan's one. And Keenan's team lost two men. Will and David; they're gone. Now second platoon is down 7 men. So I'm combining Keenan's team with Adam's team and leaving this building to your team. The building is enormous on these lower floors, so stay on your toes and keep your head on a swivel. Your mission will be to prevent the enemy from re-occupying the premises. I'll leave it to your discretion as to how you go about doing that. There's going to be more men in the field soon. Some time tonight you'll be relieved, at which point you will contact me and we'll regroup. Probably at the next spot, or the one after, would be my guess. The objective is to clear out these buildings one by one. Then we're going to hold them. If we can do that, then the enemy has got no place to hide."

"Roger that. When you moving out then?"

"Soon. Get your men down to the third floor. That's your choke point. Second floor is too wide open. Whatever happens below the third floor, don't worry too much about it. Just know where your exits are. Break a window and throw a rope out of it, if you have to. Any of you got a rope?"

"Jacob does, yeah. But we'll be exposed that way."

"I know. But I don't know what to tell you. Hold your ground. Make them eat explosives. Spray and pray. Use your imagination. Listen. If you walk out the way we came in and take a left then we'll be in the next building over. But the goal is to clear that one plus the one next to it. That second one is a monster. So, one door down and two doors down, to the left. That's where we'll be. Hell. I don't know. I got to go."

"Happy hunting, sir."

Richard Rose 157

BLACK CAT SUNRISE

"Thanks," said Darby, and then he addressed the crowd; "Gentlemen, Yoshic's team is guarding this building. The rest of us, we're on to the next one. Get your gear together. We move out in five minutes."

Yoshic pulled his guys down to the third floor and they watched Darby uneasily as he and the men came down and kept going. Positioning themselves under their space blankets, the rest of the Second platoon- of Delta company of the Long Island Battalion- rushed out the door and went on their way.

"This seems too easy. What's the catch?" Paul asked.

Jacob said, "The catch is there are six stairwells down here, and only four of us. That, and we don't know what's coming. The samurai are going to want this place back. They're going to want all this territory back."

Yoshic said, "Yeah. And we better be ready. That's why we're on the third floor. The stairwells are our choke points. Only ways in. Only ways out. Problem is there's six stairwells. Paul and Jacob, you're on the east side and we'll take the west side. Start throwing furniture down the stairs. If you hear anybody tripping around on it, use your mirrors and get positive identification, you know, before you blow them to shit, or whatever."

Using their headlamps to see, they were able to find a good supply of office chairs and smaller cabinets to throw down into the stairwells. But they didn't feel comfortable on the third-floor landing, so they went up to the fourth to increase the distance between them and the hypothetical threats. They didn't know what to think, or what to expect. The task was a good escape

BLACK CAT SUNRISE

from the shit, but it felt wrong to be sitting pretty while so many others were out there dying.

Jacob mentioned this to Paul and Paul told him, "We can't fight if we're dead. We're not dead. We can still fight. This is good. The guys who got lasered, who got their hearts stopped. That ain't right. That's a sad way to die. We killed some neeps today. Today was a good day."

"You killed a neep. I didn't kill any neeps."

"Yeah, but you shot out those heart-stoppers. You probably saved a couple of our guys, just by reacting fast as you did."

It was a lot of work moving all that furniture and they needed a break. Paul took his helmet off and shone its lamp into a corner to light up that stairwell a little. His pale- and once handsome- face was gaunt from thin rations and over exertion. Scar tissue covered much of his head and throat; an ugly red hue and textured like crinkled plastic wrap. The blonde stubble of his hair was growing out longer than he preferred. In the dark, his blue eyes reflected the blue headlamp beams. His boots were coming loose and he tied them better. His pants, too, had to be tied better at the bottom. Body armor made sitting somewhat unpleasant unless he sat up rigidly; so that's what he did. After reloading the two grenades he'd spent, he opened a packet of beef stew and dug in to eat.

Jacob topped off his rifle's ten round magazine and then dug into a packet of chicken and rice; happy to be alive and with his friend Paul. Paul gave Jacob a lot of comfort because he was never a jerk and was consistently open and warm. Jacob's black hair fell over a circular face with light brown skin and dark brown eyes. The hair was wavy and greasy; having not been

Richard Rose 159

BLACK CAT SUNRISE

washed in a long time. He too sat straight up rigidly; with his helmet beside him and lighting up the hallway. This was the nice thing about soldiering. Doing nothing. It didn't happen too often. But when it did, it was nice. In a few minutes they'd have to get back to patrolling the stairwells.

Their eyes flitted up and around, listening to the different sorts of explosions. Feeling many of them in their bones. Listening for lasers and feeling queasy to hear them. Paul wanted to be back with all the men they'd come out of the hole with. He didn't like being split up all the time. First, they split up the battalion. Then, they split up the company. Then, they split up the platoon. And now, they split up the fireteam. He said to Jacob, "You know. A thousand of us crawled out of that wormhole today. And now there are two of us. Where did everybody go?"

"I guess they're all doing the same thing we're doing. Or, some variation of it."

"Yeah. That. Or, they're dead."

"Right. Or, they're dead."

They finished eating and tossed their garbage in a bin in the next room over. Paul wished he had a heartbeat detector. They should all have them. But Paul had a lot of wishes and almost none of them ever came true. He wished to not die, and he wasn't dead. So, that was pretty good, he thought. They walked from one stairwell, over to the next, and back to the middle, and back to the first. Stopping to listen each time. And repeating this process was how they spent the next couple of hours; kindling no small measure of resentment that Yoshic had a digital device to warn of intruders, and all they had was their ears.

BLACK CAT SUNRISE

Then they heard a shout rising up from below, "Hello! Hello? Second platoon, delta company, Long Island? That you? Hello?"

"Second platoon! Fireteam Yoshic!" Paul called back.

Paul and Jacob joined up with Yoshic and Elijah. They crept downstairs, climbed over the chairs and tables and cabinets, and found that the second-floor landing- a windowless and vacuous cavern of elevators, information desks, and waiting areas- was full of soldiers and weapons and gear. Paul noticed at a glance that a lot of the men had their faces in their hands, or their arms wrapped around their legs, or they had angry far away glares in their eyes; indications of battlefield malaise. Surely they'd taken losses. Paul and Jacob had heard them taking losses, he now realized. Yoshic's team was greeted by a short and swarthy man with a grizzled appearance, eyes set too far apart, and a mystified grin. There were two red bars embroidered on the collar of his black shirt, but no other indication of rank could be seen.

Paul and Jacob noticed the bars immediately and stood at attention, but they did not salute him because nobody saluted anybody in the warzone. The captain said, "At ease, boys. You're relieved of this building's garrison. You're to reconvene with your platoon at once."

'Yes, sir,' they said.

But Jacob couldn't resist asking the man a question. "Sir, have they breached the moleholes yet?"

"No, they have not. Too many drones in the sky still. We don't want to lose the assets. But that orange witch of ours, she'll get them down, sooner or later. And then the city will be ours."

Richard Rose 161

BLACK CAT SUNRISE

"What's left of it," Paul joked.

And the captain laughed and, agreeing, said, "Right. What's left of it. You gentlemen are dismissed," and then he turned and disappeared back into his company; the entirety of which seemed to be crammed into the area. Or, the entirety of what was left of it, more accurately.

Yoshic radioed Darby, ascertained the whereabouts of second platoon, and- without hesitation- the fireteam was running two doors down with their space blanket over their head. Passing through a landscape alien to them; white stone and well-kept streets, yellow hydrants and blue booths and complicated scaffolding and grey meters and metal carts. A foreign place in time and space. Yoshic wore a grim expression- his long chiseled face; stolid, with piercing eyes that seemed to see beyond the peril and into the resolution. Somewhere out there there was peace, and he always suspected that peace was in the mind. In the moment. In the now. Even in moments like these. Especially in moments like these. Tilting his head, Yoshic listened carefully. Hell's symphonic score roared from every direction unceasingly; buildings crumbled, bombs burst, energy weapons raged, machine guns sang their sweet melody; but he wasn't listening for any of that. He was listening for a whistle. A whirling saucer's whistle of doom.

Stepping over dead bodies; Paul felt his heart sink into his stomach as a murder-hornet warbled overhead. But this time was different. This time it was only them out there, caught out and alone. They all realized it as the murder-hornet was honing in on them. "Fucking... run!" Yoshic ordered. And so they ran. It zoomed by high up, came down lower, and

BLACK CAT SUNRISE

zoomed by again. They adjusted their camouflage with white knuckle determination; constantly throwing it down or pulling it up or twisting it around. And then the murder-hornet came in lower and zoomed by them again. They were realizing that soon it wouldn't be over them- it would be beside them. And then, like fish or birds, or human prey, they collectively ducked into the door that would prove to be their salvation. Still, they fled, further and further inward, until it was evident there were no windows around.

"What the fuck?" said Elijah.

"Yeah. I guess we should've seen that coming," said Paul.

Jacob said, "There's got to be a way to stop those things."

"I'm sure they're trying to come up with something," said Paul.

"Yeah. Or, they're not," said Yoshic.

And the guys couldn't help but to deflate and hang their heads and sigh in sad agreement. But Yoshic added, "Look. We survived. Don't get no better than that. Let's quit dicking around. We got to find the others."

A few floors up, they found Darby waiting by himself. Darby informed Yoshic that Yoshic was to be the acting sergeant now; now that Deville was dead. And he needed him to help him look over the maps and give him his opinion. Paul and Elijah and Jacob were instructed to catch up with Adam, who had been given the responsibility of clearing out the west side of this building. A building with no immediately evident name which they'd taken to referring to as 'the monster' due to its colossal size. The smaller building next door had taken a fair amount of time to clear,

Richard Rose 163

BLACK CAT SUNRISE

even though they only found one neep stationed there. Said neep having been dispatched with a frag grenade. And Keenan's team of five was left behind to garrison those premises. So, Adam's team- about 10 men now, including the three additions- wasn't very far into the process of clearing these floors. Before they had left him back with Darby, Yoshic had passed off his heartbeat detector to Paul; along with his ear piece, some foggers, the laser light, and a couple other items.

Adam seemed like a guy who was always trying to catch up with what was going on. But actually, he was sharp and well-attuned. He was simultaneously out ahead of everybody while- under the surface- he was ruminating over past events. Trying to understand things others didn't even think about. A tall and strong man- blue eyed and blonde haired- with a slim build and angular features like a woman. His primary weapon was an automatic AK107. When Paul met up with Adam, Adam decided to split his team into two teams of five with Paul leading one. The new additions to Paul's team were Dennis and Jerome. Dennis was a lanky man with pale skin, shaggy blonde hair, thick black rimmed eye-glasses, and a nervous neurotic demeanor; carrying an M4 with a single shot M203 grenade launcher module. And Jerome was a strong and solid man with oily black skin, a symmetrical and even build, a round bald head with round eyes, and a serious disposition; carrying an automatic shotgun that used ten round magazines, each loaded with 3-inch oo buckshot shells.

The monster's floors had three doublewide stairwells and three main halls. They searched each hall of each floor. For many floors, they didn't find anybody. But high up in the sky, in a stairwell on the

Richard Rose 164

BLACK CAT SUNRISE

63rd floor, Paul put his fist in the air to call a halt and they all stopped suddenly. Three new heartbeats. Three neeps. He showed the others the glowing readout. Usually, the heartbeat detector detected the heartbeats when they were on the floor with the targets. So the targets must be on that floor. Paul whispered into his microphone, "I got three beats on 63. Three beats on 63. Front stairwell. Front hallway. Adam, what floor are you on?"

"48. You want to take them, or you want to wait until we get up there?"

"We're going to fall back and wait. We need you to cut off their retreat," Paul said.

"Copy that. I'll radio when we're in position."

Paul signaled the others to get back, but sneakily he peered in through the glass in the window of the door to the 63rd floor. Then he jumped back because he saw they'd set up a circuit breaker to stand sentry in the center of the hallway. Paul had some frag grenades. Each confederate soldier had a cloth tube holding three grenades. It was worn either on their pack strap, on their pack, or on their belt. A grenade would have to suffice. He didn't dare look again. The circuit-breakers were proving more ineffectual than he would have dared to hope but he didn't dare to underestimate the things, either. More importantly, he thought he glimpsed a hint of artificial light close to where the device was. And he was learning something about the predictable mentality of the slave soldier. Apparently, they had no concept of subterfuge. And they seemed devoid of situational awareness, at that. Paul retrieved a grenade.

Adam radioed; "We're in position. What's your plan?"

Richard Rose 165

BLACK CAT SUNRISE

Paul whispered, "You guys should keep to the 62nd and 64th. There might be bullets flying. There's a circuit-breaker in the hallway. I think they're in the room directly adjacent to it. I'll take the breaker out with a grenade. Then I'll have our M249 lay into their general vicinity. All you have to do is make sure they don't get away."

"Copy that."

Paul returned to the door and signaled for Elijah and Jerome to come join him. He had made sure the others had heard him talking to Adam, so he didn't have to repeat himself. It hadn't been mentioned, but Jerome didn't have to be told; he was their last best line of defense. If the automatic shotgun couldn't take down the neeps then they may well all be dead anyways. Paul radioed again and said, "Engaging the enemy."

"Copy that."

Paul pulled the pin, grasped the door handle, popped off the grenade handle, cracked the door, and with a flick of his wrist he carefully chucked the grenade to about where he thought it needed to go to. He signaled Elijah to come hither, and then he made a sweeping motion to remind Elijah what side the neeps were- probably- on. The fragmentation grenade detonated and the building shook. Paul opened the door and Elijah stepped through; leveling his M249 belt fed machine gun. Nobody had verified the circuit-breaker was destroyed, so Elijah was essentially doing so with his life.

The grenade had made a lot of smoke. And dust. The headlamp beams could barely penetrate. Elijah scanned the hallway. Looking for something. Anything. There was a laser sight mounted on his weapon. He

BLACK CAT SUNRISE

turned it on, but couldn't see any evidence of anybody. Although, the circuit-breaker wasn't killing him, and this occurred to him, and he shrugged and nodded with heavenly gratitude. Paul had said he thought the neeps were over by where he had thrown the grenade to. So Elijah squeezed the trigger and put a few shots into those walls. This- predictably- caused the neeps to- as they panicked- start chattering. The chatter gave Elijah an idea about where they were. But he wasn't going to waste ammunition. After marching around carrying all that weight, he had a certain respect for each and every cartridge. A mindset for which they'd all always been conditioned. So, carefully he fired some exploratory shots through the walls. He'd shoot and listen, and shoot and listen. And after a few cycles of that he felt like he could almost guess exactly where they were. So, he began releasing three, four, or five shot bursts into their location. They cried out in excruciating pain and he knew he had them.

Except for one of the neeps who suddenly came tripping into the hall and into a wall. Paul had been crouched down behind Elijah and as Elijah opened fire on the man, Paul launched a grenade; exploding the neep into chunks of meat and showers of blood. Paul had done that because he didn't want to risk having a god-collar or circuit-breaker out where they might be exposed to it. The explosives were chaotic, but they'd proven useful for neutralizing the enemy's weapons. Jacob called out, "How many heart beats, Paul?"

Paul could hear the moans and groans of painful suffering. He checked the detector and called back, "Still one too many. But it's red negative." Red negative meant failing slow and red positive meant failing fast. Red negative was far less likely to be a threat than red

BLACK CAT SUNRISE

positive. Red positives couldn't be trusted; they could be false-positives coming from alarmed individuals. Red negatives could only mean the person was about to die.

Elijah said, "Hang on. I can see through the holes. I got him."

And after he fired about ten more rounds, the neep went silent. Elijah looked back to Paul and Paul signaled him to fall back to the stairwell. Radioing Adam, he told him, "We're all clear, Adam. You got paint to X out the door over there?"

"Yeah. We got it. Nice work."

"Thanks. We're going to keep on keeping on. Got a lot of floors left, I guess."

"Yeah. I guess so. Over and out."

They Xed out the doors to the 63rd floor and then walked up the stairs until they were on the 79th floor. That seemed to be the highest floor that wasn't utilitarian and locked off. On the 79th floor, they stepped out of the stairwell and into the interior to take a look at what was going on outside. It was hard to look at, but oddly satisfying. It was late in the night now, but time wasn't relevant. Paul thought of his childhood. Of his life of service to the cause and nothing else. This war. These witches. This world. This was what it was for. Or it seemed that way. Something like this. This had to be important. But he couldn't fathom how. How this mattered. How anything mattered. A fog of noxious smoke was draped over the city like a pall. The moonshine only occasionally penetrated as the hazes shifted. Entire swaths of the city were burning by this point. There was no way to extinguish the flames. Lasers were still flashing down below. The murder-hornets were relentlessly

Richard Rose 168

BLACK CAT SUNRISE

persistent. Paul noticed that, occasionally, red laser bolts came shooting down from turrets positioned on the corners of buildings. He hadn't known those were there.

Upper New York Bay was out to the southwest and it wasn't exactly visible but the area was oddly placid except for the plasmoids which were darting up out of the water. He wondered how the confederates would stop the enemy's submarine drones. Paul reasoned- correctly- 'we don't have any way to attack their submarines.' He didn't know whether or not the confed had even one submarine. Even if it did, it wouldn't be a match for these. For a minute he was wondering how they could hit the things without torpedoes. Or depth charges.

The skyscrapers were still burning- more now than previously- and they lighted up the endlessly sprawling metropolis which was otherwise bleak and black and overgrown with vines and weeds. The roads; choked with rotted out automobiles. The city was a wasteland before they began decimating it. By the time they were finished, it would be a razed and ruinous blanket of rubble and wreckage pockmarked with bomb craters and bespeckled with skeletons. The sky seemed eerily inactive. There weren't any kuki drones stalking about. Nor could he see any kumo in the field. And this bothered Paul. The bakufu was holding its strength in reserve. Same as the confederate.

He wondered how many of the Quinetucket Killers were still underground. More than half, he guessed. Delta company was everywhere, split up into its smallest parts. Below; that other company, whatever it was, it was all together. Probably that's how it would be. They'd send out platoons to clear out the neeps and

Richard Rose 169

BLACK CAT SUNRISE

then use the buildings to warehouse the division. Both teams were transfixed on the vision of the battleground outside. It sucked to see the laser bolts picking men off. But otherwise, it was a surreal vision to behold. It was hypnotic, to watch the city burn. And funny, too, because nobody really cared about the endless array of structures being decimated. Maybe the bakufu cared. But that was all for the better.

Adam called out, "Hey...! Hey! I can't reach the lieutenant! We got to get back down there! Right now! Fall back! Double time!"

As a matter of course, Adam and his team took the west stairwell and Paul and his team took the right stairwell. They practically flew down the steps. They weren't used to running down stairs, but they were used to running down craggy mountains, and this was easier than that. Paul felt so stupid. They were staring out the windows like dickheads, and now Darby was out of contact. Darby was a good guy, and he had Yoshic with him. It hadn't occurred to Paul at the time, but it was a serious error for those two to stay behind like that. The teams arrived at the second-floor landing and ran out into the reception area, to where- sure enough- both Yoshic and Darby were sprawled out over their maps; fallen over each other and dead. Each of the men reacted differently. But they all readied their weapons. Paul gripping his MP5. A lot of guys felt themselves getting choked up. Everybody liked Darby. Some guys were numb to death and didn't feel anything more than a dull resentment toward the war. Some guys started looking around and checking heartbeat detectors. Jacob unclipped Paul's detector from Paul's shirt. Somebody needed to monitor it and Paul was concentrating on the dead bodies. Like he

BLACK CAT SUNRISE

was trying to solve a riddle. Really, he was trying not to weep.

Yoshic was his friend. They loved him like a brother. They were each other's brothers. They didn't have anybody else. They were it for each other; the end-all be-all of human affection and adoration. Paul approached the corpses, and, at a glance, it looked like their hearts had stopped. Which was typical. But he examined them more closely and realized there was a small trickle of blood coming out of Yoshic's ear. And then he found the same trickle coming out of Darby's ear. Somebody had to figure out why they were bleeding from their ears. It may as well be him. Paul knelt down, saw what caused this, and pinched the offending foreign object; a small black ball. Then he pulled it out. The blood came spurting thereafter. The object, it turned out, was a slim five-inch spike of gleaming steel. These had been driven through their foam ear plugs and into their brains. One for each man.

Chapter 10
Japs
Earlier that day, just after attacking the teki on the bridges, but before the teki heishi came up from their wormholes; Moto returned from Ryker's Island and stepped out from beneath the glass of the transport pod and into the stainless-steel transport landing. Her black hair hung over her hinomaru headband. Her cheeks were chubby. She was five foot one and a little bit plump and didn't look like her sister; her face was rounder and Maya's face was more angular. Moto's mood was perturbation and her slanted eyes were looking around like those of one lost

Richard Rose 171

BLACK CAT SUNRISE

in thought. She lit a cigarette. Maya and Kazuki and Xander were waiting there to greet her.

"So they're spread out then?" Maya asked her, anxious to hear anything promising.

"The heishi dorei? Yes. The city is crawling with them. The teki won't be able to throw a rock without hitting one. But nobody is confident in them. From what I am told, they haven't improved since we last inspected them. They're still timid little creatures. Essentially, frightened rodents. They're slaves, not soldiers."

"The bushi had two weeks to train them," said Maya.

"They needed two years, not two weeks. But it doesn't matter. There isn't much we can do about it now. We expected this. We're not relying on them; we're relying on their cardio weapons. The teki will chew them up easily enough, but it will cost them dearly. The heishi dorei are basically human booby traps. I am more concerned for the bushi. They're so few and far between. They're out there with little to no tactical advantage."

"So what are you doing about it?" Maya asked.

"I issued the quasar rifles and void generators. Beyond that, I left it up to their discretion. I told them that now that they have positioned their dorei heishi, they are free to fight however they see fit. We've always been inferior in number, and now, thanks to their phantom majo, inferior in artillery. Drastically inferior. I told the bushi that our hopes for holding the city rest entirely on their fighting spirit. I told them to leave the dorei heishi to their own devices. I told them to remember they are bushi. The bakufu is theirs. Theirs to defend. Theirs to lose."

BLACK CAT SUNRISE

"Good. Or, not so good. The dorei will fail. It's inevitable. What about the ninja?" Maya asked.

"They're descending upon the city as we speak."

"Excellent. We can breathe a little easier."

Kazuki said, "And if you think about it; it's really not as bad as it seems. We lure them in. We wear them down. We turn them back. We want them to attack us! How else can we destroy them? There's no better way."

Moto and Maya looked at her and smiled. She was right in that. And Maya agreed, saying, "This is true. We will do what we can, but even if we fail, the bakufu will not fail, because the majo will not fail the bakufu."

Moto asked, "Do the teki know they cut a tunnel through our tunnel?"

Maya said, "If they did, then we'd be in chains right now."

"Did you evacuate the Freedom tower?" Moto asked.

"Yes," said Maya.

They walked to the low table and sat on their knees at it. Moto poured a sake and offered to pour for her sister and niece, but they both refused. Kazuki instead set about heating a pot of tea. Maya gazed into the portrait of the sprawling garden and remembered her own garden atop the Freedom tower; feeling like she was losing everything. Suddenly so grateful for Kazukichan. Xander was pouring over tablet screens in the conference room in the bunker; over by where the drone sphere was located.

"Mama. I want to fly the drones," Kazuki said.

"Absolutely not."

"Why not? They're just going to be destroyed."

BLACK CAT SUNRISE

"It will antagonize the teki majo. Now is a time for humility and acceptance. Not a brazen display of bravado. We don't know what's going to happen. It may come to pass that our lives will depend on the good will of our adversaries. We will be on our best behavior. We've done everything we can. Let the pieces fall where they may." Kazuki frowned and scowled and looked away; pouting and pensive. Maya asked Moto, "How are our operators?"

"As good as can be. Morale is low, because they feel there's nothing they can do. I told them to do their best. I told them the marshall won't dispatch them unless there are high value targets available."

Xander slid open the shoji and entered. He wore the same plain white clothes and hinomaru headband as the others; his bald head reflected light as he bowed, and- with a tablet in hand, he said, "It's begun. They're emerging from their holes. We're getting the first reports of contact. I received three transmissions in rapid succession. Midtown, the east village, and the financial district."

Maya looked away and down and began to drum her fingers on the table. Her black hair fell over her eyes. She felt a sadness wash over her. It was a shameful sensation. This was her fault. Because she wanted Long Island. For no reason other than pride. Tears filled her eyes, and she told Xander, "Release the BD-14s."

"Hai," Xander said, and walked away.

BD-14 was the technical name of the so-called 'muder-hornet.' It stood for Battle Drone 14. The fourteenth and latest version of the bakufu battle drone. It had always been a saucer, but it was constantly being made faster; with upgraded targeting

BLACK CAT SUNRISE

and more effective laser bolts. Moto poured herself another cup of sake. And Kazuki said to her mother, "There's nothing left to do here. When are we going to Bosuton?"

"We'll leave when we are defeated. If we leave before we are defeated, then we'll lose face with the coven. How ridiculous would we look if our forces win the battle and we're not even here to see it?"

This terrible day passed in much the same way as Maya had feared and expected; an abhorrent and catastrophic affair. She watched her own forces bombard her own city in a haphazard attempt to dissuade their determined foe. A blunder she'd personally ordered. As much out of nihilistic remorse as out of practical benefit. Her beloved city. The bakufu, the majo; these were above her. The slaves. The bushi. These were beneath her. It was her city that she was losing. It was herself. She was her city, in a way. They were attacking her. Bombarding her. Burning her. Occasionally, she'd remind herself, 'You did it to yourself.'

They'd known the enemy would arrive in full force. And now that they were there, it was a sickening sensation. However, there were a couple promising facts about what had transpired. Their computers registered a few battlefield statistics and these were promising. They could see how many heishi dorei they were losing. It was a lot, but not as many as she had feared. There were tens of thousands at their disposal. They'd only lost 2,000. And those 2,000 had claimed over 4,000 heishi teki. A two for one exchange rate. Of the five hundred bushi, only 15 had gotten themselves killed so far. Maya couldn't figure out if that figure was

Richard Rose 175

BLACK CAT SUNRISE

prudent or cowardly. The assorted laser systems; kuki, kumo, umi, turret, XT-19, and AD-14; these registered over 15,000 hits combined. Those numbers were good. But they didn't change the fact; Nyu NyuYoku was being overrun.

Maya figured that the teki had sustained ten percent total strength losses. Meanwhile, the bakufu had sustained something like seven percent total strength losses. And also, these figures weren't accounting for the ninja's numbers. There wasn't any way to know how many losses the ninja were inflicting. They didn't submit reports and weren't subject to inquiry. Similarly, she had no idea what the majo were doing or what sort of losses they were inflicting. As far as she could tell, neither the bakufu majo nor the teki majo were doing much of anything. Which was unusual, but that was their prerogative and these were unusual times.

The teki didn't seem to realize that there were hidden cameras everywhere. They couldn't make any moves without bakufu intelligence marking the changes. Watching the cameras is what the Naito had been doing all day. Occasionally the 5th dan bushi would contact Moto for a brief consultation, but mostly the Naito weren't participating. Only observing. The bushi didn't seem to be participating, either. And Maya wasn't happy about that but she wasn't anxious to get them killed, either.

Finally, Maya grew weary of her frustration and lamentation and poured herself a cup of sake. And poured another for Moto. And one each for Xander and Kazuki, too. She drank it down and asked, "What are they waiting for? They're just sitting underground.

Richard Rose 176

BLACK CAT SUNRISE

Why don't they bring out their tanks and their artillery? Their numbers?"

Kazuki said, "They're clearing out the heishi dorei. And the heishi dorei are making it too easy for them."

Moto- slurring her words a little- said, "You know, you're absolutely correct. The bushi are failing in their duty. This is unacceptable." Moto picked up a small silver cylinder and transmitted a message to the bushi, saying, "Motosama desu. These are your new orders. You're to compel the dorei to engage the enemy. We're losing dorei too easily. It's unacceptable. You're going to have to start shocking the dorei. Make it clear to them that cowardice will be punished severely. Any dorei who is found to be cowering will receive a 110-volt shock from their collars as a warning. If the cowering continues, they'll receive a 220-volt shock as a punishment. I want you watching these people whenever you're not otherwise engaged. They are your weapons. You have to use them. They're our best line of defense and we're wasting them. Stop wasting them. Make them count. All they have to do is hold their cardio ray out in front of the teki. Or hide in a shadow where the teki are walking past. It's not that complicated. I don't care how many times you have to shock them. Shock them until they're wishing for death if you have to. 110 volts as a warning. 220 volts as a punishment. Ping my device to confirm you understand."

Her communication device displayed hundreds of pings received and that was satisfactory. Meanwhile, none of the Naito dared to bring up the obvious question. This situation was an ominous precedent. Now that their shields were down, they were greatly diminished, and the Naito knew the predetermined conclusion to this situation. A couple of weeks ago, it was a reassuring notion. Now, it was a disturbing premonition: When the time came, and the cause was lost, the bakufu would initiate the nuclear option. Not the literal nuclear option. As that was not an option. This was the figurative nuclear option. A universal slaughter. The shinobi.

Paul held the spike that had killed Yoshic in one hand and his MP5 in the other. His grenade launcher; slung over his shoulder. The men around him were transfixed on the object he had pulled out of his dead friend's ear. But he'd been distracted for too long and his training kicked in and- realizing something wasn't right, that it wasn't right to be so distracted for so many seconds- he picked his head up and looked around. He saw the others looking at the deadly spike, but he also saw something incongruous. At the corner of the sprawling reception area. Moving in their direction. A pasty skinned and crazy eyed man whose teeth were exposed by lips that snarled like a rabid animal. The man wore white. With a red circle over his forehead. In one motion, Paul flung the spike away, slapped Jacob and pointed at the enemy, and lifted his MP5; trying to get a shot, but unable to and- diving for cover- calling out, "Heart-stopper! Heart-stopper! Take cover!" There was cover available; in the form of a plethora of courtesy desks and ancient blue couches and big plastic pots with big fake trees in them.

This neep had caught the entire platoon off guard. Jacob saw that people were already dropping. He let the apparently unreliable heartbeat monitor slip from his hand, jerked his head, twisted his frame, and

BLACK CAT SUNRISE

shouldered his rifle. There were men between him and the neep. Some dropped in place. Some scattered; jumping through the air toward wherever they thought might be safe. As his body stilled, and as his breath escaped him, Jacob acquired the target in his scope and pulled the trigger. He'd been trained as a sharpshooter since the first day they put a gun in his little boy's hands. The .308 cartridge exploded, the rifle kicked, and the bullet found its mark. The god collar. And the throat. The neep's neck burst apart in a pink flash of sparking metal and splashing gore.

Jerome watched the neep's circuit-breaker fly through the air and drop. As soon as it stopped sliding across the floor, he squeezed his trigger thrice. A single oo buckshot round was equivalent to 9 9mm rounds going off at once. The shotgun had obliterated the deadly device by the third round- but he fired a couple more to be certain. 5 rounds total.

Paul stood up and surveyed the scene. When he saw what had happened, he almost threw up; except his throat was too dry. It wasn't the dead neep that made him sick. It was because Elijah was dead. And Dennis. And Adam. And a few other guys he didn't know particularly well, but whom he had liked well-enough; Charlie and Darius and Christopher. Hell. Elijah was one of the best of them. If the day's events were any indication. Again- Paul's training gripped him tightly; all emotion drained from him in an instant and he felt a desperate animal instinct take over. Paul said, "Darby is dead. DeVille is dead. Yoshic is dead. Adam is dead. I am assuming command of this platoon. Take their machine guns. And get their grenades. We have to get back up to the 79th floor. We don't know what's

BLACK CAT SUNRISE

going on down here. We have to get someplace secure
and call for reinforcement!"

Paul went over to Elijah and knelt down beside
him, and as he unslung the M249 and the case of belts,
he told the dead body, "I'm going to miss you, Elijah. It
won't be the same without you." And Yoshic was
nearby, within earshot; so he added, "You, too, Yoshic.
See you on the other side." Some of the guys heard him
talking to the dead, but they thought nothing of it.
They just watched their heart monitors and kept their
eyes on the exits. Some of the confederates had faith in
old world religions. But none of the religions had any
official position in their lives. Just an informal
presence, at best.

Paul took a quick headcount. 10. Down from 25
to 10. He couldn't believe it. After they got away from
the murder-hornet, it had seemed like everything was
going so good. It had seemed like things were going to
be alright. Another soldier- Terry; a hulking and
grizzled redhead with a wild beard- was pulling an
M240 off of Charlie; who was also somewhat hulking,
before he became dead. The men had gotten most of
the grenades, and Paul couldn't take the suspense any
longer.

"Guys! We got to fallback. Now! Let's go.
Upstairs!"

As they ran upstairs, Jerome called up to him,
"Hey! Paul! Why we going up all these flights! Why
didn't we go into the basement?"

"We cleared these floors! I have no idea what's
in the basement! There's something in this building!
Something other than that last neep! Whatever killed
Yoshic and Darby! I don't know what did that! It wasn't
no slave neep, though!"

Richard Rose 180

BLACK CAT SUNRISE

But that was a lie. Because in the back of his mind, he did know, but he didn't believe it. He didn't want to believe it. The others had to be thinking the same thing. It was a frightening prospect in a warzone full of frightening prospects. Jacob chimed in, "The heartbeat monitor! I was looking right at it! That neep didn't register!"

"Was he too far?" asked Habib; a slender man of Indian descent with a thick mustache, a prominent cheek mole and a strange body odor that was different from most guys' body odors. Habib's primary weapon was an M110 with a tactical scope.

"I don't think so!" Jacob answered.

They passed the Xed out door on the 63rd floor and soon they were back up on the 79th. Panting and gasping to catch their breath. Paul could feel his exhaustion pushing against him. If he was tired then the others were tired, too. There was an open area in the center of the building. An office space that had nothing in it except for an old vacuum cleaner and some trash bins. And there weren't any windows. Four doors in and out. Paul led them in there, took a look around, and then told them, "Alright. We need one man on each exit; the rest of us in the middle. We sit back-to-back, we stare at whatever door we're facing toward. Keep your weapons ready, but not too ready or you'll fall asleep and shoot somebody. I'll take that door. Jacob, you take that door. Jerome, you take that door. Habib, you take that door. The rest of you; circle up in the middle. I'll see who I can get on the horn and find out when they're going to back us up in here."

Confederate headsets were programmed to select from different channels to reach different positions going up the chain of command. Right now,

BLACK CAT SUNRISE

Paul's was set for the other platoon's fireteams; but the other fireteams were nonexistent. So he pressed the up button four times to change the channel and then he was able to reach Delta company's radio dispatcher. "This is Paul with Second platoon. We've sustained heavy losses. We need reinforcement."

'You're at forward fighting position delta five, is that correct?'

"That's correct, we're on the 79th floor."

'Is the building clear?'

"We thought it was. Now we think there's ninja here."

'There may be. There've been reports of ninja activity in every sector in the warzone. How many of you are there up there?'

"There's ten of us."

'Damn it. Yeah; we're getting tore up out here. Alright. Hold on. I'll talk to the captain, see what he says. Over and out.'

Paul looked back to the guys- whose tired eyes only barely managed to meet his. They watched the doorways with their heads hung and their shoulders slumped. Then Paul realized he was standing for no reason. He needed a break and his body all but collapsed beneath him as he half fell over and half sat down; practically squashed beneath the weight of his gear; his pack, the grenade cartridge bandolier, five grenades, bullet magazines, more and heavier bullets in belts, a submachine gun, a machine gun, and a grenade launcher. The adrenaline had been gripping him so tight, he didn't even realize he was carrying all this stuff up all those stairs.

Clutching the MP5, he waited; for a call back or for death. He didn't know which. And then the ear

BLACK CAT SUNRISE

piece crackled to life, 'Second platoon, delta, come back.'

"We're here. What's going on?"

'I'm being told all those buildings are more or less connected. Sounds like the battalion engineers have been blowing out the doors and passageways in the basement floors. They're about to get to your building. Captain Matthews says that if you can get down to the basement, he'll have delta company rendezvous at your position. But, listen, Fourth platoon is across the street and cut off. Their numbers are better than yours, but there's no way for them to get over there.'

"They don't got mylar blankets? Send them out under the murder-hornets. That's what Darby did to my fireteam."

'Yeah. Maybe. It's up to the captain. I'm just letting you know, we got a platoon cut off. Besides yours.'

"Okay. We're moving to the basement, then. Thanks."

'Over and out.'

"Who wants to hump the pig?" Paul asked them.

A guy named Aaron stepped in to take over Elijah's M249 and its burden of bullet belts. Aaron had hazelnut colored skin, long eyelashes, dimples in his cheeks, shaggy brown hair- under his helmet- and he was a strange individual because he always wore a smile; even now. And it seemed like he was dumb but actually he just liked being here. Some guys were like that. This was what they'd been looking forward to since they were children, and now they were here. Aaron was already encumbered by an M16 and Pistol,

Richard Rose 183

BLACK CAT SUNRISE

but Paul had to operate the grenade launcher; so the M249 had to be handed off. The M16 was discarded.

"Alright! We're going down to the basement!" Paul said.

"I fucking told you!" Jerome said.

"Yeah, well, I don't want to hear any shit about it. I did what I thought was right."

And Jerome said, "Nah, you're alright, man. Fuck it. Who gives a shit? Really...."

Paul kept going, "We're going down to the basement because the engineers are blasting out the walls and the doors and connecting all these buildings at the subterranean level. Or, I guess they already were connected? I don't know. But come on. Let's get the fuck out of here."

They pulled themselves together and hurried down the stairs but they were collectively overwhelmed with exhaustion and it was more of a slog than a jog. The stairs twisted and turned around and around and it was dizzying and it seemed as if the world was spinning and spinning and they were falling and falling. Their headlamp beams swung about wildly and blended together. Darkness and light swirled and swirled together and apart and together and apart again. Always, a sense of impending doom was draped heavily over their shoulders; a dismal and demoralizing weight. Habib called out, "Hey! Wait! Stop! Wait! We lost Toad!" Toad wasn't Toad's real name. It was a nickname, because Toad was short and squishy and ugly; with acne-scarred skin and mushy features. Paul held up his fist to call a halt and they stopped and looked back at Habib; who had turned back up the stairs and was searching with his high-powered rifle at the ready.

Richard Rose 184

BLACK CAT SUNRISE

Some guys followed Habib. Some guys looked to Paul for instructions and he signaled them to follow Habib. Just loud enough to be heard, Jacob said, "We got to stick together!" They'd gone up three flights of stairs when Habib announced, "I found him! He's gone!" Toad had been dragged just a little ways away from the stairs and left just out of sight. Habib had almost missed him entirely, and then they may not have found him at all. Now, they all stood over Habib's shoulder and saw what had become of Toad. A small trickle of blood was running out of his ear and his eyes were white because they'd rolled up into his head. Terry stepped aside and laid into the vicinity with the chugging M240, raging, "Japs! Japs! I fucking hate Japs! Die! Die! Fucking Japs! Die!" But he stopped himself before he wasted too many bullets. Then he began to sob uncontrollably. Toad had been Terry's best friend. They could feel his pain. They'd all lost good friends by now.

Paul noted what floor they were on- 52- and then he said, "We don't have time for this; we have to move. Come on!" And so they went, and, as they ran, Jerome called out, "We got to stay close! Watch your back! Watch out for the guys around you!"

The building had become a frightening menace and each floor they traversed was a welcome subtraction to the distance they were trying to go. And then, at about the 24th floor, the building quaked beneath their feet and shook so violently that those of them who couldn't grasp a railing were sent tumbling down the stairs and onto the next landing. Landing in a pigpile.

"I hope your weapons are safetied," Aaron said; from amongst the heep with the others.

Richard Rose 185

Jacob- also in the heap and wrapped around his rifle to protect the scope with his body- asked, "What the fuck was that?" The shock continued to tremble the floors and the walls and it was immediately evident that something was seriously wrong, because the icy night wind was now howling through what had previously been a stagnant stairwell. It was possible to look up through the center of the stairs' cases- which rotated 180 degrees back and forth. The soldiers peered up through the opening and saw that something- everything- was burning up there; and indeed, molten materials were beginning to drip down through the same hole they were looking up through.

Paul had picked himself up, was helping Terry to stand, and he told the others, "Keep moving! We have to keep moving!" And Aaron said, "They shelled the fucking building! They hit it with a plasmoid!" And Jerome said, "We can't be here! We have to get out of here!" And in a senseless terror they took off running downward as the building vibrated and trembled beneath their feet. And they were lost in their own private abysses. And so nobody noticed when Luis was wrenched off of his feet and dragged into the interior of the 14th floor. Luis was of Mexican descent; a muscular man of stout build with a black beard, a deep scar from where shrapnel had torn through his chubby cheeks, and a generally cheerful demeanor. Kind of like Aaron; but more willful and defiant. He had a kind face. Some guys never noticed how miserable their lives were. Because every day among the living was a good day; from their perspective. They were grateful for the breath in their lungs and the rhythm of their heartbeats. Luis was that way.

BLACK CAT SUNRISE

The platoon didn't stop running until they were down where the staircase ended. In the basement. And of course, the door was locked. A freezing whirlwind whipped around them; sometimes burning hot air became intermingled with the cold. Paul was hammering on the door with his fist and Jacob was checking the heartbeat detector and the others were just catching their breath. And Aaron said, "Luis! We fucking lost Luis!"

And Paul asked, "Where? When? How?"

"Do we go look for him?" Habib asked.

"You can. If you want. Look... He's probably dead," Paul said.

And Jerome added, "He's not probably dead. He's definitely dead. And if you go after him, you're going to be definitely dead, too."

"What the fuck is out there?" asked Marcus; a gaunt charcoal skinned soldier who was taller than everybody else, with sunken eyes, a wide smile, and two Uzis 9mms he carried with one in either hand.

Jacob answered, "It's ninja. It's got to be. There's nothing else it could be. They don't show up on the heartbeat monitor. I've been watching it the entire time. I haven't seen anything. But it's going off the charts now. Our people are here."

Paul kept banging and sure enough, the door opened. They were greeted by engineers who carried things like plastic-explosives and drills and crowbars and fire-axes. Their helmets had face-shields. The door opened up into what had been designed as a parking garage but which was never used as such because cars were never allowed on these streets. Paul warned them; "They hit the building with a plasmoid. We have to get out of here."

Richard Rose 187

BLACK CAT SUNRISE

The engineer he spoke with told him, "Only if it burns. It doesn't always burn. Sometimes it does. Sometimes it doesn't. We have eyes on it. Try not to think about it."

"What if it collapses?" Jacob asked him.

"They don't collapse. They burn. There's no way to collapse one of these buildings. Not unless you lace the columns with thermite; cut the beams on a diagonal. They can blast it with plasmoids all they want. They'll shoot it all to shit, but it won't collapse."

"But it will burn?" Habib asked.

"Oh, yeah. You haven't seen outside? They're burning to high hell all over the city. This one might burn, too. Or, it might not. I don't know, I can't say," said the engineer.

Chapter 11
Combat

Luis

First and Third platoon emerged on the other side of the parking garage; from a section they couldn't see into. Paul led the others over to them and he tried to guess at their numbers. Maybe about 30 or 35. Those were comparable losses to their own. And so it stood to reason the other men of Delta company were equally as shell-shocked as Second platoon was.

Even Captain Matthews looked like he was about to crack. Captain Matthews was over the age of thirty. Field officers were often over the age of thirty. He'd spent a few years in Valhalla and now his children and woman would be compensated for his commitment to redeploy and further rewarded if he never returned. Matthews was pasty and doughy and

BLACK CAT SUNRISE

bald under his helmet, and he wore standard-issue black-rimmed eyeglasses. As he walked over to greet Paul, Paul saw that his eyes were spinning, and he seemed to be limping. And he was walking slowly; almost in slow-motion. And then Paul realized he himself was walking in slow-motion, also.

"Come on, boys," Matthew called to them, adding, "We're going to rendezvous with Fourth and then shut down operations for the night. Time to get some sleep. We done enough dying for one day. I'd say."

"Music to my ears, captain," said Jerome.

Paul asked, "What's your plan to meet up with Fourth, sir?"

Matthews said, "That's up to the engineers. Last I heard there's a subway tunnel between us and them. They're going to try to blast their way through it. For now, we're falling back to FFP delta four, letting the engineers do their thing, and then hopefully we'll be on our way. Easy." With that, Captain Matthew called back to the other platoons, "We got 'em! Now fall back! Give the demolition team some room to work!"

They plodded away and traveled through a short tunnel into another underground parking garage which was smaller but just as empty. There they took a break. They drank water. Some men who couldn't keep their eyes open dozed off on their packs. Others ate and stared vacantly at nothing. Antonio had taken the cigars off of Darby when nobody was looking; he gave one to Paul and lit one for himself. And they shared these with whoever was nearby. Antonio was of Italian-American descent. He had a handsome face with smooth tan skin, but his nose had been broken and it never healed correctly. Antonio was a grenadier, like

BLACK CAT SUNRISE

Paul. And so he also wore a bandolier of grenade cartridges. But he didn't have a six shooter. He used a pump action launcher that could hold four rounds. His sidearm was a full auto Glock 18 with an extended 33 round magazine.

"Man, that four shot looks a lot easier to carry around than my six shot. This thing is cumbersome as shit."

"Yeah, but there might come a time when those two shots make all the difference. If I ended up in that situation. I wouldn't make it out."

"Doesn't seem likely. I used to carry an M-79. Never even used it. But that was before the shields went down."

"Yeah. Whole new world. Now. Our world," said Antonio.

"Man, I hope so," said Paul.

Shortly thereafter, Paul saw something that made him jump to his feet. Jerome and Habib and Jacob also noticed. Everybody else was too out of it to realize what was happening. It was Luis. He wasn't dead after all. Jerome hurried over to him and wrapped his arms around him. Luis said, "What the fuck, you guys just left me up there?"

Paul said, "Holy hell... No! I mean, yeah. We thought you were dead. We'd been getting picked off, we lost so many guys. We thought they got you. What the fuck happened? Where were you?"

"I don't know. I been looking all over for the platoon. I don't know what happened. We were running down the stairs. And they caught me. They put something over my mouth. Gas. Or something. I don't know what. I passed out. I woke up. I didn't know where I was. I started looking for you guys. The

BLACK CAT SUNRISE

building was on fire. I was freaked out. I didn't know where you were. Eventually, I got down here. The engineers told me you're all over here. I came over here. Now I'm here. Can I smoke some of that? I feel sick."

"Yeah. Here. Go tell Captain Matthews what you just told me. He's over there," Paul said, handing him the cigarette and pointing.

Luis took the cigarette and walked off. By this point, the entirety of Second platoon was on their feet and watching Luis. "I'm a fucking asshole," Jerome said, "Habib wanted to go look for him and I talked him out of it." And Jacob told him, "It wasn't just you. It was all of us. We were all too chicken shit." And Terry said, "I'm still too chicken shit. There's ninja up there. I don't want to die."

They stood there, watching Luis, and then an instant later there was a sharp and sudden explosion and they were all blown over onto the cement. Soldiers were screaming in agony. And others were crying in anguish. Paul had been struck hard by- something, an airborne rifle, maybe- and his body was throbbing so bad he could hardly force himself to move. But he knew he had to, so he clutched his MP5 and got up to his feet. Through the smoke, he saw bodies scattered; body parts and gear and weapons. And blood splashed like paint across the floor. There was nothing where the bomb had detonated. Where Luis had been standing and talking to the captain. It was just burned and black and the carnage radiated outward from there.

Paul wondered, 'Who triggered it?' And with all his equipment disheveled and hanging off of him, he started wandering around and peeking around corners

BLACK CAT SUNRISE

and looking out for who might be watching them. Then he noticed a camera. Small and hidden within an inconspicuous fixture. Jacob had gone off with Paul to cover his back. And Paul pointed out the camera to him. "Spray paint it," Jacob said. "I got to stand on your back." Jacob got down on his hands and knees and Paul stood on him to get the paint can close enough to black out the lens.

"They've been watching us the whole time," Paul told Jacob.

"Not surprising. The cameras must have a direct current. Or something. Come on. These guys are bleeding out."

"Oh. Right," said Paul. His head was ringing from the blow he took. He couldn't think straight. He was punch-drunk.

Back with the others; some of the men had bandaged and tourniqueted some of the other men. Several of them were in serious condition and probably wouldn't survive. Others were in bad condition but could probably tough it out long enough to get treatment. It was mostly guys from First platoon; the captain's platoon. Paul felt guilty on two counts. For leaving Luis behind, and for sending him over to the captain. But First platoon was too bereaved to point fingers at Paul. Paul realized their captain was gone, and so he sat down. Some of the others were arranging to evacuate a few wounded men; one missing an arm, one missing a hand, one with his face cut to shreds and burnt to hell, and another with a sucking chest wound. Third platoon still had a lieutenant- Lieutenant Jameson, and Jameson authorized them- and the other severely wounded- to go and try and get back to the medics.

Richard Rose 192

Hinata

The bushi had their own way of fighting the fight. Their primary responsibility was to position the heishi dorei and then ensure that the heishi dorei were- in fact- being effective. Beyond that; their generally agreed upon strategy was to hang around out of sight until all the dorei were dead, all the drones were destroyed, and all the ninja had gone home, or died. If they were mortal. Hinata didn't know. Nobody really knew anything about the ninja. They came and they went. They killed. They didn't seem to die, but probably they might. The bushi weren't so fortunate. The bushi's time would come. And so Hinata found himself wishing he were a ninja. Because he was expected to fight, and he didn't expect to survive it.

None of the bushi were especially hopeful about their prospects. Not with the enemy hordes descending upon them. Ever since they were children, the bushi were instructed in bushido. Loyalty to the bakufu was their highest priority. Endlessly, they were reminded of honor and of sacrifice. Of the banzai charge, and of the kamikaze. These were outdated modes of fighting, but the spirit of sacrificing one's life for the greater good was very much relevant. Like bees, who die when they sting. There weren't enough bushi- there were few, actually- for suicide attacks to make any tactical sense. But, nonetheless, each bushi loved the bakufu dearly and whole-heartedly. They'd grown up in a world in which the bakufu was ascending to ever greater heights. But, like Icarus- not that they knew who or what Icarus was- the bakufu had flown too close to the sun, and now their wax wings were melting.

BLACK CAT SUNRISE

The bushi were operating out of bunkers, barracks, pill-boxes, and safehouses. These were strategically placed across the city. These refuges were connected by a maze of subway tunnels and assorted passages. From inside their hideouts, they utilized tablets to control their assigned cadre of dorei heishi; transmitting messages and discipline from a distance. The dorei had collars and the collars performed a myriad of functions, including video recording. So, bushi could see what dorei were seeing. So, infuriatingly, bushi could see dorei hiding instead of fighting and dying. The bushi also had access to most of the cameras in the city; a supplemental means of monitoring their charges.

The plan was that when Moto- or one of the 5th dan- gave the order; they'd initiate a tactical withdrawal; essentially, fighting their way out of the city. Some would live. Most would die. Hinata was stationed in a bunker under Foley Square; specifically, under the fountain with the abstract statue in the center of it. Through steel eye slits he could see a squat building with Greek looking pillars and carved into it was a clever statement about how justice is the... pillar... of good government. There was a park situated beside the fountain. And a variety of 20, 30, 40, 50, and 60 story buildings were towering all around; with his dorei cowering within the structures.

The fighting had begun and he'd been listening and he'd been watching his tablet as his dorei heishi- who were scattered about somewhat at random- were giving a lackluster, at best, performance. It wasn't surprising that a slave would lack courage in the face of destruction. They'd been conditioned to be sniveling and pathetic. Some of the dorei, however, were

Richard Rose 194

BLACK CAT SUNRISE

behaving surprisingly admirably; but those never survived very long. Still, at least they inflicted losses. The meek were just wasting good weapons, not to mention their own lives.

And then. Something bad was happening. Something worse than the skirmishes raging outside. It began as a sound. Imperceptible at first, and then louder. Coming from his escape route; his only way in or out. A tunnel that crossed through a subway and made its way to a bunker that had another tunnel that connected to the bushi base in this sector. Hinata was the only person in his pillbox and the rapidly escalating commotion made his blood run cold. He knew what it was, but he didn't want to believe it. It was an unlikely and disturbing turn of events.

The air was cold, but, all the same, sweat began to drip down his face. Hinata was slant eyed, but pale. He looked western, but was handsome in an eastern way. Half nihonjin, and half amerikajin. Most bakufu were hafu. The pure nihonjin had always been few and far between, and now they were getting old, as well. His name- Hinata- meant, 'toward the sun.' But there wasn't much sun in his bunker. He had water, food, a bucket, his rifle, his grenades, his wakizashi, his tablet, his pack, and a sleeping bag. And an abundance of dank shadow. He wore all white; jacket and boots included. Stupid clothes for a man hidden in darkness, but it was a matter of pride, and, also, they didn't have any clothes that weren't white. They all dressed exactly the same. This was what they wore. His winter hat had the red hinomaru over his third eye. He assumed the teki would see it as a target; and he wasn't wrong.

Apparently, he was about to find out. This wasn't what he wanted. This wasn't the way it was

BLACK CAT SUNRISE

supposed to be. But, this was war. And he was samurai. If he must die for the bakufu, then he would do so graciously. As it was, there were teki heishi running desperately through the streets; evading the murder-hornets as best as they were able to. Glancing out at the street one last time, he noticed there were more strewn about corpses than the last time he had checked. That was good. But his life was over now. It was his time to die. But he'd had a good life. He'd made three beautiful children with a lovely woman. It didn't get any better than that. He was ready to go. In death, he could be reborn. Living again. Dying again. Living again. The great cycle. Samsara.

The XT-19 rifle was an icon of Nippon innovation. And the VZ-12 grenade struck fear in the hearts of all who knew about it. Hinata couldn't guess what was coming, but he knew he didn't want to face it. The rifle had hinges in the middle and it had sensors that- if in a certain mode- would automatically bend the business half of the weapon around curvature and angles. So, he didn't have to face his foes head on and could instead let the curvature of the tunnel shield him as he made his stand.

Hinata sent an SOS signal to the other bushi, who he knew wouldn't- and probably couldn't- do anything to help him. What he heard coming was non-human. And he knew from the reports of others; it was some sort of robot. And maybe the dorei couldn't fight these robots, but he was not dorei. He was bushi. He could fight a robot. The XT-19 could, more specifically. The teki's radio-controlled vanguard drone made inhuman sounds that echoed down his tunnel; its tracks' motor whirring electronically.

Richard Rose 196

BLACK CAT SUNRISE

The tunnel was dark, and he didn't dare to light a light, and so he approached it, not knowing exactly where it was, because the viewing screen on the rifle butt was set to thermal. So he set it to night vision. But it didn't matter because the rifle targeted the robot before he ever noticed it on-screen; discharging several laser bolts and destroying the teki contrivance without any difficulty. This elicited a certain hushed and muffled commotion from the enemy in the distance.

Now Hinata knew that they knew that he was there. And he realized they'd have to grenade him before he grenaded them. So, he resolved to grenade them before they grenaded him. And the VZ-12 grenade was nothing like the teki fragmentation grenade. The teki fragmentation grenade was ferocious, but the VZ-12 was catastrophic. Hinata kept the rifle trained around the bend with one hand and with his other hand he pressed his thumb to the fingerprint reader on the VZ-12; holding it there in order to keep the device primed until he was ready to throw it.

Hinata could sense them before the screen on his rifle displayed their position. He didn't wait. He released his finger, lobbed the grenade toward where their tunnel opened up at, and then he ran as fast as he could, back toward the little bit of light that was trickling in through the distant eye-slits. The shockwave hit him and instantly knocked him unconscious and lifted him off of his feet and threw him forward; his body hurtling violently through the air and back into his bunker beneath the fountain; which was filling with dust that was wafting out into the streets. Although, the dust didn't draw any

BLACK CAT SUNRISE

attention because the only people out there were trying not to get murdered by the AD-14s.

The VZ-12 concussion grenade had succeeded in collapsing the enemy tunnel; crushing dozens of men who had just had the life jolted out of them. The collapsing teki tunnel also destroyed the micro-TBM which had dug it out. Unfortunately, if and when Hinata awakened, he would find that his escape tunnel, too, had collapsed. There'd be no way out except for to be rescued, and that was an unlikely scenario for several reasons. Maybe he could contrive an escape through the steel slats. But- for now- Hinata had stopped the emergence of a teki battalion, killed dozens of teki heishi, and even survived the encounter. Albeit, barely.

Deitrick

Deep in the shallow woods, with trees all around, Dietrick cowered in a cylindrical hole big enough for one man. The bakufu had been nice enough to give him a blanket, but still, it was freezing outside. Looking out from over the trench's rim; he was eye level with the snowy ground. The chill had penetrated him to the core and he tried to do like the bushi and be zen and not feel it, but his entire body was rattling and his teeth were chattering and the misery was unending. But, once in a while, the wind would shift and bring a current of hot air and smoke. And it was hard to breathe- choking, even, at times- but the warmth felt heavenly. The collar around his throat was actually hot in one spot, but the rest of it was icy against his flesh. The trees were devoid of leaves and their branches clacked together in the breeze as well as in the wind of the shockwaves. And

BLACK CAT SUNRISE

he didn't know which was which except for by the heat
that accompanied the latter. One time, a thick hot
wave of ash came blowing through and he worried he
would suffocate and die, but he was able to breathe
using his shirt as a filter and eventually the ash
dispersed and settled.

Deitrick didn't have any fat to keep him warm.
He felt weak and tired, but he couldn't sleep, standing
up on his feet, like he was. Last night, before he
crawled into this torturous vertical trench, they had
given him a few rice balls and some water, but he'd
eaten it all and drank it all basically immediately.
Thankfully, he could eat snow to hydrate, but his
stomach turned for want of nourishment. The trench
was cylindrical because his unit had used a sort of
auger to bore it out. There were other men in other
holes- other slaves- in the forest with him. Positioned
at points a hundred feet apart. In a hexagonal pattern.

Through the bases of the trees and saplings, he
could see a pond off in the distance. There was only
one other slave who he could see through the trees,
but when their eyes met, it was like two dying animals
watching each other. Deitrick wondered if the other
could see others, but dared not ask. Out beyond the
trees, machine guns rang unending and bombs went
off and lasers tweeted their rage and the buildings he'd
known so well were now being destroyed by weapons
he couldn't imagine. In his memories, he remembered
washing their windows. That was his job. He had been
a window washer. All he ever knew was washing
windows for the bakufu. It had been a pitiful life, but it
wasn't all bad. Because he spent his days hanging high
in the sky. Looking out over the city, out over the
water, and out over the whole world. And he knew that

BLACK CAT SUNRISE

if a rope snapped, and he fell; it wouldn't be that bad. Because it wasn't a life worth living. No hope for a woman. No hope for a family. At best, they might allow him to breed. But that was as much a matter of luck as it was a matter of being selected.

Deitrick thought highly of himself. They didn't feed him enough to give him strength, but he was agile and sinewy. And his cheeks were sunken, but if they would have just fed him more, then he would have been handsome, because his head was perfectly spherical and his teeth were naturally straight. He had thick and silken black hair. And vibrant green eyes. Nobody else he knew had green eyes. That should have qualified him for breeding. And he was tall, but not overly tall. This was his only wish. All he wanted was a chance to breed. All they gave him was washing windows. And now they gave him this hole to die in. It didn't make sense. They wanted him to kill the confederates, but there weren't any and he might freeze to death before there were.

There were other memories that came to mind. The bakufu had sought to deprive him of his humanity. They wanted to make a machine out of him. And in some ways they had. But they couldn't deprive him of friendship. He'd had good friends. Other damned souls. Those whose work was equally basic. Like, street sweepers. Or, rat harvesters. The slave masters had sought to stifle their natural sexual urges. Feeding them food cured with saltpeter. But they kept him and the other men like him all rounded up in dormitories. And so inevitably they turned to homosexuality as a way to expel their yearnings. And so, in this manner, Deitrick had known love. Forbidden love. Not

BLACK CAT SUNRISE

forbidden because it was gay, but forbidden because it was illicit behavior.

Gay sex was the best thing that had ever happened to him. And a lot of the other slaves would have shared that sentiment. But all they ever really wanted was to know the touch of a woman. Because they'd all seen women. From afar, usually. But, what's more, some of them seemed to know a thing or two about women; so they had a mythology built up around what it was like to be with a woman; wild notions about pleasures and sensations. They would pontificate for hours about what breasts must feel like. And if women peed out of their vaginas or not. How long were women pregnant before the baby was born. These were not intelligent people, obviously. Most never learned reading or writing or arithmetic. This was a male bakufu slave. He didn't know much about the lives of the females, but he knew it must be better to be them. These men started adult life at the age of 3, when they were torn from the arms of their mothers. Gardening and tending animals, at first. Working in kitchens after that. There was an assortment of menial labor to be done. Perhaps some time mending clothes, or cleaning bathrooms. And then they went into whatever duty had been pressed upon them. The more training their position required was the more highly skilled they were thereafter; and thus the more valuable they were to the bakufu, and so the better of a chance they'd be selected for breeding. Deitrick's job didn't require much training. Some, but not much.

So; he dreamt about being up on a bosun's chair, cleaning the windows in the sky, looking out over the great ghost of a city and daydreaming about getting split in half by the love of his life; Leroy. No last

BLACK CAT SUNRISE

name. None of them had last names. It was these visions- this imagery- that clouded his mind as he faded in and out of consciousness. They were allowed to get out of their hole and stretch, and so he had been doing so; to keep his numb and sleeping legs from atrophying. But even this became too much, because he was too weak; the pain and the cold- it was shutting down his faculties; making him witless and delirious. "Leroy? Is that you?" he was saying, with his head against the hole and his body slumped and lifeless.

He'd heard footsteps. He didn't even know he was hearing them. He was half dreaming. And then he heard the thump of a man falling to the ground. The other slaves in the other holes; they were in a similar condition. So they weren't poking their heads up and betraying their positions. Also audible was the sharp and piercing electric jolt of laser bolts discharging in rapid succession. Men shouting. Men shrieking. Men screaming. Men wailing. Near and far.

Deitrick realized; Leroy wasn't there. But he didn't know where there was. There was here. In a dirty hole in the freezing ground. But he couldn't figure out why he was in a dirty hole in the freezing ground. The bakufu. They'd made him a soldier. They said that if he survived, he could breed. He could be a bushi, if he survived the battle. To become a bushi was a wish that a slave wouldn't ever have thought to wish. The enemy was here. They were out there. He couldn't lift his head up. His eyes, looking down, saw the CD-7 in his hand. CD; cardiac disruptor. But there wasn't any way to lift it. He hadn't control of his extremities.

The enemy was screaming unintelligibly and had most assuredly fled into his woods in a blind panic; hoping to find shelter from the lasers of the

BLACK CAT SUNRISE

drones. Still, Deitrick couldn't lift his head. His entire body was fused into a crumpled-up posture; it felt like. If he could've picked up his head, he would have seen that the enemy soldiers had stumbled into the trap. The late model dorei heishi collars were working passably and inflicting some enemy losses. And the soldiers were so panicked by the lasers- which they were failing to hide from- that they weren't capable of counteracting the effect of the trap. Deitrick began to wiggle his fingers and toes and the pins and needles in his extremities were excruciating. But this was the only way to circulate his blood enough to allow him to move. Soon, he could move his wrists and ankles and elbows and knees and hips and shoulders and then he raised his CD-7 up over the hole. By this time- he hadn't even realized- the imperiled enemy soldiers had gone silent. But he suspected they were still out there. So for many long minutes Deitrick continued to hold the heart stopping device up where it might find a target to dispatch. Nothing was happening. So he put his hand back down and for the next hour he tried to find the courage to lift himself up out of the hole. Eventually, his body was falling back asleep and he felt like if he couldn't move then he would rather die anyways. So- with sickening trepidation- he lifted his head and looked around. There weren't just a few bodies. There were dozens in his vicinity alone. Some had laser wounds, he saw. And others did not. The other slave soldier he could see nearby- he saw- was watching him. Their eyes met and they stared at each other for a little while. They wouldn't have known what to say even if there was anything to be said. They were alive. These enemies were dead. So many; dead. And what was better; there didn't seem to be any

BLACK CAT SUNRISE

enemy soldiers left alive in the vicinity. This was a good day.

Kuro

Kuro jettisoned from the transport saucer sometime around midday; falling through the clear blue sky toward the snow-covered city below. Manhattan smoked like it was infested with volcanoes; burning buildings and smoldering craters. The ninja wore aerodynamic photochromic goggles to protect his oriental eyes and to allow him to see through the wind. The yellow-brown skin around his eyes was the only area of his body that was exposed to the light. Looking around the sky, he saw the other ninja falling in a dramatic profusion. They were just specks, but there were several thousand of them. The ninja uniform was a black jumpsuit; form-fitting but stretchy, warm but breathable, especially suited for their style of combat, and equipped with a myriad of miniscule and deadly devices to complement their martial skill set.

On either wrist Kuro wore a six-inch-long bracelet like strap and on either ankle, he wore a similar anklet. Each strap contained a lightweight low-profile anti-gravity propulsion device that angled outward from the body. These effectively enabled him to fly, but flying could be dangerous if done in excess; so, the system was primarily utilized for landing in drop zones and attaining the escape saucers; secondarily, for emergencies and necessary adjustments of position. Certain ninja used the propulsion system more than others and got exceedingly excellent with it, while certain others succeeded in injuring or killing themselves. Kuro was a flier of average ability. There was no shame worse than

BLACK CAT SUNRISE

to die outside of battle. And the shame was what a ninja feared; more so than the injury or death which a crash would inflict.

By tapping a code into a code-reader, and by holding his arms and legs in a certain outstretched fashion, and by tensing his little fingers and middle toes just so; he was able to control and slow his speed of descent to such a degree that he gently lofted down onto the rooftop of the building which had been assigned to him by bakufu intelligence. Kuro's objective was similar to the teki heishi's objective. Seek and destroy. But, he wasn't hunting frightened slaves. He was hunting trained killers. But, he too was a trained killer, and his training surpassed that of all known human combatants. By far. His greatest strength was genetic; purebred nihonjin- his bloodline reaching far back into the Nippon annals. These were men who could be stabbed or shot or broken or maimed and betray no outward expression of anguish whatsoever. Men who could stand atop a wooden beam on one foot from sun-down to sun-up. Men who could run to the summit of Mount Fuji without stopping or even slowing. Men who could drop ten meters and land on their feet uninjured. Men who could scale shear walls and hang from ceilings. Men who could tip-toe across creaky floorboards without making a sound. Men who killed with unmatched speed and precision. Their eyes; trained to see in the dark. Their ears; trained to hear what their eyes could not see. They were hunters, more than fighters. Fighters were fools. Hunters were wise. Fighters rushed in and died. Hunters waited- hidden and patient- and vanquished with calm and calculated assurance.

BLACK CAT SUNRISE

Stealth was their shield. The element of surprise was their weapon.

After placing his goggles into a pocket on his thigh; Koru surveyed the skies. Something of a no man's land. The bakufu had no forcefields. The confederate wasn't sacrificing the limited supply of aircraft they were in possession of. He peered over the edge of the building- a 65 story high rise- and observed the BD-14s shooting down the teki as they crawled up out of hell or scurried about like rodents. Occasionally, a roof-top turret fired a laser bolt off into the sky and hit an indistinct object at an indeterminate point. Teki surveillance. The turrets were shooting down teki drones. So the teki had eyes in the sky... So Kuro could assume they knew he was there... The rooftop entrance to Kuro's engagement was locked. It wasn't supposed to be, but it was. His right bracelet had a tubular void generator built into it; he tapped a three-beat code and then braced his right wrist with his left hand and tapped again to fire a singularity at the door jam where the bolt held it. A void appeared and the door's locking mechanism disappeared. Kuro went inside. The void generator wasn't much bigger than a pencil, but it was capable of rapid firing and could inflict extreme losses on enemy forces.

Be that as it may, it wasn't in accordance with ninjutsu. Not only was it a good way to invite an early death, but such an ignoble attack would gain little prestige, and so too; little honor. The ninja believed a man should be killed by as direct a means as possible. This meant that hands were better than steel and steel was better than projectile. The exception to this rule was when attempting to eliminate multiple combatants at the same time. In which case, there

BLACK CAT SUNRISE

were no rules. It was shameful to shoot one man with a void, but there was no shame in shooting two men with two voids. It just wasn't ideal. Kills were currency in their world; but to have a high value, each kill required a certain high quality. Being nihonjin; they had an elaborate system for assigning said value. When the battle was over and he submitted his report, the high council would promote and reward him in accordance with the value of his deeds. And a ninja would never lie about what he had accomplished. To lie to gain glory would go against everything they believe in, against ninjutsu, and it would be a death sentence if caught, besides. To unjustly- or justly- accuse another of lying was a violation of code known to insight fratricide. Another crime, also punishable by death. To lie was unthinkable.

Kuro contacted his intelligence team to make an inquiry into how many dorei heishi were occupying this location. Just two. One on the fifteenth floor and one on the 35th. Trends indicated these two dorei would be dispatched without inflicting much- if any- loss on the teki. Kuro asked why they weren't motivating them, and intelligence said that that was up to Motosama and she hadn't given the order yet. Really, it didn't matter what the dorei did. The ninja expected them to do nothing. If they did anything, it'd be a bonus.

This building used to be a lavish apartment building. That was a long time ago. Now it was just a shell of its former self. Like the city itself. Kuro proceeded downward to where he found a favorable position by a floor to ceiling window and this offered him an informative view of the proceedings below. There he knelt and watched and cleared his mind.

BLACK CAT SUNRISE

Waiting for the sun to go down. It wasn't their way to kill men in the light of day; for tactical reasons as well as for traditional reasons. He would observe the scene and clear his mind of apprehension and doubt. Later, the premises would be breached by teki forces. This did not much concern him. Teki used heartbeat detectors to locate their pitiful quarries. Ninja used suppressors to mask their cardiac signatures. Kuro was informed that the teki had arrived on the scene. This aroused his killer instinct. He stood to his feet. The teki would locate and ultimately eliminate the dorei heishi. This was as it should be. They would then think themselves to be safe. They may or may not know of his presence, but they wouldn't search the building room to room; even though they should and would have to, eventually, if they chose to linger.

The walls shuddered somewhere far below as a spat of gunfire broke out. The fifteenth floor. It was very faint. If it were nearer, it'd be less faint. So, he waited for the second spat to break out. Which, in due course, it did. After that, Kuro continued to wait. Waiting was an important part of his methodology. For one thing, the men coming up those stairs were on guard and expecting an encounter. For another thing, it wasn't dark out yet. Kuro listened as the search party approached, disregarded, and passed by the floor that he was on. They continued upward and then, after some delay, they returned. This time, Kuro's interest had been piqued. So, he tip-toed over to the door of the apartment he was lingering in and listened to the pattern of their footsteps. Four men. A fireteam. Their smallest unit. He knew. They continued onward and he crept out into the hallway to listen to them go. They weren't talkative and he couldn't glean any other

Richard Rose 208

BLACK CAT SUNRISE

information about them. But he could guess. They'd have knives. They'd have guns. They'd have grenades. They be slow and dumb and make stupid mistakes. They'd wander about haphazardly and divide their strength absent-mindedly. They'd be oblivious, except for when they were spooked. They'd be hungry, and physically and mentally exhausted.

The problem was this was just a vanguard unit. There could be hundreds more coming. Or, no more coming. Those four could be leaving the highrise. It didn't matter. Whatever happened. It was all the same to him. All he had to do was survive; the rest was just details. It wasn't dark yet. There was nothing to do until then. So, Kuro went back to the window, knelt down, observed the chaos, and cleared his mind of disruptions. This was a west facing window. The city, by now, was shrouded in smoke and ash. One building in sight- across the street and down the way- was engulfed entirely in flame. Others were, too- elsewhere- he saw.

The sun sank behind the skyline and the glowing of the fires cast dancing orange light throughout the shadowy streets; which were littered with dead and dying. Tomorrow- he reasoned- this situation would escalate. Tomorrow- he reasoned- the teki would release its full strength. The bakufu would throw their full force against it. The teki majo would destroy the bakufu drones and perhaps destroy the bushi bakufu. The teki would overrun the city. And then the real mayhem would begin. He sensed these things because he could feel them coming. It was the inevitable course of events.

Darkness, eventually, fell upon the warzone. Kuro stood up and stretched his body like a cat. The bones in his shoulders, neck, and spine; popping like firecrackers. Orange firelight illuminated the otherwise darkened room. Stepping out into the black hallway; he stopped to listen. The first thing to do was to visit the corpse of the nearest dorei heishi. So, he descended to the 35th floor. The halls were pitch black, but there was a red flashlight sewn into his mask and he used it because he knew there was nobody up there. He would have heard them. At the dorei corpse, he picked up the cardiac disruptor. The collar; he wanted that, too. But it was locked around the man's body. Kuro carried a straight blade shirasaya tanto sewn into the calf of his legging. Withdrawing the blade, he grasped the man by the shirt and lifted him so his skull fell backward. Then- in a single stroke- he sliced the head off at the neck, cleaned the blade on the dead man's clothes, sheathed it, and picked up the bloody collar. Now he had two cardiac disruptors.

Creeping downstairs, he listened, and he heard... nothing... This building had been abandoned. The teki were gone. So he went back up to the roof and examined the three buildings closest in jumping distance. The night winds blew hot air and noxious smoke and the towering infernos lighted the cityscape orange. Extrapolating known teki emergence points; he clipped the cardiac weapons to his belt, jumped from that building and landed on the roof of another. One which he had figured would have a decent sized contingent sheltered within. From high up in the air- to his surprise- he had spotted two guards down below. These had not been visible previously; out of sight behind a massive HVAC system. The guards had not seen him; so, he positioned himself where he needed to be and then dropped down beside the rooftop

BLACK CAT SUNRISE

entryway which the guards were standing in front of. Thundering explosions emanating from near and far made his quiet motions inaudible. The cardiac disruptors had the men clutching their chests. They were already dying as Kuro killed them. He removed a steel hatpin from a pouch sewn into his shoulder. Sneakily, he drove the pin into the first man's ear. And the second; all he saw was a blur because in a single fluid motion Kuro had fingered out another hatpin, gripped the teki's throat, pulled him toward him, and driven the hatpin through the hearing protection and into the brain. Dropping him with a swishing thud.

Kuro felt no semblance of remorse about taking these men's lives. But he did feel pride to know these two kills would shine at the opening of his report. The door wasn't locked. He put his ear to it and listened; hearing nothing. Taking the CD-7 in his hand, he opened the door and looked in with the device held out before him. Just a dark and empty stairwell. He entered cautiously. Listening, he stepped down the steps. At the top floor, he heard nothing, and on the next floor he heard nothing, but on the floor after that; he heard them. Dozens, perhaps. Too many to confront. So he went back upstairs and wondered what to do. Then he remembered about the dead soldiers on the roof. They had grenades. He needed those grenades. So he went and got them, and that completed his plan.

Returning to the area where the teki were; he stood against the wall by the open doorway. An open door. So foolish. It should be closed and locked. He used a small mirror to quickly glimpse their physical arrangement. Most in the center with their gear. Some against the walls. Kuro had six grenades now, and this

BLACK CAT SUNRISE

presented a logistical problem because he only had two hands. So, he gently positioned them on the floor in a row. One after another, he hurriedly removed the pins, popped off the handles, and threw them in. The first was exploding as the last was leaving his hand, and as he stood up he reached for his tanto. The first man who came out did so with grenades exploding at his back; knocking him off balance. And this teki- as he was practically falling out of the door- couldn't possibly raise his firearm fast enough to prevent Kuro from driving the tanto upward through his throat and into his brainstem.

Kuro pulled the man from the doorway in order to not give any extra warning to the next heishi. He didn't know what was happening inside the killzone, but he could guess. Stepping back; another man came running out and Kuro gave him the tanto, too. Downward through the neck and into the chest. But this man's heart stopped before the grievous wound could end him. Dropping the second atop the first, he backed up again. Standing his ground, he awaited another assailant, but there wasn't one. There was a lot of commotion coming from within, however. And smoke was pouring out. 'Help!' men gurgled. 'He's bleeding out!' they pleaded with each other. 'Where's my arm?' one was desperately asking. Kuro walked in with his blade flipped up and hidden behind his wrist. It was difficult to see through the smoke and dust and nobody noticed him. The cardiac disruptors did the rest. One by one they were falling, and one heishi asked, "What the fuck is happening?" and he must have known because he tried to run; only to drop dead an instant later. Kuro watched as the teki heishi died so helplessly. And he even smirked, under his mask.

Richard Rose 212

BLACK CAT SUNRISE

When he was sure they were all finished he fled back up to the roof and jumped back over to the apartment complex because he knew that was a sort of safezone. Kuro watched and waited and when a detail of 4 teki heishi was dispatched to the killzone building's roof top- to secure the area- he fired the void generator across the sky and into the collective mass of them. Over and over he delivered voids unto them. Until they were just a bloody pile of gruesomely disfigured corpses.

Chapter 12

Bombardment

Xander had been monitoring enemy troops movements; with sunken eyes, pallid flesh, wrinkled clothing, and a foul smell about him- he reported to Maya, "They've breached their moleholes. They're moving their tanks in."

Kazuki and Moto were sleeping on the big futon in the master bedroom. Maya was awake; kneeling at the dinner table, pouring over the data, drinking matcha, and considering her options. Endlessly, she considered her options. Her limited options. And she asked him; "What are they going to do with tanks? All the dorei are hidden. All the bushi are hidden. All the ninja are hidden. What good is a tank going to do them?"

Xander knelt beside her and she poured him a cup of tea. He considered the question and said, "It will give them a false sense of security. Boost troop morale."

"They can't hurt us with morale."

"No. But they can hurt us with majo."

BLACK CAT SUNRISE

"Yes. It seems they're going to have to," said Maya.

Maya wore a fluffy pink bathrobe open at the throat and her cappuccino skin was moist and glistening in the dim lights. She had blow-dried her hair, but it was still a little wet and wispy. She seemed vulnerable. She'd been lucky enough to get some sleep. Having been so exhausted for so long that after she drank the sake, she just passed out. When she awoke, she checked the battle statistics and showered. Xander observed her. Admiring her timeless beauty. Forty-eight years old, but hardly aging at all. The angles of her face were sharp and distinctly oriental. Her mournful eyes expressed her supple femininity. He longed to feel her touch and know her affection, but she didn't think the same about him. Not whatsoever. There'd been a time when they were close, in a clinical way, but she got older and became disinterested and it'd been moot ever since. Xander wanted to hold her. To violate her. In a way, it was refreshing to see her stricken. Usually, she was so domineering; it was kind of off-putting. The teki had humbled her, it would seem.

"Maya?"

"Yes, Xander."

"We have to evacuate. When are we going to evacuate?"

"I'm not done fighting yet."

"What are you planning to do?"

"I promised the drone operators high value targets. Now we have high value targets. Activate the financial district taiyo kumo. Put a tsuki kuki on standby offshore."

BLACK CAT SUNRISE

An elongated spider drone crawled out of the parking garage where it had been stationed. Erecting itself, it stalked through the streets menacingly; quaking the earth with its weight. Teki heishi peered through windows to get a glimpse of it. Teki tanks were scattered about. The kumo blasted the seething prismatic beam of its radioactive heat ray at the first tank it encountered. Instantly incinerating much of it. What was left was aflame and red hot or molten. The crew were charred or gone. A second tank fired its cannon and hit the taiyo kumo forcefield. The blast produced the phantom majo, and she destroyed the kumo by slicing through its hull with her antimatter essences. Hovering above the wreckage; the scintillating nude figure of a voluptuous nordic vixen of ethereal orange energy surveyed the scene and found what she was looking for. The Freedom Tower. Her vexing target. Closer than ever. She charged through the maze of the streets, making her way toward the tower; taking a couple wrong turns, but gaining distance fast. What's more, the tsuki majo wasn't coming to stop her.

A camera on the tsuki kuki drone broadcast video to Maya; who watched with detached abhorrence as the phantom majo flew in and out of the base of the Freedom tower. The building did not fall. But Maya knew it would soon. The phantom witch again flew in and out of the base of the tower. Over and over, again and again, in and out and in and out; vaporizing all the iron columns and the steel girders and the cement; disappearing the very materials which were keeping the colossal structure upright. And then, with one final pass through- shooting in and out; the majo and Maya alike watched the tower pitch toward the interior of

BLACK CAT SUNRISE

the city and plummet downward and northward; sidelong across lower Manhattan.

This last part, Maya didn't so much mind. Lower Manhattan was teaming with teki. However many bakufu that majo had just annihilated; it wouldn't be close to the number of confederates she'd dispatched as well. It was a fitting consolation that the tower should kill so many with the wrath of its death throw. But it was a big city and so the giant skyscraper- in effect- only dented a single sector. Really, though... The tears were coming to her eyes. She would have cried if Xander wasn't there. That building had been her home since she was Kazuki's age. Furthermore, her beloved garden had sat atop it.

Suddenly, Maya had an idea and pressed the communication button to reach the tsuki kuki operator, saying, "Operator, take your drone to an altitude of 300 kilometers. Full throttle." The phantom majo had been stunned into stillness by a deeply gratifying sense of satisfaction. But she could sense the shield of the kuki and so gave pursuit when she realized it was pulling away. The drone broke through the sound barrier with a sonic boom that rattled every man in the warzone and all the slaves in White Plains and everybody else in this region of the planet.

The phantom majo was fast but the kuki was faster; attaining the desired position well before the majo could possibly catch up. 'It's done, daimyo sama,' said the operator. "Are your targeting systems functional from that distance?" she asked. 'Seems to be. We'll have to try.' "Good. Yes. Try. The tanks, please."

Then she turned to Xander and said, "We'll see how their morale feels about this." On the largest

Richard Rose 216

BLACK CAT SUNRISE

tablet- of the variety of tablets spread across the table- they switched over to an array of airborne surveillance drones on patrol. The city looked astonishingly different than it had the day before. Especially now, with the blazing wreckage of the freedom tower clouding the streets with choking ash and dust. It had even torn down much of several other buildings when it went over. And so many other buildings had been shelled and burned. It was almost unrecognizable from two days ago.

Maya could see some tanks, but not many. So she switched one screen to view the view through the kuki's targeting apparatus; just in time for the pixelated visage of a tank to disappear as the tsuki singularity struck it. Leaving behind nothing more than an eerily smooth crater of dirt in the asphalt where the tank had been.

"Excellent work, operator. Continue eliminating those tanks, please," she said into the microphone, before asking Xander, "Do we have eyes on the phantom majo?"

"I've been trying. If you look here, you can see her. But if I zoom in, I lose her. You think she'll make it up that far?"

"I hope not. I really hope not."

The phantom majo ascended higher and higher, but she didn't realize she was disappearing. The ionosphere was eating away at her. At the quantum level, it was dissipating her. Her target was growing closer, and she was reaching for it maniacally; as the substance of her being was fading into oblivion before her eyes. All she needed to do was to get to the kuki's forcefield. But the ionic interference was too powerful and the distance too great. With fifty kilometers to go,

Richard Rose 217

she found herself fading back into that other dimension- which only the physicists and the covens knew the name of; that incomprehensible realm that was the progenitor of her.

Maya was observing as a second and then a third tank was struck with singularities; vanishing into voids. And Xander said, "Maya. I think we did it. I think she's gone."

"No. I don't believe it."

"It's true. The kuki is still operational. And I don't see the phantom anywhere."

Maya pressed the button for the kuki operator, 'Operator, lower your altitude by 200 meters. We could be in violation. Bring it down, but don't let off on those tanks. Destroy them all, if you can."

The violation in question referred to the grey coven's code of conduct regarding terrestrial objects in space. This was why there were no satellites nor any of the technologies which satellites enabled. There were fleets of communication drones to relay signals, but they were somewhat ineffectual compared to what satellites were capable of.

Soon, the tsuki kuki was shooting incoming teki missiles out of the sky, but there wasn't any chance of penetrating the barrage of laser bolts it defended itself with. It was too high up. With too much line of sight. And after just three attempts the teki stopped wasting missiles on it. They did, however, begin moving their tanks into parking garages, placing them under the trees in the parks, or- just as often- simply driving them through the lobbies of skyscrapers. Anything to keep them out of sight of the kuki's targeting apparatus.

BLACK CAT SUNRISE

Maya was keen enough to know to follow up on her victory. However, her options seemed to be limited within the city because the teki had evidently slunk back out sight. Or, so she thought. The obvious solution was to search for targets outside the city. She transmitted to the operator, 'Operator, I am going to link you a new target. This is their supply line. The primary tunnel is marked by the red X. It is about time we closed that tunnel."

"Hai, daimyo sama!"

The teki supply chain was exposed to the open air at a certain section about ten miles to the west. This was the point where the teki were forced to march over land. From up in the stratosphere, the kuki only had to make a slight adjustment to target the target. There were troops moving into the tunnel alongside fighting vehicles and support vehicles. The kuki operator realized before Maya that a void could not destroy a void. A tunnel was a void. So, instead, the kuki fired the tsuki cannon at the earth at the base of the tunnel rather than at the earth above the tunnel. The soldiers were- naturally- aghast to see their peers and their body parts disappearing before their eyes. However, this bombardment became complicated as it required several discharges of the cannon to close the tunnel. The best the tsuki void generator could do was to fill the bottom of the tunnel with the dirt that had been above it; thus cutting the tunnel open at the top, at its entrance.

Meanwhile, the teki began to fire missiles at the kuki, but, again, the kuki's lasers easily defended it. Interestingly, however, and unbeknownst to the bakufu; the teki had anticipated something like this might occur and they had a special weapon in place for

BLACK CAT SUNRISE

the occasion; located at the mouth of the other tunnel, where the teki were surfacing at; a railgun on a turret on a power-plant on tracks. A high explosive incendiary tipped high velocity projectile was propelled forward by means of electromagnetism surging through a relay of copper-alloy rails. The projectile moved at 9,100 kilometers per hour guided by fins that kept it on course. Many orders of magnitude faster than a laser bolt- which, after all, was not an actual laser. The projectile struck the kuki's shield in a tremendous burst of blue flame and orange phantasm and with enough force to not only generate the phantom majo, but also to send the kuki hurling through the sky so as that the majo had to overtake the flailing saucer in order to destroy it. Which she did, and did.

Maya had watched this through the camera of a surveillance drone that was out that way. It bothered her, but what bothered her more was that now the phantom majo- the nubile feminine figure of orange liquid light- was careening toward Manhattan, and Maya said, exasperated, "This majo. I hate her. She is unrelenting." Xander said nothing. Maya pressed the button for the operator and said, "Send a raijin kuki out there and lure her up into the ionosphere again. 300 kilometers. Same as last time."

This was done, and the phantom majo was apparently not very smart, because it worked flawlessly. "They're like dogs," Xander said. And Maya said, "Like bitches. Witches. Bitches. I don't want to play this game anymore."

Moto seemed to sense her sister's frustration because she came to the table- also clad in a pink bathrobe- and poured herself a sake and lit a cigarette

Richard Rose 220

BLACK CAT SUNRISE

and said, "So. What did I miss?" And Maya filled her in on the details of what had transpired since she had been asleep. Moto said, "We have to take out that railgun."

Xander said, "They've pulled it back underground. And now they know we know about it, too."

Moto said, "We have to hit both tunnels with a dondon. Or a senso. A tsuki was the wrong weapon."

"It's what we had in the field at the time. We have two dondon kuki remaining. Three senso kuki. We'll send a senso. And we'll send the raijin kuki down into the city as a diversion. Hopefully we can blow out the tunnels before the phantom majo gets the senso. Xander; locate the greatest thermal concentration of heishi teki. Dispatch the raijin to that point."

This maneuver worked exceedingly well for the senso and less well for the raijin, which wasn't expected to escape anyways. The raijin was able to land among the enemy at midtown, and- because their profusion was such that they had difficulty remaining out of sight- to inflict losses in profuse quantities; with each weaponized bolt of lightning eliminating entire platoons or more, and the laser bolts even more still. But a tank hastily got into position and fired into the kuki's shield; thus attracting a dissipating phantom majo eager to re-energize, whom in turn eliminated the raijin kuki, before next shooting up into the sky to locate the senso kuki, finding it, and heading toward it.

By then the senso kuki had completed its objective and was retreating to the safety of the ionosphere. The senso cannon had been able to completely demolish both openings of the supply chain tunnels. Blasting massive craters into the earth,

BLACK CAT SUNRISE

making wastelands of the areas, succeeding in destroying a good measure of tunnel length, plugging up some, too, and killing thousands of men besides that. The phantom majo then chased the senso kuki up into the sky to where she dissipated and disappeared while the senso kuki remained unmolested; subsequently returning to a lower altitude of 100 kilometers.

This was a satisfying outcome, but it was followed up by an unfortunate turn of events. Kazuki came to the table as Xander was reading through bushi field reports and verifying the messages with surveillance footage. Kazuki wore a bathrobe identical to her mother's and aunt's. Fluffy and pink and soft and warm. With fuzzy pink slippers, too. But she was unshowered and her long curly brown hair was messy from her pillow. Her eyes were scrunched up and she was still half asleep. Kazuki never was a morning person. Not when she was four and not now, either. But Xander was happy to see her beautiful face; smiling through her foggy deportment. Always a smiley girl; she was. Except for when she was angry, that is. Xander stopped what he was doing to ask her if she slept well and she said that she had. Young people are good at sleeping. He wished he was, too.

"A lot has happened," Maya told her.

"And more is happening," said Xander. This turned their attention to him and he continued, saying, "Apparently, they have got nets now. They're hanging them from buildings and covering up the blocks where they're concentrating."

"Nets? Nets for what?" Kazuki asked.

"For the battle drones," Maya answered.

BLACK CAT SUNRISE

Moto said, "If they're hanging nets from buildings, then just destroy the buildings."

Maya thought for a second and said, "I agree. We won't have a choice. The BD-14s have been more effective than anything else in reducing their numbers as well as in keeping them on the defensive. We can't afford a disruption in this regard."

"Isn't destroying a building to take down a net an overreaction?" Kazuki asked.

Moto said, "These aren't any buildings. These are the buildings at the places where they've chosen to congregate. Raining down glass and steel and cement is a good tactic. If we have them where we want them. And because they think they're safe; they're going to be out in the open. Where we want them. Xander, send a message to intelligence and request a report detailing which umi will have to hit which buildings and from which directions. Get the report to umi operations. First priority."

"Hai," said Xander.

Maya added, "Yes, and in the meantime, let us allow them to feel comfortable and drop their guard. They're not destroying the battle drones, so there isn't any extra urgency."

Kazuki said, "The urgency is they're overrunning our city."

"Yes, but there is only so much we can do. We're stretched to our limit," said Maya.

"What about Obachan? Why isn't she doing something? Or the other majo? What are they doing? They're not doing anything!" Kazuki said. She was clearly becoming upset, so Moto poured a cup of sake and passed it to her.

Richard Rose 223

BLACK CAT SUNRISE

Maya told Kazuki, "The majo have their own ways. We don't know what they're doing or not doing. It's none of our concern. It's not our place. It's not our business."

"Of course it's our business. What about Obachan?" Kazuki asked, drinking the sake.

Maya said, "Your Obachan isn't human. She is majo. I don't know where she goes. I don't know what she does. I presume she is with her coven. Maybe she is in the city."

"We have to know what's happening! What our kovun is doing!" Kazuki shouted.

Moto said, "We can only know what we can know. We can hope the majo are killing many many teki. But we have to draw up our plans as if they're killing very few teki. When we feel the pressure, we will know there is a problem."

"I feel the pressure. I know there is a problem," Kazuki said.

Moto said, "This is not the pressure. I was forty-five feet from the taiyo majo, protected by phantasm and nothing else. All my team was dead. That was pressure. This is not pressure. We are safe. We are good. We are doing what we can. Doing all we can. Try to relax."

These were words of wisdom- or foolishness- and Kazuki didn't have the maturity to understand them or refute them; but she seemed to be reassured by her aunt's disposition. So she calmed down and went to take a shower while the plan to destroy the battle drone nets was being put together.

Moto said, "Maya, we have a kuki senso on stand-by. Why don't we use it?"

"What will we use it for?"

Richard Rose 224

BLACK CAT SUNRISE

Xander said, "I have an idea. But you're not going to like it. Or, maybe you will. It's something we should have done yesterday."

Maya asked, "What is it; what are you talking about?"

"Look at the map. They've got all their moleholes spaced apart. Each has its own area of operation. One molehole per sector. Ten moleholes, ten sectors; right?"

Moto realized what he was saying as soon as he said it and so she finished his line of reasoning, saying, "No, wrong. Nine moleholes, nine sectors. One sector has zero moleholes."

And Maya said, "The prisoners. They're going to release the prisoners."

The prisoner of war camp was located 250 meters directly above their bunker- in the Bronx. Inside the camp's razor wire fences there were 15,000 individuals who had been captured in various war-zones all across the planet. The camp was run by a special cadre of bushi, a unit of slaves, and about one hundred security drones. The prisoners subsisted on bad food, lived in apartments, and performed good works in order to earn rewards like blankets or clothes or improved rations or games or whatever else was available.

Moto asked, "So, what are you saying? You want to annihilate the prisoners."

"I don't want to, but I am suggesting that, yes. 15,000 men. That's a division and a half extra heishi teki. We're obviously having trouble with the legions they've sent heretofore; do we want to allow them to absorb another 15,000 men into their ranks."

Richard Rose 225

BLACK CAT SUNRISE

"That's one of our escape routes. If we blow it, then we'll only have one way out," said Maya.

Moto said, "The teki may have tunneled up into there already. Xander, bring up the camp's video feeds." He did, and they examined them. The feeds showed a ghetto that used to be a neighborhood; a long time ago. The homes were mainly brick duplexes built as near together as possible. With garages; where people also lived. But the residents were clearly restless; as could be expected. They wore black uniforms to represent their status as teki. And they were standing on their rooftops; looking out into the warzone that was encroaching upon them and- to some extent- surrounding them. Or, they were out in the streets and meeting up in clusters. Or, they were walking up and down the razor wire, looking out and trying to see what they could see. The AD-14s wouldn't attack the prisoners inside the fencing, but the heishi teki couldn't get close without inviting death by laser bolt. What the teki could do was to ram a tank through the barricades. But it stood to reason that the slaves didn't want to get hit by drone lasers, and so they had to be waiting for a tunnel. And surely a tunnel was forthcoming.

Maya reviewed these images carefully. And she reviewed the teki positions. There was no doubt that the teki had designs on the camp. Then she said, "We have to go. Now. We can't be down here when we destroy it. We don't know what will happen. It's time to go to Location D." Location D being the bunker beneath Rikers Island. Get dressed. Collect your gear. Get your go bags. We're getting out of here. Now. We have to do this fast."

Richard Rose 226

BLACK CAT SUNRISE

And so that is what they did. Within a half an hour they were all in their standard issue bakufu dress- holding baggage and cases of electronics; walking into the stainless-steel pod tube station, stepping into their pod, and settling in. The door slid closed and suctioned shut. Maya pressed the button and they zoomed away down a tube that flashed with white light and intermittent darkness.

Stepping from the pod, they walked out of the little station and found themselves in another bunker that was exactly the same as the one they were in previously except for that the mural displayed a different garden than before. And Kazuki felt silly because she was really happy to see a new mural. Moto lit a cigarette and went off to find the sake. And Maya called after her, "Where are you going?" "Sake!" she called back. "Is that all you think about! I am about to slaughter 15,000 human beings! I could use your support!" And Moto called back, "I am supporting you. I am finding the sake! Give me a minute." And Maya couldn't argue with her logic. They knelt at the table and got out the tablets and Xander casually mentioned, "They found a hoshi kumo and destroyed it." And Maya said, "Well. It was only one. I'm surprised they haven't found others. Where was it?" "In the garage at the city museum."

Moto knelt at the table and poured each of them a choko of sake from the tokkuri; leaving her cup empty for Maya to fill- which she did. "Do we have to do this, mama?" Kazuki asked. Maya drank her shot and didn't say anything. Moto answered and said, "It's 15,000 heishi teki in those fences." "Not yet, they're not heishi, yet." And Maya said, "They were before they were captured. And they will be again soon. Any

Richard Rose 227

BLACK CAT SUNRISE

minute now. If we allow it." And so Kazuki asked, "Then what were we even keeping them alive for?" A perplexed expression came over Maya's face. And Moto had a similar look. And Maya looked to Moto, and Moto looked to Maya. And then Maya looked to Kazuki- who was watching both of them- and said, "You know, that's a good question." Moto said, "They were supposed to be hostages. Bargaining chips. Like we trade them for a favor or a concession. To gain a strategic advantage." And Kazuki said, "So? Why don't we trade them for a favor or a concession then?"

Maya said, "That's not a bad idea, but we're not in contact with the teki."

And Moto said, "Even if we were in contact with the teki; there's 15,000 men in there. Heishi. Heishi teki. Our intelligence estimates the teki invasion force at 160,000. Or, less, now, of course. My point is, what concession would be worth increasing the teki's strength by ten percent?"

They thought about this for a minute. And Xander said, "The obvious answer is their immediate withdrawal from the city. Would be worth it. There's nothing else we want from them. We're trying to destroy them. Not make peace with them."

"Ah, so so so," said Moto, adding, "And if the teki are willing to lose tens of thousands of lives; why would they vacate the city to rescue fifteen thousand?"

Kazuki said, "We're positively certain there's no strategic advantage we could trade for?"

And Xander said, "I can't seem to think of one."

And Maya said, "Kazuki. This is not a card game. We're not haggling over a fish at the market. This is war. We are at war. We are trying to exterminate them. They are trying to exterminate us.

BLACK CAT SUNRISE

That's it. Those prisoners were a political contingency. The time for diplomacy is over. Now, please don't make this any more difficult than it already is."

Kazuki didn't say anything else; she just held her choko out toward her aunt who promptly refilled it. And Maya did the same. And she poured for Xander, too. And then Xander poured for her. "Kanpai," Xander said. 'Kanpai,' they said.

They drank and then Maya pressed the button to communicate with the senso kuki operator, saying, "Operator, I am transmitting a target. Commence bombardment. Don't stop until there's nothing left." 'Hai. Wakata.' And she sent him an image- essentially an archived schematic- of the compound which used to be called 'East Bronx,' with a thick line around it to designate the fence boundaries. Xander was swapping video feeds on the tablets; then he settled on a few acceptable ones. One camera watching the kuki. Several cameras on the East Bronx prisoner of war camp.

By now, the sun was setting on day two of the teki offensive. Maya was pleased to see the daylight dimming. So much of her hope for the future rested with the ninja. But she knew it was false hope. There was no real hope. All she could hope for was a secondary life in Boston where she could try to be useful enough to earn a position in the coven. One screen flashed as the senso kuki fired. An instant later, the other screens flashed as the plasmoid collided with the earth; sending hundreds of thousands of tons of debris up into the sky, obliterating about 250 square meters of cityscape, and burying a certain blast radius in dirt; besides. Maya wondered if this was the right thing. She really didn't know. If the coven shunned

Richard Rose 229

BLACK CAT SUNRISE

her, for this, or for anything... She'd have to seppuku. All she knew was that she was the daimyo, and this was her decision. Her call. Flash, bang. Flash, bang. Pika, don. Pika, don. The blue light of plasmoids; streaking beautifully through the sky. The camp- full of helpless men; erupting like so many volcanoes releasing their hell.

Chapter 13

Demonic

Paul's fireteam hadn't gotten much further than the building across the street from where the ninja had blown up Luis and the captain. There was nowhere left to go. Not for them. Not for a while. The confederacy kept bringing in more soldiers, and the soldiers kept filling up these vacant buildings, but it didn't seem to be accomplishing anything. They were killing slaves- in small numbers- as they went along. But that was the extent of it. Paul had only seen that one dead bushi. And nobody had seen any dead ninja. Meanwhile, the ninja were inflicting tremendous losses on them. A lot of the guys believed the ninja weren't human. And Paul didn't disagree with them. He didn't know what they were. But he knew they were extremely intimidating. There were stories of a single ninja eliminating entire platoons or even multiple platoons. And Paul had seen enough to believe it. What was more frightening than the ninja was being in a city that was collapsing down around them, and going up in flames as it did so. Paul had to wonder at the logic of sending an army into this doomed place; but, it was probably the only way to push the enemy out. Still, it seemed like they could have firebombed it. Or bombarded it with heavy artillery. It was frustrating because they weren't

BLACK CAT SUNRISE

accomplishing anything except getting themselves killed. Or, that's what it felt like.

Delta company had been holed up at 37 Wall Street. A building that was more like five buildings welded together; a little one, three medium ones, and a big one. Now, Delta company wasn't Delta company any longer. It had been absorbed into Bravo company; which had suffered similar losses. Bravo company shared the premises with the rest of the battalion. Formerly; six companies. Now, only three. Alpha, Bravo, and Echo. At least the Long Island battalion was still together. Even if it had been reduced by half. Much of the 46th infantry division was similarly sprawled out across the sector. But, too, much of it remained back in the tunnels; having not yet tasted the delectable horrors awaiting above. And it was a relief for everybody to remember; they were the vanguard. The majority of confederate strength remained; yet to be unleashed.

Related to these vanguard horrors was the need to stay up on the upper floors because- as a result of the Freedom tower toppling, as well as due to the added effect of other buildings burning- there was now a four-story high pea soup haze of turbid hot ash and acrid smoke churning on the ground level. The engineers had succeeded in connecting every building Paul had come through via the basements and subways, and they were now attempting to connect the entire division, but that would require more time; probably days. Even more time still, because their work was at a standstill as they waited for the noxious dust to settle. As it was, the only way anybody could move from one location to another was by using gas masks or oxygen tanks.

Richard Rose 231

BLACK CAT SUNRISE

One positive bit of information was radioed up and passed along; the supply chain had expedited barrier netting forward. These barrier nets would- supposedly- stop the murder hornets; thus, enabling the soldiers to move around in the streets. This was an uplifting bit of information, because it meant they could get out of these buildings and get around town better, and, in a sense, too, it meant they were claiming that much more of the city for the confederacy. This was supposed to be a morale booster for them. However, the nets evidently didn't change anything; because lower Manhattan was a wasteland in their sector. They had no use for the street because the street was indefinitely uninhabitable.

So; Alpha, Bravo, and Echo were all stuck in the upper floors of this highrise. At some point, the soldiers learned that the murder-hornets weren't programmed to fly higher than about 300 feet in the air. So, the soldiers were actually free to hang around and stare out the windows while they waited for the dust to settle. If it ever would. This was a tedious day. Occasionally, a drone fight would break out, and they'd watch- if they could- to try and figure out what was happening. Sometimes bad news would radio through. Sometimes worse news. But, presently, nothing terrible was happening to them directly, so they really couldn't complain. In the daylight; the fractured cityscape was appalling and hideous to look upon. Skyscrapers that had been glinting and gleaming and glassy yesterday, were blackened and charred and skeletal today; their materials smoking away into nothingness. The building they'd been in before this one- the one across the street; it had a thirty-foot diameter angular hole through it; they could see

Richard Rose 232

BLACK CAT SUNRISE

straight through it. The dust clouds in the streets were yellowish-tan and evil looking. They knew that if they were forced down into them, it would probably kill them.

More bad news came, but it fell on deaf ears. The tanks were being destroyed. The supply tunnels had been closed. The prisoners of war were all dead. By now the soldiers had seen so much death. Death was on their skin like a slime. Their perspective was devoid of depth. Death was skin deep. It rolled right off them. What struck them was the sun setting. Darkness was upon them. And they feared the return of the ninja.

Paul and Jacob and Habib and Terry; this was Paul's fireteam. Paul was a sergeant now. But they were all privates in their hearts. Lieutenant Jameson had been kicked up to Captain. Jameson was pale skinned and pale haired and blue eyed. He carried a double-barreled shotgun and wore a bandolier of shells. He had a face like a turtle's. But, he, too- in his own quarters- hung around like the rest of them. Waiting for something to change. Waiting for a ninja to slaughter them. Waiting for the dust to settle.

There were dozens of floors to be occupied. There were dozens of soldiers on every floor. Paul and his fireteam were with their platoon on the same level as the captain. The 58th floor. Which was divided into small offices, and so each fireteam took up residence in an office of their own; sharing the more open spaces down the hall. And this floor happened to have a balcony. A lot of the guys were too shellshocked or superstitious or paranoid to go out there. Paul liked it out there. There was usually somebody out there with a cigar to share. The only problem was that the air in the city was bad, and it made smoking unpleasant.

Richard Rose 233

BLACK CAT SUNRISE

Everything tasted like asbestos- or something. As the darkness crept in, many soldiers were gathering in the lobby area; hushed- they were lacking for words. They all seemed to think that if they were quiet, they would hear the ninja coming. They seemed to think they'd be safer if there were more of them in one area. Paul sat with the group for a while, but as the darkness grew thicker, and as the city began to glow orange with flame; he had the sneaking suspicion something wasn't right.

Returning to his fireteam's office; he sat down beside Jacob- who hadn't left the room since they'd entered it and who was sleeping soundly besides Terry who was also sleeping. Paul had slept a little, earlier, before the sun had come up that day, and he wanted to sleep some more, but it just wasn't an option. Darkness had fallen. The hour of the ninja was upon them. Habib must have realized this, too, because he returned not long after Paul.

"Habib, you tired?"

"Yes, man. Of course I am tired."

"Get some sleep. I'll take first watch. Then I'll pass it to one of them. After that, I don't know."

"I only need a couple hours. If I get a couple hours, I'll be okay."

"Let's hope we all get more than a couple. Because if we don't..." and his voice trailed off.

And Habib said, "Yes, Paul. I hear you." And just a few minutes later he was asleep and Paul could hear him breathing softly and rhythmically.

Paul didn't know what he could do that wouldn't make any sound and awaken his team. He wanted to organize his gear, or sharpen his knife. Or clean his pits and crack. Instead, he listened to the song of the warzone. Normally it was a battle hymn. Now it sounded like a lullaby. It was astonishing how little he slept these days and- all the same- he felt like he could stay awake forever. Or, that was what he thought. Shortly thereafter, his eyes were closing and he was drifting off to sleep. He'd kick and start. He'd rub his face. He'd pinch his hand. He'd stand up and walk back and forth. He'd drink water. Anything he could think of to keep from falling asleep.

Paul listened for screaming, for bullets, for explosions. These were an omnipresent din drifting within from outside, but he was listening for sounds coming from this building. Listening for impending doom. For enemy contact. For an assault. For anything. Nothing was happening. It was eerily quiet, in fact. He could sense the sleeping soldiers. A lot of guys, that was the only time they were quiet; when they were sleeping. And it seemed like, when they finally shut up, the whole world went silent with them.

Terry shot up straight; clutching his machine gun and hyperventilating. Looking around with wild eyes. Dim orange light shone in from a torched high rise in the distance. Paul watched as Terry tried to figure out where he was and what was going on. Terry saw Habib and Jacob sleeping and Paul smirking at him, and then he relaxed and leaned sideways against the wall.

Paul said, "If I don't sleep, I am going to pass out. Can you take over the watch, Terry?"

"Yeah. Sure. Paul. Get some sleep, man."

Terry stayed awake diligently as he had had a nightmare and it had so jarred him that he could not have fallen back asleep even if he wanted to. All these soldiers were trained in the habit of staying on watch.

BLACK CAT SUNRISE

So Terry sat up and stared at the wall while the others slept. What he thought about was dying. 'Live to war. War to live.' No. Die to war. War to die. That's what the patch on his arm should say. Some variation of that thought- and its grizzly related imagery- ran on repeat in his mind.

Jacob woke and Terry passed the watch off to him. Jacob felt rested enough. And Jacob didn't like sleeping in the warzone anyways. He wasn't used to the mayhem- not that anybody ever could be- and it felt unnatural to be unconscious when he very well might wake up dead. It was the middle of the night- sometime after 0100 hours- when Jacob first heard something alarming. What it was, he couldn't imagine. It sounded like an animal. An angry animal. But it was faint. Coming from outside. At first, he thought he imagined it. He thought it was probably nothing. Listening better, he heard it better, because it became louder; closer. Angrier. Whatever it was, it was incensed. The sound was like... dogs... Wild dogs. Growling. Wild growling dogs from hell. More like a demon than a dog. That's what it was. It was demonic.

Jacob punched Paul and punched Terry and kicked Habib. They all awoke and none of them understood, but when they saw Jacob with his finger to his lips; they listened. And then they knew. Whatever it was. It was bad. It was shrieking; outside the windows. Close by and far off; by the sound of it. They grabbed for their weapons and clutched them and pointed them at the window or doorway. But Paul motioned to put them down, because he wanted to look outside and see what he could see. And an instant later he jumped back wishing he hadn't seen what he did.

Richard Rose 236

BLACK CAT SUNRISE

"What was it?" Jacob asked him.

Paul just shook his head. 'No.' He couldn't say what it was. He didn't know. There was a word for it. He knew he knew the word, but he couldn't remember. It was an inky black shadow. An oily black shadow. And it had pale white claws that seemed to glow with their own inner source of illumination. Skeletal talons, alive with... moonlight... With red eyes like energized laser light. Glowing within a hood or beneath a shroud. And the mouth; howling lamentations- ovular; with a red thermonuclear reaction within. Or, maybe it was hellfire in its mouth and eyes. The worst part was, there was more than one. More than two. More than three. However many, it must be a lot. But he didn't think any of the creatures saw him. They were flying; in graceful arching arcs- this way and that. Up in the sky. Circling the sector. Circling the city. Listening; he tried to guess how many there were. Five, or ten. Twenty. Or more. He couldn't tell. And he couldn't remember the word. But Terry was moving toward the window; trying to look out. Paul had to hold him back, whispering, "They'll see you."

And Terry whispered, "What the fuck are they?"

And just like that, the word jumped into his mind. "Wraiths. It's wraiths. They're wraiths."

What Paul didn't know was that it wasn't just wraiths out there. There was a woman. An old Japanese woman. Shrouded. Airborne. Circling. Wailing lamentations of her own.

"What the hell is a wraith, man?" Habib asked him, urgently whispering.

"A demon," Paul said. Then he put his finger to his lips, because he reasoned that silence was an urgent necessity. On and on these things screamed.

BLACK CAT SUNRISE

Until a rasping raging resonance was ringing in the men's bones. Ten minutes. An hour. Two minutes. Whatever it was, it stopped. All of a sudden.

Paul got up and peaked his head out into the hallway. Other men were doing the same. He could see; nobody knew what to do. This was outside the realm of contingency. Returning to their room, he pushed Terry aside and glanced out the window. It was silent now. There was nothing out there. Paul's heart beat fast and hard. He could feel it in his ears. Looking at the balcony; he studied its features. It had iron fencing with spikes. The iron cemented into the wall. That could hold weight. And he remembered that there was another balcony maybe twenty feet below, and also a flat rooftop probably 35 feet down if they went over the narrow side. Paul inspected their gear. Jacob had a long rope. Paul checked the window again, and- seeing nothing- he didn't hesitate. Taking the rope; he stepped through the window and out onto the balcony. He ran over to the corner of the building to where they could get down to the other rooftop. Tying the rope off and chucking it over; he ran back as fast as he could.

Then they waited. And Terry said, "We should have a goddamn flamethrower."

And Paul said, "Don't fight it. Just run. I saw them. They're not living. You can't kill something if it's not alive."

Urgently, they stopped talking and listened; hearing the silence of the entire building anxiously waiting for whatever was going to come next. Hoping nothing was coming next. Paul stood up and strapped his gear on. Making sure his pack and slings were

BLACK CAT SUNRISE

secure and his clothes were fitting good. The others saw what he was doing, and they did the same.

Atop the high-rise- like on many buildings in the city- there was a fifty foot tall HVAC unit. It had eight turbines situated around a vent. The Japanese woman had lofted down atop this unit. Her wraiths; they'd flown off to other buildings. There were over 6,000 high-rises in the city. Many of which remained intact. These high-rises had become the temporary barracks of entire battalions of confederate soldiers. This one included.

The Naito majo stood atop the building; watching as her wraiths descended upon the whereabouts of other confederate soldiers. One by one, they disappeared into one building after another. Soon, the silent death knell reverberated in her ears. Souls splashing into the night like mists and vapors. Her essence tingled; sensing the ghosts. Then, she vanished. Then, she reappeared on the highest floor which the confederates could be found on; in a spacious room full of weary men carrying firearms. Now, her talons were reaching in and out of a soldier's gushing throat. One soldier fired a gun at her, and she blinked out again. And his bullets struck his fellow soldiers. Again, she reappeared; ripping another man's throat out. Again, she disappeared. Bullets zipping and zooming. Hitting the very men they'd been intended to protect. When she reappeared, it was as an indistinct black smear- moving as a sable apparition; all flashing talons and blurring trails. Splashing blood through the crowd. Too fast to be targeted and too translucent to be struck; the soldiers continued to empty their weapons at her- while the more intelligent ones

Richard Rose 239

BLACK CAT SUNRISE

screamed out 'Cease fire! Cease fire!' and fell bleeding with those words on their dying lips.

And when she had felled most of the men in the vicinity, she slithered off to find more; and this was not hard, because they were behind every door on every floor. And they fired bullets at her or slashed her with knives, but they couldn't hurt her, because she wasn't there; because except for her claws, she may as well have been made out of thin air. Reaching and piercing and tearing and reaping. Fluidly wafting with ethereal grace. Some men saw her as she was. An old Japanese woman, cloaked, and with a serious expression on a joyless face. Others didn't see anything at all except for the other scared men and the dead men they were becoming. Some saw the ghastly sable smear streaking through the darkness and shadows; moonlight white talons stabbing at them. Their own blood flung in black ropes and droplets.

And, of course, the men on the floor below heard the screaming of the men on the floor above. And, too, they had previously heard the demonic chorus of hell's angels singing in the night sky. And some, too, had looked out the window and seen what was out there, what these things were, and what was surely eradicating the troops on the floor above. So, they did the only thing that made any sense; they fled. The problem was that the Naito witch was fast and after she claimed one or two or three; she could then float up over their staggering remains and drift across the heads of the next swath of the panicking herd; ripping more throats out as she went. Many of the men were still throwing their gear together when she came for them; such was her forward momentum. And there was a lot of soldiers on this floor- and on all the floors-

Richard Rose 240

BLACK CAT SUNRISE

and they were having trouble funneling into the stairwells.

Her claws were everywhere and the bullets were flying wildly. Same as above, the soldiers kept shooting each other while others were screaming 'Cease fire!' A carpet of dead bodies lay upon the floor. Each with their throat torn open; their blood staining their skin. And staining their black uniforms. And staining the walls and the ceiling. And pooling beneath them, as well. Down below, the officers were calling for a full retreat, but they weren't saying where anybody was supposed to retreat to. The lower floors were a death trap of toxic smoke. However, the troops didn't need much persuasion to run for their lives. It was more or less understood that a bloodthirsty wickedness was upon them. All they could do was flee, try not to get shot, and try not to get killed. One by one in rapid succession; men would feel the hot spray of blood on their face, and look over to see a dispassionate old oriental woman whose hand was inside their skin and ripping their jugulars out. Piteous souls cried incomprehensibly- pushing and shoving; trampling over one another and crushing each other underfoot. But it'd be those who had been stepped upon who would prove to be the survivors. The witch never stopped moving; with otherworldly speed she reaped human lives as fast as she was able.

This onslaught went on and on without end. Until the commotion of panic-stricken men had arrived at Paul's floor. Paul and his team listened to what was being said, 'Run!' 'Run for your lives!' 'She'll kill us all!' 'Go! Go! Go!' And Paul said to his team, "Come on. It's time to go. And Jacob said, "Should we tell the others?" And Paul said, "They'll get us killed.

BLACK CAT SUNRISE

Come on." Paul's fireteam stepped out of the window and walked toward where they'd flung the rope over. Some other guys had also thought to go out on the balcony for safety. So Paul waved them over. He was on the side of a skyscraper, in the middle of what used to be the greatest city on earth and was now a demon infested hellscape. This situation didn't strike him as odd, or even strike him at all. If anything; he felt a feeling of belonging here. A sense of culmination. The moon shone bright. The orange fires cast light and shadow in all directions. Skyscrapers toward overhead; some were torched and flaming, some were burned out husks, some had gaping wounds that smoldered, and some were simply unharmed. Lifting himself up over the chest-height iron spikes; Paul came down on the outer ledge, with a 35-foot fall at his back. Then he clutched the rope and rappelled down the side of the tallest structure of the composite and onto the roof of the second tallest structure of the composite. Jacob came after him. Then Terry. Then Habib. Then some others. And another, and another, and another. There was fifteen of them down there before more stopped coming. No Jerome. No Antonio. No Aaron. No Jameson. Paul didn't know any of these soldiers. But he was sure glad to see them.

From outside, on the outside of the wall; they could hear the screaming coming from inside. Hundreds of men were dying in there. There was nothing any of them could do except be thankful they were still alive. Thankful, or bitter... More than one of them was beyond their breaking point. A couple had collapsed in fits of heaving sobs. A couple sat hunched against the walls with their arms around their legs and their faces smashed into their elbows; weeping and

BLACK CAT SUNRISE

whimpering and wishing this would just end and wondering why they'd fled out here only to die in a minute or an hour or a day. A couple cigars were passed around and they smoked as their fellow soldiers died. More than once, a person jumped out of a window and fell screaming to their death. And out in the open air they could hear similar terrified screaming- either faint or prominent- coming from not just their building but also from multiple other buildings; both close and distant. These were hardened confederates screaming in mortal terror. Hundreds and thousands of them.

Terry walked up to Paul and said, "Hey man. Those things was outside. Now they's inside. Don't you think they're going to be outside again at some point. You know, outside- as in here- with us. Out here."

And Paul said, "What are you suggesting?"

"There's this door. This is pretty much a separate building we're on. We should break in the door and go in there and hide. There ain't nobody else in there. The demons probably won't go in there. So... Let's go in there."

Considering this, Paul listened to the night air; alive with the squealing of men being slaughtered like hogs. Terry was right, he knew. The door was locked; so they found a crowbar in one of their packs and pried it open to get inside. They went in and- in the darkness- they snuck down the steps to the top floor. Nobody dared to use their flashlights. But they had nowhere to go, anyways. And they had nothing to say, either. They sat in silence. Through the walls, they could hear the extermination carrying on, but, eventually- thankfully- it came to an end. And then, again, came the hellish howling of demonic dogs.

BLACK CAT SUNRISE

Airborne and ravenous and raving in the night.
Nobody dared to look. But they listened intently as the
howling entities multiplied in number. None of the
soldiers were immune to the disturbance of this and to
a man they felt as though something about this satanic
song would somehow be the end of them; and they
grew to fear it as much as anything, and they plugged
their ears with their fingers. And they closed their eyes,
too, as if that might quiet what was happening. It
wasn't painful. It was maddening. A maniacal urge
swelling in the mind. Reaching a fever pitch. Like a
devil breathing down their neck. Its bony hands,
reaching down their throats. But then, before they
even realized it, it was over.

Nobody dared say anything, but they could all
see that one of their number had driven his own
combat knife into his own heart. A young man.
Probably only 16 or seventeen. A black skinned boy
with wide white eyes. His mouth; full of blood that
spilled down his chin. His dead fingers still clutching
the hilt of the blade. Paul and some others had the
impulse to creep to the windows and look out at the
sky. The wraiths were gone, it appeared.

One of the other soldiers said, "We have to get
back over there; there's got to be survivors." And they
all knew this was true. They had to get back over there,
whether there were survivors or not. They belonged
with the others. Or with their corpses. And another
soldier asked, "Do we go back up the rope, or try to
find a way from this side over to that side?"

And Habib asked, "Is this one building or two
buildings?"

And they all looked to each other for an answer
that none of them had. And somebody said, "I think it

BLACK CAT SUNRISE

is five buildings." And Paul said, "We try to find a way over. If we can't, we go back up the rope. Agreed?" 'Agreed,' they said. And they turned on their flashlights and started combing the corridors; searching for a passageway. Soon, they became familiar with where this structure ended and the other began, but all they were finding was walls. But, then, they found something else, too. One of the others. A short and stocky fellow with chipmunk teeth and soft pale skin. Dead. With a steel spike driven through his ear protection. They released a collective groan and Terry put his fist through the drywall in anger and frustration. "Take his grenades," Paul said. And Jacob asked, "Was this building ever cleared?" And one of the others said, "Yeah. But there ain't no way to clear out the ninja." And they'd all heard the stories from the night before; so they knew that the ninja would have circuit-breakers and god-collars from the dead slaves. And grenades from the dead soldiers.

Paul said, "Fuck this. We're going back up the rope. Stay close together. If you hear any sound that's not the sound of us getting the fuck out of here, dump your fucking clips into it. If you see that piece of shit Jap fuck. Fucking kill it." As they moved, Paul thought, 'He probably heard me say that. But then he thought, 'Whatever, they probably don't speak English.'

They moved through the building as a single organism with many eyes. They shone their lights into every crack and crevice as they went. Some walked backward. They looked at the ceiling. They looked at the floor. They looked under the furniture. Nobody said a word. Nothing happened. When they were back up on the rooftop, they hurried toward the rope and started climbing. The steel door slammed behind the

Richard Rose 245

BLACK CAT SUNRISE

last man; who was certainly relieved to be back on the rooftop again. He was Henry. Henry was of Hebrew descent. Henry hurried toward the rope, also, but he fell dead with a circular section of his torso completely disappeared. And the steel door had slammed shut a second time before anybody knew what had happened. Then, Henry's body was spotted. Paul was waiting to ascend until the last of his guys- Habib- had made it to the top, and then he called out, "Keep your guns on that door. Keep your eyes open."

Chapter 14
Survivors
After Habib had made it up and over the fence; Paul was next. Climbing; he didn't even notice the weight of his weapons and ammo and gear. But he looked over his shoulder and saw the hole in Henry's back. That's what he thought about. When he got to the top, the next man started up, and he told his team; 'we got to cover these guys-' but they were doing that anyway. Except for Terry, who was helping people over the spikes, because he was a hulking giant and it was his duty as such. Paul was staring at the steel door where they'd come out of. An angry stare. A glare. A glower. He could sense it; that ninja had to be in there. It had picked off the last of them to come out. With his grenade launcher in his hand, his trigger finger was itching.

He said to Jacob, "I should demolish that stairwell enclosure."

"What if we need it again?"

"What if he's inside? What if he needs it more than we do."

Jacob thought about this and said, "Yeah. Do it."

Richard Rose 246

BLACK CAT SUNRISE

"I can't. Not until everybody's up here. The shrapnel. It's too close."

There were still seven soldiers remaining below and waiting their turn to climb up. One of these spotted an object falling from above and shouted out, "Grenade!" But it wasn't a grenade. It was a bug-zapper. All the same; Paul pulled Terry back and Terry lifted a man bodily up over the side and the three of them dropped back on Jacob and Habib. And the bug-zapper discharged with a deafening crack and a blinding jolt which lit the vicinity blue and blasted a hole in the building and blasted the stairwell enclosure door inward and off of its hinges and essentially obliterated the soldiers who had been the weapon's targets. Paul and his companions had been in a position to survive the blast but the concussion had been powerful enough to knock them senseless; so as that when they stood up, they did so dizzily and had to squat back down in order to not fall over the edge. Paul, however, fell against the building and used it to support himself as he shoved off and lurched over the others. And when he got to where he wanted to be he plunked six grenades into the rooftop stairwell enclosure. These explosives detonated in rapid succession and afterward nothing remained but a smoking heap of bricks as well as bricks which were flung outward in all directions. Terry appeared beside him with his M240; looking for a target, but there was nothing there. Jacob called to the others, "I'm getting off this ledge! I'm going inside!" And the others followed. Except for Terry and Paul. Terry was searching for the enemy, and Paul was reloading his grenade launcher. When Paul finished reloading, he told Terry, "If he's out there, he'll kill us. Come on.

BLACK CAT SUNRISE

Let's go." And he pulled on Terry's shoulder to get him away from the edge. They left the rope behind, not even noticing that it was 80 percent shorter.

Back inside, the air smelled of blood and piss and shit. And the temperature was balmy for some reason. Maybe just because they had been out in the cold. Or maybe because all the dead bodies were releasing their heat. There were so many corpses on the ground that no matter how hard they tried not to step on them, they were still stepping on them. They noticed survivors; more than they dared to hope to find. Some were rifling through the belongings of the dead. Others were smoking. Others were crying with their faces in their hands. A sad and sickening sight. A feeling so familiar. Nobody seemed to know what to do next. But Jacob had some ideas, and he said to Paul; "We have to get everybody together. We can't be scattered out like this. And we have to get back to the tunnels."

"How?" Paul asked him.

"Can you radio the captain? Or the lieutenant colonel?"

Paul tried, and said, "No."

"Then we get to the top, and herd everybody down to the bottom."

"That ninja. He'll come for us," Paul said.

"We have to get to the tunnels. What if just you and me go?" Jacob asked.

"Now you're making sense. Come on."

Terry and Habib were quick to follow. They didn't ask any questions. Paul and Jacob started walking, and they started walking, too. Paul knew this was cowardly, and possibly wrong. But that ninja was coming. And ninja had killed as many soldiers as

BLACK CAT SUNRISE

anything else, and nobody- as far as he knew- had killed any of the ninja. After everything that just happened; there wasn't anything more important than self-preservation. They were cut off from the corps. Their numbers had been cut down to practically nothing. Their officers were incommunicado; probably dead. It didn't make any sense to stay up there and die. They had to live; to get a chance to fight another day.

They struggled to keep their balance. Clutching the railings. Tiptoeing; slowly. The air became noxious and unbearable. Their flashlight beams swept across an unending procession of deceased soldiers. Open throats; all of them. They all had the same sad eyes of men who know their blood is draining out of them. No shock or surprise; just unfortunate acceptance. Paul got the impression that it wasn't so hard to die when everybody else was dying, too. And that's usually how it was, he reflected. Or, the hatpin through the ear. That seemed relatively easy, too. The bug-zapper; turned to nothing in an instant. That had to be the best. But slogging down stairwells where there were no stairs because the only places to put your feet were on the corpses of those who were your brothers in arms. Surely, this was a bad way to die. Some men had taken a laser bolt through the head right when they first came running out of the underground. Some of them had never known battle before that moment. That must be the good way to go. Paul always wanted to fight the enemy. But, now that he had, he realized, it was worse. The waiting to die. The watching the death. The torment of anticipation.

This was the sixth floor. They couldn't go any lower than the sixth floor. And the cadres of corpses, those had stopped at about the ninth floor. So, now

BLACK CAT SUNRISE

they were alone. With nowhere to go. And they realized; this was a problem. Paul said, "We gotta stop. This won't work." And Jacob said, "I didn't think it'd be this bad. I thought we could get further down. I thought we could get to the engineers and use their gas masks." And Habib said, "We can go to the top floors. We can gather up the others on the way. We can concentrate our forces. Try to get back to the molehole, when we can." And Terry added, "We can kill that fucking cocksucking Jap." And Paul said, "We can try, at least. Anyways, it's the right thing to do. Come on. Let's go."

At the ninth floor, they collected four survivors. At the tenth, they collected two. At the eleventh, they collected five. At the twelfth, just one. And it went on like that. Nobody had disturbed them when they were going downstairs, but all were eager to join the regrouping as it was heading upward. Soon; Jacob and Paul were simply two among many again. These were a defeated lot; devoid of any semblance of fighting spirit. Except for maybe Paul and his team; who'd not experienced the wraiths up close. In the stairwell, these men were a trudging drove. Hauling their own weight; higher and higher. With every step; more and more forgot that there were dead bodies between their feet and the stairs. At each level they called out; 'Any survivors?' and there usually was, and invariably the survivor joined the macabre procession.

Up around where they had been before, on the 38th floor; there was a commotion at the front of the drove and several of the men fell over with voids where their organs had been. And others called out, 'Ninja! Ninja!' and 'Grenade! Grenade!' The drove turned and tried to run, but there was nowhere to go and they

BLACK CAT SUNRISE

collapsed into a pigpile that took up two flights. The grenade exploded and killed and maimed several men who were unfortunate enough to be atop the pile. Now there was a lot of screaming from some who were in extreme pain. And not a little shrieking, too, from men who were just afraid. And Paul's mind was instinctively telling him; if the ninja is up, then we have to go down. He wasn't the only one to have thought of this. They dragged themselves and their gear and their guns away; scraping and grinding against each other- with the nauseating remains of the dead as the only purchase their fingertips could find.

Paul felt a minor sense of relief when he was able to stand up and clutch his MP5, but it was short lived. Their situation was hopeless. Habib was gone. Dead; Paul could see in his flashlight beam. And Paul's head felt like it was being squeezed by a goliath. But Jacob came up to him and said, "Hey. I have an idea." And Terry was there, too; anxious to hear Jacob's idea. And Paul said, "Okay. What is it?" "The ninja. It's all by itself. It's using our numbers against us. We have to split up. Cover as much ground as we can. Tell everybody to do the same thing. We got nowhere to run; so we hide." Paul and Terry exchanged a look. They knew he was right. A gunshot rang out and then another, and then the caterwauling of the suffering was silenced. Paul whispered to Terry, who had heard Jacob plainly; "We split up. We hide. We kill the ninja. Pass it on." And Terry did as he was told. And Paul told a man he recognized just from being around; "We split up. We hide. We kill the ninja. Pass it on." But Paul wasn't about to lose sight of Jacob; so he backhand slapped Jacob's arm and waved him over with two fingers. They were moving toward the other side of the

BLACK CAT SUNRISE

building. Terry watched them go, and then went to find his own spot to hide.

They needed to do this quickly. The most obvious place was over by the stairs across the floor. There had once been some sort of clinic on this level. It offered a waiting room, a reception area, a confusing sprawl of hallways, and a lot of examination rooms and offices. The stairs could be seen from the waiting room. And from the reception area. The waiting room was open to the stairs and the reception area's door was held open by a corpse. Most corpses were in the stairwells, but also, they were all over the place. The walls looked to have been painted by some psychotic splatter painter. Paul reached down into a puddle of blood and smeared some on his throat; to blend in. Jacob did the same. In the reception area was a jacket closet; Jacob, by pointing toward it and toward his rifle, indicated that he'd take that spot- in order to shoot through the open door or through two tall and wide windows- and then he gestured a circle toward the ground nearer to the stairs. And from there, Paul could cover both directions it might come at them from.

There were six corpses in that room, and Paul pretended to be the seventh. Upstairs; they heard; explosions and gunshots and cries of terror and pain. Adult men in agonizing torment; wildly wailing with their final breaths. They heard men shouting to one another but couldn't make out the words. Then it was quiet again. Paul wondered who was down on this level with them, and how far the word had spread, and what would happen next. What happened next was nothing. Nobody moved. Nobody made a sound. No more gunshots. No more explosions- not from inside the

Richard Rose 252

building, that is; lots from outside, as per usual. And eventually the sun rose and cast hazy light through the yellow fog of smoke which hung over the city. They waited until they were sure the sun was up; not just purple or blue light, but clear white daylight. The dead were reeking and stiffened and as gruesome as anything else. But such was their fear of the ninja and such was their battlefield conditioning; they didn't smell the stench or abhor the sight. The dead were one more indignity to be suffered, and little else. Eventually, they stood up and stretched their strained and stiffened bodies. "God. That was a bitch," Paul said. "Yeah, but we're alive," Jacob said. And Paul looked at his companion; a 5 foot 4 inch tall, dark skinned, vaguely Hispanic soldier, with blood on his throat and a smile on his face and a gleam in his eye. Jacob was looking at him, too; Paul, his stalwart friend and his only friend in the world; with a blockish face burned ugly on one side, blazing bright blue eyes, and a hint of a blonde beard growing in on the handsome side. It had been a bad night. The worst night. But they were still together and that was an obvious blessing. And Paul said to Jacob, "You know... Your idea saved a lot of us last night." "Yeah. Maybe. But they'll get us next time." "Yeah. Something will. Probably."

Paul remembered his radio ear piece and tapped the button until somebody came through, saying, 'You got the major general's line. Who am I speaking with?' "My name is Paul. Second platoon. Bravo company. Long Island Battalion." 'Oh, right. What's your situation?' "Nobody told you?" 'No. Nobody told us. But we know it's not good. So, what's your situation?' "We're trapped at 37 Wall Street. We've sustained heavy losses. Probably 95 percent losses. Or worse. We

BLACK CAT SUNRISE

can't get down through the bad air." 'Alright. We hear you. We're on it. You can expect an evac team within the hour. Just get to the south end, and get down as close to the basement as you can.' Jacob was looking out the window. The yellow dust had visibly settled since last night; but it was still a threatening presence that seemed to inhale and exhale with a life of its own, and- having had breathed it and tasted it- Paul's stomach churned and his throat heaved just from the sight of it.

     Later on that afternoon; Xander and Maya and Moto and Kazuki were enjoying a nice lunch of chicken yakisoba, miso soup, and cucumber salad. Xander was ever vigilant about monitoring the situation, and he told the others, "I think it's time. They've got a lot of nets up. And a lot of troops wandering around in the habitable areas." And Maya was keen on accepting Xander's opinion, so she consulted her tablets, radioed her drone command, and told them; "Send a dondon up to 100 kilometers. Fast, to avoid molestation." And they said, 'Hai. Wakata.' And she added, "We're going to commence bombardment on the targets we outlined earlier. But I want you to send out a kumo, as well. Deploy the hoshi kumo positioned at 45 Rockefeller Plaza; Kumo-7. Kumo-7 is to target the teki concentration at Time's Square. Synchronize ground attack with commencement of aerial bombardment." 'Hai. Wakata.' "Repeat that back to me." The administrator repeated her orders back to her and then she instructed him to initiate. They watched what transpired next with an air of satisfaction. The teki had become too comfortable and overconfident now that

BLACK CAT SUNRISE

they were free of the murder-hornets. "If they were smart, they would just stay underground," Kazuki said. And Moto said, "They're not smart. They spend too much time underground. All they want is to get up to the surface. It makes them do foolish things." And Kazuki said, "What are they even trying to accomplish? They're just getting themselves killed." And Moto said, "Maybe killing themselves is what they're trying to accomplish. The majo love blood sacrifice." And Maya said, "Yes. They're making it easy. But they will learn, and soon, too." And Moto- lighting a cigarette- said, "Maybe not as easy as we think. They're learning right now." And indeed, the teki were learning; because the dondon was firing into their numbers with dramatic effect; blasting craters that reached down into the subway tunnels. And the senso, too, was claiming multiple platoons with every blast it released. The city shivered so violently that Kazuki asked, "Are the walls shaking?" And Xander said, "Yes. I think so."

A tank fired its cannon into the kumo as the kumo was firing the hoshi into the crowds of soldiers; who were succumbing to that weapon's dazzling display of electric sparkles- hitting the ground one by one or two by two or ten by ten, and convulsing with electricity coursing through them. The tank round burst red hot against the splashing and shimmering neon orange phantasm shield, and again the neon orange liquid light phantom majo appeared and destroyed the spider drone a moment later. Maya dispatched an order to release a raijin kuki to lure the majo up into the upper atmosphere; as well as for the senso and dondon kuki to climb to 300 kilometers. This strategy worked; the phantom majo bolted off into the sky in pursuit of the kuki and again her

BLACK CAT SUNRISE

effervescent form dissipated in the ionosphere. And Maya was grateful that at least the vexing majo was predictable. She issued a further order to bring the kuki back down to a lower altitude and resume firing on the teki concentrations; but there were no teki concentrations- not in the open- because they'd all ran off and found shelter to hide in.

Realizing this; Maya told the others, "I'm done fighting. I've killed enough teki. I am getting sick of it. I'm ready to evacuate. I want to start our new lives in Bosuton. Try to find peace. Try to forget this ever happened."

And Kazuki asked, "What will we do when the teki come for Bosuton?"

And Maya said, "When the bakufu is finished with them, they won't have an army in our region for 20 years. And by then, you'll be in my position. You'll be in Potorando. Or, Setsuri. Maybe Firaderufia. And it will be your responsibility to eliminate them before they destroy your city. Not after. That was my mistake. I was too soft-hearted. I underestimated them."

"When will we make the jump?" Moto asked.

"Anytime. They haven't found us yet. They haven't moved against Rikers. We can go today, or we can go tomorrow. Or the next day."

Kazuki said, "I don't want to look back on this period of time and think that I could have done more. I want to keep fighting. I am not finished yet."

And Maya said, "Fine. You do that. I am finished. But, when I say it is time to go, I don't want to hear any backtalk coming from you. I say we go. We go. Wakata?"

"Hai," said Kazuki.

BLACK CAT SUNRISE

"What do you intend to do here; that we have not already done?" Moto queried.

"For one thing; the dorei. They're still hiding and waiting. Look at this map." And she indicated a tablet which displayed dorei and bushi positions as well as the estimations of teki positions that were constantly being updated by the office of intelligence.

"Ok, and...?" Moto elicited.

Kazuki began pointing with the tablet pen, saying, "Here, here, here, here, here, here, here, and here. And a couple other places. These bushi should banzai their dorei out into the main bodies of the teki."

Moto smiled and looked to Maya who was also smiling, and said, "Smart kid. Why we didn't think of that?"

And Maya said, "We haven't had access to heishi teki concentrations before now. They were underground. Now they're above ground. But very well. That is a good plan of attack. Although; we'll have to do it fast, before the positions shift. Xander; start with the largest concentrations. Select the dorei and notify the corresponding bushi."

And so, as the heishi teki were huddled together in buildings, hiding from the AD-14s; the bushi began to issue orders to select dorei to run out into the thick of the teki. The dorei were- of course- reluctant to do this, and so the bushi were compelled to shock them once, twice, ten times, or as much as it took to convince said dorei it was better to die than to suffer such extreme torment. Like enraged and psychotic zombies, the dorei charged into the teki; with crazed eyes and snarling lips- holding their CD-7s out before them. On numerous occasions the dorei succeeded in penetrating into the confused masses of soldiers, and

BLACK CAT SUNRISE

there their effect was devastating. The WV-9 collars and the CD-7 devices inflicted grievous losses before the slaughter could be neutralized. Countless friendly fire losses resulted from heishi shooting into each other in an attempt to bring down their adversary. By the time their bullets or their grenades could neutralize the bakufu cardiac disruptors; stacks of dead bodies would be piled up around the dorei heishi remains. And this maneuver was performed so many times and in such rapid succession that the teki were often forced to return to their underground tunnels, or to venture out under the AD-14s in search of safety.

As the attacks were coming to an end, the family Naito examined the numbers and the teki positions. It had been a fine offensive. They lost 163 heishi dorei, but they gained 1,946 teki losses. So, an average of about 12 teki for each dorei. Plus, the spike in AD-14 kills. Plus, the friendly fire kills they couldnt quantify. Furthermore, the bushi began to relocate dorei from places where there was no threat to places where there was a threat; or the threat of a threat or the anticipated threat of threat. And, now the bushi knew how to use the dorei to their fullest potential. The trick being in waiting for teki concentrations to coalesce.

What was more was that the bakufu now had air supremacy again. So, the teki had no way to go out into the streets and were essentially forced back indoors and underground. With regard to this, Kazuki asked her mother, "They're trapped underground. Why don't they just leave?"

And Maya said, "You don't know the teki. They are like chiggers. Impossible to get rid of. Except worse, because chiggers have a weakness. If you burn one, the entire colony will go. The teki; we can burn them until there is only one left, and that last one, it will keep coming at us."

"Then they'll take the city eventually?" Kazuki asked.

Maya sipped matcha, and thought about the question. There were candles lit. The bunker was warm. They were relaxing on their futon on the tatami in the bedroom. Wearing white pajamas and white socks. With white blankets around them. The lighting was yellow and soft. Xander was in the other room; at the table with the tablets, like always. And Moto was out there with him; chain smoking and sipping sake, like always. Kazuki held a plush momonga she'd loved since childhood. A momonga is a dwarf flying squirrel. A symbol of taking a leap of faith into the unknown. That'd be them soon. They didn't talk about it, but none of them wanted to go up into the danger zone. That'd be a leap of faith, in and of itself. Maya's expression was far-off and troubled; her hazy gaze lingered on the ceiling and her mouth contorted with consternation. Kazuki's eyes were downcast, saddened, and dull, and her lips were always pouting; thinking about the men the bakufu had killed and wondering why they wouldn't just go away and wishing they would. Looking at her momonga, she wondered about her family and their future.

She'd forgotten she asked her mother a question, but Maya answered her and said, "The ninja, and the kovun, and the bakufu; they will stop the teki. The city is ours, even if it is in ruins. It is ours."

"How will they stop them? There's too many."

"It will be a hideous affair. The hinomaru will exterminate them. Like termites."

BLACK CAT SUNRISE

"How?" Kazuki asked.

Paul and Jacob awakened to boots kicking their boots. A flush of dread and despair washed over them as they remembered who they were and what was becoming of them. A familiar feeling. Above them stood their new lieutenant; Lieutenant Adams. A tall and pale man of nordic descent; with a clean-shaven face, a helmet under his arm, and well-kept blonde hair on his head. On his hip was a steel pistol with an ivory handle. Over his shoulder was a Benelli M4 tactical shotgun. And like every shotgunner; he wore a bandolier of shells. His uniform was clean but had tears and worn spots; evidencing he'd been out in the shit even though he'd gone to some length to look clean, calm, cool, and collected. Paul and Jacob had been sleeping head-to-head; on the glassy floor, along the side of a tunnel where a lot of other soldiers who'd returned from above were also sleeping at. It was an area at a confluence; serving as a hub. The air was hot and wet and echoing with the din of soldiers on the march. They stared up at Adams as he stared down at them; reading their names on their shirts. Sarkowski, Gindlesperger. Long Island Battalion doesn't exist anymore. It's been absorbed into the Quiet Corner Battalion. You're in my platoon. Third platoon. Charlie company."

"What's the mission, lieutenant?" Jacob asked.

"We're going up there to die. So, don't be surprised when we do."

"Okay, but, seriously. What's the mission?" Paul asked.

"We're here to occupy the city. The neeps are giving us hell, but we're making headway. We've got

BLACK CAT SUNRISE

the subway tunnels damn near cleared out. And we've taken up residency in half the buildings, too. The ones left standing, that is."

"Did the nets work?" Jacob asked.

"They worked at getting a lot of men blown to shit. That's about it. Neep cocksuckers figured out the phantom hex couldn't take out their shield if they flew up into the sky high enough. That's what they been doing. Any hope we had of capturing air superiority is gone and gone again."

Paul grinned and said, "That's the way it's always been."

"Yeah. The more things change, the more they stay the same. But we're here, and we got the underground. That's all the enemy ever gave us and that's all we ever needed. If the commanders had a brain, they'd quit sending us up there to die. But they want us stationed at all points across the grid and we can't do that from down in here. That's why they're marching us out under the east river. Up into the Bronx. Toward over by where they blown the PoWs to hell. They want us in the houses and the shops. They're sick of sending suicide squads into these skyscrapers. So get on your feet. It's a ten-mile march. We move out in 20."

"Hey. Lieutenant. Am I still a sergeant?" Paul asked before the lieutenant could walk away.

And the lieutenant asked him, "Do you want to be?"

And Paul said, "No."

And the lieutenant said, "Then you're not." And he turned and walked away.

They found their platoon nearby in the number seven molehole staging area; essentially a secondary

BLACK CAT SUNRISE

tunnel running out from and back into the primary tunnel. But it wasn't just their platoon; it was their entire battalion. It was a sea of faces decorated with cuts, bruises, gouges, scorches, gashes, abrasions, and every other manner of flesh-wound. Their hands and clothing, too, showed signs of disrepair. Some limped and some hobbled. And some seemed as though they'd collapse at any second; like they couldn't move without the help of another soldier to hang onto. Seeing this; Jacob could feel his injured ankle aching and Paul could feel his burnt skin tingling.

Terry was there, though, and he came over with a big smile and grabbed them both by the shoulders, saying, "I am glad to see you guys."

"Oh, yeah... Terry. How are you?" Paul asked.

Terry was a towering and brutal man- like a mangy lion with that mane of hair- but they could see now that he was soft on the inside, and he told them, "Ever since they killed Toad. And all them other guys. I feel like I don't know nobody no more. But I know you two. And we're in the same platoon. So, when they split us up into fireteams, I'm going to be in yours. Whether the lieutenant likes it or not."

And Jacob said, "Hell yes, Terry. It'll be good to have you around. When the ninja come for us; you'll give us something to hide behind."

They filled their canteens at the water truck, emptied them into their bellies, and then filled them up again. At a supply station they were issued field rations and ammunition. Then they were on their way. Paul felt incredible. Having finally gotten some real sleep. And they'd been given triple rations, too. Because there was more food to go around now that so many were dead. With regard to that, every man

BLACK CAT SUNRISE

wondered how many of their number had been killed off. It was obviously a lot. They'd all seen a lot of dead soldiers and they'd all asked each other if they'd all seen a lot, too, and they all answered in the affirmative. They'd also all seen the endless procession of casualties being dragged back to the rear. That wasn't easy to look at but it was more interesting than staring at the wall. And besides; the screaming never let up, so it was hard to ignore. There were medics amputating limbs and performing operations in the backs of trucks. Sewing up holes, removing shrapnel, trying to staunch bleeding, setting broken bones. Removing bullets, unfortunately. It was important these men be kept alive; not only for moral reasons, but for practical reasons, too.

Chapter 15

Assaulted

Their boots moved like a river of stomping feet. They walked beside a slower moving parade of military vehicles. Tanks. Fighting vehicles with gatling guns mounted on them. Surface to air missile trucks. Anti-aircraft gun trucks. Medic trucks. Supply trucks. Their exhaust stank, but nobody noticed. The lightbulbs overhead came and went and came and went in a flashing blur. Sometimes the men talked. Mostly they were silent. Their gear clattered and clacked and clanked. Sweat dripped down their faces. They breathed heavy and hard. These grueling tunnel marches were a relatively happy time for the soldiers. Nothing was trying to kill them. And they weren't dead. It was warm and moist, there was a cool breeze blowing gently, and ten miles wasn't far. Just a half day and they'd be there. Not that they wanted to get there.

BLACK CAT SUNRISE

At the end of the march, Lieutenant Adams divided them into fireteams. Not caring much who wanted to join up with who; he allowed Paul, Jacob, and Terry to remain together and they picked up a new guy, Zachery. Zachery had red facial hair, pale skin, hunched shoulders, a low forehead, angry blue eyes, and muscular hands; because- as he'd told the others- he used to be a mechanic but management decided they needed another dead body more than another mechanic and so they stuck him out there with them. His weapon was an M16A4 with a tactical 3x magnifying optic. Plus, a .45 caliber striker fired pistol on his hip. Really, Zachery was 28 years old and had never been on the receiving end of a drone strike and the commanders didn't want him to go to Valhalla without first testing him under fire. This was a common enough thing. But it didn't occur to any of them. So they just assumed it was in order to get another swinging dick in the field; and that was part of it, too. Confederate numbers were obviously down by a lot. Everybody knew that, but none of them knew how bad it was and they probably wouldn't have dared to guess because they wanted and needed their morale to be lifted, not lowered.

Adams received his instructions from his superiors and then he briefed his men, explaining; "The whole battalion is using the same wormhole. The enemy has been closing them up just from shelling us. They probably don't even know they're doing it. But they got a hard on for this sector because they know we're in the vicinity. Murder-hornets out here... it's not like it was back in lower Manhattan. There's not so many of them. But, if we group up, they'll come after us. Murder-hornets, or they'll send the slaves. But it's

BLACK CAT SUNRISE

going to be dark here soon. And you know what that means. Fucking ninjas." He stopped talking and handed out maps to the team leaders. Then he said, "Those are the maps for your team. The X marks the wormhole. Your team's position is in red. The red dashes from the X to the red zone; that's your route. The platoon is in blue. The company is green. The battalion is the black. Your objective is to dig in and hold your positions. That's it. The company will resupply the platoon and the platoon will resupply your fireteam. When possible. But don't expect the resupply to be on time; you'll be lucky if it comes at all. So, sit on your rations. And never take more than a sip of water at a time. Think of each sip as your last drop. The water truck is up at the mouth of the wormhole. We're going to drink until it's coming out of our ears, and then we're going to get in the hole and go. Any questions?"

There were none. Nobody cared. What he was saying was bad, and they were sure it'd be worse than it sounded. To a man, they felt as though they were dying for no reason. Best case scenario; dying so another soldier could have a toe-hold. No man expected to be the one who survived. No man expected to see the enemy's death apparatuses overthrown. It didn't matter. After everybody they had lost. After how far they had come and still with nowhere to go and nothing to do. This was as good as it got. So, they did as instructed and drank water like fish on dry land. Then they were shoved into the wormhole and scrambling upward; anxious to get out into the open air, because the wormholes were cramped and exhausting. Some wormholes could be quite long and this one was one of those. Nearly a mile in length;

BLACK CAT SUNRISE

crawling on their bellies in the narrow confines. Terry suffered the most because he was the biggest. If his machine gun or ammo box shifted, then he could get stuck. And getting stuck in a wormhole was a serious problem; not just for one person, but for everybody. The rule was; the person in front of the stuck person would have to crawl out and then crawl back in and help fix the problem. And then crawl out backwards afterwards. In a warzone; this delay could have serious consequences. And so for that reason, large men weren't usually allowed to use them. Terry was at the maximum size allowance. And, too, the hole was bigger than it seemed. It was their gear that could make it seem overly small. And Terry- being aware of this- packed his pack as diligently as possible.

They emerged into a thick fog of smoke and dust and it tasted as much like dirt as it did like ash. This was an area much different than lower Manhattan. It looked like a hundred other places Paul had been since he'd first been marched down to Long Island and then marched up into upstate New York and then marched back down into the city. However, these neighborhoods were especially cluttered and congested. This was a sprawling residential area overgrown with vines and shrubs and trees. With evergreen trees being the only real color, as the deciduous leaves hadn't returned and the buildings were dull grey, sulfuric yellow, dingy white, or faded brick. Eight and ten story apartment complexes occupied a lot of the space. Houses were built close together. And a lot of structures were dilapidated; with broken windows, collapsed porches, and caving in roofs. And some structures- for reasons he couldn't discern- looked pretty well maintained, albeit with

BLACK CAT SUNRISE

faded paint. Utility poles were often broken at the top and power lines hung in all directions like cobwebs. The streets were full of skeletal motor vehicles with busted out windows, and trees grew up out of the asphalt wherever they could. So, in a way, to call the streets 'streets' was a misnomer. The whole region was essentially an ugly wilderness that used to be a civilization.

The temperature was unusually warm that day and the sky was overcast with low hanging black clouds. The air had an electric quality and the pressure was wrong. It seemed as if at any second the sky would open up and drop a deluge on them. But it was rain weather and not snow weather, and that was a blessing. The snow on the ground was turning to slush and had already melted away in places. Paul hadn't forgotten what might rise up out of the water and neither had anybody else; so they avoided puddles carefully. The entire company was to move in the same direction; so, for now, they were just following the lieutenant. Paul clutched his map in his hand; realizing they were making slow progress and that the daylight was failing. The wormhole came up in the West Bronx, but they could tell- from the unusually hot breezes, from the smoke, and from the reeking stench- that the East Bronx wasn't far off. There were even dead bodies in the trees and on rooftops or tangled up in scrub; the corpses were dressed in black prisoner clothes and the only explanation for their presence was that they'd fallen out of the sky. Similarly, there was debris littered about but it blended in and could scarcely be noticed.

All in all, the landscape was significantly difficult to traverse. They had to filter through the remains of the dead city and it was slow going. But it

BLACK CAT SUNRISE

didn't seem too bad as far as battlegrounds go. They weren't being assailed by murder-hornets. So, that was good. And eventually their route led them out onto a concourse which was somewhat more spacious and easier to move along; although, just as littered with rusted-out vehicle husks as anyplace else. But the trees were bigger and shaded out more area and this prevented shrubs from gathering. Paul looked up at the shadowy rows of apartment complexes that were built along the concourse, and he thought; 'All these buildings were apartments. Places full of people. Living above ground. So many buildings. Endless buildings. It doesn't seem real. It seems impossible.'

The rain began to fall. First, as a pitter-patter of heavy droplets. This signaled the men to reach for their rubber ponchos and put them on. Then, it came down as a torrential downpour. With hoods covering their helmets, the draping rain-gear made them look amorphous and inhuman. Like lost souls wandering through purgatory. By now dusk was upon them, and- with the shade and the rain- visibility was low. This had been a hypnotic trek up to this point. The anxiety of impending doom intermingled with static anticipation and anticlimax to create a mind-numbing effect. None of them dared to think they'd make it to their destination unmolested. And in this they were correct. For, as they deviated from the concourse they headed east and came upon a relatively open intersection with the remnants of urban shops on two corners; the gateway to and beginnings of their destination on a third corner- that is, a weedy cement sprawl with a brick gatehouse and an iron fence around the perimeter of some train tracks which led out to a wilderness with the wilderness itself being the

BLACK CAT SUNRISE

central feature of their- hopefully- soon to be domain which they were to be stationed around the perimeter of. And on the fourth corner of this open intersection there was a seven-story building that was taller than everything else in the immediate vicinity.

The one-hundred-man company marched in a file, two by two. In the driving rain, nobody heard the electronic groan of turret tracks as a laser cannon came out of hiding and positioned itself on the ledge of the seven-story building's rooftop. The weapon unleashed its double-barrelled fury and the soldiers scattered. The laser bolts were high energy and so fired slowly, but a slow firing laser was still scary fast. The blazing red bolts tore through the darkness and the men alike; blasting off limbs, creating gaping holes in chests, removing the tops of skulls, or maybe just burning gouges into muscle tissue. There were trees and cars available, and so they took cover behind these. Jacob and Paul had found a good spot behind a rusty old work van. A moment later and they could no longer hear the piercing chirp of the turret's discharging; nor the crashing impact of laser bolts colliding with whatever object was behind the targeted human.

"Hey, block the rain," Paul told Jacob. And Jacob stood over him so he could inspect the map. Doing this, he triangulated their position with their destination and the laser weapon; divining a new course to escape by. Over the rain they could hear men screaming in pain and shouting in confusion. But, also, he heard Terry calling, "Paul! Where you at, Paul?" And Paul shouted back. "Behind the van. You see the van?" Then lasers started raining down on them from another direction; from where they were not protected except by the trees that were growing up out of the

BLACK CAT SUNRISE

road. This was a laser rifle and it was shooting at some others close by. Close enough that the sound of laser bolts punching through meat was audible. Thankfully, Paul could clearly see the second story window which the bolts were coming out of. So, he pulled Jacob over to a better position; crouching low between the van and a car. Then he equipped his grenade launcher and dared to step out into the laser rifle's sights. It had to be done. In his head he calculated distance and trajectory and unleashed three fragmentation grenades at the window in question; blowing the building apart in that spot and carving out a cavern there. The dead body of a bushi lay in the rubble on the sidewalk below. And- surging with adrenaline- Paul didn't even realize he'd just fulfilled his highest ambition in life; killing a bushi. Jacob looked over his shoulder, saw the smoking ruin, punched Paul in the arm, and said, "Nice fucking shooting, bro." Smiling, Paul pulled Jacob back to the better spot behind the van, and called out, "Terry! Zach!" Terry came hurrying over wrapped in a mylar blanket. Zach called back, "I'm fucking pinned down!" Paul called back, "You ain't got no space blanket?" "No!" And then, somebody else inserted themselves in their conversation and said, "Just chill out! We got a M72 over here." And a moment later they heard the ignition of a rocket firing, the rasping soaring whistle as it flew off, and then the blast of the shell exploding into the laser turret; demolishing the thing.

With the threat neutralized, they came out of hiding; using red LED headlamps to survey the scene. They found the lieutenant crouched down beside a medic who was working on a soldier whose right leg had been shot off just under the knee. The maimed

BLACK CAT SUNRISE

man was unconscious. The medic had wrapped a tourniquet above the knee, and severed the ragged flesh and jagged bone with a gleaming steel cleaver and a flat wooden chopping block. Proceeding to then roast the wound with a blowtorch. 'It smells delicious. Hey. I'm hungry,' Paul thought, unthinkingly. Then, when the wound was cauterized, the medic sealed it up with jelly and bandages. The lieutenant ordered Jacob to make a stretcher out of tree branches and a tarp. As this was being done; the medic tended to some flesh wounds and the company got back into formation. Terry and Zach hauled the body. And they joined up with the fallen man's fireteam for the duration of the interim. There was no way to evacuate the wounded man; or, more accurately, it wasn't their way to backtrack for the sake of casualties. Unfortunately, he'd have to recover in the field. He'd lost a lot of blood, and his complexion was ghastly, but the medic had said he'd pull through if he stayed hydrated. And thankfully, it was raining and there'd be water available.

The brick gatehouse was locked up and overgrown and impenetrable. But the gate was only waist high; so a few guys stacked up some chunks of concrete and made a platform that everybody could easily jump over from. Now they were on train tracks. Turning off their headlamps, they followed these in night blindness. Soon they were passing by a university campus. It was there that they saw something nobody had anticipated but which they should have expected. There were strangers lingering in black prisoner clothes. Not many, but some. But in the windows of the buildings, staying out of the rain, there were many, and more. The captain called a halt and went over to

BLACK CAT SUNRISE

speak with these onlookers. There was a subway station with a canopy and the soldiers took shelter there while the captain drew the PoW camp survivors a map to guide them out to the wormhole. From there, they'd be safe. At least for a little while.

Ten minutes later and the troops were on their way; walking out into the rain that was intermittently a torrential downpour and a gentle shower. They went past a college sporting arena and then climbed up out of the train tracks; arriving at what used to be a botanical garden; or, so the signage indicated. Their maps told them that they were on the edge of a forest which stretched along a parkway with the devastation of the East Bronx on its eastern flank and a more amorphous border to the west; where they were. As far as forests go, it was a tiny thing, but in this place, it was a valuable asset to any men trying to subsist in the area. Such as Charlie company. This was where the company split up at. The fourth platoon went to a preparatory school. The second platoon went to a convention center. The first platoon went to a conservatory; where they were certain to be uncomfortable, surrounded by a botanical wonderland that had been more or less dead for about fifty years. And for some reason- perhaps one of those classic lapses in military logic- the third platoon was separated from the others' somewhat centralized locations and sent a full click further up the road to a library.

Adams' platoon had been angry about this decision when they realized what was happening, but when they got to the library itself, they felt overwhelmed by a sense of relief for a couple reasons; first, because their trekking was over and all they had

Richard Rose 272

BLACK CAT SUNRISE

to do now was to sit and wait for a fight or a plasmoid or a new marching order or a detail assignment. Second; because the library was enormous and beautiful and spacious. Hidden within vines and trees; it was an eighty-foot-tall building with white brick walls and pillars and two wings. Each wing with a depository attached to it. None of them knew how to read, but they could burn the books to stay warm; if they were so inclined. Out front, hiding inside some overgrowth- there was a fountain with a statue of baby angels riding horses that were going to trample over some naked people who were swimming with alligators. Paul remembered well the terror of being cut-off from reinforcement, and, too, he remembered the terror of being stalked by a ninja. So, it was nice that the building was nice, but it didn't matter because the situation was not nice at all. One death trap was much the same as another. A few men with machetes hacked through the vines to get to the entrance. Then others threw rocks through the glass of the doors and undid the locks. Then they all stepped inside.

Inside, their red headlamp beams displayed a forgotten facility caked in dust and cast in gloom. Overhead, high up, was a dome that was glass at its apex. There were complicated abstract statues which were offensive to the confederates' sensibilities because they couldn't understand what they were or why they were. They had no concept of art. Each fireteam possessed a heartbeat monitor but it was impossible to determine an accurate reading, because everybody was spreading out. All the same, it was evident nobody had been in this area because there would have been footprints in the dust. Upon further exploration, the platoon found that much of the building was a weird

BLACK CAT SUNRISE

museum, but always the artwork seemed stupid and frivolous to them.

Once they'd gotten settled in, and finished their assigned tasks, Paul and his team took up a position on the first floor- at the southeast wing; in a corner near the front yard. Nobody was particularly excited to venture up into the upper floors. They all wanted to stay close to the ground. Frank's team had assumed a position not far from Paul's team; stationed at a back corner with an overgrown parking lot outside the windows. Frank's team had the legless man; Steven- a small man, not taller than five-foot one inch, who wore wiry glasses made for kids, and who was drifting in and out of consciousness; drugged out on morphine. Frank was a nice enough guy. Quiet and unassuming. Average physique. Pale skinned. Pointy facial features. Carrying an AK107 with a 50 round drum magazine.

Lieutenant Adams dropped by Paul's unit to inspect their situation. There wasn't much to see. They watched him looking them over. And he said, somewhat unnecessarily, "I want one of you awake at all times. We had an easy day today. But we're not aware of what the enemy is aware of. Maybe they got eyes on us. Maybe they don't. If we get through the night, it should be a good day tomorrow."

And Terry said, "Yeah. A good day, or they hit us with a plasmoid."

"Right, or that. Anyway. We got the extraneous doors sealed shut and we got the rooftop door booby-trapped. So don't go up there. And we got the trip wire tight around the perimeter; so don't go outside. Except to the latrine. You all been to the latrine yet?"

And Zach said, "Yeah. I dug the thing. It's a great latrine. Best latrine ever."

Richard Rose 274

BLACK CAT SUNRISE

And Adams said, "Don't bullshit me, son. That latrine is mediocre and we both know it. Anyways. Sergeant McDouglas is out filtering water. So, he'll be coming by to get everybody a drink. Don't shoot him. Don't shoot anybody on our side, for fuck sake. He'll have his red light on. Other than that, keep it dark. It's night. We're all creeped out. Stay in your position. Keep your fingers crossed. Have a bite to eat. Get a drink. Get some sleep. First thing tomorrow, we'll be fortifying the perimeter. Paul. Nice shooting with that samurai. How did it feel?"

"I was just glad he was dead, sir. But, now that I think of it... dream come true, really."

"Yeah. I'd like to tag myself a samurai, one day. Fuck, I wish any of us could tag a goddamn ninja. Anyway. I'll see you in the morning, and hopefully not before then." And with that, Adams walked away.

"Who wants first watch?" Paul asked. This was a loaded question. First watch was the best for getting sleep if there wasn't any danger, but the later watches were the ones they wanted to be awake for if there was going to be some shit going down. While they were thinking about it, Zach said, "I'll take first."

Shortly thereafter, the sergeant came by with a five-gallon jug of water and a funnel. They drank their fill, hit the latrine, and pretty soon they were dozing on their backs on the hard marble floors; holding their guns even as they slept. It was quiet. But the rain fell outside and Zach was happy to hear it. It was a nice sound and it gave him something to listen to. Somewhere in the distance, a plasmoid struck the earth like the hammer of a god. This woke all but the deepest sleepers, but they didn't think much of it and so went back to sleep. Zach's watch ended and Jacob

BLACK CAT SUNRISE

took over. In the quiet night's silence, he remembered the shrieking of the wraiths. Thinking back on the city, it seemed like they were in paradise now; just to be out of there. But again, a plasmoid or a dondon struck the earth with a ferocious impact and again the others awoke. The impact again seemed distant, but at the same time, too close to be pushed out of mind. Paul radioed the lieutenant; "That's not our company, is it?"

Adams radioed back, "No. It's not our company, but it is our battalion. North north-west. By that other forest up there." Paul communicated this information to the others; who were watching him. Then they went back to sleep. Terry took the next watch and Jacob was unconscious as soon as he put his head down to slumber. Then they heard an explosion and it woke them all. This hadn't come from a plasmoid from the sky. It had come from a claymore mine at the front door. Paul said, "On your feet, soldiers. We got a live one." And Jacob said, "You mean a dead one?" Throughout the building; the other soldiers were also standing and gripping their guns. Except for one-legged Steven who would pass out every time his eyes opened. Red headlamps flashed around as the men searched the building. Paul decided this might be a good time to try out the night vision goggles, which he'd been reluctant to do, heretofore. Then he said, "I'll go and come back. Hold our position." Then he was gone; clutching his MP5 and walking slowly and quietly. Frank- also begoggled- too, was joining him. The scene in the goggles was green, but the image was smooth and clear. They found the lieutenant and the sergeant and a few others standing around and observing. The front door had been blasted inward because the claymore had been mounted on it. The

Richard Rose 276

BLACK CAT SUNRISE

smoke was still clearing, but Paul could see a scorch mark on the cement beyond the threshold as well as a man blown to pieces in a fan shaped pattern all across the stairs and out over the driveway.

"Looks like it was a slave, don't it?" the sergeant asked. And the lieutenant agreed, saying, "Frank, here's another claymore. There's the wire. Reset the trip wire. We'll cover you." This was done and they went back inside and then Sergeant McDouglas- a tall white skinned man who looked like he might be literally starving; so skinny with eyes so sunken, and whom carried an M4 with an M203 on it- asked, "So, what do we do now?" And the lieutenant said, "Let's just go back to sleep." And the sergeant asked, "You don't think there's a ninja? Or a hex?" And the lieutenant said, "Could be. Could be they know we're here and they're going to hit us with a plasmoid. Unless we all want to go sleep out in the rain, I don't know what else we can do."

And Paul said, "Sir, we should split up the men. Cover more ground. Make it harder to take us out all at once. Put up a fight, if we can." And Adams said, "Alright. Let's do that. But if we're doing it, then we better do it right. Open up the closed off areas. Tell your guys to hide as best as they can but emphasize that they are not to shoot at anything unless they know exactly what it is." None of them had wanted to say it, but they were all thinking it; 'Ninja, ninja, ninja.' This was night time, after all. But still, there were worse things than ninjas.

Paul told his crew the orders and they went out into the library's book depository. The books were still there. Floor upon floor and row upon row of countless shelves of books. Zach asked Paul, "Paul. If there's a

BLACK CAT SUNRISE

ninja out there, and he's killing our platoon; are we supposed to stay here and hide, or are we supposed to go fight it." And Paul said, "As far as I know, nobody in the entire army has killed even a single ninja. And the ninja have killed thousands of us. If you want to go fight it, then go fight it. But I'm not going to force anybody to go and die." And Terry said, "Then why don't we jump out the window and hide in the trees." And Zach said, "Wouldn't be right. Disrespectful to the dead." And Terry said, "We'll be the dead, if we stay here." And Jacob said, "Let's call hiding in the trees Plan B. At least if we stay here, maybe we can trap it." With that in mind, they hid behind desks and flipped over tables and Paul positioned each man so that they could create as much crossfire as the book stacks would allow for.

Not long after, there was another explosion. Muffled and distant but intense enough to rattle their brains. A claymore's ball bearings shattered windows and tore the building's walls apart. This blast had come from the rooftop. And then they knew for certain. Slaves don't descend upon you from above, but the ninja do. Shortly thereafter there came a few bursts of automatic gunfire. Paul received a transmission from Adams. 'It's here. The ninja's here. Good luck, boys.' And Paul whispered, "It's here. It's a ninja." Nobody said anything but their stomachs turned with fear. Paul remembered that this strategy had worked for them last time. The ninja wasn't willing to fight them when they were ready and waiting for it. He wondered why it had sent that slave into an obvious trap. But it wasn't his place to know the mind of a creature of the night. Probably reconnaissance, he figured.

BLACK CAT SUNRISE

And in that, he was half correct. The ninja knew there were men in there. It was obvious from the mutilated vegetation at the entryway. The ninja also knew there was a dorei nearby; across the street in an old police department. The ninja wasn't interested in getting close enough to visually confirm the existence of a trap. If the slave could march in unhindered; great. If it set off the trap, he'd lose the element of surprise on one hand, but he'd make them afraid on the other and that was advantageous in its own way. Or so the ninja reasoned. When the enemy rewired the trap, the ninja understood better how he'd made a tactical error, but it was what he had chosen, and so he decided to follow through lest he be accused of wasting the dorei for no reason. It was now imperative it be demonstrated that wasting a dorei and alarming the target was beneficial to his purposes. Or else he'd be judged poorly by his superiors.

With that in mind, he jumped out of a treetop and landed on the roof. The rain poured on him, and it was night, so it was cold out; but his uniform was waterproof, windproof, and warm. Here, too, was another booby trap. A wire and a claymore mine. He didn't have to set it off, but, again, he wanted to. So, he jumped to a different area and- using his void generator- he hit the wire's bracket with a singularity; exploding the mine. Then he disappeared a section of rooftop to create a hole through which to enter the library. However, before he could use it, the heishi inside was shooting a machine gun up through the ceiling- albeit at the wrong area- and so the ninja had to jump to a completely different section of the rooftop.

Chapter 16
Kunoichi

At this corner of the rooftop, the ninja was able to make another hole, and safely inspect it, and safely drop down into it. Thinking that maybe if he admitted he had made a mistake, then they would forgive him and not inflict demerits for the sloppy work he was doing in this place. He'd done good work before. He could do good work again. This place was a failed experiment. But he could still make it right. Listening; he heard the soldiers listening. And he tried to sense where they were hiding. The room he was in was an art exhibit. Or, it used to be. The floors were carpeted. He wouldn't hear footsteps easily. The corridors seemed to be like a maze; as there were several jutting out of that area. He drew his black-bladed tanto. The next part required patience. Or, maybe not. He stalked to the main- larger- exit of the room he had come down into. Some foolish soldier came creeping through the hall and the ninja spotted him in his tiny mirror. Probably, the man had been drawn to the sound of rain falling through the ceiling. Either way, the ninja drove his blade in through the throat and out through the brainstem and dragged the limp body into the room with him. Taking the grenades and clipping the pouch to his body; he pulled the trigger on the soldier's machine gun and released a burst of fire into the wall. Then he watched in the mirror as another man came to investigate the area. The ninja stepped into the hall and fired a singularity into the man's chest and he fell dead in a bloody mess with a disgusting hole about the middle of him. With the flopping dead weight of the departed having had made a gruesome thud; yet another man came to the deadly corridor; this one

BLACK CAT SUNRISE

more resolute and foolhardier. But the ninja- having located what hall they were coming out of- repositioned himself so as that he was behind this next heishi when he came through; and then he drove a spike through the man's ear protection and took his grenades, as well. Now he had 6 grenades and this was excessive, so he found the stairwell and examined it quickly with his mirror; indeed finding yet another soldier hiding in there. Hurriedly, the ninja armed and threw a grenade at him. This left the heishi with no choice but to flee toward the ninja who was waiting with his tanto; driving it up into the man's chest as a booming explosion shook the building to its foundation. With the dying man convulsing at his feet, he threw another grenade down the center of the stairwell as a means of attacking whoever may or may not be standing at the bottom. He slowly backed away- to where he'd made a hole in the ceiling- and then jumped back up onto the roof. From there, he stepped over the ledge and wafted eighty feet to the ground. Choosing an arbitrary spot, he shot two singularities into the wall and waited for gunfire or commotion, but there was none. So then he stepped inside and crept into the next room over, to where the rain wasn't so loud. And here he listened. And he heard whispering. And he ascertained where it was coming from in a general sort of way. Tip-toeing toward these unintelligible voices. By the time they stopped speaking, he could guess where they were. In rooms like offices, but for study. This entire hallway was lined with these. But he narrowed the target down to just one or two of them. Both of which had closed doors. A closed door was a simple obstacle but it presented a serious problem. Opening a door may seem like a

BLACK CAT SUNRISE

quick and easy thing, but in a combat scenario, that one or two second difference would mean the difference between life and death. So, instead of attacking them directly, he threw a grenade into an unoccupied room nearby. When it exploded; one of the men was foolish enough to come running out- as the other was calling after him; "Don't go out there!" The ninja did two things; he armed a grenade and threw it behind the bolting heishi and through the open door from which said bolting heishi had emerged. And then he rushed at the running man and thrust a spike into his brain through his ear. The active grenade exploded as the secondary combatant was making for the hallway; the force of which sent the heishi flying into a wall at breakneck speed. This heishi may or may not have been dead, but the ninja drove his tanto through the throat to be sure, and it turned out he was indeed alive because his eyes shot open and he jerked, choked, gurgled, and spasmed as the lifeblood gushed out of him. About twenty seconds later and the heishi was lying still. The ninja stepped into a room that was closer to the stairs and he listened. The material over his ears offered protection from high decibels but allowed low decibels to pass through without resistance. So, he knew the teki were coming down on him. Two, by the sound of it. By the sound of it, nobody else was moving in the vicinity. But, they could certainly be hidden close by. The teki methodology had evolved over the past couple days. But, too, they were still swimming into his open jaws all the same. Two heishi arrived at the bottom of the steps and hurried toward their fallen companions. They didn't see him hiding behind an open door, watching them through its rectangular window, waiting for the right

BLACK CAT SUNRISE

moment, and then stepping out and firing a string of singularities into them before they could even aim their rifles at him. A head fell from a body as a neck disappeared into a void. An arm came off as a portion of a chest disappeared. Portions of the waist. Portions of the hip. Blood pooled beneath the discombobulated carcasses. The ninja walked back into the study room and thought of how many heishi teki he'd killed here so far. About eight. So, he could assume that 17 remained. Probably less, but possibly 17. Then he had an idea; looking upward- he fired a string of singularities up into the ceiling over his head; removing the floors, the ceilings, the debris, the display cases, the furniture, the falling books. Over and over, he shot these voids upward until after about thirty seconds the rain was raining on him and he could see clear out into the night sky. Now, he didn't hesitate; he lifted straight up through these eight floors. Looking around as he went; locating at least two more men. Then, he stood over the hole; looking down through. The nearest soldier was two floors below, and so would have to shoot through a significant mass of material to hit the ninja. This was not attempted. What was attempted was what was anticipated. With his void generator pointed down into the hole, the ninja waited. Soon, a head appeared; a helmet with a black face and bright white teeth. The rain was getting in the heishi eyes as the ninja fired a singularity into him. The helmet and the head disappeared altogether. The body; hanging half over the edge of the hole and draining its blood to the floor far below. The ninja knew this zone was becoming questionable and unstable. There were a couple solutions to the problem which the enemy's strength was confronting him with. First option: Leave,

Richard Rose 283

BLACK CAT SUNRISE

and call in an airstrike to wipe the library off the map. This wouldn't gain him any prestige. Second option: He could fight his way through these men with grenades and singularities. That would gain some prestige. But, in order to extract maximum prestige from this particular offensive; there was only one option. The third option: Ninjutsu traditional fighting style. Steel. Stealth. Surprise. That'd be the only way to rectify this botched operation. So that was what he must do. And with that in mind, he jumped over to the opposite end of the structure. To the south south-east end. Where he knew they weren't looking for him at. Then he heard a window break. Peaking over the edge of the building, he saw a soldier down there; fleeing or changing position or possibly hastily searching. The ninja stepped over the edge and floated down through the rain- adjusting his trajectory to intercept that of the man. At the last instant he dropped upon him and drove his tanto down through the neck and into the heart. The soldier gave three of four jolts and then died. From this spot, the ninja saw the window which had been broken open and through which the soldier had made his escape. Ducking over to over there; he listened to what was going on inside. Hearing nothing; he checked the area in the mirror. This was tricky because of the rain, but he managed. There were two men in there. One laid out and injured; asleep- by the look of it. The other- rifle in hand- guarding the injured one. The ninja fired a singularity at the bracket that was holding the tripwire that would set off the claymore and the supersonic explosion lit up the night and made the earth shake beneath his feet. Checking the mirror again, the ninja saw the able-bodied individual walking away from the injured man and

BLACK CAT SUNRISE

now this soldier's back was to him and so he was vulnerable. Three seconds later there was a hatpin in that man's brain and the ninja was inside again. The injured man remained unconscious. An abstract statue gave the ninja a place to hide behind as footsteps could be heard to be coming from multiple directions. The nearest heishi came out of one of several corridors and the ninja caught him off guard and drove the tanto up under his chin and into his brain. There was a help desk close by and so the ninja ducked behind it to stay out of sight; hauling the victim out of sight with him-trailing a negligible blood trail. Two more men entered this main foyer. Walking together and carrying machine guns; turning their heads and searching all around, but staying close together as they went. They didn't see the previous victim's blood because they were focused on the smoke from the explosion. They stopped looking around and began peering into the darkness outside. The ninja lunged forward and thrust a hatpin into the ear of the man on the right and then grasped the helmet strap of the other with his left hand; pulling back on it and throwing his victim off balance completely. With his right hand he drove his tanto down into the heart through the throat. Unfortunately, in dying, the man's finger had squeezed his weapon's trigger and now the machine gun was releasing a magazine full of ammunition into the walls and into the ceiling. Glass began falling from the dome above, but the ninja was already darting out into the night, and so escaped before a glass shard could cut him down.

It was early morning, and they felt the time to depart was upon them. It would have been better to go

BLACK CAT SUNRISE

in the night. But day time had advantages, as well. Conducting operations had carried on in such a way that Kazuki kept insisting upon personally monitoring the drones; vigilantly searching the tablets for any troop formations that were worth firing on. And, also, she was too invested in the dorei and the bushi to walk away before she was assured the confederate strength had been adequately weakened. And to that end, she was never satisfied, but she did what she could. Now, Maya had declared they were to evacuate, and that was that. Every hour the teki were bringing more heavy machinery into the field and the situation grew ever more precarious.

They stood at the vertical lift in the stainless-steel tube station of the underground bunker; about to step in and ride to the surface. They wore parachutes strapped to their backs, and white jumpsuits instead of regular clothes- with warm garments underneath; and they had on white jump helmets with the hinomaru over the forehead. Void generating devices had been sewn into the fabric about their wrists. They carried minimal baggage in duffel bags. But Xander- as he reached out to press the button- felt a bad feeling sweep across him. Pressing the button, the steel doors opened, and the air rushed over them. Xander turned and told Kazuki; "Hey. I'm very proud of the young woman you've become. You're the best thing that ever happened to me. I've been blessed to be your father. You're going to make a ferocious majo, one day. And I love you. More than words can express."

Of course, Maya and Moto heard this, but they didn't say anything. Instead, they exchanged a despondent glance. Knowing what Xander was thinking, and feeling the same. Feeling the same

BLACK CAT SUNRISE

ominous burden of imminent danger. Wanting to say so much, and so saying nothing instead. But, too, Maya was bothered that Xander would betray the knowledge of their perilous predicament to Kazuki. Kazuki took it in stride, and said, "I love you, too, dada. And I love you, mama. And I love you, too, auntie." And Maya and Moto told her they loved her, too, and they all forced smiles as they stepped into the lift. Then the doors closed and they shot upward.

They came out of the lift in a cluster. The tube opened into an unassuming building at the edge of a landing pad on Rikers. Kazuki stopped to hug her father- and she hugged her aunt and her mother, too. They found themselves exposed to the open air for the first time in a long time. It was rainy and gusty and that must have been cleansing the air of smoke, because the city was visibly burning in every direction. The brackish east river sprawled out around them; vast and gray and salt-scented. The drone hangers were nearby, but hidden beneath parking lots. On this landing pad- still marked with a yellow 'H'- there were two flight pods waiting for them. Hurrying; they wasted no time. The flight pods were two seaters, so Xander and Moto split off toward one craft and Maya and Kazuki took the other.

These pods resembled futuristic helicopters with no propellers and they had bulbous bulletproof windows wrapping around the front and these allowed for a 270-degree view. Each unit was attended by reprogrammed AD-14s that flew too fast to be shot down, and by kuki drones that flew too high to be shot down but low enough to cover them with laser fire, and also by umi drones that were protected by the water. Even humble security drones had been

BLACK CAT SUNRISE

retrofitted with void generators and reprogrammed to shadow their evacuation from ground level. So, as they lifted up into the sky, there was a veritable swarm of activity surrounding them.

The antigravity drives silently lifted them into the sky. As soon as they were up above the skylines and tree lines, they were immediately greeted by the firing of anti-aircraft guns; M61 Vulcan gatling guns mounted on tracked armored personnel carriers and M45 quadmount fifty calibers and 40mm Bofors, as well. The tracers flew all around them but the sky was big and the bullets missed and the guns were exploding just seconds after opening fire as the kuki honed in on them with laser bolts and the AD-14s descended upon the crews of the weapons. Similarly; a barrage of red-hot surface to air missiles and orange-white hot air to air missiles were coming at them from all around; but these were also destroyed by the laser bolts. But the motion of the AD-14s flitting about wildly was disturbing the flight pod guidance system and they were veering off course; decidedly to the north.

Kazuki saw her first- a woman wearing black; falling out of the sky- and she cried out, "Mama!" But the woman- the majo; she wasn't coming at them. She was heading for Xander and Moto. Kazuki didn't know who it was, or if she was friend or foe; but Maya knew immediately and said nothing. The only thing Maya could maybe do to avert disaster was to take over the pod's controls; but she wasn't good at operating these things and Kazuki had never learned.

Moto knew how to fly them, though, and she, too, had noticed the majo descending through the rainy overcast sky. Moto took control and initiated

BLACK CAT SUNRISE

evasive maneuvers. But the majo was made of nothing and flew through the air like a marlin swims in the water. And Moto saw that even as she dipped, and dashed, and darted, and rose, and dove and twisted and turned; the majo was always on her. Moto looked to the old woman, and saw. It was Helga. The old woman of the kovun teki. This previously cheerful old face was now a mask of malice and maliciousness. Moto watched her and she watched Moto watching her. The majo's black gown rippled in the whipping winds. Her long white hair trailed her haggard old face. Her wrinkled bare feet dangled in the blustering draft of her body. And Moto watched as Helga reached her hand toward the flight pod; a bony hand with just a veneer of skin. Xander gripped the armrest and watched the women watching each other. His body; frozen with terror. And Helga was looking Moto dead in the eye when she suddenly clenched her outstretched fist. In that instant; the anti-gravity drive disengaged and the pod lost power.

And Moto said to Xander, "We have to jump! Now!" And Xander, said, "Hai," because this was self-evident. His stomach sunk as the pod fell like a penny thrown off the Empire State building. Moto pulled the red latch. The pod's window popped off, caught the wind, and blew away. They undid their safety belts, stood up through the G-forces pinning them down, and got violently sucked out into the sky; opening their parachutes immediately thereafter. Their altitude was about one kilometer.

"Mama. I'm scared," Kazuki said.

And Maya said, "Don't be afraid. Anata wa kunoichi desu yo." A refrain from Kazuki's childhood. The nihongo words meaning, 'You are a lady ninja!'

BLACK CAT SUNRISE

Helga bore down upon them. And Kazuki was suddenly appalled to realize she'd been foolish enough to believe this woman was her friend. Helga had been so nice when they met. Even Obachan liked her. She was Obachan's friend, too... Kazuki thought. As if reading her mind, Helga looked Kazuki in the eye and drew her decrepit finger across her waddled throat in a threatening gesture. Then Kazuki remembered why she hated these people and she was suddenly as angry as she'd ever been.

Helga saw Kazuki's reaction to her and this caused the old majo to smile grimly as she reached out a grasping hand and clenched her fist and destroyed the anti-gravity drive of this flight pod as well. In that instant, a sparkling white blur appeared from nowhere; crashing into Helga and sending her tumbling through the sky; the black cloak and the white cloak spinning like a yin-yang through the air. Kazuki and Maya were spiraling downward, and Maya shouted; "We're jumping! Try to land where I land!" And then she pulled the red latch and the window popped off. They undid their safety belts and gracelessly half-leapt and half-spewed out into the sky. The wind was roaring and the raindrops felt like needle pricks as they pelted her. Kazuki pulled the handle of her parachute. The fabric was flung out into the air behind her. The chords caught and jerked her harness. There was a tremendous whooshing as her descent slowed. Looking around, she saw the world in slow-motion; taking it all in in a single glance. The parachute was white with a giant hinomaru on it. Very subtle. The teki majo was plummeting to the earth; fighting with Kazuki's Obachan. Her aunt and father; far away and small and almost impossible to see against the scenery of the

BLACK CAT SUNRISE

sprawling city. Wild tracer bullets glowed in the dim light and danced with the radiant laser bolts that were seeking out their sources. Their flight pod; exploding against the asphalt- far below. And her mother; frantically waving at her- inaudibly calling for her attention. And when Maya saw that Kazuki was seeing her, she pointed and made a circle with her hand; indicating a pond. There was ice on it, and the ice probably wasn't safe, but it was the only place where there weren't trees to be impaled on or buildings to be broken against.

This wasn't the first time Kazuki had parachuted. During peace time- or what passed for peace time- they had done this for fun on several occasions. She never wondered why her mother wanted her to know how to maneuver a parachute, but, in retrospect, it made sense. And Kazuki suddenly remembered who she was. And she renewed her lifelong vow- promising herself that if she lived through this, she would devote her life to exterminating the teki and she wouldn't cease or even ease up until there wasn't a man, woman, or child remaining who might call themself a confederate or wear the symbol of the hissing black cat. And there wasn't a witch on earth or in heaven who would stand between her and her calling. Now, the ground was coming at her faster; so she steered toward the water. Or the ice. Not knowing which it was. Careful to aim closer to the shoreline.

Moto had been flung out over the Bronx; a burning battleground of a sprawling and uninhabited cityscape overgrown with trees and vegetation and decorated with raging structure fires. In some areas it

BLACK CAT SUNRISE

was a moonscape of smoldering craters; such as in the East Bronx. There was no way for her to maneuver her parachute to the water. She'd have to try to come down in a tree. Better to smash into a tree than to smash into a building or a house. There was a park she could aim for. But it was more like a small forest. Moto felt overwhelmed by a livid rage gnawing at her raw mind as well as by a callous and unfeeling disbelief in her heart; to have seen the other pod falling out of the sky, and her niece and her sister parachuting into the warzone. They were so far away; there was nothing she could do for them. Not right then, anyway. Xander, too, was somehow descending in a completely different area than her. She could see his parachute but he was exceedingly far off. Moto had no idea how she could possibly hope to find him, but, once she landed she'd be able to communicate with him through a link sewn into her suit. Moto and Xander both knew every bushi stronghold by rote and there were dozens in every area; so she figured she'd find one and he would find one, too. And then they could find each other. And then together they could find her sister and niece.

As Moto aimed the parachute for the tiny forest, she couldn't help but notice there were heishi teki marching hither and thither like trails of ants. It didn't strike her as immediately important, because her mind was preoccupied with the task at hand; finding the most welcoming evergreen in the forest and steering herself into it. It didn't occur to her- the danger- until the bullet ripped into and out of her torso; punching through bone and organs alike. A heishi teki down on the ground had stopped in place, told the man next to him, 'Hey, watch this,' lifted his sniper rifle, aimed, led the target- Moto- and then fired in that single instant

BLACK CAT SUNRISE

which he knew he had had her. It was a powerful bullet and it killed her instantly. The soldier never considered he might be gunning down bakufu royalty, or the commander of the samurai. He hardly even noticed it was a woman, and was just thinking how Japs look like women. It was clearly a Jap; as evidenced by the giant Japanese flag of a parachute. He'd shot her from over a hundred yards away. They weren't going to diverge from their route to go pull a dead Jap out of a tree. And that's where she was. And that's where she'd stay. In a conifer. In the tree she'd been aiming for. Her parachute tangled up high. Her body dangling down low. Her white parachute; stained with the red of the hinomaru. Her white jumpsuit stained with the red of her blood. Her eyes closed. A serene smile on her face. Her world was so ugly. She'd always wanted to die. Death was so beautiful.

Xander only barely knew how to control his parachute. He collided with the canopy of a maple and fell down through all the branches; landing on a decrepit old car. The parachute was tangled up overhead. As he fell through the tree; Impact after impact had made him see shocking sparkling visions of light. The pain was extreme and he felt a suffocating darkness pulling him down into sleep; but he forced himself to become aware. Even though his body was seizing with throbbing agony. To become aware of what; he didn't know. He didn't know where he was, or how to get help. There was a comlink in his clothes. He tapped the code and pressed it; not thinking about his extreme pain or his exposed position out in the middle of who knows where and presumably surrounded by teki. "Moto? Maya? Zuki-chan?" There was no

BLACK CAT SUNRISE

response. He hadn't seen what had happened to them. There was a tension in his eyes; a sensation like he could cry for his daughter. And a pressure in his chest gripped his faculties as he began to exchange hope for quiet desperation. A crushing feeling of helplessness and defeat. A tremendous sense of loss. Sitting up; he knew a rib was broken. Maybe two or three ribs were broken. Struggling with the stabbing pain; he succeeded in getting to his feet. A second later; he heard boots stomping toward him- wet snow sloshing. And then there was a rifle in his face. And then there were heishi teki standing all around him. Ten or fifteen angry black cats on as many red patches sewn on as many uniforms. He'd worn that patch, too, once upon a time, and he remembered well the sacred words; 'war to live, live to war.'

A grim looking soldier smoking a cigar came up to him and they examined each other. Xander had known a thousand guys like him; when he was younger. Mean, hard, cold; blue-eyed, blonde-haired, jar-headed, square-jawed, squinting, sneering, and hostile. Xander didn't know what to do. He put his hands up; even though it hurt to. They were in a street, but it seemed like they were in the woods. The streets and the woods were one and the same thing, apparently. The teki officer had two stripes on his collar, and he commenced questioning him, "What's your name, sir?" "Xander." "Xander. Why you done fell out the sky just now?" "Sir. With all due respect. I'm not going to share my business with you. I am obviously with the bakufu. Look at my helmet. I obviously just parachuted into occupied territory. If you want to know more than that, then you can deliver me to your superiors. I'll have to speak with your

BLACK CAT SUNRISE

commanding officer. Or, just kill me now. It makes no difference."

Then Xander's shirt collar started talking. 'Dada! Auntie!'

This caught the captain's attention, of course. He drew his knife, reached for the shirt, cut out the comlink, and inspected it. Not knowing how to use it. Not knowing it required a tap code. Kazuki's voice came through again, 'Dada! Auntie! Mama says to be quiet. Call me if you're there.'

And the captain offered it back to Xander, saying, "You're here. Call her back."

And Xander said, "It wouldn't be right, sir. You understand."

The captain replied, "I don't understand nothing." And then he threw the comlink into a puddle and continued, "I don't have time to deal with you. Xander. Whoever you are. Whoever your kid is. Her mama. Her auntie. I don't know. And I don't care. Greg! You and your fireteam. You'll have to join up with another outfit. I need you to... deliver... this guy to the Lieutenant Colonel. I don't know who he is; but he ain't no ordinary neep. And he ain't no samurai, neither. Probably a pencil pusher or something. Whoever he is; he fell out of the sky, and that ain't normal. Search him. And then drag his ass back to the underground. Get him to the lieutenant colonel. Expressly. That's an order. Dismissed."

Chapter 17
Specter
Helga had succeeded in preempting Yoshiko; who wasn't able to precognate the teki majo's intentions. But, when Helga attacked Moto; this

BLACK CAT SUNRISE

disturbed Yoshiko's stasis and she sped into action; manifesting in the clouds and bearing down upon Helga. By this time, Yoshiko could see that Helga had already disabled both of the attack pods and her descendants were compelled to parachute downward. The rain drops moved through her like she wasn't there. And the city was a blur below; as she descended like a falcon. Yoshiko's skeletal fingers morphed into moonlit talons. Her mouth spread wide- practically to her ears- and her teeth morphed into a gnashing array of over one hundred slender moonlit spikes. Her eyes glowed radiantly purple and blue and white- flashing like an arc welder. She struck Helga like a bullet; driving her off into the distance in a flailing and spinning mess of thrashing and snarling. Two individuals who could teleport through solid ground and effortlessly fly through the sky; they were nonetheless susceptible to the forces of their equals. Yoshiko sunk her teeth into the back of Helga's neck; biting down with crushing pressure. And she dug her talons into the teki majo's shoulder and flank; drawing no blood but disrupting the conduit of the flux of phantasmosis. Helga's face, too, took on a ghoulish transformation; her eyes emitted a smoldering orange radiation- and her mouth became a swirling vortex of blazing orange-red and glistening black; emitting a high-pitched monotone. Helga's frail fingers turned jet black and stretched out in long and thin tendrils that became wrapped around Yoshiko and penetrated her with needling tips. Now Helga seethed with volatility. Pulsating with a repellent energy that ionized the air and created an arcing specter between them. This neon green specter glowed vibrantly at Yoshiko's hands and mouth. As well as at ten points inside of her body. It

BLACK CAT SUNRISE

was essentially the only possible way they could harm one another; but it hurt Helga as much as it hurt Yoshiko. They didn't definitively fall, because they were also floating. And they didn't definitively float, because they were also falling. When the specter was flowing into Yoshiko, they were driven earthward. But when the current of the specter reversed, they were lifted skyward. And Yoshiko continued to bite down like a pitbull; undeterred. Even though Helga's tendrils had pierced her at points all over her body with penetrating and squirming fingertips that jolted with an interdimensional voltage. And now they were locked together; and drifting out to sea on the winds. Both were helpless to defy the other. Nor could either possibly undo the cosmic entanglement they'd unleashed upon one another. They tremored and spasmed and started and shuddered and convulsed and kicked and bucked and jerked and at times became still. The fight was draining them of the phantasmagorical charge which allowed them to exist in this world to begin with. Not long thereafter and they were all but still. Yoshiko's teeth and claws; buried in her enemy- who used to be her friend. Helga's snaking tendrils embedded in her enemy, who'd believed she was her friend. Helga had always known; Yoshiko was evil. Yoshiko never thought of herself as evil, and so couldn't see why her dark sister would think that. But, she reflected- as they drifted in stillness and silence, out over the ocean- she remembered that her mother had once warned her this might happen. But it was just an offhand remark, and one made so long ago. When she was still human. A simple remark; 'Never trust the majo teki. They will love you as a sister and then strike you down when you

BLACK CAT SUNRISE

are vulnerable.' And Yoshiko simply hadn't given it much thought at the time. Perhaps she always knew, and chose to remain willfully ignorant in order to retain some semblance of a sense of control over her domain. The majo of the teki coven were deceptive, by nature. This was known. Meanwhile, the majo of the bakufu kovun were brutally honest; with no use for trickery. At any rate; Yoshiko was fading away. With her teeth buried in Helga's neck. Still, she refused to believe this animosity could be real. Even if her and the majo teki were set against each other; they were of a single essence. And this essence was separate from this world. And it had an agenda higher than the agenda of this world. Like the agenda of fire, to consume. Or the agenda of liquid, to be fluid. The phantasm yearned to break free of its confinement beyond the veil. Yoshiko wondered what part of her remained human; an old question, amplified in this cruel moment. She knew sisters fight. She was wondering if sisters forgive. Surely they must. Or else, they'd be angry forever. And then Yoshiko felt it, and she knew; Moto was dead. And in that instant; the two majo disappeared. Back into the ether from whence they had come.

Paul and his fireteam had just woken up. Upon a tarp set between hastily dug drainage trenches. Beneath a shelter of mylar blankets which they'd strung in the trees. For warmth, they slept in a tangle- like a clutch of flying squirrels. Last night, back in the library, when they'd heard the telltale sounds of their companions being slaughtered; Paul ordered his team to jump out of the window and run to the woods to hide. They ran and ran until they reached a body of water. Then they stopped. And it was a good thing they

BLACK CAT SUNRISE

had done this; because not long afterward a kinetic projectile struck the library like a meteor; obliterating the structure entirely. Brick and rock and steel and dirt came raining down upon them, but the grove of fully grown evergreen trees protected them from the worst of it.

The rain hadn't stopped, but it was daytime now, and they didn't think the slaves or the samurai would be out in these trees. So they made a fire to get warm by and with which to dry their clothes before beginning their trek back to find another unit to fall into. It was a relatively quiet morning; gunshots and explosions could be heard in the distance, but the trees muffled that some. The fire was going hot now after a tedious struggle to get the wet wood blazing. And they heard a sound coming from overhead. They stood up and clutched their weapons. They were near enough to the water's edge that they could sense what was happening, even if they couldn't see it. A paratrooper. Immediately, Paul's team was on its feet and hurrying over. They held their weapons at the ready. But what they saw was disarming. It was a woman. An older Japanese woman. And Terry said, "It's a fucking Jap. I'm taking the shot." And as he raised his weapon, Paul reached out and put a hand on the barrel and pushed it down. Telling Terry, "That's a woman, Terry. We don't kill women." And this enraged Terry, who then said, "It's a fucking Jap. We kill Japs. Don't fuck with me Paul." But Paul didn't move his hand and restated himself, "Terry, stand down. That's an order."

Terry released the grip of the M240 and punched Paul in the nose. A gushing torrent of blood burst from Paul's face as he spilled bodily into the branches of the underbrush. Then Terry again lifted his

BLACK CAT SUNRISE

weapon to fire, but before he could, Jacob pulled his pistol out of its holster and shot Terry in the head at point blank range. The bullet entered through the brainstem and exited through the top of the helmet; ejaculating white chunks of bone, grey bits of brain, and a red spray of blood. Terry toppled to the ground in a heap. Then a second parachute came swooshing down onto the wet ice. Jacob pointed the pistol at Zach and Zach put his hands up in the air and said, "Hey, man. I don't care what you do. I'm a mechanic, not a fighter. But, yo, look." And the mechanic pointed out onto the water, to where the Japanese woman was. And now she had with her a stunningly beautiful young lady; with crazy windblown curls of brown hair, slanted black eyes, high cheekbones, blood-red lips, pale skin, and rosy cheeks. There were the red circles of Japanese flags on all of their gear. And they were looking toward Paul's fireteam; pointing their fists and clutching their wrists. Evidently aiming some strange weapon.

Paul was getting up to his feet. Blood had gotten into his eyes and he was staggering; trying to regain equilibrium. He'd heard the shot, and gleaned what had happened. Wiping his eyes; he saw Terry's corpse. Then he saw the woman and the young lady. Being in the woods, it was easy to see out over the ice. Out on the ice, it was difficult to see back into the forest. Knowing this, and knowing the gunshot must have frightened them; Paul called out, "We're not going to hurt you! We just want to talk! Lower your weapons!"

And Maya called back, "We will talk, but we will not lower our weapons!"

Richard Rose 300

BLACK CAT SUNRISE

And Paul called back, "That's fine! We're used to it! You should get off the ice! Before it breaks! We have a fire going here! You're welcome to share it!"

Maya considered his words. She considered that they were soaking in freezing water and sitting on thin ice. And then she helped Kazuki to unlatch her parachute and Kazuki helped her to unlatch her own. Then the two females walked over to the shoreline. And Paul said, "Jacob, you keep your gun on them. Zach, help me drag these chutes off the ice, so nobody sees them." This was easily done, as the chutes were close to the shore.

The soldiers led them away. Maya and Kazuki had come from a climate-controlled environment, and fallen through the winter sky, and landed in puddles of freezing water; so, their teeth were chattering, their cheeks were windburned, and their numb fingers were aching in their gloves. Kazuki was shocked to see the dead body, but Maya was able to intuit what had happened here, and so when Kazuki jumped back, she just squeezed her hand and- in gasping freezing breaths- said, "Come on."

Zach threw more and more dead branches on the fire and for many minutes Maya and Kazuki squatted and knelt and stooped and bent in weird positions over the fire; drying the different areas of their soaking clothing. Which is exactly what the soldiers had been doing all morning. After a while, when she could breathe normally again, Maya asked Paul, "So. What did you want to talk about?"

"Who are you?" Paul asked.

"We are your enemy," she replied.

"Yes. I can see that. But, why did you fall out of the sky?"

BLACK CAT SUNRISE

And Maya said, "I will tell you, but first, you tell me. Where is your commanding officer?"

"Dead. Or, maybe a click to the south. I don't know. We were about to go figure it out. Then we found you two."

"Then maybe this day is not so unfortunate as it seems to be. Your friend? The dead one... He was going to kill us?"

"Yes," Paul said.

"And you saved us?"

"Jacob did. I got punched in the face. As you can see."

"Indeed. Well. Thank you. You're a fine set of gentlemen. But, I have to ask, is it not your duty to report us to your superiors?"

The three men exchanged a look and kind of shrugged. And Jacob said, "I don't think we thought that far ahead." And this was the first time Jacob had spoken to them. And it was also the first time Kazuki had glanced up from the fire. With a smile on her face, nonetheless. And this subtle indication of potential was not lost on Maya.

Paul asked, "What's going to happen if we bring you to our superiors?"

"We'll be executed," Maya said.

And Paul asked, "Why? Who are you?"

"Can I have your names, first?" Maya asked.

"I'm Paul. This is Jacob. This is Zach."

"My name is Maya, and this is my daughter; Kazuki. Now. Paul. What if I told you that I could get you three out of the war? You could join our side. Guaranteed to never have to fight again. Never have to die in combat. You could marry a bakufu girl. You could have bakufu children."

BLACK CAT SUNRISE

The soldiers exchanged glances. Their faces shared a similar sickly expression of consternation. This woman had just tempted them with their deepest desire; by putting them in the position of becoming the thing they hated the most: The enemy.

Zach said, "I'm two years from Valhalla."

Kazuki asked, "What is Valhalla?"

"It's where the confederate women are. Where we can have children," Zach said.

And Maya asked Zach, "Do you think you will survive two years? Do you think you will survive two days?" And to this he said nothing. Each man hung their head and sighed.

Then, Jacob lifted his chin and said, "Paul. Do you remember what Yoshic used to say?"

"About what?"

"About this. He used to say- I think he was talking about deserting to the middle men- but, he used to say that, if we ever got a chance to get out of the war, to find a place with good people who were living good lives, then we should take it. Because the confederate is just going to throw us into the meat grinder to die."

Considering this, Paul asked, "We'd be samurai?"

"Bushi. We call them bushi. But, yes. And with a special provision; to keep you out of battle," Maya said.

"Bushi have women? Children?" Zach asked.

"Wives... And children. Yes. And they get full shares of bakufu profit and benefit. Kazuki's father is a man such as this. He was raised as a confederate. Just like you."

Paul asked Jacob, "You think Yoshic would agree to this."

BLACK CAT SUNRISE

And Jacob said, "I know he would."

Paul asked, "Zach. What do you think?"

And Zach said, "This was my first time on the battleground. My first night. And we just lost our whole platoon. You guys have been out here longer than I have. I'll go with whatever you decide."

Paul stared down into the fire and said, "We'll do it. For Yoshic. And because these two are women. And they're in distress. And if we're not fighting for women, then what the hell are we fighting for? The confederacy doesn't care about us. That's why Yoshic is dead. And the others, too." Paul pulled his combat knife out of its sheath, sliced the hissing black cat patch off of the arm of his uniform, and threw it into the fire. Then he walked over to Jacob and sliced his patch off and handed it to him. Jacob threw it in the fire. Then Paul sliced off Zach's and he threw his in the fire as well.

Kazuki watched these men. She'd never seen heishi teki in person. Not in uniform, anyway. Only as slaves; cleaning toilets and sweeping sidewalks. She felt her frailty when she looked at them. They were rigid and brutal. Paul was horribly scarred and his face was lined with dried and cracking blood; but he commanded the respect of the other two. Jacob had skin colored similar to her mother's, and he was handsome and slender- and sweet... Zach looked fearsome; powerfully built- with excessive musculature and exotic red facial hair, but he was kind and friendly and warm. They wore helmets, boots, and backpacks. They were covered in armor and weapons and ammunition. These were the men she'd sworn to destroy, and they were essentially pledging their allegiance to her. These were the same men she'd been

BLACK CAT SUNRISE

killing by the hundreds and the thousands. And now they were endeavoring to save her life. Kazuki cast her eyes back to the fire and watched as the patches burned. Absent-mindedly, she read the words aloud, "Live to war. War to live."

And Zach said, "Yeah. And they meant it unironically."

Paul asked, "So, Maya. Lady from the sky. Where do we go from here?"

And Maya said, "We have two options. There's a place called Yonkers. It's northwest of here. Outside the confederate area of operations. There are bakufu resources there. If we can get there, then we'll be alright. The other option; we wait here. When darkness falls, we can signal the ninja. And they'll escort us to safety."

Zach laughed, and said, "Hear that? Ninja's going to escort us to safety."

Paul- grinning- said, "The confederates are going to reinforce these positions. They're going to come for this water source."

"Probably not today, they won't," Zach said.

And Paul asked him, "Are you sure?"

Jacob said, "If we're moving. We'll be easier to spot. If we stay in one place, it'll be easier to hide, but harder to get away if they find us."

"How many of you are there?" Kazuki asked.

And they all kind of smiled and laughed and rolled their eyes. It was a funny question. And it sort of gave Paul the answer he needed, so he said, "We're like ants. We go marching two by two. But there's more of us than... um... I don't know... ants in an anthill, I guess. Probably a hundred thousand more. Based on what I've seen. We're losing a lot of people, but we're

Richard Rose 305

BLACK CAT SUNRISE

learning how to survive. Way I see it, if we go, they'll spot us. If we stay, they'll find us."

And Maya said, "I can arrange a diversion. We can draw the army to the south, and then you'll help us get to the north. Carefully. Because I'll be trusting you, Paul. You seem like a capable leader. So, lead us to safety."

"I don't even know where we're going," Paul said.

And Maya said, "I know where. I'll guide you. You lead us. And when you succeed, you'll be rewarded more splendidly than you can possibly imagine."

Because there were no satellites; confederate communications traveled along cables, radio signals, and transmitters. At the forward command post, a call was made to the rear command post. To where Olga was working over a paper map with a pencil and eraser and various wooden figurines in the forms of cannons, tanks, and soldiery and the like; and these represented conglomerations of confederate assets in the field. As reports came in, she marked changes; and when the changes changed, she erased and remarked her markings. She drank strong black tea. Her black uniform was unlaundered and odorous. The rear command post cave was shadowy except for the lights blazing down on her maps. Her long black hair was in a braid that was working itself loose. A 9mm was fitted into a hip holster on her belt.

She answered the phone; rolling her bright blue eyes and squeezing her eyelids open and shut and open and shut. There was a frown and a grimace on her handsome feminine countenance. She expected bad news, as per usual; "This is lieutenant general Sauer."

Richard Rose 306

BLACK CAT SUNRISE

'Yes, hello, madame. This is brigadier general Sommer. We've received a prisoner. An enemy prisoner. An administrator, by the looks of him. He won't talk to us or tell us exactly who he is. But, we do know his name is Xander. He wishes to speak to the woman in charge. I'm being told he came down on a parachute.'

"Yes. I know who he is. He is Xander Naito. Regional high command. A bakufu shogu. If I remember correctly. He came down on a parachute because we shot his escape pod out of the sky. Send him to the rear. My brother and I will see him at once."

Then she hung up the phone and said to her brother, Arnold; "We got one."

Arnold looked up from the maps and said, "What are we going to do with him?"

"What do you think he would do with us?"

"I don't know. I don't understand the thought processes of neeps. Boil us alive? Put us in a jail cell made of paper and wood?"

Olga said, "I want to know where the samurai are hiding. I want to know how to stop the murder-hornets. I want to know how to end the battle."

"You should have let the brigadier general deal with him."

"You shouldn't be such a pussy," she told him.

Arnold shrugged and went back to examining the maps. His hair was getting long, but the strands were tight curls and so it just looked a little puffier than usual. And his facial hair was growing out, but it was wispy and sparse. Brother and sister shared the same caramel complexion and it was glowing from so much time down in the tunnels. The more time in the tunnel, the more a person began to glow; so a lot of the

BLACK CAT SUNRISE

confederates had glowing skin. These two, less so than most. As they had lived relatively affluent lives outside of the tunnels. Arnold's pistol was identical to Olga's; black gunmetal, with a hissing black cat on a red grip and the words 'Live to war' emblazoned on one side of the barrel and the words 'War to live' emblazoned on the other side.

It had been a brutal campaign. Something they'd been warned about since childhood and raised to anticipate. Somebody had to send all these men to their deaths. They were the ones to do it. If this was as bad as it got, then they'd know they did alright. But they both expected it to get worse. And neither expected it to ever get better. They'd studied the campaigns of confederate generals before them. There was a foregone conclusion, and both refused to believe it. This fight could kill them all. But they didn't make the orders. The coven decided. And this was what the coven had decided. The witches didn't care about the humans. They cared about the territories. The confederate coven wanted this area of land devoid of bakufu more than it wanted this army to be alive. The idea was to push the enemy out of their strongholds and concentrate them into fewer and fewer locations. Meanwhile, the loss of human life was incomprehensible.

Olga and Arnold ate lunch together in Arnold's quarters. They shared a roasted chicken with carrots and potatoes. They talked about the next influx of troop strength; what areas they'd forfeit and what areas they'd reinforce. And Olga was realizing the truth of what Arnold had been saying the entire time; they'd have to flood the underground with soldiers. And forget about the aboveground until solutions could be

BLACK CAT SUNRISE

found. It was lucky New York City had an extensive subway system. They should be utilizing it better. Still, not a real solution. They needed a real solution. That was the bottom line. That, and they needed the witches to do better. To destroy the murder-hornets. To destroy the artillery drones. To destroy the ninja. The slaves and the samurai had been bad, too, recently, but at least that problem was showing signs of abating. It seemed as though no matter how many confederate soldiers the enemy slew; there would always be more. But this was not so. Eventually, all would be lost. And it was a grueling ordeal to witness it transpiring.

"What do you think it will be like, when the fighting is over?" Arnold asked her.

"I don't know. Depends how many men we have left. When this fighting ends, some other fighting will begin. The coven will want us to take Boston, or Philadelphia; but we'll have no resources. No men. We'll have to rebuild the army. Consolidate equipment."

"I want to get married. Have a family."

"You will. I want to do that, too. It will take five or ten or fifteen years; to replace all the men we're losing here. So, unless they send us units from the west, or from the south... We'll have nothing to do for a long time."

"Do you think we'll actually take this city?"

"Not unless something changes. They chew us up. But we can't hit them back. We could lose the whole army this way. And their witches haven't even bothered us. Or, not as bad as I expected."

BLACK CAT SUNRISE

"Our witches could win the fight. And they don't bother to help us. I was hoping for better from them."

"I guess that's the way it is. The way they are. We're nothing to them. Just a sacrifice to the bloodthirsty gods of whatever hell-hole they crawled out of."

Her radio chirped. It was an orderly; saying, 'Madame general. We have the prisoner in the brig.'

"We'll be right there." They washed up at an improvised sort of campsite kitchenette, and then they walked out into the controlled chaos of troop movements. Some soldiers bowed to them. Most didn't notice them. Most were marching toward the front. Some were going backward in truck-beds; maimed and mangled and moaning or muted.

The brig- like every other room in the tunnel- was a cave carved at an angle that jutted off from the main tunnel. In attendance was a four-man detail assigned to escort the prisoner, as well as Olga's orderly. The orderly- Jay- had acne scars and an unusual hunching posture, with blonde hair and blue eyes; carrying an M4. The brig itself was a series of cubic iron cages installed against the back wall. Xander was leaning against the back of the cage. Still wearing his white jumpsuit; but without a helmet or parachute pack. Olga noticed the hinomaru over the breast before she noticed anything else. Xander's hands were cuffed behind his back. As she approached him, Xander stood up straight to greet her. She examined him. Xander's expression was sullen. She observed his shining bald head. His naturally wan face and gaunt cheeks. His brown eyes met her blue eyes. And he

Richard Rose 310

BLACK CAT SUNRISE

thought, 'how beautiful this woman is...' But he did not smile at the sight of her. There was a lot on his mind.

"Xander Naito. I'm lieutenant general Sauer. I'm told you were anxious to parley. I don't particularly enjoy speaking with traitors. All I really want to know is whether you're going to help me bring this battle to a resolution, or if you're just going to waste my time."

And Xander said, "I'm going to waste something..." The soldiers who had searched him had not found his void generator. They'd placed their hand right on the weapon, but thought it was his wrist bone. Xander slowly twisted his body so as that nobody realized what he was doing. From behind his back- clutching his wrist in his fist- he discharged a singularity which passed betwixt the prison bars and into Olga; removing a large portion of her lower waist, hip, and upper thigh. She released a guttural cry; but fell silent in an instant, as she fainted and collapsed into a mess of her own spilling blood. Arnold had his pistol out and was firing before the other soldiers even realized what was happening. Squeezing the trigger over and over, he filled Xander's body with bullets until there were no bullets left in the magazine. Then he holstered the gun and knelt down at his sister's side. Her blood was everywhere. He was kneeling in it. On her face; a blank expression. Her mouth hung open and her eyes were wide; staring into the ceiling. His head fell to her chest and he burst into tears, crying, "My sister! My sister!" His twin sister was obviously dead from catastrophic trauma and blood loss. Arnold's anger took hold of him; the whole world seemed to compress into the space inside his head. And his vision had become a shade of red. Bright red, and flashing like an alarm.

Richard Rose 311

BLACK CAT SUNRISE

Arnold stood to his feet and rushed the orderly; punching him in the head, yelling, "How could you let this happen?" The orderly lifted his M4 to defend himself, and Arnold snatched the weapon out of his grasp. He racked the slide, clicked off the safety, and fired several shots into the orderly's body. The attending soldiers had the presence of mind to flee. They feared Arnold and they feared this entire situation. Arnold turned his head and saw them running away; then he looked back down at his dead sister. He thought of the war; the men going forward and coming back diminished, or not at all. And he thought of their grandmother; literally a witch- not even human- obligating him to send these men to their doom. Then he put the barrel of the rifle under his chin, pulled the trigger, and fired a bullet up through his brain and out of his skull.

Chapter 18
Traitors
When the flight pods crashed, the attending murder-hornets returned to their default setting; which was to patrol Manhattan. The kuki drones were still in the sky overhead, but their laser systems couldn't target down into the trees; or else they would have shot the three soldiers. Maya used the radio in her collar to contact a subordinate at the drone facility. She instructed this person to call off the drones. As well as to notify the bushi that her and Kazuki were downed in this area and would be hoping for an extraction. The subordinate informed her of the whereabouts of the nearest prospective bushi who could facilitate. But he was far away and when they contacted the man, he was discovered to be in poor

BLACK CAT SUNRISE

physical condition; suffering from two bullet wounds and with the enemy closing in on his position. The next nearest bushi was in better condition, but this person confirmed the suspicion that the area was crawling with teki heishi. The subordinate wanted to position the kuki to cover Maya's movements, but there was no way to prevent the laser bolts from targeting Paul, Zach, and Jacob. And Maya had made a promise to them, and it would be against bushido to break her word. But, not only that; she was certain she would need them as much as she'd need cover fire from above, and presumably more so even. In this scenario, she was completely out of her element. She was a woman in a man's war. With no instinct for- or concept of- what would be necessary to keep her and her daughter alive.

Maya was connected- via radio relay- to her brother in Bosuton. And it was he who informed her that Moto was dead. The bakufu officials had thought it to be more proper to have Michio give her this information. Kazuki had asked about her father, and, at the time, Xander was still alive, but evidently captured. And so even though they had lost Moto, they took solace in knowing that Xander was not dead. Maya, of course, was deeply affected by the news, and so Kazuki took over the radio communications; as there was still the matter of creating a diversion. A complicated problem because if she lashed out at the teki too hard, then they might run right to where she didn't want them to be. And if she lashed out too softly, then they might not react at all. It seemed obvious that lashing out was the right thing to do, though. Paul suggested that they should shell strategic locations between the former library and Yonkers. The

BLACK CAT SUNRISE

confederates had a tendency for lingering within targets of relatively high value. So Kazuki instructed her subordinate that he was to utilize a senso cannon to destroy the major buildings between where they were and where they needed to be. Not all at once, but rather in a cascading succession of decreasing intervals as the entourage approached their destination. The timing was important, because the unusual strike formation could give the teki an indication as to what was transpiring. And an escalation of force would be crucial toward the end of the journey; if for no other reason than to continue the ongoing distraction.

The senso strikes were to be aimed to the south of their trajectory because the heishi teki would be predisposed to fleeing to the south because that was where they'd come up out of the underground at. Alternatively, the forces to the north of their trajectory- in theory- would be predisposed toward avoiding proximity with the intimidating explosions. Furthermore; the senso strikes had to precede the entourage by enough distance that they wouldn't be crushed by the shrapnel that was falling about them, or become collateral damage in the blasts. Kazuki had suggested they get airlifted out of there; but Maya wasn't willing to put them up in the sky again. Not after what happened last time. However, as a last resort, they'd arranged for an airlift and a airstrike-force to be on standby. And, meanwhile, they'd arranged for a squadron of murder-hornets to descend on their position within one minute of activation. Probably, though, the murder-hornets would get the three traitors killed.

Paul decided that their best course was to travel through the backstreets. Using the main roads would

BLACK CAT SUNRISE

increase the likelihood of encountering opposition. Jacob snuffed out the fire by shoveling frozen dirt and snow over it. Zach traded his M16A4 for Terry's M240. Paul traded his MP5 for Zach's M16A4. Maya and Kazuki were given some earplugs to put in. After that, they departed; moving away from the pond, through a narrow strip of forest, and out into the scrubby vegetation of the train tracks; to where they came up against a high cement wall on the other side. This wall they followed north for a hundred meters before finding an opening where a street dead-ended into the tracks. This was when the first plasmoid impacted. About a kilometer and a half to the southwest. The women dropped to their knees as the earth shook but the men only smiled because as far as terrible explosions went, this one was negligible. They were surrounded by trees and rotted out cars and dilapidated old buildings; but looking up, they could see embers and smoke rising into the sky. It had been an academy, that was struck. A catholic girls' school; once upon a time. "Come on, ladies. We have to move. Stay close," Paul said. Kazuki was shaking like a leaf. Nothing in her life had prepared her for this. Her shoes were already soaking wet again and they hadn't even gotten anywhere yet. Paul had a compass in his pocket. And he had a map, too. He'd made a cursory examination prior to getting underway, but there were too many streets to memorize adequately. However, he had a general concept of where to go and how to get there. But progress was slow. It would have been difficult for three men to move with any haste, but the women were afraid of every branch that got in their face, and they kept getting halted by obstacles a man wouldn't even notice. Like downed tree limbs, or

BLACK CAT SUNRISE

chain-link fences, or a particularly congested area of cars. But there was no sense in rushing them, because they were obviously trying their best.

Eventually the group came upon a bottleneck. Paul had been concerned about this area. It wouldn't be a bottleneck to any given strategical confederate mind; only from Paul's unusual perspective would it be considered as such. There was a parkway to the south and a modest sized ovular sporting arena and city park hybrid to the north. Both these areas would be attractive to the confederates. The bottleneck was two city blocks wide. The area itself was about half a kilometer from where they'd begun and they had required almost two hours to get there. At this rate; night would descend on them before they ever got to Yonkers, or found a bushi, but perhaps that would be to their benefit. As a ninja could rectify this situation easier than Paul could. As it was, Paul didn't know what to do next. But as he was trying to figure it out- trying to keep them hidden and quiet and moving- a senso plasmoid ripped through the sky overhead; tearing into a 65-story apartment tower. The sonic booming of the plasmoid was enough to drop the ladies to their knees, but the concussion of the impact was extremely turbulent at this proximity and Kazuki was clutching her head and weeping by the time the rumbling subsided. The tower was over a thousand feet in the distance and it was good that the drone pilot knew to aim the plasmoid away from them because if it had come toward the entourage then they might have been absorbed by its damage path. The tower was near enough that they could see its flaming wreckage by peeking through the gaps in the trees and the buildings. There were actually two identical towers,

BLACK CAT SUNRISE

but only one had been struck. And even with a ten-story hole through half of the middle of it, it was still standing.

A rusted old street sign read, 'Rochambeau Avenue.' Zach and Jacob had been following slowly behind the women, and Paul was out in front. Paul held up his fist, as an indication to stop, but he immediately realized the women might not understand this; so he used the more universal sign-outstretched fingers and a thrusting open palm- to signal, 'Stop! Stop!' Once they took the hint and stopped; he then used a different sign- an arcing open palm swoop- to indicate that they should duck out of sight and hide. Maya and Kazuki were near to a trashy three-story house with rotted out steps, peeling and faded yellow paint, and an ajar door that dangled from a single hinge. Maya suggested this place with a point of her finger and Zach and Jacob nodded affirmatively. The four of them hurried in there and Paul- who had been further ahead to scout- carefully slunk down and out of sight; into the scrub and the tangle of cars.

What Paul saw was what he had expected to see. There was evidently a contingent of confederate soldiers stationed at the recreation center at the park. And some of these had wandered out into the street to watch the tower burning. But they couldn't get a good view, so they were moving around brazenly; trying to see. It was four men. A single fireteam. They were five-hundred feet ahead, in the middle of an intersection. Thankfully; their attention was focused toward the other direction, or they may have noticed the commotion their appearance had caused. Paul could watch them through the bare branches and busted-out car windows. And Jacob and Zach were watching Paul

Richard Rose 317

BLACK CAT SUNRISE

from the doorway of the house. One of the confederate soldiers- a man with oily black skin and blindingly white eyes and teeth- began looking around. Paul didn't flinch, but he squinted his eyelids. There was no way this person could see him through so much cover; because he was out in the light and Paul was hidden in the shadows. Still, the man evidently had some sort of sixth sense, because he said to the others- at a volume inaudible to Paul; "Let's go back. We should go back."

Paul calculated in his mind that because that was just a fireteam and not a whole platoon; his entourage could probably get through the bottleneck without interference, but- on the contrary- there were probably other fireteams in the area. Because probably a platoon was spread out around here. These soldiers could be anywhere. But, hopefully, they'd be spread out around the park, and not along the parkway. After waiting a further five minutes; trying to feel the ever-rumbling air for stillness or disruption- Paul made a quiet vocalization and waved the others back onto the street. They continued moving but even more carefully than before. Paul examined every facet of every direction; scrutinizing each detail systematically. In this way, he led them through the bottleneck.

Not long thereafter, they came upon another problematic area. To the northwest, there was a tall building. It was a hospital, but Paul didn't know that. He only knew that it stood high above the surrounding area and so would be attractive to the confederates as a vantage point. The obvious thing to do was to stay out of sight of it by avoiding open areas. They actually accomplished this by taking a detour through a back alleyway which was barely passable. The alleyway was filled with furniture and scrap metal and trees and

BLACK CAT SUNRISE

foam rubber and all kinds of things. But they had to stay out of sight of those high windows and this was the only way to do that. It was a trying stretch- especially for Maya who was aged and out of shape- but it didn't last long. When they came out of the back alleys, they were too close to the parkway. And there was a stretch of park that ran along the parkway, and Paul couldn't decide if it was better to move through the forest that had overtaken this park, or to try to get through the buildings. These buildings used to be long stretches of side-by-side shops and there was no way to get between them. And the roads- overgrown, but barely so, due to being shaded by overhead subway tracks; the roads were clearly pathways where the confederates would choose to march if they were in the area.

Apprehensively, Paul chose to venture into the forest. But he felt wrong about it because he couldn't see into the trees and he knew he was just guessing as to if there'd be opposition in there. But that's the way they went. And when they were safely hidden in the thick of the wood; he consulted his map. Now he realized that this patch of forest was just a precursor to what was ahead. They were headed into a sprawling patchwork of park, timberland, and golf-courses. Paul didn't know what a golf-course was, but he knew that it would be heavily forested; same as the parks tended to be. Furthermore, just across this narrow park and out beyond the parkway- there was a high school. About 600 feet distant. Far too close for comfort.

At this point, Maya's radio crackled, and she received a message in nihongo; it was short and concise. Paul whispered to her; "What was that?" "It was a bushi commander. Our bushi contact is close.

BLACK CAT SUNRISE

But there is a dorei trap blocking our course; 200 meters ahead." "What the hell is a 'dorei...'?" "Slave. A slave trap. You three cannot go through there. You will die. We have to go through the buildings." "Where is the contact?" Paul asked. Maya exchanged messages with the man on the radio. Then she told Paul, "There are many slaves in this area. It is very dangerous for you. The confederates are in the high school- there," and she pointed at his map, continuing, "But this triangle of buildings, here, this is where the bushi is. This is where we need to go; but it is full of dorei. Slaves. But wait. There is one thing we can do." And Maya issued a command to the man on the radio. Then she said to Paul, "Okay. Bushi command has remotely powered down the cardiac disruptors. We can now proceed. Our contact. He will be exactly here; in the interior." And she pointed to the map.

They continued on their way; creeping carefully and quietly. Looking through the trees, Paul could see where he needed to get to, but then something caught his attention, and his heart skipped a beat. Down in the leaf litter and deadfall. There were bright blue eyes looking up at him. And when he saw these eyes, he saw there were confederate corpses, too. Their legs, arms, packs, boots, helmets and guns; all tangled up with each other. About three or four deceased soldiers. The slave's eyes were in a skull that was down in a hole in the ground. And the skull- or, deteriorating head- looked more dead than alive; but it was gasping for air and blue with cold. These eyes were watching him, but the head wasn't moving. Maya said, "Come on." And Paul told her, "You people are demented." And she said, "This is war. We do what we have to. Come on. There's the way in." She didn't want him to realize that

BLACK CAT SUNRISE

there were undoubtedly dozens more slaves such as this further off in this narrow stretch of woods. When Kazuki saw the dorei, she wondered if he could guess who she was; but he seemed too near to death to be thinking much of anything at all.

The alleyway used to be blocked by an iron gate but the iron gate had been ripped off by a pickup truck. Both gate and truck remained in this involved arrangement. Now, instead of a gate, the way was blocked by trees and saplings and these they were able to squeeze through. They maneuvered along a walkway with the high walls of apartment buildings on all sides; turning left and then right, as a bushi was making a catcall to guide them over. The bushi signaled them in through the door where he was. Leading them down into the basement. And from the basement he led them to a bunker which was actually once a fallout shelter. It was a dismal place with a cot and minimal supplies, but this was where he'd been staying and he'd actually cleaned up a bit out of respect; hiding his two excrement buckets elsewhere in the building. However, Maya had a sensitive nose and could sense that this man had been living in his own filth. But she didn't care. They began speaking in nihongo and Paul couldn't understand anything of what they were saying.

Exchanging glances with Zach and Jacob; they couldn't help but smile at the absurdity of consorting with the enemy. And Jacob pointed with a flash of his eyes; there was the bushi's rifle. A reaper. A fearsome weapon. But one without any dignity. It shot itself. All the bushi did was hold it and point it in the general direction of what he intended to kill. The confederate traitors observed the bushi, too. He was weirdly pretty;

BLACK CAT SUNRISE

like a bald woman. The skin was metallic caramel. The head was spherical and small. And the eyes were so slanted that Paul had to wonder how he could see.

Maya informed Paul; "We wait here. Until it is dark. The bakufu will send a ninja. To escort us. It's all forest between here and the tunnel. The tunnel is at the edge of the forest. No more walking through the city streets. But it's a long forest. And it will be dangerous. That's what the ninja is for. He will clear the way, and we will follow behind."

Jacob had a thought, and said, "Excuse me, Madame. You said the ninja is a he? Is the ninja human?" And Maya and Kazuki both laughed at his question, and Maya answered him saying, "Of course, he is human. You thought ninja are not human?" "Some of us thought yes. Some of us thought no. We never knew," Jacob said. And Paul said, "I knew. I always said they were human." Zach said, "They sure don't fight like humans." And Maya said, "No. They certainly do not. That's why they're special."

Soon thereafter a call came through from the shokicho; Maya's brother, Michio. He informed Maya that Xander had been killed. And Kazuki was right there; plainly listening. And so Maya couldn't protect her from exposure to the information. And when Kazuki heard the words- suddenly, she was a little girl again, and she was in her father's bed; he was reading her a book, and she was brushing her dolly's hair, and when she looked up to smile at him and see his smile in return; she realized he wasn't there. Her father had disappeared and she was back in a warzone with three teki traitors and a bushi she didn't know. Kazuki stood up and walked out of the fallout bunker and away through a basement that was disgusting with decay.

BLACK CAT SUNRISE

And when she got far enough, to where she didn't think they'd bother her; she thought of her Dada. He was the best friend she ever had. And she cried for a long longing long while; remembering many warm memories. The sorrow; only ever increasing with each tear to fall. After a while, her mother came to her side and held her. And they wept together. Xander was never Maya's lover, but she had always loved him. He'd given her the greatest joy she'd ever known; her daughter. And he'd been there when her mother became majo and she became daimyo. Xander was loyal to her, and devoted to Kazuki. And while they were crying; they cried more for Moto, as well.

Eventually, they returned to the bunker. Their eyes still red, but their faces dried of tears. The bushi-Ryo- had some white tea and he prepared it and offered it to them. The bushi and the soldiers had been devising a way to utilize the dorei. The dorei in the scorpion holes were as good as dead, but those which were stationed in these apartment complexes remained fully operational. Twenty-two in total. The first step of the plan was for the bushi to visit each dorei and show him on the map which direction he was to march off toward. Certain dorei were to have their cardiac disruptors reactivated, but others were to have their weapons remaining non-operational; for their purpose was to function as something of a minesweeper or icebreaker or human shield or early warning system. So, as the bushi instructed the dorei, he also took down the numbers of those which were to be reactivated and those which were to remain deactivated. This information was organized into a chart. Essentially, the plan was to dispatch the dorei in a radiating palmate formation. Thus, creating an

Richard Rose 323

BLACK CAT SUNRISE

additional problem for every confederate in the
vicinity. But first, the dorei needed to relocate to
different commencement locations, and so that was
what they did.

The soldiers ate their rations and napped sitting
up against each other in a corner. Dusk came and went
and darkness fell. A ninja landed on the roof of the
apartment building and used his void generator to
bore a series of holes down through the different floors
and into the basement. Then he lofted downward and
located the entourage. All of whom had heard the
sound of debris falling inward. The soldiers had since
awakened and were on their feet grasping their
weapons nervously. The others were just watching and
waiting when the ninja approached the doorway;
peering in hesitantly. The ninja's combative eyes
focused on the soldiers and he pointed at their
weapons. The soldiers took their hands off their guns
and the ninja entered the dimly lit room and stood
amongst them. Each person fixated their eyes on him
but they each had a different thought. The ninja didn't
care what they thought. He lifted his eyebrows and
searched their faces; waiting to see if anybody was
going to do anything. His gaze lingered on the bushi.
The bushi should be leading the others, but wasn't. So,
with a wave of his hand, he instructed them to follow
him. As the others filed out behind the ninja, the bushi
entered some information into his tablet; initiating the
dispersal of the dorei.

And it wasn't only one ninja assisting in this
operation. It was actually a team of seven ninja with a
collective goal of eliminating all opposition between
Gun Hill Road, where they were- and the intersection
of Broadway and Caryl at the border of Yonkers; where

Richard Rose 324

BLACK CAT SUNRISE

a secret tunnel would lead them to an old sugar factory. The sugar factory was on the Hudson River. And there an umi transport would be waiting with an escort of umi attack drones. And it was this umi transport which would deliver these people to safety.

Up in the main hall on the first floor; the ninja shot a series of four singularities into the building's walls and opened up a way through. The ninja did this even though they obviously could have just used the front door. Paul put on the night-vision goggles. Each person carried an illuminated red flashlight in their pocket and this created a dim glow which allowed them to keep track of each other without betraying their position. Although, the light in Paul's pocket was white- because he was leading the group. Because he had the night-vision. Out in the street; the ninja jumped up and flew out over the trees and completely disappeared. But he'd gone in the same direction as they were to go. Then, a senso shook the sky like thunder and crashed into the nearby high school like a meteor; generating an earthquake under their feet. A mushroom cloud of red flame rose up into the heavens; lighting up the entire area with an orange glow. When the turbulence calmed; they set off on their way. From the sidewalk of the road, they walked up five steps and found themselves in a dense wood where little of the fading firelight came through. Paul set about identifying the path of least resistance, guiding the others, and checking his compass as they went.

Soon, they found the ninja waiting for them. At an indistinct spot in the woods. When they'd all caught up to him, the ninja again jumped up and flew out over the trees and away. Machine guns were rattling in the distance. And grenades were exploding. Men screamed

BLACK CAT SUNRISE

in terror and pain alike. It was a flurry of activity and coming from every direction. But not from anywhere uncomfortably close. Or so they hoped. The dense forest muffled the action and made it difficult to estimate the exact whereabouts and proximities of these flare-ups. Worse; pushing through the underbrush would have been difficult in the daytime, but in the night, with minimal light and two oligarch bakufu women in tow; it was a dreadfully slow process.

Another blazing blue senso tore through the black sky. This one hit further away than the last. Obliterating a college called Manhattan College- even though it was in the Bronx. The fighting was breaking out all over the place, but that was to be expected. Paul was content it wasn't happening in their vicinity, but part of him realized that all this activity would cause a reaction in the confederate ranks, and the commanders may well endeavor to reinforce the area. These officers would chart the contact points and realize something was happening out here. They might start launching mortars at them. That's what he would do, if he were them. But, for now, their luck was holding. Albeit it was nerve racking with firefights breaking out in every direction. Paul guided them through the woods and they followed. Again, the ninja was waiting for them, and again- when they caught up- the ninja jumped up through the trees and flew to a point further forward along their trajectory. But unlike last time- Paul could hear; their ninja had found a fight.

"Down! Down!" Paul whisper-shouted at the others. In the green night-vision, he saw that they understood. He slunk backward to get closer to the women; but not too close. And Zach and Jacob did the

BLACK CAT SUNRISE

same; so as that they were in triangular formation with Maya, Kazuki, and the bushi in the center. Maya had shoved Kazuki down into the frigid wet mud beneath a thick dead log. They were in a relatively deep forest. How deep; nobody really knew. It was disorienting. They could be anywhere. There were fires of all sizes burning in all directions near and far, and these provided enough ambient light to see by. But the omnipresent smoke created a distorting haze. Zach saw there were three confederate soldiers creeping through the trees; not far away. These men were moving, so they were easy to spot; whereas the entourage was standing still and so remained as yet unnoticed. The confederate soldiers were- interestingly- coming up on them from behind; and it was only then that the entourage realized there was a glaring vulnerability at their rear. Fortunately, however, Zach had the M240 and he was astute enough to know to seize the initiative while he had the element of surprise. So he clicked off the safety and clutched the dual pistol grips. The M240 was heavy, but the hundred round belt was well-contained in a slender pouch, and its mechanisms were smooth, and its cartridges were powerful. The weight of the machine gun remitted its recoil. Fireballs flashed at the tip of the barrel. The noise was all encompassing. Zach became an army of one; immersed in a rapid succession of sonic concussions. The bullets punched holes through the confederates and their blood danced through the night air in ropes; one spinning and crashing to the ground and another sailing backward and landing in a shrub.

So the first two were dropped and bleeding-out but the third had rushed behind a tree to where there

Richard Rose 327

BLACK CAT SUNRISE

was cover from the machine gun. Aggrivated; Zach shouted, "Fuck!" But Jacob had his sight on the third confederate and put a bullet through his helmet, skull, and brain. Neither Jacob nor Zach stopped to think about the moral implications of killing confederates. Because it didn't feel wrong. It felt the same as killing neeps. A 'better you than me' kind of feeling. The enemy was the enemy, no matter which side they were on. Ultimately, even neeps were human. Humans shouldn't be killing other humans no matter who was who relative to whom.

"Got him!" Jacob called.

Zach called back, "I got to finish them off." And without waiting for a response, Zach put down the machinegun and half-crept and half-crawled over to the men he'd shot. The one in the shrub was visibly dead, but the one down in the red snow; he was writhing in a contorted position and gasping and struggling to not die. Zach shot him in the face with his pistol and then rushed back to the machine gun. Which still had about 70 rounds in it.

Paul was a little further out ahead and he could see through the trees; there was another fight happening about 35 meters away. Lifting his grenade launcher; he hesitated to fire. It seemed like that fight was the ninja's fight; and so, it was not much of a fight at all. Especially because the confederates the ninja was assaulting were distracted by the perceived threat coming from not far off; specifically, Zach's machine gun. Now that the three men who'd snuck up on them were dispatched; they just waited while the ninja was fighting these others. Probably there was a squad out there. In the green of the night-vision, Paul saw the ninja driving his sword in and out of these men's

Richard Rose 328

throats before leaping up into the trees and releasing a hail of singularities. The ninja never stayed in one place long enough for the soldiers to aim at it. It jumped from treetop to treetop and if it couldn't find a treetop that it liked, then it jumped straight up into the sky. Paul hadn't wanted to interfere, but- because he had seen the ninja ascending- he thumped three fragmentation grenades into the midst of the confederate squad.

One man had heard the launcher discharge and turned toward Paul and even seemed to see him; but a grenade exploded by his feet as he raised his rifle and so the body was torn to shreds which landed in the branches overhead. Similarly- in the light of the explosions- Paul could see limbs popping off and bodies hurtling through the underbrush. A couple survivors were stumbling through the bodies, the craters, and the trees; their rifles shouldered- desperately searching for a target. A few seconds later and the ninja descended; landing directly on top of one confederate and plunging its sword downward through the throat and into the body; and then, in a single motion- lifting its arm and swinging it out backward; it decapitated the final soldier before he could swing his rifle around and take aim.

Chapter 19
Overrun
Paul scanned the area. Paying special attention to the rear now. It seemed that their position was secure; at least temporarily. And he told the women, and the others; "We have to move and we have to move faster." The bushi had been standing guard over the two women; evidently somewhat rattled. But he

BLACK CAT SUNRISE

was quick to grasp their hands and help them to stand; saying, "Onegaishimasu. Hayaku."

It didn't take long for Paul to notice that a change had come over the women. They weren't holding the group back anymore. If anything, they were too hot on Paul's heels. Maya and Kazuki were running scared. They were cold and wet. Kazuki was frightened out of her wits. Maya was afraid for Kazuki. They didn't notice the tree branches sticking into them. And they didn't care that they were trudging through muddy swampland. And when the streaking blue light of a senso plasmoid cut through the sky and blew up a school down the road from the college; it hit hard enough and near enough to bowl them over with its shockwave. But the women just stood up like nothing had happened and continued moving with raw determination.

The fire-fighting continued from all points, but Paul could hear from the patterns and discern from familiarity; these were the sounds of ninja eliminating soldiers. And perhaps soldiers eliminating bakufu slaves, as well. Their escorting ninja- on foot now- continued to scout ahead at about 150 foot intervals and soon was leading them off course. But Paul could see that there was a body of water out there and they were being guided around it. Soon they crossed over what used to be an interstate but was now just an automobile boneyard; as well as a place where stunted trees struggled to burst through the asphalt. The crossing went smoothly. The ninja had to disappear a section of brick wall for them to make it through, but nothing more eventful than that. It seemed like they were breaking free of confederate gains, and also, it seemed like the confederates were satisfactorily

Richard Rose 330

BLACK CAT SUNRISE

overwhelmed. The firearm and grenade reports were decreasing and Paul could recognize the meaning behind that fact. There was nobody left to fight the ninja. They'd all been destroyed. Or, if they were smart, they were hiding. But this situation- he knew- was in flux. There'd be a backlash, he guessed.

Passing into a golf course, they found themselves in a different sort of forest. The trees here had grown fast and tall and strong and so more easily shaded out competition. So it was easier to move in this forest than in the forest they'd just come out of. The trunks of the trees were far enough apart that- in some directions- it was possible to see a substantial distance ahead. The confederate- for their part- had a sprawling urban area to occupy. This urban area stretched far out in every direction. And over the past days, many thousands of soldiers had flooded into it. Paul knew they were out there and he knew they were going to be coming for them. He couldn't help but feel like a fundamental miscalculation had been made. The ninja continued to lead the party northward through the golf course because it was easier to cover distance; rather than trying to push northwest directly. Paul kept their pace set fast, as- from all directions- firefights were sporadically breaking out and dying down. Then- somewhere beyond visibility- the forest exploded and a tree fell over. This was what Paul had been afraid of. Again; another explosion. Closer this time. More trees crashing to the ground. The confederates were firing mortars at them.

Paul didn't know what to do, so he just continued to hurry forward; reloading his grenade launcher as he went. The mortars didn't often come too close, but the shrapnel was audibly zinging

BLACK CAT SUNRISE

through the branches. Paul knew the enemy knew where they were. The enemy. The confederates, anyways... And then one mortar landed in a bad spot, and- over the thunder- Paul heard Jacob release a guttural groan and go spinning to the ground; still clutching his rifle. Fearing the worst; Paul ran to his friend. There was a chunk of metal in Jacob's thigh, but he seemed okay besides that. "You want to leave it in, or pull it out?" Paul asked him. "It's in the meat. Pull it out," Jacob seethed.

The ninja realized the group was no longer moving forward, and so it seized upon the opportunity to jump up through the trees and fly high into the sky. The mortar shells created a subtle tracer effect as they flew through the air, and, with that, the ninja was able to discern where the mortar team was operating from. Flying to that spot, he dropped down on a rooftop nearby the old gas station umbrella that the unit was operating beneath. From there, he unleashed a barrage of singularities on the weapon and its operators; leaving nothing behind but mangled chunks of bloody meat and some useless scraps of metal.

Paul had just finished field dressing Jacob's thigh when the ninja landed close by; indicating the direction to move. "You good to go?" Paul asked. "It's just a flesh wound," Jacob said; grasping Paul's hand and pulling himself up off the ground. Their unit resumed its previous configuration, and- at the northern edge of the golf course- the ninja led them back into the dense forest and then across a small open meadow and then back into the dense forest and then across a parkway covered in rotted out cars and small trees and then back into the dense forest. Suddenly, a light flared up in the sky; it was a white phosphorus

BLACK CAT SUNRISE

flare drifting to earth on a little parachute. And Maya had a sudden intuition; 'The teki. They know I am here.'

The ninja continued to draw them forward. The idea was to cover as much distance as possible in as little time as possible. Each member of the entourage had become accustomed to slipping between tree trucks, reaching out to divert branches from their faces, twisting about to free up entanglements, feeling each step to not trip over deadfall, trudging through mud as if it wasn't there, and pushing forward unrelentingly. For three and a half kilometers the ladies had struggled against these forests and finally it was becoming easier. Of course, for the men it wasn't a challenge in the first place. Except for Jacob who'd recently developed a stabbing limp. Another phosphorus flare lit up the night; making it difficult for Paul to see in the night vision. Difficult, but not impossible. Paul realized the ninja was standing amongst them. And it was signaling for them to get down. Each of them instinctively moved a little closer to one another. But not too close. They didn't want to be taken out by a single lucky grenade or anything like that. Looking over each-others' heads, they tried to see if an enemy was approaching. The ninja jumped up into the sky and hit the flare with a singularity. Then the night was black again. Paul had no idea how, but-somehow, in the darkness- the ninja relocated them and came down amongst them again.

Paul offered Maya his pistol, and she said, "No. We have weapons. Void generators." Kazuki had observed this exchange and she clutched her wrist; remembering what was there. And Paul said, "Ok. Just be ready to use them." Naturally, the four men and

BLACK CAT SUNRISE

Maya formed something of a circular formation, with Kazuki in the middle. The ninja jumped up into the sky and disappeared to somewhere where none of them knew where. Nearby, the woods suddenly erupted as a dondon careened to earth and exploded; quaking the earth, sending a dirty fireball into the sky, and raining down rocks that would be deadly if a person was unlucky enough to be struck by the wrong one. Zach called out, "Cover your heads!" And a moment later they were pelted by many painful stones and dirt-clods. The dondon was followed by a senso plasmoid fired toward roughly the same location. And after that they heard a smattering of laser bolts; followed by relative quiet as men were panicking and screaming and sometimes shooting at fleeting shadows.

Both confederate and bakufu alike were monitoring the situation from cameras on surveillance drones. The confederates were closing in from all sides; and they were moving in force. The bakufu laser bolts weren't able to target them because they were hidden by the trees. But the bakufu were using infrared cameras to register heat signatures and with this information they were able to hit them with heavy artillery. The senso and the dondon created gaps in the forests and the targeting systems were able to acquire soldiers on the peripheries of these craters; not a few of which were already de facto deceased before the lasers hit them. Meanwhile, several programing specialists on Rikers were busy adjusting the AD-14s to patrol certain areas which wouldn't compromise the safety of the confederate traitors.

The ninja- for their part- were honing in on the stragglers; picking off those who were lagging behind. And to inflict heavy losses in this manner wasn't too

Richard Rose 334

BLACK CAT SUNRISE

difficult of a task because the ninja could hover silently above the treetops, and because the soldiers weren't in the habit of looking up, and because the ninja had excellent night vision in conjunction with highly sensitive auditory reception, and because the ninja could drop down and kill one or two or three men and be back up in the sky before anybody else realized what had happened. And, plus, if the ninja had an open shot, they could shoot a further one, two, or three men in the backs with singularities. Being as that eight ninja were performing in this way; the confederate horde found itself somewhat reduced even before it got very far away from the cityscape from which it emerged.

    At the northern periphery of the forest, an assortment of confederate tanks and armored vehicles were gathering. But their cannoneers and gatling-gunners couldn't get eyes on their target, and there were too many soldiers closing in to open fire blindly. It was those infantry units which were shooting the flares up into the sky; in an attempt to spot Maya and her entourage- who they knew to be close. But each time a flare went up- the nearest ninja would zip over and snuff it out. Some of the soldiers were shooting buckshot at the ninja, but they were too high up- and moving too fast and too hard to see- to be struck down in this way and there was no other way. The bakufu drone operators, meanwhile, had realized high-value heavy targets were in play and soon a tsuki kuki darted out of its hanger; taking up position in the lower upper altitudes. The confederates continued to occasionally launch surface to air missiles in hopes of hitting the kuki, but it was a waste of good missiles because the kuki lasers shot them out of the sky invariably. The

BLACK CAT SUNRISE

tsuki cannons fired peak-potential singularities at the tanks and armored vehicles. Peak-potential meaning that if the power were any higher then the singularity might start sucking the surrounding area into the void; which- of course- wasn't acceptable.

Confederate onlookers observing the bombardment saw that, in just an instant, perhaps half of a tank- or nearly the entirety of a truck- would just vanish into thin air; leaving behind burning wreckage and bloody body parts. The crews of these vehicles fled in all directions. The AD-14 murder-hornets discharged laser-bolts into these exposed men. Survivors joined up with the infantry in the trees. And it was this additional influx of men which was succeeding in making contact with Maya's party.

Paul saw them first in his goggles; shadowy figures creeping cautiously with their rifles held at the ready. He hit Zach in the arm to get his attention. Then he shot a full complement of six 40mm grenades in their direction; attempting to position each shot in such a way as to repel the onslaught. With the obscured light of the flashes of these grenade explosions- in conjunction with the ambient glow of a sky full of firelight; Zach was able to identify his targets. They were nothing more than backlit blotches of rushing black figures. But that was enough. The M240 kissed the enemies and they went down. But Zach's machinegun gave away their position and Jacob knew this and so he was watching for soldiers who remained combat effective. Such soldiers were split-seconds away from returning fire, and that was unacceptable. Not even feeling the scorching pain in his leg; Jacob identified a murky threat, got his

Richard Rose 336

BLACK CAT SUNRISE

diagonal ironsight on the dark target, and put a bullet into the soldier's head.

But now there was zinging metal coming from other directions. Blind shots taken by soldiers who were still out of sight, but close enough to know their objective was in range. These red-hot projectiles zipped through the air and thunked into trees. Way off, but way too close, too. Paul roughly estimated where he needed to put his grenades and commenced to return fire. And because he had night-vision, he wasn't firing blind. He could see their movement, and their shape. The earth was shaking from the dondon and the senso. A deafening din seemed to be emanating from the air itself. Dirt rained down from the sky. Discharging guns clapped ears painfully.

The bushi- for his part- had been booting up his rifle. It wasn't a reaper. Paul and the others had thought it was a reaper, but it was much more than that. It was a quasar rifle; an EQ-29. The EQ-29 rifle utilized a singularity harnessed within a negative gravity chamber in order to generate a quasar. The antigravity chamber was made of glass and it lit up neon green; clear lenses along the length of the weapon's black frame lit up neon green, also. A ninja came down beside the bushi and put out his hands expectantly. The bushi passed the weapon to him; thankful to be rid of it. Then the ninja pinged a special code into a communication device which essentially notified the other ninja of an urgent necessity to relocate to the sky.

Paul fired the last of his grenades; placing them with precision, to the detriment of the confederates. Jacob quickly and methodically identified urgent threats and neutralized these. Zach had finished his

BLACK CAT SUNRISE

first belt of ammunition and was loading the second; even though his hands were shaking to the point that he was fumbling with the task. The ninja had been performing their duty basically in the crossfire; coming down on the opposition hard, keeping to the treetops and only going below to make kills- inflicting losses furiously; and it seemed as though no matter how many soldiers they eliminated, the difference was insufficient and there was always more teki filtering into the forest. But now- in heeding the emergency signal- the ninja took to the sky and rained down singularities from on high. Maya was searching for movement and firing her void generator at anything she thought might be a target. And Paul had taken up his rifle and was laying down suppressive fire in much the same manner. Kazuki was also shooting singularities into the dark forest, even though her mother kept shouting at her, "Kazuki! Yamete! Shita!" And the singularities, for their part; were occasionally hitting the teki, but mostly they were felling the trees. The falling trees were as dangerous as anything else.

Then, an unfortunate bullet found its way in through their defenses. Probably attracted to the flashing of the muzzle of Paul's rifle. This unfortunate bullet tore through the fleshy part of the throat at the base of Paul's skull. Jacob jumped to Paul's side and pulled the night-vision goggles off of his friend's face. As Paul lay dying, he lifted his hand and grasped Jacob by the shoulder. Unable to speak, he tried to say with his eyes; 'It's okay. Soldiers die. Just live, Jacob. Just live.' But all Jacob saw were the eyes of a man who knew he was seconds away from expiration. The last thing Paul saw was a violent torrent of vibrant neon green energy pouring down with extreme turbulence.

BLACK CAT SUNRISE

Paul's final thought was, 'What the hell is that?' And then there wasn't enough blood in his brain and he felt a falling sensation- like he was descending into a cosmic abyss- and he heard some sort of electric crooning; like a robot singing a death chant. And then he was gone. Jacob- seeing this- picked up his rifle, slapped in a fresh 5-round clip, and continued searching for targets; suddenly bewildered by the wild green waves of neon radiation which were washing over the wilderness.

A lot had changed in the last sixty seconds. With the quasar rifle in hand, the ninja had flown up to a height of about forty meters. Aiming the weapon; he carefully fired into the earth. The quasar rifle was going to disintegrate a lot of wood, and those trees were going to fall all over the place. He had to be calculating to be sure there'd be enough standing trees to catch the falling trees to prevent them from landing on his charges. The neon green energy beam tore through everything in its path; penetrating about four feet into the dirt before dissipating. The ninja oriented his ankle jets in such a way as to slowly rotate his body. And he cut through the forest in a slow and methodical spiraling motion. The teki- realizing an unearthly nightmare was upon them; turned and fled. But they didn't have a prayer of reaching safety soon enough. Whether one at a time or a dozen at a time, the neon green quasar obliterated humans the same as it obliterated trees. If it caught a man by the foot, he might pitch backward into the spectral ray and disappear entirely; or, he might pitch forward and survive with a missing limb and a cauterized wound. But most soldiers were being caught about the torso, and there wasn't any way to survive when missing

BLACK CAT SUNRISE

everything below the lungs. The quasar illuminated the night for a mile in all directions; creating a gusting wind as confused hot and cold air currents whirled toward the ray and away from the ray simultaneously. Beneath the ninja the forest remained intact, but everywhere else there were trees fallen on trees like matchsticks sprinkled in a spiral pattern; with steaming rifts of dirt trenches spiraling in between the wood.

The ninja took his finger off the trigger and the night was a lot darker suddenly. But it was still possible to spot movement below. There wasn't a lot of movement in the immediate vicinity, but there was some, and even more further off in the distance. The battlefield was properly decimated. The trees had fallen and so the kuki and AD-14 targeting systems were more and more finding soldiers to eliminate; so more and more a hail of blazing red laser bolts was coming down upon the teki, as well. Many soldiers who survived the quasar had been crushed by trees and those who survived the trees and the quasar and the lasers were invariably injured and crawling pitifully; if they were moving at all. Further off in the distance, the teki numbers were somewhat more intact; albeit in retreat, as well. The ninja set about aiming the celestial torrent at the livelier of the survivors and dispatching them wherever they could be found. And, too- out at the forest's edges- where there were entire bands of soldiers fleeing; the ninja aimed the quasar beam and fired and eliminated these droves of teki with as much ease as was humanly possible. Other teki remained on their lonesome- or in duos, or in trios- and these, too, he dispatched as he spotted their pot shot muzzle flashes.

BLACK CAT SUNRISE

One last thing the confederates tried, was to fly a couple UCAVs- unmanned combat aerial vehicles- out into the vicinity, to shoot missiles at Maya's entourage; but the commanders were only willing to spare two of these and there were still kuki drones up in the sky and these kuki shot down the confederate UCAVs before they could even attempt to deliver their payloads. After a little while, there wasn't anybody left to fire the quasar rifle at. The ninja pinged the code to end the ground level emergency and then he descended back into the midsts of the entourage. He noticed the dead confederate traitor. But it didn't mean anything to him; other than being a miniscule black mark on his pride. The bushi put out his hands for the ninja to return his weapon to him and the ninja glared at the bushi but did not return the weapon. The bushi put his hands down and shrugged.

In the dull orange glow of the burning trees; Maya saw that they were surrounded by an impenetrable barrier of lumber and trenches. It was only thanks to the days rain that the area hadn't gone up in flames. The steam was thick. The smoke was thicker. Jacob didn't think anything of the obstacles, saying, "Maya. We have to go. That way." And he pointed through some branches toward some buildings; which were actually not that far away, now that they could see through the forest. The ninja jumped up into the sky and occasionally fired a jarring quasar off into the night. The other ninja continued to patrol the surrounding areas in search of any confederate who was stupid enough to come out of hiding. The bushi and Jacob and Zach helped Maya and Kazuki to cross over the trees and the trenches; and this- as it turned out- wasn't especially difficult,

Richard Rose 341

BLACK CAT SUNRISE

because the trenches were only between two and three feet wide and there were many tree trunks to walk on and outstretched hands to grasp for balance. The arboreal ruin that used to be a forest was much reduced from what it had been an hour before. Blood coated the felled wood. Entrails decorated the branches. There were human remains everywhere they looked; heads, heads and necks, heads and necks and torso, single legs, double legs and hips, headless bodies, bodies halved vertically, full upper bodies connected to full lower bodies by just a thread of their mid-bodies. There were hundreds of these in their area alone. Nevermind the rest of the forest. And Kazuki thought, 'There can't be anybody left alive out here.' And in that she was pretty much correct.

Stepping out of the smoldering woods; Kazuki was relieved to feel asphalt under her feet. Jacob had held her hand to help her over the downed forest. He'd been holding her hand and helping her along so much that she had started to enjoy his touch. She didn't want him to let go. So, when he let go, she grabbed back at him; keeping his hand in hers. And in that moment- even though Jacob would not have ever guessed what she was thinking- she was thinking; I always had a confederate of my own, and now that man- my dear father- is dead. I know my father would want me to have a confederate by my side- and this is the one; this man will be the father of my children. Jacob would steal glances at her and find her watching him, and smiling at him. And he would smile back at her. And she would squeeze his hand. But still, Jacob didn't dare to dream that this exquisite female specimen would ever want him. Then Jacob's mind suddenly remembered about his friend Paul. Paul had died a

BLACK CAT SUNRISE

good death; defending these bakufu ladies. It was a death that meant something. That was all Paul had ever really wanted. A meaningful death. But he didn't get it because of the confederacy; he got it in spite of the confederacy. So many meaningless deaths, they had seen, fighting in this hopeless war. Almost invariably, they'd all been meaningless deaths. In the confederacy, meaninglessness was meaningful; and meaning meant nothing to a dead man.

Zach watched Jacob holding hands with the girl and he couldn't believe what he was seeing. All things considered, stranger things had happened and so Zach was happy for his companion. Zach was sad that they had lost Paul, when they were so close to getting out of there. Paul had had the guts to rebel against everything they'd ever known. The confederates would call them traitors. But Paul would always be a hero in Zach's mind. And seeing Jacob with that girl; Zach knew-absolutely positively- that they had made the right decision, back at that fire that morning. Every other confederate in the area was dead. And Zach was still alive. Alive and with the promise of a real quality life ahead.

From this point, it was only two city blocks until they were free of the ominous open air above. The laser systems had since been called off, but the ninja were up on the rooftops and drifting through the sky. There wasn't any threat; just the scattered remains of destroyed confederate assets; burning portions of vehicles and deformed weapons and disheveled gear thrown about. Gruesome dead bodies and gory body parts. Soon enough they entered into a nondescript building which the bushi had been aware of, and then they went down some stairs into a basement, and in

BLACK CAT SUNRISE

the basement they found a door, and the door opened up onto some more stairs, and the stairs led down into a tunnel. There was no light in the tunnel but they still had flashlights in their pockets and so they used those to see by. The tunnel had numerous exits to other tunnels that led off toward bunkers and pillboxes. But there was a yellow line painted down the center of the main hall and this was leading toward their destination. The sugar factory.

Or, what used to be a warehouse for a sugar factory. Windowless- it was more like a trellis for ivy vines. One of the walls had crumbled into rubble and a fierce wind whipped in off the Hudson River. Out on the water, Kazuki could see the umi attack drones. They were a comforting sight. Their laser systems were powered down, but the teki wouldn't know that. The sky was just beginning to turn purple in the east- out beyond the raging structure fires. On the other side of the river, it was dark and placid. It seemed nice over there. Quiet and peaceful. They made their way through a parking lot full of rotted out shipping containers and truck trailers. Over to the actual sugar factory, which was next door. And there there was a dock where raw materials used to get shipped in at. At the dock there was an umi transportation pod. A lengthy submersible with ten seats in it. And there was even a pilot. A bushi gentleman. The entourage halted; expecting Kazuki to step down first. But she stopped and turned back. She looked to the ninja- who had reappeared; still holding the quasar rifle, which was still glowing green. Kazuki waved, shouting, "Arigato gozaimasu!" And then she bowed to him. And then the ninja bowed to her. And then the entourage piled into the vessel. A plexiglass dome came down over them

BLACK CAT SUNRISE

and the anti-gravity drives hummed and the transport
sank down into the black water with a commotion of
bubbles.

Kazuki sank into her mother's arms. Maya was
astonished at how dirty they'd become. Their clothes
were soaking wet and covered in filth and grime. At
least the transport was climate controlled. The pilot
blasted the heat to get them all warm again; but the
hot air combined with the moisture in their clothes
and made the vessel almost unbearably humid. Maya
abhorred the wet dog scent of the two confederates.
They smelled like a shower drain. And they were
sharing some kind of ration and the odor of the food
was almost as bad as the mildew odor of their bodies.
The bushi pilot was asking Ryo about the fight, and
Ryo was animatedly explaining the horrors which had
recently transpired. This bothered Maya, too. She
wished he would just shut up. But then she thought
about it and realized; her and Kazuki were lucky to be
alive. They'd fallen out of the sky. They'd been exposed
to hundreds of whizzing bullets. So many teki- maybe
a thousand of them; they had all perished in a failed
attempt to claim her life. Her beloved sister was gone.
Her faithful companion, Kazuki's father- Xander- he
was gone, too. Her city- the only home she'd ever
known; it was a smoldering ruin. What had once been
her pristine and glistening domain; it was now infested
with teki. And then she remembered about the dorei.
Not the heishi dorei. But the tens of thousands of dorei
in White Plains. Probably they'd escaped. Probably
they'd be teki soon. But that didn't matter. She was
happy for them. And she wished them well. The things
she had done. The hordes of lives she had ended. All
for the glory of the majo. She couldn't help but feel like

BLACK CAT SUNRISE

it would have been better to have surrendered the city and conceded the fight. But that would have been impossible. It simply wasn't the way of the world. And what was coming next. That was a horror that she couldn't even comprehend. And she was grateful that she wouldn't have to be around to see it.

The sun was coming up. The ninja were flying off into the sky to board their transport saucers. The bushi were retreating along their own channels; off toward clandestine escape pods of their own. The heishi dorei were being abandoned to their own devices. Their collars; deactivated and unlocked and left forgotten where they came undone at. The drone operators at Rikers had dispatched every flight-capable bit of technology- and, too, the seagoing varieties- on a course for Bosuton. And soon all the bakufu staff at Rikers would be boarding transport saucers and pods and following their gadgets off into the sunrise. Some of these pods might be shot out of the sky. The saucers could defend themselves. The teki would wake up to find a startling absence of resistance. They would allow themselves to be deluded into believing that they'd won; that they'd taken the city. But they would be sorely mistaken. Because they'd never known an enemy such as that which was inbound. They'd never known... But they were going to learn... Soon... They'd all know... And even the majo teki will have wished the army had retreated when it still had the chance.

Chapter 20
Shinobi
Shinzen Naito was Maya's father. But she'd never really known him. Not since she was a little girl. Yoshiko always told Maya that Shinzen held a very

BLACK CAT SUNRISE

important position in the bakufu. Such an elevated position of such importance that he couldn't have any access to his family; because it would be a danger to everybody involved and even to the bakufu as a whole. So, Maya always believed that her father had made a tremendous sacrifice in order to advance and secure their way of life. And this was absolutely true. Maya never really knew him and she never really knew much about him. Maya never knew Shinzen was a ninja. And even if she could guess, she never would have guessed he was among the highest ranking of the ninja. A 9th dan of ninjutsu. This illustrious status was held by few men and because of this ranking Shinzen was chosen for induction into the bakufu kovun. But Shinzen was no ordinary man. And so he was no ordinary majo. Shinzen had become something more. No human knew of his status, ability, or nature. To the majo, he was known as the Shinobi.

The shinobi was a creature of legend. Few confederates had seen him and lived to tell about it. He wasn't visible in surveillance footage. And his appearances coincided with instances of universal slaughter and maddening fear. He was thought to be a phantom. And that was basically true; because he was as much of a phantom as every other witch. What the confederacy knew about him was equal to what the bakufu knew about him. Both sides considered it bad luck to talk about him or even think about him. He was an unstoppable force that descended upon overrun cities. He was an apocalyptic annihilation. He was Shinzen Naito.

The sky was black with night and clouds. Gusting winds blew with gale force. The rain was a torrential downpour. Now was the time. Within the barren crater of a long-shattered volcano called Mount Iwate; the shinobi manifested from thin air. His uniform resembled that of the ninja but its substance was the same as that of the clothing of the majo. A special material that looked like clothes, was worn like skin, and didn't actually exist in any physical sense. His flashing eyes were spectral orbs of purple, blue, and white light that crackled and sizzled with prismatic radiation.

The shinobi jumped and flew up into the sky; the rain drops passing through his body as if it wasn't even there. He ascended into the dark clouds and beyond; far out into the dark night he thrust himself. The moon was a waning gibbous. Higher and higher he flew. A neon green streak caught his attention. The tsuki majo was intercepting him. The shinobi stopped and waited; wafting in the thin atmosphere- high above the air currents. The tsuki majo was a young girl; still a teenager. Her nude body was slender and delicate. Neon green radiation sparkled and shimmered and this was the essence of her. Even her hair was a floating and waving mass of delicate strands of radiation. Radiation that wasn't radiation as much as it was phantasm. The shinobi observed her. The tsuki majo observed the shinobi. This was their ritual. The shinobi was resented, but tolerated. The tsuki majo was respected and exalted by all. The shinobi bowed to her solemnly. She didn't bow back. Instead, she bolted away like a shooting star; disappearing just as fast as that.

Traveling at a speed many times that of the speed of sound, Shinzen was soon out of the night and into the daylight, with the baby blue skies above and the deep blue sea below. His mind was clear and his

BLACK CAT SUNRISE

eyes smoldered. Soon he was passing over the Aleutian Islands, and then he was up above the Alaskan mountain range, and then he was out over the northern lowlands of Canada- in teki airspace..., and then he was out over the great lakes; and onward, across the Allegheny range, and then, soon, the urban areas were becoming more common; and finally, he had arrived in the city of Nyu NyuYoku.

Shinzen drifted over to the top of the Empire State building; wrapping an arm and a leg around the tip of the lightning rod. The teki were moving in the streets below; troops marched victoriously and vehicles rolled on wheels and tracks. None of the confederates were encountering any sort of opposition and so a foolish notion had spread among them; that the battle was over. And they felt a false sense of security as though there was nothing left to fear. Shinzen gazed down and around; taking in the scene and absorbing the energetic emmenations of the human bodies. And the shinobi's vision- as one might expect- was radically different than the vision of a person; like an eagle that can see with high acuity, or like a viper that can detect infrared, or like a spider that sees with eight eyes, or like a bat that sees with its ears, or like a cat that can see in the dark, or like an x-ray camera that can look through solid objects; there was nothing the shinobi could not see and even if he couldn't see it- he could sense it by scent or by vibration or by sound. Looking down at the city; he didn't notice the smoke or the dust or the destruction or the inferno. The shinobi was a grim reaper. A harvester of men. He honed in on human lives; for this was his purpose. The shinobi was the final check against the conquering nature of humanity. He was the pivot point between freedom

BLACK CAT SUNRISE

and war. It was his purpose to drive the confederates back into the holes which they had crawled out of. And to do so in such a way that they would not dare to return. He'd done this in cities all over the world. But it wasn't lost on him that this was his daughter's city and these were the people who had stolen it away from her.

Bone white spikes appeared through the fabric at the tips of his fingers. The spikes were alive like moonlight. The shinobi hopped and skipped down the side of the building and held fast to the facade upon realizing there were men within the structure. He could feel them without thinking about it. These doomed souls called out to him; touching him with their quintessence. His fingertips plunged through the glass of the windows and- stretching and snaking- searched out the teki heishi; his fingers elongating further and further and turning and twisting until they reached what they were reaching toward. These lengthy tendrils pierced the confederate soldiers through the ear; penetrating their brains. Some entered the brain through the brainstem or through the eye or from under the chin; but usually the bone- white spike-tipped tendril was seeking out the ear. And while it seemed the fingertips moved with a mind of their own; this was an illusion. The shinobi could sense the differing circumstances of each finger individually and process the feedback simultaneously and unconsciously.

And in this manner, he embarked on a methodical campaign of systematic extermination. Occasionally- and, inevitably increasingly more often- the shinobi's snaking tendrils would happen upon a concentration of heishi teki. A single finger could then be tasked with eliminating a dozen men or more; and

BLACK CAT SUNRISE

while that could be done manually, doing so manually wasn't practical. Such an instance occurred before he was even one third down the height of the building. What happened then was that the shinobi's eyes sparked and flared and flashed; lit up like welding arcs- and then these malevolent fingertips emitted elaborate webs of jolting lightning bolts. The lightning reached in and out of several men with each discharge. Popping explosions broke windows and fires started wherever there were any remotely flammable materials; as the air around the electricity was heated to several tens of thousands of degrees Fahrenheit.

By the time Shinzen was approaching the ground level, a collection of men had already gathered down below and these were firing bullets up at him. But the bullets went through him just the same as the Iwate raindrops had. Over fifty people were dead inside the Empire State Building. The crowd down below him would constitute the next objective. The shinobi aimed one deathly appendage toward them and the fingertips suddenly stretched the 25 yards downward; penetrating skulls and releasing lightning storms that dropped half of the teki and sent the others running; some of whom had been set aflame and were becoming engulfed as they fled.

Once his feet were on solid ground; the shinobi took off walking along the nearest widest street; which happened to be west 34th. He walked like a determined killer. But with his palms flat at 90-degree angles to his body; kind of like a dainty dancer. And to the men who were firing rifles and grenades and rockets at him; it seemed like his hands- outstretched as such- made him look a little bit silly. But the shinobi's murderous tendrils had a range that seemed

Richard Rose 351

BLACK CAT SUNRISE

to know no limits. And then, too, the lightning he emitted could jump even further distances. So even as a torrent of ordnance was erupting around him, he was reaching out and touching men with death, and discharging lightning claps wherever he found more than a few targets. The electricity would touch the men and drop them or throw them or make them explode or cut them in half or set them on fire. Thus, the electricity proved to be a grizzlier demise than the relatively clean death bestowed by a piercing digit. Because the arrival of the shinobi was a ghastly spectacle, it didn't take long for a panic to break out, and the panic was so pervasive that it actually circled completely around Shinzen's position and sent heishi fleeing directly into his clutches.

Confederate soldiers were trying everything they could think of to destroy him. Snipers were putting bullets through his head; to no effect. Rocketeers were blasting away sections of buildings high overhead; trying to rain steel and cement down on him. Tanks were firing their cannons at his feet; exploding craters beneath him without even faltering his steps. But compelling him to hover as the ground below him disappeared. The only facets of the shinobi's being which were material were his talons; and these were indeed being blown apart one by one or even sometimes all ten in total and at once. But his immaterial essences allowed him to effortlessly regenerate these talons over and over. And because he'd been ninja in life, he wasn't susceptible to energetic fatigue like every other majo. The kovun would have liked to have made every majo out of ninja except for that the ninja were almost entirely men; but, this small fact was changing with the times. At this

BLACK CAT SUNRISE

moment- somewhere in Japan- there was indeed a kunoichi being groomed to become a shinobi. And one day- perhaps- maybe all the bakufu majo would be shinobi. And when that time came, the third coven would have to get involved to prevent the bakufu kovun from dominating the confederate coven.

By now the word had spread through the teki. They didn't know what to call him; so they just called him a witch, or a hex. And they didn't know how to describe him, so they said things like, 'It'll kill us all,' or, 'It's killing everybody,' and the soldiers knew this to be gospel. And with that cognitive shift in the opposition's morale, the shinobi was no longer being showered with victims, and so had to begin seeking them out. His purpose was to eliminate as many heishi teki as it required to drive them out of this area. And it wasn't in his nature to fail at his purpose.

Confronted with this reality, the confederates' instincts told them to run back to their wormholes and moleholes, and so this was what they did. And the shinobi could sense the flowing channels of lifeforce these men were creating; like when water runs over the desert and creates rivulets in the sand. It wasn't Shinzen's intention to be chasing down a few men over here and a few men over there. His intention was to position himself where the rivulettes were coming together and forming a flood. And to achieve this purpose he needed to be at an elevated position; to see which soldiers were where. So he jumped up into the sky and hovered in place for a while; observing and waiting for the panic to disseminate throughout the horde. It was immediately clear where the teki droves were fleeing toward, but he delayed his assault in order

Richard Rose 353

BLACK CAT SUNRISE

to give their numbers more time to coalesce; as necessitated.

The confederates were making for Madison Square Park. That's where the sector's macro-TBM had chosen to break through the surface at; for the simple reason that there wasn't a building built on top of that spot. There was a coliseum with a lot of open space. Now that Shinzen knew where they were going toward and had given them some time to get over there; the shinobi came down into their midsts. And now assailing storms of lighting were bursting out of the shinobi's eyes; loud, like staccato gunshots. These destroyed the soldiers in big quantities. The deathly fingertips leaped out in all directions; ravenously searching for victims and dispatching them nearly instantaneously. The fingers flickered about in search of the next man and the next and the next; releasing popping lighting strikes as they went. And the soldiers didn't know where to run to, because every time they turned around they were greeted by a man with fountains of sparks coming from where his eyes used to be, or by a man with eyes rolled back into his head and an inky black snake coming out of his ear, or by a man who was burned to a blackened char before gravity could even pull him down to the earth, or by the bright purple flash of an arcing bolt blinding him and deafening him and scorching his flesh, or by a man who was more like a bonfire than a soldier, or by a spray of blood coming from a man whose organs had superheated and exploded out of his chest cavity, or by a pig-pile of individuals who were being pierced by dancing snakes with glowing white noses and falling dead upon one another just as they were scrambling to climb over the men who had fallen dead beneath them,

Richard Rose 354

BLACK CAT SUNRISE

or by the webs of electric bolts that were flickering through their companions in the same instant as they were blotting out the soldier's own mind, or by the absolute vacuum of death. The shinobi's tendrils were reaching out around nearby corners, into caves and caverns and cracks and crevices, and down into the tunnel itself. Shinzen hadn't moved from the spot where he'd descended to, and now there were throngs of dead bodies piled up around him. Some on fire. Some charred black. Some blasted into pieces. Pools of blood were draining into the gutters and running down the streets. Purplish clouds of static electricity zapped and sparkled with brilliant strands of electric residue crackling within. Blood burned up in the air.

Now the shinobi was faced with a decision as to whether to follow the teki into the tunnel or to pursue them out into the streets and find the next tunnel. In the tunnel the teki were concentrated and in the streets they were dispersed. For the time being, the tunnel would inflict more severe losses and thus have the greater effect on the total. Many soldiers had gotten a head start; but they were retreating into advancing columns; shouting things like, 'Run!,' 'Go back!,' 'Turn around!,' and 'We're all going to die!' Stabbing fingers preceded the shinobi by about twenty meters; flitting and thrashing and darting and snaking and slinking and stabbing and stabbing and stabbing; and shocking, shocking, shocking. Zapping, zapping, zapping. The soldiers were combusting and igniting. The electricity was scorching and searing. The tunnel echoed with a cacophony of screams and these screams could be heard from back where this tunnel joined to other tunnels and from further back than that, too.

BLACK CAT SUNRISE

Many soldiers decided to take their chances by crawling up into the wormholes to escape. And, astonishingly, that actually worked. Actually, mostly it didn't actually work. But, for a small fraction of lucky individuals; crawling up into a wormhole was their salvation. Shinzen's devastating fingers pursued most of these soldiers up into most of these wormholes, but the shinobi was mainly focused on the main conduit of the molehole. Thus, some soldiers did- against all odds- survive. Furthermore, some of those who'd been struck down by electricity- these, too- for whatever biological or physiological reason- also survived. Albeit, such instances were relatively rare.

Occasionally; a brave soldier would about face and face the shinobi's face. He'd be greeted by the glare of two sizzling orbs set in the eye sockets of a shadowy figure who stood amidst tangles of corpses and flaming corpses; as flickering tendrils- black as tar and white tipped- flitted about and whipped all around. This soldier would raise his rifle and fire; the automatic cycling of rifle cartridges deafening in the cramped tunnel. Then bolts of lightning would leap out of Shinzen's face and enter through the aiming eye of the soldier; scorching his brains.

As usual, a line of military vehicles took up a lot of space in the center of the tunnel, but the fleeing men were running up and over these- the ones that weren't on fire- as if they weren't even there. The vehicles' drivers were abandoning their conveyances to join the desperate retreat. But no matter how fast these humans could run, it was nothing for the shinobi to rush forward- hovering over a burning and bleeding carpet of the slain- and again be back in position to continue ravaging the army. The tunnel was filled with

BLACK CAT SUNRISE

the pulsating purple light of an electrical fury; casting dismal shadows of flailing sufferers. Deeper and deeper, Shinzen descended into the tunnel; overtaking them as the ranks of the advancing transformed into an exodus of the retreating.

Shinzen bore down unrelentingly. Driving terrified men before him and trailing a thick matting of carnage behind him. A thousand. Two thousand. Three thousand. It is impossible to account for such a figure; but scarcely a man was spared from the wrath of the bakufu. The confederates knew this was going to happen, and they went through with it anyway. Because the simple fact of the matter was that the confederacy wasn't any less evil than their enemies. They were pawns of the wicked witches; no different than the bakufu.

Eventually, this tunnel came to a point where it merged with another tunnel; creating a fork. One branch led back up into the city. The other branch- the main channel- led further down into the underground. The men who'd gone back into the underground were going toward where the bakufu wanted them to go to. The men who'd fled back up toward the aboveground; these were going against bakufu wishes. Shinzen turned the corner and went into the ascending tunnel, but- for a time, and for good measure- he utilized his left hand to continue to destroy those who were fleeing downward; whilst subjecting those going upward to the punishment of his right hand. And then, about a minute later, he subjected the upward bound to both flashing and stabbing hands. Onward he moved steadily forward as he continued his mass-murder.

The teki formed something of a wall as they fell. Those in the rear were invariably running faster than

Richard Rose 357

BLACK CAT SUNRISE

those further to the front. And those in the rear were motivated- and compelled- to scramble over those before them as if their lives depended on it. At the rear of the panic, the trail of dead bodies unfurled like a flaming red carpet on the heels of those who were to become the substance of the aftermath. The electric storms were absorbing those who were falling behind; wild and amorphous arcs burned the air and rippled in beautiful designs. This- in tandem with the onslaught of the ten bony protuberances of Shinzen's demonic fingers- was driving the delirious teki forward with calculated efficacy. As they ran, the soldiers in front were falling dead from the searing of electrical shocks. Falling dead at the feet of the soldiers in back who were falling dead from jolts and penetrations. Falling dead as they tried to scramble over those in front. And still others in both the fore and the rear were simply being trampled and crushed down into the high-voltage blood pools below. And the electric arcing was seething and smoldering in fits and starts; as if for dramatic effect. As well as for murderous effect. This rear portion of the panicking herd consisted of more than a hundred humans at any given time; and these were divided by the stopped military vehicles that occupied the middle of the tunnel. Some of which vehicles were prone to bursting into flames due to the electricity coursing through them; not dissimilar to the humans. But the vehicles didn't explode like blood-filled water balloons, and sometimes the humans did. For instance; a man might be running through a tangle of evil snakes attempting to pierce him, and crawling over men who had been- or were being- stabbed in their brains, and scurrying over the dead and dying- with blinding electric flashes sizzling and snapping and

BLACK CAT SUNRISE

popping at his back, and having a man's jugular burst in his face and cover his exposed skin in hot red blood; and all before just an instant later suffering the exact same fate; feeling the paralyzing sting of the high voltage as his chest exploded its red and rancid contents onto some not yet dead but soon to be dead other.

And this carried on for an extensive period of time- as the tunnel was long and the surface was far away; but, at some point, there was a divide. The men out in front of the slaughter succeeded in separating themselves from the men at the rear of the men out in front who were being sucked back into the slaughter. And this phenomenon of men escaping and surviving occurred because there simply wasn't any tangible way for the shinobi to eliminate a greater number of persons any faster than his method allowed for. And so- out toward the front- a certain minority of individuals were able to break out of the gravity of the culling and escape to the surface. But even then, it wasn't as if those people had gotten to safety. Many of them had only succeeded in postponing the inevitable. Shinzen found himself at the head of his trail of burned and bloodied dead with nobody remaining in front of him. And so his elongated finger tendrils made the journey back to his hands. Clenching his fist; his knuckles cracked. And this was an odd detail, but there were many odd details and he was used to such incongruities. Cracking knuckles were a residue of mortality. He didn't actually have knuckles. But they cracked just the same. The concourse was black; all the lights had burned out. His eyes cast illumination before him, but he didn't need light to see. Besides, the

BLACK CAT SUNRISE

light at the end of the tunnel was appearing ahead. He carried on without hesitation.

Back up on the surface, it was about midday and the sun was shining bright. Shinzen could sense the presence of many men. Men who thought they were hiding, but who- to the shinobi- were plainly evident; even if they were down in basements or up in skyscrapers.

This area was somewhat more decimated than the first area he'd been at. The air was a haze of smoke and dust, and the ground was covered in a coating of dust and ash that could be a foot deep in places. There were toppled skyscrapers draped over lesser skyscrapers. There were the scattered skeletal remains of sections of skyscrapers that had fallen from the heavens. There were skyscrapers that were blown apart like swiss cheese but still standing. There were humans all around, but none in any sort of concentration. So Shinzen took to the air and alighted upon a relatively short building which possessed a roof reminiscent of that of a cathedral. Down below there were old government buildings- city hall- and a sizable park- city hall park. Shinzen saw the decimated cityscape stretching out before him. And he felt the teki crawling through it like rats. He could locate several concentrations of the infestation at several locations; but, he realized that if he attacked these concentrations then they would disperse. The best way to force them together would be to round them up- after a fashion- and, in order to do that, he would have to go after the outliers. It wasn't as important to slaughter the teki as it was to drive them out of the city. It was crucial that- as much as possible- they fled back into their holes and not out into the city. With

Richard Rose 360

BLACK CAT SUNRISE

that in mind, Shinzen decided on his next course of action.

For the next portion of his crusade, speed was of the essence. There was a lot of ground to cover. There were soldiers in every direction. They were up in the buildings and down in the subways and scurrying through the side streets. They were hiding in cracks and crevices and in sewers and in ventilation ducts. Occasionally, they were out in plain sight and stealing glimpses of him. Those who saw him would have seen a ninja with smoldering purple eyes who was leaping from the side of one building over to the side of another building and shoving his hand through the glass windows and filling the facade's interior with flashing purple light. Then they'd see him jumping down to a lower floor and shoving his hand through the glass down there and again filling the interior with light. Or, maybe not filling the interior with light. And a lot of these onlookers would be firing weapons at him and he would scarcely notice the bullets or the explosions. And then; after scanning his surroundings- he'd jump out in the open air and fly over to a different building; again- ramming his hand through the glass and attacking whoever was inside there. The fingers; penetrating drywall and concrete effortlessly and seemingly with a mind of their own- striking down all the soldiers in reach and electrocuting them when they proved too numerous.

The shinobi floated back to the Earth's surface and moved like a dashing and darting blur as his fingers lashed out at whoever was so unfortunate as to find themselves in his vicinity. And in this way he covered a lot of ground; only hesitating when he came upon a platoon or a company, as these laser units

BLACK CAT SUNRISE

required 'X' amount of time to exterminate. All the while the soldiers would be shooting bullets into him and hitting their fellows on the other side of him; or they'd be firing rockets into him and blowing each other up. And men with flame throwers would attempt to get close and then themselves conflagrate when the sensually undulating electrical current struck their fuel tank; showering fountains of flames. It was a scattered endeavor. The shinobi flowed toward wherever the men were, and- as it turned out- they were all over.

Into the subways he pursued them; filling the dark tunnels with crashing purple flashes as well as the screams of the dying. Happening upon a company or two companies or even an entire battalion; it made no difference. The subways were packed with them and they all died the same. More or less, the same... The shinobi stood starkly still as his ten spikes did their grizzly duty. Only his flashing eyes betrayed any semblance of life as their intensity fluctuated with the influx and output of electricity, as his cosmic essences generated zero-point energy and dispersed it through the killzone at his fingertips. A dying man found himself firing his final bullets at a soulless executioner who didn't seem to care how many thousands of living beings were succumbing to his violence.

And when all were dead in this stretch of subway tunnel, Shinzen went back up into the sky; leaping from tower to tower as a monkey leaps from tree limb to tree limb. Lashing out at the defenseless troops with his claws, or zapping them with lightning bolts, or scorching them with arcing electrical currents. When back down below on the solid ground, he gave chase to those who were fleeing helplessly before him. But it wasn't much of a chase. The

BLACK CAT SUNRISE

lightning caught them. The talons caught up with them. And he shifted position with near-instantaneous lunges that made him look blurry. His course took him north through the west side, out to where he found a third molehole. And there was where all the soldiers in this sector were retreating to. A congested area crammed with nearly an entire division jostling and pushing and shoving against one another in the frenzied hope of getting down into the tunnel that had opened up at the south end of Morningside Park. All semblance of order having had deteriorated into nothing. The shinobi jumped up into the sky and came down into their midsts. His eyes were releasing electricity and it was burning the air and enveloping him in superheated clouds of high-voltage; incinerating and exploding the humans in his midsts. Shinzen held his hands up over his head and his tendrils began to perform a sort of spiraling ballet. Striking and sparking and leaping and lashing and whipping and flicking and flitting and striking and sparking. And the teki bodies became scorched and flaming and charred and exploding and dismembered. And as they fell, the dead would be still or convulsing or flailing or strangely contorted or bursting at the seams with superheated organs, or they'd have flames coming out of their eyes, or they'd have half their body burned away to nothing and the other half eerily untouched, or any combination of such conditions. And these dead were gathering in interlocked clusters with pools of blood accumulating beneath them. The electrical arcs took on a living aspect when feeding off the dull bioelectric charge of those being consumed. And as the sinister hands reached out further and

BLACK CAT SUNRISE

further, so too did the electrical onslaught advance further still.

Those at the outskirts of the dying mob- these had the opportunity to escape; but the spectral currents seemed attracted to they who were gaining distance and space; and so the arcs were eager to jump after them and cut them down. Fifty, one hundred fifty, two hundred; this many perhaps escaped. But the dead in this specific kill zone alone numbered well over two thousand. Many of which were eliminated by ill-informed friendly fire. And that was before Shinzen followed the escapees down into the tunnel.

Chapter 21

Suffering

Down in the tunnel, Shinzen repeated the tactics he had used in the other tunnels. The same tactics he had used on all the teki, heretofore. The only tactics necessary. The retreating teki fell before him like crops before the harvester. The men went into the tunnel as insects and as insects they were destroyed. Dismembered arms held rifles with gloved hands. Booted feet kicked around on dismembered legs. Split open torsos had backpacks still strapped over their shoulders. Eyeless heads still had their helmets on. The trucks burned and roasted the bodies that had fallen on top of them. A haunting shadow stalked through the tunnel; gliding over the burning, smoldering, steaming, smoking, and slimy carcasses of the departed. And the soldiers- as per their inclination-continued to take shots at the electric whitish-purplish eyes; firing through the blinding haze of radiant and squirming arcs. And maybe these soon-to-be-dead men saw the serpentine death-givers whipping toward

BLACK CAT SUNRISE

them, and maybe they didn't and maybe they saw the electricity arcing at them, and maybe they didn't.

The shinobi pressed further and further. The bodies lay splayed out behind him, as well as before him. But only to a limit. Eventually, there wasn't anybody left living in the tunnel. But he could hear- further down, there were more. However, instead of pursuing them deeper inward, he instead turned back and- in a single swooshing swish- returned to the surface. Back at the surface, he jumped up into the sky. And from there he looked toward the ground. Whereas he used to be seeing an infestation of heishi teki, he now saw an elaborate display of dead heishi teki. Although, there were still way more teki than was acceptable; but it seemed as though they were beginning to take the hint and commence retreating en masse. To the north, they were fleeing to their tunnel there. To the east- in Brooklyn and Queens- the teki were unacceptably undiminished. And they weren't retreating into their holes, either. To the south- where he'd killed the most of them- they were trending toward crawling back down from whence they'd come- enduring the indignity of marching over their fallen brethren. Certainly, an unpleasant moral to reflect upon.

The shinobi- for his part- wasn't an especially contemplative individual. He didn't stop to consider why or why not the enemy in the east hadn't fled into the underground. If it was defiance or ignorance; it made no difference. It was obvious that he'd have to attack them in downtown Brooklyn, so he endeavored to fly over there; hovering in the sky above them.

The confederate molehole in this sector was in a park called Fort Greene. The largest concentration of

BLACK CAT SUNRISE

confederate soldiers were out in the street at the intersection of Flatbush and Tillary. When the shinobi positioned himself above this area and looked down at them- he saw something he'd seen on another occasion; but only once. The soldiers- perhaps more than ten thousand of them- were crammed close together in a helter-skelter formation; but they were on their knees, bent over in a kowtow, with their foreheads touching the ground. And while the shinobi wasn't human, barely even actually existed at all, and didn't possess any known vulnerabilities; he wasn't immune to novelty. There were many thousands of soldiers down there begging for mercy. It had to mean something.

The shinobi descended before them. Some peered at him subtly, with hidden faces and upturned eyes. Many clenched their eyelids shut and kept their heads down; trembling and sobbing. Some urinated in their pants. Some shat in their pants. All who had felt his ominous aura were mortally afraid. All had heard the rumors. All were cognizant of the losses this thing had inflicted upon them. In begging for mercy in this fashion they were providing an opportunity for their fellow soldiers to escape as well as giving themselves an opportunity to survive.

Shinzen observed them. His eyes; smoldering. His hands at his side; clenched into fists. Then, he raised his arm and pointed a finger at them. This single finger began to elongate; moving like a sidewinding snake through the air. The shinobi was taunting them. They were a mass with no discernable shape, but one of them had to be the nearest to him and it was this one whose brain soon had a white talon plunged into it. Those nearest to this one flinched and trembled; but nobody moved. The sun shone bright overhead. It was a warm day with a gentle cool breeze blowing in off the water. The rains had melted much of the snow. Shinzen left his finger in the exemplary soldier's skull. Then his eyes flickered blindingly white and purple as electricity coursed through the outstretched finger and into the man's head; bursting out of his facial orifices. The lightning hit like the hammer of Thor; sending multiple bodies flying through the air while exploding some and torching others. Then; he drew his moonlit talon back to his hand and observed.

Still, the soldiers did not get up and run to safety. The shinobi lifted his hands up over his head; his white-tipped fingers pointing toward the sky. The purple of his eyes began to sizzle and crackle and emit white sparks that jumped out of his face. And at his fingertips, too, the purple-white electricity sparked. A surging electrical hum was emanating from him. And the sparks at his fingertips began to grow into lengthy arcs that were wriggling and writhing and waving and squirming and undulating and popping louder and louder. There were electric arcs streaming out of his eyes, too, and they were twisting and wiggling and jiggling and branching apart or joining into one or just kind of dancing in the breeze. This electricity was exceedingly loud. The volume; gaining in decibels as the ferocity increased. Each pop produced a loud bang and there were many arcs popping and it sounded like rapid semi-automatic gunfire. And the electrical sizzle was like the hissing of an alien reptile. He was able to position his fingers in such a way that the lightning arcs were making a spectacular spiral design. He could control their form, it appeared. And he twisted his wrists to create a rotational effect. Then he guided this

BLACK CAT SUNRISE

high voltage performance art downward and thrust it all out before him. Nobody dared to look, but the shinobi delighted in creating a beautiful display at such a surreal moment. This was a kind of message he was trying to send to them. The ninja weren't normally a talkative sort. But the teki had sent a message to him, and so now he was returning the sentiment. The electric arcs stretched out over the bowed heads of the kowtowing men. They could feel the hair-raising energy, and the heat was blistering hot, but they weren't yet burning from the exposure, and all things considered- that was a positive indication.

And then the shinobi let the electricity fizzle out and vanish into the air; drawing his hands back to his sides. There he stood, with eyes flaring blue-white; gazing out over the horde of soldiers. He clenched his fist and waited. And the shinobi wasn't thinking anything about what these people would or would not do. But the soldiers were thinking lots of things, like; 'What do we do now?,' or 'So, he's not going to kill us?,' or 'We should run... He's giving us a chance to run... Why aren't we running?' Shinzen saw that these people were paralyzed with fear. And while most weren't looking at him, some of them were. The whole of them seemed to have acquired a near-religious belief that to pay homage to this evil being, they must keep their heads bowed no matter what. And so even though they all wanted to get up and run away, none of them wanted to be the first one to do it. Nobody dared to move.

Shinzen still had a lot of killing left to do, and he didn't want this episode to take up more time than was necessary. This homage was appreciated, but it was time to carry on with the day's events. With this in

BLACK CAT SUNRISE

mind; Shinzen- not above humility- stooped, knelt down on the asphalt, placed his hands out before him, and touched his head to the ground. And then he touched his head to the ground again. And then, one last time, he touched his head to the ground. This was an ancient Chinese tradition, but he didn't expect the teki to know the difference between China and Japan, and- ultimately- it didn't matter at all. So if kowtowing would help to hasten the teki out of the city, then it was a simple and worthwhile device. After he had touched his head to the ground three times; he rose up on his knees and sat down on his feet with his hands on his thighs. In this position, he observed the teki. Slowly and hesitantly, the teki sat up and replicated his posture. They were watching him now. In their faces he saw their fear and their hatred and their anger and their disgust and their impotent rage. It took a moment before he felt he had the majority of their attention. A lot of them were too afraid to look at him. While- in contrast- many of them exhibited a reluctant curiosity, as- for the moment- it seemed like they were going to be spared. With as many eyes on him as he was likely to get; Shinzen lifted his hand and pointed his finger toward their molehole; which wasn't far off- over at Fort Greene park.

The soldiers seemed to take his meaning. They were not interested in lingering about anywhere near where the shinobi was. One by one and two by two and ten by ten and fifty by fifty; they stood to their feet and shuffled off toward their molehole. Shinzen remained in position; observing them as they went. Occasionally, men would look over their shoulders at him; trying to catch a glimpse in order to remember what he looked like for when they were talking around the campfire. It

BLACK CAT SUNRISE

took a while, but eventually all the soldiers had hurried out of there and gone back down their hole. This detail would be forgotten in the legends and lore that sprang from the battle of New New York City. Legend would have it that the shinobi slaughtered the entirety of the army. Eventually, they'd forget who and what the shinobi was. The confederates would never even learn the word 'shinobi.' All they'd remember was that some terrible evil descended upon them and slaughtered them mercilessly; leaving nobody left to fight. And even these present soldiers- who on this day had bowed their heads in submission- these would be incapable of correcting the unofficial official story and setting the record straight. People would believe what they were inclined to believe. It was a simpler and more compelling story to say that the army was slaughtered to the last man. And it served coven purposes as well. Even the bakufu would believe the teki had been slaughtered to the last man. Even though they should know better.

The shinobi didn't care what anybody thought. He'd accomplished what he'd set out to do. He'd driven the teki out of the city. The obvious question pertaining to this situation is why the shinobi would allow the bakufu to fight the confederates in the first place. When from the beginning he could have forced them back single-handedly. This sort of conundrum assumes that a man can understand the mind of a witch. Or the mind of a woman, for that matter. Of the behaviors of witches and women; no man can understand. But, it is theorized that the witches require bloodletting to endure. They're not interested in the physical properties of the blood. What they require is the spiritual essence of the blood. The soul of

Richard Rose 370

BLACK CAT SUNRISE

the blood. This is why witches could never be content with pigs and goats, or dogs and cats. Pigs and goats and dogs and cats have no souls. Humans have souls. Or, some of them do. And, to clarify; it isn't as though the covens are wandering about with shovels and collecting souls in wheelbarrows. These are cosmic beings. And souls are cosmic essences; unavailable when trapped inside the humans, but easily collected when dispersed throughout the magnetosphere.

The bakufu has to fight or the balance would be disrupted. And while the bakufu primarily exists to drain the life out of the confederacy; it's not exempt from the established order. Bakufu losses are token, but they're essential as well. And if they didn't fight then they wouldn't die. And that was that. Only the third coven- and the middle-men- were exempt. But the middle-men were as imperiled as the confederates, if not more so; just in different ways. The bakufu- it would seem- gets off easy; but this is a necessary condition of the arrangement. If the confederacy had no enemy, then they'd have nothing to die for. The blood was in the friction. The friction was essential. If the two sides were equal, then they'd destroy each other. And for that reason, the bakufu was given an extreme advantage in power and an extreme reduction in numbers. It was a simple system and its primary purpose was to keep generating generations to genocide. And its secondary purpose was to prevent the humans from breaking free and turning against their overlords. Which may or may not be possible, depending on whether or not the humans were willing to leverage their existence against their freedom. And if there were too many humans, or if the humans were

BLACK CAT SUNRISE

allowed too much idle time to consider their options; then they might do just that.

Shinzen stood to his feet. There were heishi scrambling in the periphery, he knew. But these were negligible. They were evidently heading toward their molehole. Some time had passed since he had accepted the surrender of this division. It should have been enough time for the word to have spread throughout the army. But Shinzen wasn't naive. He'd done this before. He knew of their persistence. He knew that even though these soldiers in this area were in retreat, and even though other soldiers in other areas were in retreat; the confederate commanders were still going to be forcing troops up into the areas where he'd not visited yet. Perhaps even some of the same men which he'd forced downward were now being forced back upward in the face of duty. The teki didn't realize that the shinobi could do this for as long as it takes. And he thought how they should keep some kind of a record- like, an oral history or something. Not for his sake, but for their own sake. But then again, if these men were being sent to die, it was because the majo wanted them dead. And it wasn't his place to contradict their intentions. Certainly, the teki forward momentum would break soon.

Back up into the sky, the shinobi ascended. And sure enough, he found their defiance immediately. There was a molehole in north Brooklyn. At Saint Michael's cemetery. And there the men were going in the wrong direction. Instead of going down into the hole, they were coming up out of the hole. Furthermore- he realized- they were taking boats out on the water; with designs on Rikers Island. Presumably with some sort of reconnaissance or espionage in mind. All of this bothered him; but Rikers Island was a bakufu installation and the active trespassing irritated him more than the ongoing defiance in Brooklyn. So he flew off toward the east river. The boats had apparently been inbound for some time; coming from wherever they could be commandeered at. There was a sparse trail of them incoming from Long Island Sound and they were swarming about the shores of Rikars as well as ferrying people across the narrowest point between the island and La Guardia.

The shinobi set in on them at this place where the ferrying was happening. He flew in low; at a height of about seven meters. His body; like a plank and arms outstretched like a child playing 'airplane.' Some men fired weapons at him. Some men steered their boats away and gunned the engines. Others- on land and on sea- stood still in stunned disbelief. The shinobi flew slowly and did his deed methodically. His fingers took on lives of their own and lightning bolts exploded like VZ-12s wherever there were extra teki to eliminate. At first, Shinzen had caught them off guard and they went down easily. But an instant later and they were fleeing in all directions. The snaking fingertips caught many and the lightning and arcing current caught more; but the island was littered with these people. And it was a convoluted complex in a practical sense as there were buildings of all shapes and sizes positioned in many different arrangements. The shinobi pursued the trespassers in the most efficient way; which was to kill whoever was closest to him and to rapidly proceed through their numbers. The teki ran away screaming and shouting and they hid in the cleverest places they could think of, but there was no way to hide from the

BLACK CAT SUNRISE

shinobi and he dashed and darted about as his vile fingers moved in all directions. He created a killing field, one hundred meters in diameter.

Shinzen soon eliminated all the teki who were caught out in the open and now the island was bedazzled with bloodied, burnt, and bursted bodies. Next, he commenced leaping around like a lemur in order to get over to where he knew the teki were at. Coming down on them as they cowered in fear in office buildings and in crumbled old prison blocks and in drone hangers and in bushi quarters; wherever. It took extra time to be so exacting but he wanted to be sure to punish all those who dared to trespass on hallowed ground. Eventually there wasn't a living person remaining on the island; although, several had been difficult to root out, even for him; having had scurried deep into various shafts and silos. And there were still boats out on the water and there were soldiers in them and they may or may not have had designs on the island; so Shinzen flew out over the salty river to make sure they wouldn't venture onto the island after he went away. Killing some. Scaring others.

Then he went away. Not far. Just over to North Brooklyn. To the cemetery where the molehole had opened up at. Shinzen landed amongst their ranks and, for a second- even though he caused an immediate panic- he was distracted by something interesting. The tunnel boring machine had unearthed ancient skeletons. Basically shoving these remains up through the earth at the edges of where the tunnel pushed through the surface. Shinzen found these bones quite entrancing and for a little while he didn't even notice the typical chaos which accompanied the task at hand. There were soldiers firing bullets point blank through

BLACK CAT SUNRISE

his head; but he was too bewitched by the skeletons to react. One soldier tried to tackle him and his body passed right through Shinzen's body as if Shinzen was a ghost. This was enough to ruin the reverie, however. Shinzen's talons jumped into action; making sounds like swinging swords. And his eyes began to fire off explosive lightning that devastated those who hadn't run away when they had the chance. The crowd and the shinobi were out in the open in the cemetery. The teki were fleeing through- and tripping over and into- the gravestones. The humans moved like a threatened school of fish as he came at them. Human bodies exploded in fountains of blood; throwing organs through the air. Human bodies burst into flaming torches that either ran about crazily screaming or silently dropped like stones. Human bodies disintegrated; in part or in total. Human bodies fell dead with bleeding ears. Human bodies convulsed and vibrated as their eyes bulged and their flesh roasted. As with all of the shinobi attacks; it was an electrical spectacle. The lightning flashed brightly and popped loudly. The arcs raged maliciously; scorching and shocking whatever they came into contact with. Miniscule sparks gathered into clouds that enshrouded the dead and dying. Coupled with the useless gunfire and the useless grenades; it was an explosive ordeal. The ground was so often erupting beneath him that he scarcely noticed. Shinzen stood within a small volcano. The teki never seemed to realize he had no substance and couldn't be eliminated.

Eventually, there were no more crowds of soldiers to exterminate. Not up on the surface. On the surface, it was only outliers remaining. Down in the tunnel, that was different. And for the last time the

BLACK CAT SUNRISE

shinobi gave chase to those he drove before him. His lashing fingers doing their devilish stabbing within a holocaust of high-voltage. And so, here, too, Shinzen killed the droves of the horde.

And this particular slaughter was the definitive conclusion of the battle of Nyu NyuYoku. Shinzen flew up into the sky and hovered out in front of the setting sun in order to disguise himself. He didn't want to distract the teki from their exodus. Not that any soldier was keen on staring at the shinobi. He observed that- to his satisfaction- the teki were in full retreat. There weren't any humans moving away from any of the moleholes; although, many were opting to crawl down wormholes instead of marching over the corpses of their butchered brethren. And many of those were discovering that many of the wormholes were plugged up with corpses; and for those soldiers, that was an ordeal in and of itself. Shinzen remained in the sky for several hours. Ensuring the message had been made plain and clear. And eventually he decided that- to his satisfaction- this battle was over. Night had fallen. The city was devoid of life. With the exception of a smattering of stragglers who were injured or lost or hiding out. It was those people who would inherit this wasteland.

The shinobi flew away; returning to Mount Iwate. The bakufu might reclaim the city. The bakufu might reclaim their equipment and abandon the city. The bakufu might abandon their equipment and the city. One week before, Nyu NyuYoku was a pristinely preserved relic of the old world. A world that was undoubtedly preferable but lost forever, all the same. Nobody built buildings anymore; big or small. Nobody built beautiful bridges; only temporary pontoon

BLACK CAT SUNRISE

bridges to move supplies and equipment. Nobody built planes, trains, or automobiles; not unless they needed them for trying to kill the enemy. They built tunnels and tunnel boring machines. They built saucers to kill and decimate; or to transport killers and decimators. They repaired and refurbished weapons from an age when weapons were still being manufactured. They still made gunpowder. They still mined led. They still cobbled together tanks and mobile missile launchers and attack vehicles of all sorts. They scavenged for scrap metal. They created laser weapons. They redesigned technology of the highest order; for the express purpose of obliterating humans. They made babies like their lives depended on it. Because it did. Because these babies were born to die. To live to war and to war to live.

Theirs was a world where witches lorded over them like gods. A future with no end. There could be no resolution. Again, the confederate would build an army. Again, the bakufu would decimate the armies of the teki. And the covens might quarrel, or again they might not; but in the end they relied on one another and their purposes were united. Even the grey coven relied on the balance between the white and the black. People had begun in a similar way as the animals. With a touch of extraterrestrial genetics to grant them a spark of the divine. But now the human race had a higher calling. Or, a higher culling, as it were. The witches' world was awash with soul substance and would be for as long as they reigned supreme. Some men had souls. Some men did not. But there was no way to know which was which until death was suffered unto them both alike.

And so the humans would forever wonder who the witches were and where they had come from and what their purposes were. And the humans would forget that they used to wonder these things about themselves. They'd forget that they once crawled out of the void of prehistory and conquered one another and created all manner of miracles through cooperation and conflict. There was no history. There was no art. There was no culture. There was only war, and an amnesiac's recollection of what used to be; back in the time before the end of the world.

NyuNyuYoku was a ruin. Ironically, it was mostly the bakufu who had destroyed the place. In their attempts to annihilate the teki. The fascinating thing was that it really made no difference if the city was destroyed or not destroyed. There weren't any inhabitants in it before, but there could be some afterward. The slaves in White Plains were free now. The city was being maintained like some extravagant collector's item. And that was really all it was. It didn't serve any purpose except as a symbol of power and a needlessly grandiose base of operations. One day the teki will have invaded all the old-world cities and the bakufu will have destroyed each in turn. But that was in the future and a lot of things could change before then. Probably the bakufu would start building cities of their own; better suited to their purposes. All NyuNyuYoku really did was serve as a connection to a time and a place that was dead and gone. This was an obvious lesson the bakufu was reluctant to learn. But, they'd lost the Freedom tower. They'd lost Rikers Island. They'd lost their underground facilities. Soon they'd grow weary of losing their investments. And probably they'd abandon their precious ghost-cities in

BLACK CAT SUNRISE

favor of impenetrable fortresses and unreachable outposts; leaving the confederates with nothing to march against. The bakufu could become free of vulnerability.

For now, the battle was over. Nobody won, but certainly the confederacy lost. The confederate army would begin the long march north. As they trudged home, many injured persons would die. A couple divisions would be dispatched to the west; to where they'd linger for several years; awaiting the battle of Chicago, or perhaps the battle of Omaha. Maybe no such battle would occur, and they'd rotate back to the tunnels beneath the Canadian wilderness. The east american populations would prepare for the battle of Ontario, or the battle of Boston. But it'd be a long wait before their numbers were sufficient to mount another invasion. They'd lost more than half their strength. Not including the militia; which remained intact. Also, the confederates had squandered an immense quantity of valuable resources. They'd need to produce new resources. Or improvise. Maybe take up sticks and stones...

As for the bakufu; what mattered most to them was Japan. And there weren't any teki forces that could challenge Japan. Not without weapons that didn't exist. And, furthermore, the bakufu domain extended to all the regions in the vicinity of Japan. The bakufu suspected that one day the confederacy would consolidate its resources and come for them in their homeland. And they also suspected that one day the third coven might decide the world could do better with five covens or nine covens or seventeen covens. All that was really certain was that the witches would continue to set the humans against one another. And,

BLACK CAT SUNRISE

an equal certainty was that the humans wouldn't ever realize their full potential. It was a lack of imagination that kept them trapped in such a hopeless scenario. And the frailty of the human physicality. Even if somebody dared to dream that by standing together they could stand against the witches; certainly nobody would ever dare to attempt it. It wasn't in their nature. They were too weak. They valued their miserable lives more than their freedom. A man simply wanted to suffer a little less than the man suffering beside him. And as for the women, they weren't suffering at all.

Author's Note:

Okay, the first thing I've got to say about this book is that it was an experiment. I like the way it turned out, but I don't love the way it turned out. If you know anything about me, then you know that this writing business hasn't been doing me any favors. Writing takes and takes and takes and gives nothing in return. I enjoy doing it. But I don't enjoy the misery it inflicts upon me. My only hope is that one day it benefits my children because I have certainly lost all hope that it will ever benefit me. And yes, I know I am social-contractually obligated to mention the spiritual benefit I derive from the practice, but honestly, the spiritual benefit can shove it. What I am failing to say is that I tried my best, but this was a weird project; even by my standards. It was just too far-fetched to work out correctly. I guess it's not the first time that this has happened. Now that I think of it, this happens more often than not, as far as my books are concerned. That's my biggest goal as a writer; to write normal books for regular people. Instead of weird books for imaginary people... I feel like when I can finally do that

BLACK CAT SUNRISE

then I will have finally mastered this craft. I guess I'm just too fond of chasing literary dragons. Don't got the extra time to write ordinary stories.

The second thing I wanted to say is this: In the author's note of my last book I was venting about plagiarism. And the things I said there were true, and I stand by my statements (as if anybody cares). But, not long after I wrote that note, I actually caught myself committing an accidental act of plagiarism. And because I have integrity, I feel obligated to say something about it and thus clear my name of any hypothetical condemnation. It should be taken as a given that I would not lie in a voluntary confession. So, I will give a brief history of the idea for this story and then I will get to the point.

My vision for this novel began rather modestly. I just wanted to do a story about toxic waste. I just thought it'd be cool, or whatever. And for a long time I had been toying with the idea of doing a witch story. And in retrospect, I kind of wish I had done something more traditional and less bizarre with my witches, but that's obviously not what happened. Anyway, I figured I could combine my witch story with the toxic waste idea and that'd be something, maybe. However, at the time, I was reading a lot of historical non-fiction about warfare. And then I thought maybe I should do a fictional military history. And then I thought, why don't I make my witch story the same story as my fictional military history story. And so that's what I did. As it turns out, non-fiction is a bad template for fiction and that's why this book was so experimental by nature. But I did alright; considering; I think. But that's not the point.

BLACK CAT SUNRISE

My point is, this was what I was thinking when I was beginning this book. I got maybe two or three chapters in when something happened that really bothered me and still bothers me to this day. I wish it never happened because if it hadn't then I wouldn't have had to write this dang author's note. What happened was that I was audio-reading a collection of short stories by Richard Matheson and in that collection, there was a story called Witch War. It was a trivial little number. Enjoyable, but not especially spectacular. Nonetheless; it was more or less exactly the story of my- at the time- work in progress. And, hand-to-God, I swear that if I had not already begun the project then I would have abandoned the concept entirely right there and then. But I was some chapters in and there was no turning back. So, now the world has two witchy war stories and I've got to say; mine is way better. I mean, let's be real; no contest.

I guess I should be less critical about plagiarism, but to reiterate, when I did it to Richard Matheson it was an accident and when the small-hats in the entertainment industry did it to me- over and over and over- it was malicious as hell; so, really, not the same thing.

Anyway. Until next time; much love, my dudes.

Richard Rose 382